Antonio Pennacchi

THE
MUSSOLINI
CANAL

Dedalus

This book has been selected to receive financial assistance from English PEN's PEN Translates! programme. English PEN exists to promote literature and our understanding of it, to uphold writers' freedoms around the world, to campaign against the persecution and imprisonment of writers for stating their views, and to promote the friendly co-operation of writers and the free exchange of ideas.
www.englishpen.org

Published in the UK by Dedalus Limited,
24-26, St Judith's Lane, Sawtry, Cambs, PE28 5XE
email: info@dedalusbooks.com
www.dedalusbooks.com

ISBN printed book 978 1 909232 24 2
ISBN e-book 978 1 909232 40 2

Dedalus is distributed in the USA & Canada by SCB Distributors,
15608 South New Century Drive, Gardena, CA 90248
email: info@scbdistributors.com   web: www.scbdistributors.com

Dedalus is distributed in Australia by Peribo Pty Ltd.
58, Beaumont Road, Mount Kuring-gai, N.S.W. 2080
email: info@peribo.com.au

Publishing History
First published in Italy in 2010
First published by Dedalus in 2013

Canale Mussolini © 2010 Arnoldo Mondadori Editore S.p.A, Milano
Translation copyright © Judith Landry 2013

The right of Antonio Pennacchi to be identified as the author and Judith Landry as the translator of this work has been asserted by them in accordance with the Copyright, Designs and Patents Act, 1988.

Printed in Finland by Bookwell
Typeset by Marie Lane
This book has been printed on Ensolux Cream wood-free paper.

Dedalus Europe 2013
General Editor: Mike Mitchell

THE MUSSOLINI CANAL

The Author

Antonio Pennacchi still lives in Latina outside Rome, where he was born in 1950. For most of his life he worked on the nightshift of a local factory before his success as a writer allowed him to leave.

His first novel *Il Fasciocommunista* (2003) won the Premio Napoli and was turned into a major feature film. His second novel *The Mussolini Canal* (2010) won The Strega Prize and has been one of the most successful literary novels published in Italy in recent years.

The Translator

Judith Landry was educated at Somerville College, Oxford where she obtained a first class honours degree in French and Italian. Her translations for Dedalus are: *The House by the Medlar Tree* by Giovanni Verga, *New Finnish Grammar, The Last of the Vostyachs* and *God's Dog* by Diego Marani, *The Mussolini Canal* by Antonio Pennacchi, *The Devil in Love* by Jacques Cazotte, *Prague Noir: The Weeping Woman on the Streets of Prague* by Sylvie Germain and *Smarra & Trilby* by Charles Nodier.

Her translation of *New Finnish Grammar* was awarded The Oxford-Weidenfeld Translation Prize 2012.

To my brother Gianni, and all our dead.

For what it's worth, this is the book I came into the world to write. Stories are not invented by authors, they float around in the air waiting for someone to pluck them out of it. From childhood onwards, I have always known that this was the story I had to lay my hands on, before it vanished. This story and no other. This story, this book; no other.

Each book that I've written – for what it's worth – has seemed to me a prelude to this present one. My other books came into being with this one in mind; and it was for this that I began to look into the more freakish aspects of this world, from Neanderthal man to Fascist architecture and land reclamation. So, here and there, the reader may expect to come upon things he has also read about in those earlier works. This book does not copy from them. Rather, it is they which were written for this one.

Naturally enough, there was no real Peruzzi family in the Pontine Marshes to whom all these things happened. Although this book contains references to historical figures, both the Peruzzi family and the series of events in which they were caught up are pure invention. But there was no family of settlers in the Pontine Marshes – whether from the Veneto, Friuli or around Ferrara – this too is a fact – who did not experience at least some of the events in which the Peruzzi were caught up.

In this sense, and in this alone, all the events recounted in this book are to be regarded as true.

A.P.

I

Hunger. That's what drove us south. Why else would we have left? Except for hunger, we'd have stayed put. We belonged up there. Why would we want to come down here? That was where we'd always been, that was where all our relations were. We knew every nook and cranny of that place, we knew every thought that went through our neighbours' heads. We knew every tree. Every canal. Why would we want to come down here?

They kicked us out, that's why. Kicked us right where it hurts. Count Zorzi Vila. Stripped us bare. Robbed us blind. Of our livestock. Our calves. Our cows, with their udders bursting. You can't imagine how much milk they produced. One squirt, and you'd have a bucketful. You'd sit down on the stool, you'd hardly touched a tit, you'd barely tickled an udder than a jet of milk streamed out, filling the pail, and you had to grip that pail firmly between your legs so it didn't fall over.

Why are you laughing? Don't you believe me? I just wish you'd been there to see it all.

11

And the oxen – our pairs of oxen could pull a plough faster than any caterpillar.

Now what are you laughing at?

Those oxen cut through that earth like butter. You just have no idea. I swear, up there we would plough a holding in one day, with just a couple of our oxen. Then, out of the blue, count Zorzi Vila stole them from us. Took over our livestock at the drop of a hat. Left us with nothing. And it was then – when they'd evicted us, then robbed us of our livestock – that Uncle Adelchi ran back into the house, and up into the loft, to take Uncle Pericles' pistol out from its hiding-place under the beam, behind the loose tile. Then he came roaring down again to the threshing-floor, shrieking and shooting. And the factor scarpered; everyone scarpered. The factor went off hopping and skipping along with the rest, and trying to hide – because it was him that Uncle Adelchi was after. 'I'll get you,' he shouted at the factor; 'I'll get you, wherever you are!' And my grandmother – the only one who wasn't scarpering, apart from the animals of course, they were standing quietly in the courtyard, all lined up to go, they didn't know what was going on, poor things, and they were just chewing the cud – my grandmother went up to her son who was shooting and said: 'Delchi – Delchi boy, Delchin.'

And Uncle Adelchi stopped shooting and stood there with the pistol in his hand and stared at it, as though wondering what he was doing. And my grandmother was saying: 'Delchin, Delchin,' and both of them were kneeling on the threshing-floor, wailing, with the others all gathered round them.

The factor came back, though, and Count Zorzi Vila gestured to him to keep clear. Then the *carabinieri* arrived. And that's how they found the pair of them, kneeling in the middle of the threshing-floor, with my uncle weeping. They put him in chains and were starting to drag him off when Count Zorzi Vila began bawling at his steward in his usual high and mighty way: 'Get a move on! What are we waiting for?' and went back to tugging on the animals' chains and off they all went, Uncle Adelchi with the *carabinieri* and our livestock with Count Zorzi Vila and his lot.

What did you say? That you can't see Uncle Adelchi in a towering rage, firing like a madman and then starting to weep in his mother's arms? That you remember him as tall and upstanding, commanding universal respect in his policeman's uniform?

But this happened much, much later, and anyway such rage runs in the family. You don't amble round all day saying to people: 'Look, I'm in a towering rage.' You keep it to yourself, hidden, coiled up, and it might never come out at all. Then, when you're least expecting it, they get you smack on the spot where it's all coiled up, and the rage comes out and gets the upper hand, and afterwards you say: 'What was that all about? I didn't mean it. Let's turn the clock back, please, let's go back to where we were a minute ago.' But nothing will ever be the same again, and please God your mother would be there for you that day, so you could weep there in her arms.

Anyway, Uncle Adelchi wasn't the saint that you remember, the man everyone turned to when a quarrel needed patching up. He was no peacemaker – he meant war, at least in his own house, which was also our own. And it was because of him, rather than the livestock, when all's said and done, that we ended up coming down here.

There was nothing we could do about the livestock. Before the business with the count and the factor, my Uncle Pericles had already gone to make inquiries at the Fascist Headquarters and the union, first at Rovigo and then at Ferrara, because the Rovigo lot hadn't got a lot of clout. It was Ferrara that mattered, and if at Ferrara they said to you: 'Look, Peruzzi, there's nothing to be done, this is how things are, it's all to do with that new 90 lira rate, the only person who can help you is Rossoni,' then you saw that was that, because the Ferrara lot were Balbo's men, they were on the side of the landowners, and if they said to you 'Go and see Rossoni' – they'd always hated him – it was to put the blame on him: 'You see? He couldn't do anything for you either.' Anyway, Rossoni was in Rome, which might as well have been Babylon. Was my Uncle Pericles going to go all the way down to Rome?

In fact, though, when he saw his younger brother being dragged away in chains by the *carabinieri* – Uncle Adelchi was twenty-five or twenty-six, whereas Uncle Pericles, who was born in '99, was thirty-two and already had a couple of kids to think about – and not only his younger brother, but the livestock with him, and my grandmother turning trustingly towards him, as though he, Pericles, were her one hope of salvation, and shouting 'Pericles, Pericles!' he might well have felt like saying: 'Well, what am I supposed to do about it?' because he would never have expected Adelchi to crack up like that. Yes, he'd seen him rushing into the house, but he hadn't taken much notice, because he didn't really set much store by that brother – always conveniently somewhere else, never around when you needed him – and he would have liked to give him a good thrashing whenever he heard him screeching and shrieking at his sisters. But when he saw him reappearing from the door which led on to the staircase and not even closing the mosquito net, and shrieking and shooting, and stumbling slightly as he came down the outside stairs, and shooting like a madman, and the factor making himself scarce and Adelchi shouting 'I'll get you,' and shooting some more

14

– well, put like that it all seems to take an age, but actually it happened in a flash – seeing his brother at that moment, Uncle Pericles actually burst out laughing: 'Just look at Adelchi.' And suddenly he felt love for him.

So when his mother turned to him with that 'Pericles, Pericles,' he would have liked to come back with 'What am I supposed to do about it?' but then she immediately added: 'Go to Rome, Periclin,' and she'd never used that diminutive before, even when he was a child. And then he said: 'All right then, tomorrow we'll be going to Rome' – and it was a matter-of-fact sort of statement, not a suggestion, directed at Uncle Themistocles, his older brother; you won't remember him, you can't have known him because his sons took him back to Northern Italy in the Sixties, to Turin. They worked at the Fiat factory, but he was too old for that.

What did you say? How many of us were there? Quite a crowd. My grandfather had produced seventeen children, eight girls and nine boys, and his brother had produced another seventeen, also eight girls and nine boys. At first we were rock-solid, just one big family, but with time the cracks began to show. They stayed up north, they didn't come down to the Pontine Marshes. But that wasn't why we split: they didn't come south because we were split already, and we never made it up. It was to do with politics. Anyway, there were seventeen of us children, and it was different in those days, children weren't a financial burden. In those days children meant prosperity, because they were tantamount to so many hands to work the land. What did you say? They were also so many mouths to feed? Of course they were, but that wasn't a problem, you just gave them whatever was around. And if a child was strong, it more or less brought itself up. If a child got ill, you didn't go off to some special doctor and buy some special medicine. My grandmother would light a candle and set herself to pray; and the child would get better, grow up and be put to work. And if it didn't get better, it would die. You'd cry, pray, bury it and have another. That's what everyone did, not just us. To work the land, what you needed was a pair of hands, there was no other way. Tractors and all those modern contraptions came later, they weren't around in those days, and if you'd been there, you would have done as we did. That was how it had been done for centuries, *saeculorum amen*. There was no welfare then, just hunger.

What did you say? That large families made things worse, they just meant more people sharing the same hunger? For us, each one was a pair of hands, what more can I say? We were hungry and we needed hands to produce food, which was our wealth. But even now, you say, it isn't just the rich who don't have so many children? Well, we don't in Italy, but in Africa – where they're still poor, and get themselves drowned trying to get to Lampedusa – they carry on having children like nobody's business. Just try telling them not to. You think they don't know that a child is all too likely to die of hunger, or of AIDS? That's why they have so many: 'Sooner or later one of them is bound to pull through.' You have children because they're useful to you, and the poorer you are, the more useful they are; it's when you're rich that you can get by with just a few.

Uncle Iseo wanted to go to Rome as well. He was the third of the male children, just two years younger than Uncle Pericles, and they'd always been thick as thieves, both in the fields and in the wine-shop. Uncle Pericles himself would have preferred Iseo to go, because you didn't flit down to Rome on some idle whim and come back the next day, there weren't any of those fast trains you have nowadays. You never knew when you'd make it back, or indeed whether you'd make it back at all, though actually at that point the Fascist regime had already brought in some degree of order, but a few years earlier, when Italy was still divided, or barely united – apart from the fact that you'd never take it into your head to go as far as Rome at all – those few people who did go there, on some pilgrimage or for Holy Year, would make their will before they left, because you never knew what kind of pickle you might be getting into, brigands on the roads, or in the woods, or illness – and the journey would be a long one. Anyway, it was better to embark on such an undertaking with someone you could really trust – who, if it came to a fight to the death, would be sure to look out for you as well as for himself. It's true that Themistocles could be counted on for this, and Uncle Pericles had always got on with him and been close to him. Uncle Themistocles had also fought in the war, he'd been involved in hand-to-hand fighting, and he knew what it meant to cut a man's throat to stop him cutting yours. He'd been in that situation more than once in the war.

But Pericles was closer to Uncle Iseo. Indeed, at a later stage – when they had set up on their own and things weren't going too well and first the Mussolini Canal broke its banks and then there was the hail – they'd both been tempted by the pay and enrolled as volunteers in the last World War, and had been sent to East Africa to defend it against the English who'd gone in from Kenya, and who had Land Rovers and armoured cars, the lot, whereas we'd got nothing, just carbines and hand grenades, our kind that is, the Balilla SRCM, which were made of tin, and all they produced was little slivers of wire, not like the English Pineapples, which were real hand grenades made with real iron. And while my uncles were attacking, amidst all those explosions and all that smoke, and people falling down and shrieking and the lieutenant shouting 'Forward march!', at some point Uncle Iseo found himself on his knees and then flat on the ground, unable to breathe. 'What's going on here?' he wondered, and then he put a hand to his side and there wasn't anything there, and his hand was all red, and he looked at it and tried again, but he felt the pain even though he couldn't find his side, and then he shrieked: 'Pericles, Pericles – Periclin.'

And Uncle Pericles was right by him on the ground: 'Just keep calm,' he urged him.

'They got me, good and proper,' Uncle Iseo was saying, and then: 'I've had it, it's you who'll have to take care of the kids.' And Uncle Pericles dragged him out of harm's way, behind an upturned truck, and plugged his wound while everything else carried on as before, explosions and smoke and shrieking, and Uncle Iseo said: 'Stay here, don't leave me alone.'

But everyone else carried on shooting, and Uncle Pericles left him where he was: 'Just keep calm, you're all right here, I'll be back soon, just wait for me here.'

'I'll wait for you all right; if I don't die, I'll wait,' said Uncle Iseo.

But that time they went to Rome, it had to be the eldest, they couldn't all go, and so it was my Uncle Themistocles who went. The women put the water on to boil and then filled the wash-tub in the threshing-area, and Uncle Pericles and Uncle Themistocles took a bath, one after another in the same water, because that's how we did things back then, there wasn't anything like a shower in those days. They had supper and then they went to bed, where each of them probably had a go at his wife. And the next morning, off they went. Actually, Uncle Pericles probably had more than one go, because he was known to be hot-blooded and had probably wanted to stock up, as you might put it, since a bit of enforced abstinence was in the offing. Come to that, she was hot-blooded too. My cousins – who sometimes got to hear how things were going, through the wall – said that she would snarl encouragement at her husband, and he would tell her to stop scratching him, in no uncertain terms. Anyway, early the next morning they set off for Rome, on their bicycles, well before dawn.

What did you say? Why didn't they take the train? Well, if we'd had the money to buy the tickets, we'd have had the money to pay the boss; it was all down to that new 90 lire rate, as I told you, and there wasn't a lira to be had anywhere, for love or money. We had sacks full of grain, but we didn't have a single spare lira, because grain wasn't worth anything either, by now. The Duce had killed Italian agriculture stone dead – industry was all right, but agriculture had had it.

Anyway, off they went, and after a lot of legwork they arrived in Rome. They took five days, or was it six, I can't remember. They must have done about a hundred kilometres a day, it wasn't the *Giro d'Italia*, where they do two hundred and fifty or even three hundred kilometres a day, averaging sixty an hour with erythropoietin. Bicycles were heavy in those days, and the tyres were worn. Every now and again you'd get a puncture, and have to stop to repair the inner tube with rubber solution. They'd taken some spare ones, but those were old too, and had already been repaired on several occasions. They'd also taken a load of bread, and some clothes. The roads themselves weren't too bad, because the Fascists had already set up Anas to take care of them, and the road from Ferrara to Rome – first the Via Emilia and then the Flaminia – was asphalted. They slept wherever they happened to stop, in cowsheds or haylofts, and sometimes there were pilgrims' hostels. Anyway, up hill and down dale, and after lot of legwork, they arrived in Rome. There they stayed at the

Casa del Viaggiatore, a place for travellers near the station, and the next morning they washed, put on the militiaman's black shirt and uniform they'd taken with them – rolled up in a package tied behind the saddle, and which they'd had ironed for them the night before – and presented themselves at Palazzo Venezia: 'Knock knock, we want a word with Rossoni.'

'What's he to you then, your bosom chum?' came the reply. 'How dare you! His Excellency Rossoni, to you! And just who are you, anyway? Do you think you can just roll up here, at Palazzo Venezia, and say you want a word with whoever you choose? With the Duce himself, why not? Troublemakers, that's what you are.'

Uncle Pericles didn't fly off the handle immediately, though. While they were walking up from Via Nazionale, and his brother asked him: 'What d'you think, are you sure they'll see us? Aren't they more likely to send us packing?' he had immediately reassured him: 'Are you joking? Send us packing? What price the revolution, in that case? Don't you worry.' But, in his heart of hearts, he wasn't quite so sure. Throughout the journey, up and down the Apennines – even during the steepest climbs, at the Furlo and all through Umbria, when they had to dismount and carry on on foot, pushing their bicycles – he hadn't known a moment's hesitation: 'Just wait till I'm in Rome, I'll have the whole thing sorted in less than no time.' But after Terni, when it was clear that they would be in Rome by nightfall, other thoughts began running through his head: 'Perhaps I won't be able to sort anything out at all – perhaps they won't even let me see Rossoni.'

So Uncle Pericles didn't fly off the handle immediately. He was resigned; it was almost as though he was expecting it. But when he saw Themistocles' crestfallen look, the one he'd so often seen on his face as a child, as though he were saying:

'Here we go again, it's hopeless, just one more wasted journey, we've been had, as always,' then Pericles really took offence, really flew off the handle. He put his hand to the knife he wore on his belt, pulled it out and began to yell, and was just about to use his other hand to swivel over the bench and come face to face with the usher on the other side. But in the meantime – hardly had he put his hand to his knife – the two brothers were set upon by four men from the secret police or some such outfit, and tied up like so much salami, and Uncle Pericles just had time to finish shouting at the usher, 'Tell Rossoni that Peruzzi from Codigoro was asking for him, you oaf!' and they bundled them straight into a cell that just happened to be there to hand. And, while they were bundling them into it, they gave them a thorough going over, kicking and punching to their hearts' content. Then they plonked them down on to the plank-bed, with Uncle Pericles still shrieking 'Peruzzi from Codigoro,' until the last the policemen said: 'Shut up now – we've got the message.'

But – just to be on the safe side – before calling the police station to have them taken away, the officer of the guard sent someone to the floor above – 'Have you ever seen the likes?' – who spoke to the usher there, who spoke to a secretary, who spoke to a clerk who, picking up a few things that needed to be signed, knocked on Rossoni's door and went in: 'Excuse me your Excellency, there are two madmen downstairs who say they're called Peruzzi. From Codigoro, I believe. I had them put inside, you can't be too careful nowadays.'

Well, you won't believe this, but Rossoni leapt up from his desk like a jack-in-the-box, rushed down the stairs, had the cell door opened, saw who was in it and held out his arms: 'Peruzzi!'

My uncles leapt up from the plank-bed where they were

sitting, jumped to attention, gave the Roman salute and uttered the one word 'Excellency,' in tones of reverence.

'Excellency nothing, you sons of bitches! Come over here,' and he threw his arms around them, saying to his secretary: 'This here is Pericles Peruzzi, watch out for him, he's a right scoundrel, I've known him since he was a boy,' and took them straight back upstairs with him, one on each arm.

None of this stopped Uncle Pericles from shouting out: 'You oaf!' at the usher as they passed his lodge for the second time.

At that time – as any history book will tell you – Rossoni was Number Two in the pecking order. Straight after the Duce; before Balbo and all the others who were ministers by name, but he was the one who did the real ministering, because he was Under-Secretary to the Prime Minister, equivalent to the American Secretary of State in relation to the US President, no less. He was the Duce's eyes and ears, his right-hand man, and he knew absolutely everything that was going on. Number Two, as I've already said. Of course, that wasn't the case throughout the whole twenty years. With the Duce, you never quite knew where you stood. Today you'd be his blue-eyed boy, tomorrow you would find yourself on the scrapheap. Look what he did to Balbo. And Ciano. Ciano was his son-in-law – married to his daughter – and he had him shot. What hope was there for a lesser mortal? So Rossoni too found himself in the doghouse, shortly after the Charter of Labour, when the Duce had him sacked from his position as President of the Fascist Unions – there was even a rumour that he had escaped to Switzerland with their funds, the 'treasure', so the rumour went; but he always denied this utterly, even though those who succeeded him found the cupboard completely bare, not a lira to be seen, nothing but debts – but in 1932 it was carrot time again, rather

22

than stick time, and it was Rossoni who was calling the tune. Of course the Duce was always breathing down his neck – just one office away – but you couldn't see the Duce without seeing Rossoni first. And as soon as he saw Uncle Pericles he threw his arms around him and almost lifted him off his feet.

What – you don't believe me? You think it sounds like the stuff of fiction, that it's impossible that someone like Rossoni should have put himself out for the likes of them, that they should have got through the doors of Palazzo Venezia – even if it was only to talk to the usher – without anyone stopping them, as though it was any old block of flats on Via Vincenzo Monti? Indeed, that two bumpkins like them couldn't even have got themselves inside a block of flats on Via Vincenzo Monti?

Well, obviously, I've given you a shortened version – I couldn't spell it all out for you blow by blow. Naturally, on their first lap, when they left home in the early morning, they went first to Ferrara. And they weren't fools – they wouldn't have set out on such a venture without thinking about the paperwork. In those days you didn't just wander all over the place just as the fancy took you: 'I've had enough of it around these parts, I think I'll give it a try somewhere else.' You needed permits. There was a Commissariat for Internal Migration, and they checked on all your comings and goings. For instance, you weren't allowed to leave the countryside and go to live in town, saying that you were looking for work – they wouldn't put you on the employment register, or give you a residency permit, they'd just send you off with the inevitable piece of paper like they do with illegal immigrants today. All right, we were peasants, we didn't really know the ropes, but anyway, before they set off for Rome my uncles had gone to the provincial Fascist Headquarters in Ferrara and got themselves a letter that read: 'Comrades Tom and Dick are coming to Rome for such and such a purpose, please help them in any way you can, Fascist greetings and thanks.' Was there any way the provincial party secretary would not have written that letter for my Uncle Pericles? You do understand who we're talking about? So, when they got to Piazza Venezia, even before they were anywhere near the Palazzo, they immediately showed that piece of paper to a policeman, and then to another couple of plain-clothes men, there in the square, and then again on several other occasions, until they got to the main door, with the sentry stationed alongside the Duce's special guard, all puffed up in his sentry box, and he let them in – the sentry, that is – and took them to the usher. And the usher didn't even bother to look at their piece of paper – he must have seen quite enough pieces of paper in his time, he'd got out of bed the wrong side that day, and when he saw those two little peasant nobodies, self-important though they were – 'We want a word with Rossoni' – goodness knows what he must have thought, and he said: 'I'll show these two country bumpkins how I snap to attention, I'll soon have them grovelling.' And it wasn't long before he learned that rage was a besetting sin in our family. You and I, though, can't go on like this. We'll have to come to some agreement. I don't know why you should want one, but if indeed you do want a blow by blow account I can give you one – I have nothing to hide now that so many years have gone by – and everything I'm telling you is the pure unvarnished truth. But at this rate we'll never get anywhere. If you want to be around to hear the end of the story, I'll have to skimp on surplus details. If I tell you that they did such and such a thing, then that's what they did, you'll just have to believe me, otherwise we'll just have to let the whole thing drop. I'm not inventing anything; at most my memory may be faulty.

Anyway, just to backtrack a bit, my grandfather had been in prison with Rossoni at the time when they were still reds and Socialists, at Copparo, in 1904, the year Uncle Adelchi was born – he was the only one to have been born in his father's absence. Although, in fact, my grandfather hadn't exactly been there when the others were born either. On mornings when my grandmother would say: 'I'm not going into the fields today,' and begin to put great pans of water on to the fire and pull out pillowcases and sheets and clean linen, he didn't even wait for her to send off the smaller children in the charge of the bigger ones, but would just say: 'What would you say if I were to go off and had a little game of cards?'

'Be off with you,' she'd say.

And off he'd go to the wine shop – and he'd sit inside, not out, he didn't want to be within earshot of any telltale noises – and play *briscola* and drink wine, until, in the early afternoon, or towards evening, some child would roll up and say to him: 'It's been born.'

'Boy or girl?' he'd ask. And, on hearing the reply, he'd go off to see for himself.

All my grandmother's children were born by day, not even one by night, because the wine-shop was shut then. And all at home, with my grandfather safely out of the way. All except Uncle Themistocles, who was the oldest, who was born before my grandfather understood the system and so could recognize the signs, she always had them in the fields, when they were getting up the sugar beet. Her waters broke while she was using a hook to grapple with a particularly large one, just when it was poised half in and half out, like the baby itself, and she said: 'What's all this then?' and left the beet where it was, with the hook attached, 'Excuse me a moment,' she said, and walked across the field to the drainage canal, sat down in the shade of a tree and produced my Uncle Themistocles. Once they'd realized what was up – the news had spread fast – the other women all went to gather round her, and she said: 'Next time I'll stay at home,' and got up and wanted to go back to finish off her work with the large beet. It was only with the excuse of wanting to wash the baby that they managed to get her back home.

Anyway, at that time we were still in Codigoro. I don't know how many years we stayed there, but not many. My people tended to be on the move. Hither and thither we went, wherever we could get contracts as sharecroppers. Where exactly my grandfather was from, I really couldn't tell you – but certainly somewhere on the Po, well before it starts to branch out, and the delta begins. Indeed, perhaps from around Modena, or Reggio Emilia. His family seems to have had a bit of money at some stage – that's what the old people said – and they were millers, so they were quite well off. Some grandfather or great-grandfather – I don't know on which side of the family – had apparently been in Russia with Napoleon, and on his return he'd built himself one of those water mills, you know, the ones you used to see on floating barges on the Po, with the river water turning the paddles. People would bring him their grain and his people would keep their share, that's how they made their money. Then it ran out. Because they had bought land; and ultimately they lost that as well. I don't know whether it was through mismanagement, or some wastrel son, or perhaps a disastrous flood which washed away the lot, mills and money both, leaving my grandfather and his brother – and their parents, too – with nothing but the clothes they stood up in, and not a penny to their names. They lived in huts made out of branches, and started to work as carters, going from village to village. And that was how my grandfather met my grandmother, going up and down the roads of what was known as the Greater Ferrarese drainage area, which, despite being called 'Ferrarese', actually also extended beyond the Po, along the delta, into the Polesine, which was in the Province of Rovigo. I've never understood why it should have been called that: perhaps the funds – the capital, and the firms involved – came from Ferrara, or else when work began the whole area to be drained was in the Province of Ferrara. At all events, in their comings and goings around Formignana, where there was a tiny hamlet called Tresigallo – not a real town, like it is now, but just three houses and a little church – my grandfather and his brother would pass an isolated dwelling, and here they would often glimpse a particularly lovely girl. I don't know if you remember any photographs of her – she was as tall and sturdy as a *carabiniere* even as an old woman – and goodness knows what she must have looked like when she was young, all dark-skinned as she was. Anyway, on those frequent sightings, my grandfather would pay her his respects. At first, she would just blush, but as time went by she started to give as good as she got – she was never one to be lost for words. And my grandfather too cut quite a dash from up there on his cart: fair-haired, a fine moustache, smoking his ever-present cigar. But my grandmother's brothers were not so keen: 'A nobody, that's what he is,' they'd tell her. And then: 'A carter?' For them, a carter was a nobody.

They were peasants – they worked the land. They owned the odd field, and held some land as sharecroppers, and had some livestock of their own. But it was those four square metres of land they owned that made them feel like gentlemen, as good as any landowner. Nobility, almost, in comparison to my grandfather. And they weren't going to allow themselves to be besmirched. Their sister, on the other hand, had taken

27

it into her head to fall for that 'shirker', as they called him, and there was nothing to be done, eventually she got her man, and the brothers put a brave face on it and set themselves to making a good peasant of him too. They even taught him to read and write.

He took some persuading – he liked his cart, his horses, and going around the roads and stopping off at the odd wine-shop. But he also liked that woman, even if he must soon have realized that she would be the one who would wear the trousers when it came to money matters. She in her turn both respected and adored him, and even as an old woman she would blush and laugh whenever he looked her in the eye in a certain way, chuckling mischievously. But when there was a decision to be made, she would listen to no one but her brothers – particularly the eldest, the one who never married – and then decide everything for herself.

My grandfather was easy-going, thoroughly sweet-natured and always laughing. He'd take his children in his arms – and, later, his grandchildren and great-grandchildren – and laugh and joke with them, whether she liked it or not. She'd tell him to get out the whip, but as often as not it was us children who had the whip hand. We never saw him angry, he never told us off; he would just give us a look – and a gentle one at that. He would do anything she asked of him with great good humour, and if anyone asked his opinion on some matter, even when we were already down in the Pontine Marshes, he would throw up his hands and say: 'She's the one to ask.'

She on the other hand made all the decisions without even asking his opinion, and then she would tell him what she had decided, and if one of my uncles felt bold enough to express a doubt – 'What about pa? Are you sure that'll be all right with him?' – she'd just say: 'I know him.'

But I wouldn't want you to misunderstand me, I may have given the wrong impression: my grandfather was no pushover, no doormat. It was just that that was the way they liked it. Indeed, at the very end – in 1952 – one morning when my grandmother got up as usual and saw that he wasn't making a move, just lying there in bed, she shot him a dark look, as though to say: 'What are you waiting for?'

He said: 'I'm not feeling all that good. I'm staying put.' And he did, and one evening, three weeks later, she sat down beside him on the bed and he said to her, weakly: 'What a beauty you are.'

'No, love,' she answered. 'It's you who's the beauty,' and shortly afterwards he died.

During those three whole weeks she was up and down those stairs, caring for him like a child, and after he died she insisted on washing and dressing him herself and the day after, at the funeral, she held herself stiff as a ramrod throughout and didn't shed a tear. In the evening, though, once they'd all gone home, she took to her bed and stayed there, and three weeks later she too was dead.

Anyway, once he was married, my grandfather stopped being a full-time carter and started being a peasant. He must have been about twenty-three. At first they lived with his wife's brothers – partly to get his hand in, as you might say, although getting your hand in as a peasant isn't as easy as it sounds, you need to have been born on the land, and if you weren't you'll always be at a bit of a loss, you'll never know the right moment to plant or harvest things, you'll have to watch what everyone else is doing, and even your movements will always be a bit stilted; and perhaps that's why he always put his trust in her. After two or three years they decided to set up on their own. She always listened to her brothers, but now she was married she wanted a separate life for herself and her family. In a word, they rented some fields at Codigoro and had a cow or two, given them by her brothers, and they also worked elsewhere, as day-labourers and, if the occasion arose, my grandfather would enjoy a bit of independence working as a carter, because when it came to the land it was my grandmother who ruled the roost.

Anyway, that famous time – in 1904 – on one of these trips, my grandfather happened to pass through Copparo. He was transporting a load of small casks of wine, tied one above the other. At a certain point he came upon a workers' demonstration – labourers working on the Ferrarese drainage system, navvies, men with wheelbarrows. And, standing on a box, yelling and gesticulating, was Edmondo Rossoni.

'Let's hear what he has to say,' said my grandfather to himself, because he'd already met him years before: tall and wiry, a beanpole of a lad, there on the square in Copparo Rossoni cut the figure of a madman. He was from Formignana, or Tresigallo to be more precise, those three houses and a little church where my grandfather's brothers-in-law also lived. Rossoni's father was one of those navvies who dug out canals by hand and built up their banks. His mother was from Comacchio, and worked as a day labourer, weeding the rice-fields and cornfields. My grandfather was eight or nine years his senior, and had known him as a little boy. Now Rossoni must have been about twenty, and my grandfather almost thirty, because he'd been born in 1875, and already had a swarm of children to his name: Themistocles, who was born in 1897, then a girl, in 1898, then Pericles, in 1899, no one in 1900, Iseo in 1901, another girl in 1902, yet another in 1903 and, in 1904, as I've already said, Uncle Adelchi.

Anyway, my grandfather saw Rossoni, all kitted out in a

student's jacket, shirt and bow tie, and he stood behind the workers and listened to him speak. It seemed that a few days earlier – in a place called Buggerru, in Sardinia – soldiers had fired on some striking miners, killing three of them. At least, according to Rossoni. But, as though that weren't enough, a few days before that, in Castelluzzo, in Sicily, the *carabinieri* had fired on another group of peasants, killing two and wounding ten. 'Whoa there,' my grandfather agreed: 'That's beyond the pale. Do you mean I don't even have the right to protest?' And no, in fact, you didn't. Now let's make one thing clear – my grandfather wasn't born yesterday. He knew how the world worked. He was a carter and didn't really have any political ideas as such, he knew that the rich and the poor had always been with us and that there was nothing to be done about it, there was no point in getting any fancy ideas, you were better off just grinning and bearing it. But when you're on your beam ends and can't feed your family, and you ask someone who's rolling in it to give you work or pay you an extra lira, that someone can't have you fired on by the *carabinieri*, or the soldiers. That's beyond the pale, was what my grandfather told himself.

But at that very moment the soldiers arrived on the scene. Right there in the square. In Copparo. Together with the Royal Guards and the local policemen. While Rossoni was talking. But they had no intention of letting him talk. 'This is an unauthorized demonstration, you're under arrest, now break it up.' Then they began to lash out, and all hell broke loose. My grandfather stayed where he was, at the edge of the square – open-mouthed with astonishment – looking down on things from his vantage point on his cart. Behind the workers.

It was utter pandemonium. A thick cloud of dust – there was no asphalt in those days – and shouts and shrieks and

31

gunfire and people running all over the place, and just when my grandfather was raising his whip to let his horse know that it was time to make themselves scarce, who should loom up, like Moses, out of that cloud of dust, but with a swarm of guards bustling and flustering behind him, and land on his cart with a sudden thud, but Rossoni, shrieking: 'Help me, Peruzzi, get me out of here.'

What could my grandfather do? He'd known Rossoni since he was a little boy. He couldn't just leave him there, now could he? My grandfather didn't even stop to ask himself the question, he reacted automatically. He raised his whip and told his horse to giddy-up. But not soon enough: the guards were already on the attack, some trying to stop the horse, seizing it by the bit, and others attacking the cart and the horse – and Rossoni – with the flat of their sabres.

I don't know who got the worst of it, Rossoni or the horse. Anyway, my grandfather flew into a right royal rage, and began lashing out left, right and centre with his long whip: at policemen, bystanders, every nearby Tom, Dick and Harry. 'Sons of bitches,' he was shrieking, beside himself.

The horse had never seen him in such a state – as I've said, he was a quiet man, mild as milk, almost ridiculously obedient; but something had really got into him that day, or rather had got out of him, and anyway the horse had never seen him like that and it took fright. Not at the policemen and the whacks it was receiving on the rump, but at its owner, and it suddenly started shying and bucking like a colt, like at a rodeo, and rearing up between the shafts, with the cart in hot pursuit, with my grandfather and Rossoni clinging to the sides and my grandfather still shouting 'Sons of bitches' and the ropes snapping and all the casks of wine falling down on to the road and the wine spilling out, and my grandfather thinking:

'What am I going to say to her?' meaning his wife, because they'd have to pay for all the wine and for the casks.

To put it briefly, they all landed up on the road, and the cart broke, too, and then the horse stopped short and the policemen grabbed them and threw them into prison, not without roughing them up first, particularly my grandfather, perhaps because he was wearing peasant gear, whereas Rossoni – for all he was a subversive and a revolutionary – was all got up as a thoroughly decent citizen, right down to his bow tie. But it might also have been as a result of those lashes – because, truth to tell, Rossoni had only been on the receiving end, whereas my grandfather had also been handing them out. Anyway, the guards too gave as good as they'd got – including a few to Rossoni – and clapped them into gaol. Then came a trial and a month inside.

I don't know whether they did their time at Copparo or in Ferrara, but I know they shared a cell – a big one, too, from what they said – and the same disgusting prison rations, and bucket, an earthenware pot in a corner of the room, where you did your business. So, they shared their bread and, as it were, their business, and my grandfather, who had never had a political idea in his head in his life – all right, he hadn't much time for priests, but he regarded politics as something for his betters – well, during that month, by dint of listening to Rossoni from dawn to dusk, he too had turned into something of a Karl Marx, even if every so often, particularly when he was curled up in his corner trying to get a bit of sleep, he would shout out from under his blanket: 'Help me, Peruzzi, get me out of here!' and everyone would start to laugh, Rossoni included. Then, after the last laughter had died down at the far end of the cell, my grandfather would add, in tones of desperation: 'Now what will I tell the wife?' Then the others would start to laugh again, but that was all he could think about and, as the days passed, and the time of his release drew ever closer, he began to dread it more and more: 'Thirty days? Thirty years, that's what they should have given me.'

But thirty days it was, and out they went. After saying goodbye to Rossoni at the turn-off for Tresigallo, my grandfather carried on on foot for Codigoro – about fifteen kilometres away – still hoping that he'd never make it, or perhaps indeed with thoughts of turning back. Mild as milk though he was, he wasn't a man to try and avoid his fate; what was done was done, and so he left the main road and took the farm-track towards home. She saw him from a distance – it was late afternoon – appearing and disappearing among the leaves and bursts of sunlight, because by now he was walking along between the rows of elms. And she was coming towards him to meet him.

He guessed that it was her – he could only see her outline, not her features, because the sun was behind her – and he quickened his step: 'Now I'm for it.' But when she was some twenty metres from him, and he saw her face – it bore no trace of anger, so there would be no trouble about the wine, or the cart, it was just happy, and her eyes were smiling even more than her lips – then my grandfather ran forwards to take her in his arms. But as soon as he touched her – just with his outstretched arms, even before he took her into them – my grandfather began to cry, and she had never seen him cry, nor indeed, as far as he could remember, had he ever done so before in his whole life. And my grandmother said to him, over and over: 'We'll pay up, Peruzzi, don't you worry,' so as to comfort him, because she thought that he was weeping with worry, about the debts and the damage. But he was weeping from sheer happiness: 'What a beauty you are,' he said to her, 'what a beauty.' My grandfather was crying because his wife was beautiful. No more no less. Well, of course he also felt a certain sense of relief, because some of his anxieties had been laid to rest; but basically he was crying because she was so beautiful, and not only was she so beautiful, but she also loved him. Well, don't such things make you cry?

It was only afterwards – that evening, in bed, when the matter of enforced abstinence had become a thing of the past – that she felt the need for further explanation. First she'd put her children to bed, keeping Adelchi, the youngest, in a cradle beside them. She'd washed herself with the scented soap she kept in the chest-of-drawers, and thrust some milk impatiently into Adelchi – 'Come on, son, drink up' – until it was streaming down his chin, and he fell fast asleep there at her breast. 'Now he'll sleep through the night,' she said, and laid him in his cradle, and then my grandfather took over at the breast, until they were both exhausted, after all that time apart, and it was only then that she asked him, chuckling, almost teasingly: 'But what got into you, Peruzzi – what got into you?' And then she burst out laughing, and had to turn over because she was heaving so much, they had been lying side by side, and she turned towards him, propping herself up on her elbow, and, again, asked him what had got into him, still laughing, because she had scarcely been able to believe her ears when people had come to tell her about how he'd shouted 'Son of bitches' from up there on his cart, and lashed out at the guards. And now there she was, propped up on the pillow, trying to imagine the scene: 'What got into you?' while he was staring through the candlelight at a damp patch on the ceiling, with his hands clasped behind his head, absorbed and serious, asking himself the self-same question.

'I don't know, either,' he had admitted to her earlier. But

now he thought about it again – while she was still laughing and already beginning to coax him back into life with her other hand – and he turned over too, and started kissing her, and said: 'It was my horse, woman. No one touches my horse!' And my grandmother sensed something hard and threatening in his voice, which, together with his kisses, sent a shiver down her spine.

After that, Rossoni disappeared. First he went to the Workers' Association in Piacenza and then to Milan, or vice versa, and now his name was known throughout Northern Italy, he wrote articles in the papers, and often there would be mention of him in *Avanti!*: 'Comrade Rossoni spoke at such and such a meeting and met with a rapturous reception, only to have the police inform on him.' When he was young, he thought nothing of addressing three separate meetings in three different places in one single day, and then it wasn't at all like it is nowadays. Nowadays no one would even think of mingling with the crowd while they were addressing a meeting. In those days you'd be out there on the square, and people would butt in and harangue and heckle you. And you had to know how to hold your ground and give as good as you got, right there on the spot. Whereas now you go on television and a nice girl smothers you with make-up, and the questions are easy, you know them in advance. And in those days there weren't any cars, either, or trains. Or rather, there were cars, but there weren't any roads. There was no direct road from Codigoro to Ferrara until 1927, and it was Rossoni himself who had it built. Before that, it took four hours by stagecoach, along the banks of the Po di Volano. Anyway, Rossoni could manage three meetings in three different squares in one single day, ranting and railing against the rich and the bosses and, above all, the priests – he'd done his schooling with the Salesian Brothers; his father had forced him to go to a seminary, in Turin, hoping to make a priest of him, but he'd been expelled. So each time he'd have to get back into his gig, hoarse from all his yelling, and hurtle down a few more kilometres of dusty road to go and get hoarse somewhere else. And that takes stamina. Goodness knows what those Salesians must have done to him in that boarding-school of theirs.

Anyway, whenever he happened to see *Avanti!* in the wine-shop, my grandfather would comment aloud on what a fine career Rossoni was forging for himself, but what he was hinting at was that it had all been his doing, 'I gave him the first step up the ladder.' In fact, at this point my grandfather didn't understand much more about politics than he ever had. He'd joined the Farmworkers' Union, of course, and would attend sessions at the Workers' Association. But that was it. As I've said, he'd always steered clear of priests, but he didn't make a thing of it – 'You go your way and I'll go mine,' end of story – not like Rossoni, who was vehemently anticlerical: 'They're the devil incarnate. They keep the poor in ignorance, in fear of hellfire, so they won't rise up against their lords and masters.' My grandfather was different: he simply left priests out of the picture, partly because my grandmother continued to have a certain respect for them. She wasn't particularly devout, but she did go to mass on high days and holidays – Christmas, Easter and Whitsun – she paid her tithe to the parish when the priest called round after the harvest, and she would always pray when one of her children fell ill. By now, though, everyone regarded my grandfather as a Socialist, a subversive, who'd gone to prison with Rossoni for his ideas. How could he not be a Socialist after all that had happened? Well, he was, and he was all for the revolution; but only from the safely of the wine-shop, while he was playing *briscola* with his mates.

Rossoni put in an appearance again in 1908, at the beginning of June. He was just passing through, he'd been holding a meeting at the Farmworkers' Union, and he came round to our house for supper. He was with another man, an elementary teacher from somewhere near Forli – a much shorter man, in comparison with him, that is – and he'd brought him along to meet us. His father was a blacksmith, Rossoni told my grandfather.

'Well, ask him whether he can mend my harrow while I'm making his supper,' my grandmother said to no one in particular on hearing this information.

The short man caught what she said, and started laughing. Put on his mettle, he took off his jacket, loosened his bow tie and rolled up his sleeves. Since she said nothing – indeed, she carried on looking at him with a slight smile, hands on hips, as though challenging him to show his worth – he picked up the hammer, stirred up the embers, blew air into the forge and mended the harrow, straightening out all the spikes into the bargain. And, while he was hammering here, there and everywhere, she was putting the supper on the table – that long table which could already accommodate all six or seven children; home-made pasta and beans, with a side dish of polenta.

This fellow – who was called Mussolini – clearly had brains as well as charm. He was only a year older than Rossoni – he had been born in '83, and Rossoni in '84 – but Rossoni seemed to hold him in great regard, drawing his attention to this or that, and at one point both of them were looking at Uncle Pericles, who was already as nimble as a hare.

Uncle Themistocles, the eldest, was rather unsociable and withdrawn; he wouldn't open his mouth unless you asked him a direct question. Uncle Pericles, on the other hand, never stopped talking; about anything and everything. Now, to grab their attention, what he came up with was: 'What we need around here is a revolution; we've got to force them to give us the land, and give them a sound thrashing,' and Rossoni and his friend laughed, but at the same time they were also watching how he moved, the speed with which he carried out his tasks in the cowshed and the firm tone he used with the animals. He was only nine, but his hands were as work-worn as those of many an older man, and he could read and write and add up, and do all kinds of work around the farm, driving the oxen and handling the bulls. Mussolini carried on glancing in his direction every now and again, even when he was talking with my grandfather and Rossoni.

There was no doubt that Mussolini had great charm, as I've already said, and my grandfather was enraptured by his conversation, because he talked even better than Rossoni: his language was crisp and clear-cut, and you immediately saw what he was driving at. With him everything seemed simple, he didn't come out with that gobbledegook you'd need a lawyer to explain to you. So, my grandfather liked him, or rather, he liked his politics. What he didn't like was the way he was looking at my grandmother, but he went on nodding and smiling a false smile as the two men carried on talking.

In any case, my grandmother was always warm and cheerful; she had a ready wit, and when my grandfather brought people home she would always be pleasant and welcoming – she wasn't the sort to be surly, or to sulk. But with Mussolini she was just a touch more affable than usual. Then, after they'd got into their cart and left, to drive the fifteen kilometres to Tresigallo, where they were expected at Rossoni's house – 'Goodbye now, and thank you for everything, you made us most welcome.' 'Do come back whenever you're round these parts,' – after the children were in bed, and they were too, and my grandmother had finished feeding the latest girl-child while my grandfather was staring at that same damp patch on the ceiling, in the light of the paraffin-lamp, and she leant over him to turn it out, it was only then that he hissed: 'You dirty slut.'

'What's that you said?' and she started to laugh: 'Are you out of your mind, Peruzzi? He was a guest in our house.'

'You dirty slut,' he said again, and then he turned her over and laid into her even as she carried on laughing.

At supper, though, while he was eating and chatting, Rossoni had said that he would be back soon, he was tired, he needed a bit of a rest: 'The day after tomorrow I've got to go to Piacenza for a court case, but then I'll be back and we'll see each other again, because I'll be staying with my mother for a while.'

Mussolini on the other hand had to go to a meeting at Meldola, which was somewhere near where he came from, around Forli-Predappio: 'So I'll be staying with my father for a bit.'

In fact, things didn't quite go to plan for either of them: Mussolini was arrested shortly after the meeting at Meldola, and thrown into prison, while at Piacenza Rossoni received a four-year sentence, plus two years of police surveillance. But hardly had the judge finished reading out the sentence than Rossoni – who'd been sitting in the public area, for his own safety, still being a free man at the time – was out of the courthouse at the speed of light, and by evening he was in Lugano, in Switzerland, and we didn't see him again for at least ten years. From Switzerland he went to France, to Nice, with Corridoni, and there too he had problems with the police,

40

and just managed to board a ship for Brazil: 'Prison wasn't for me. I'd learned my lesson at Copparo. Catch me if you can.'

By now he had sentences hanging over him left, right and centre, with new ones popping up by the day. But they never managed to catch up with him, he just slipped through their fingers like a Comacchio eel, and in fact the only time he ever did inside was that famous month with my grandfather, for the business with the horse at Copparo.

In San Paolo, in Brazil, he met up with Alceste De Ambris, a great big fellow as mad as he was. But De Ambris was the elder, by about ten years, and everyone looked up to him. He came from a well-off family, he was rich, but he'd given it all up to take up the cudgels of the poor, and even in the wineshop he was quite one of the boys. It was he who introduced syndicalism into Italy, and he too had got up to all kinds of mischief, and had had to make himself scarce.

So that was the group they all belonged to – the Revolutionary Syndicalists – and De Ambris and Corridoni were the leaders, followed by Rossoni and Mussolini. And my grandfather was one of them, since he had been in prison with Rossoni.

Excuse me, what did you say? What did the Revolutionary Syndicalists want? Well, they wanted revolution. Today, that may strike you as outrageous – 'Who were they then, the Red Brigades?' – but things were different then. Put yourself in their shoes – those of the poor, I mean, not of the rich. In those days, if you were poor, you had no rights. All you could do was work, and thank God if anyone gave you the chance, because even work was in short supply. The ships which left each day for America from Naples or Genoa were packed to the gunwales, and barely seaworthy, you've no idea how many went down, how many people were never heard of again, or thought that they were going to Canada and ended up in Argentina, or even Sicily. Right back where they'd started from. And conditions in steerage were unimaginable: great big dormitories where men and women slept side by side, and did their business in a chamber pot, like the pails you get in prison, and every morning people went round removing those who had died in the night, and threw them overboard; and, if you did manage to get there in one piece – to North America, that is – you were kicked around worse than a dog. Black labour, that was all you could get. If you took it into your head to ask for a rise, they'd kick you into the middle of next week. And if by any chance you fell off the scaffolding on a building site, and died – or even if you didn't die immediately, but could have pulled through, with a bit of medical attention – they loaded you straight on to what passed for a hearse and dumped you in a ditch in the middle of nowhere, and that was the last anyone would hear of you. They couldn't run the risk of getting a fine from the Department of Labour. I'm sorry, what did you say? They did the same thing here just the other day? Well, there you are then.

It wasn't as if our bosses here in Italy treated us any better than those in America, otherwise we'd have stayed put. You worked a twelve-hour day, even the very youngest, and not only in the countryside, either, but in the factories, with your hands in the driving-belts. You've no idea how many accidents there were. And rock-bottom wages. If you got injured, you didn't get any compensation, you just got sacked. You had no rights at all, you were worth less than a dog. The law, you say? Politics, civil rights, parliament, the 1848 constitution? All that was for the rich, it was only they who had the vote, none of that applied to you. You say that Fascism did away with freedom in Italy? But there's never been freedom in Italy, so how could Fascism have done away with it? It might have done away with it for the rich. But not for the poor. They never had it in the first place. Women got the vote in 1946, but before Fascism most men didn't have the vote either; only the rich, as I've said, while we, the proletariat, counted for less than nothing, less than the hoes in our hands, and if we banded together to protest or strike, they sent in the soldiers to mow us down. And you expect people to take it lying down? And if my grandfather didn't – and he wouldn't have harmed a fly – wouldn't you expect a spot of bother from the Revolutionary Syndicalists? That was what they were all about. They wanted revolution, pure and simple: everyone equal, no more bosses, armies or priests; no more private property; the land divided up among the peasants and the factories in the hands of the workers.

The trouble was, though, that we weren't all equal even among ourselves – not even those of us who were fighting for an equal world. It was chaos. There were the Revolutionary Syndicalists and the ordinary syndicalists from the Workers' Associations, not to mention the CGIL, the trade unions, the Socialists, the republicans, the anarchists, the reformists, the minimalists and the maximalists, each with their own set of goals; I won't go into the differences – indeed, I don't know them myself– but there were plenty of them, a bit like with the left today. Does the left today strike you as being all of a piece? Have you ever seen them in agreement? Well, in those days it was even worse, because some people wanted revolution, while today – if you think about it – even the Communists aren't so different from the liberals, they're divided because it suits them to be, otherwise people would say: 'What's the point in voting for you, rather than someone else?'

Anyway, in those days there were reformists on every street corner, people who said: 'One small step at a time; we'll edge forward bit by bit, win a minor right here and another there, and who knows, one day something might happen,' and meanwhile hope was proving a good breakfast but a bad supper, as the old proverb has it. Or at least that's what my people thought. And it's true, that night at my grandfather's, it was those same reformists that Rossoni and Mussolini were laying into – Treves, Turati, Modigliani, Bissolati; they couldn't stand them, because they kept on telling everyone to keep calm, sooner or later something would happen in parliament and what was needed was a moderate brand of syndicalism – reformist syndicalism, in fact.

Whereas our lot wanted to get things over with once and for all, by means of a well-organized general strike. Not the so-called general strikes they have nowadays, mini-strikes lasting for four hours or so and then everyone scuttling back to work, to make up for those four hours as quickly as possible. They wanted a real general strike, with everyone downing tools from one moment to the next, whatever their trade – waiter, cowherd, factory worker, street sweeper, railway worker, grave-digger – and then we'd see how things went. And not just for two or three days, either, but starting now and going on for ever, until the bosses were clean out of bread and there was no one to wipe their arses or keep the factories going or work their land or tend their cows.

Naturally, I'm not going to offer you my opinion as to the rights and wrongs of all of this. I'm just telling you how things were then, and how my family felt about it all. I don't know who was wrong and who was right. You can judge that for yourself.

Anyway, all this talk of a general strike was fine by my

grandfather: 'All you need to do is to lay in a few stores, agree on the day without letting the bosses know and you're all set, you know what's going on and they're left in the dark.' By now he was a thorough-going revolutionary syndicalist, but what Rossoni hadn't really explained to him was that the reformists were to all intents and purposes in the enemy camp. He thought we were all fighting more or less for the same cause, and so, for him, the names he saw most often in *Avanti!* – the names of people in parliament who were fighting for our interests as working people, against Giolitti and the king – were the best of the bunch.

So, from 1904–1908, during which time my grandfather had produced another four children, thinking he was doing his bit for the party, he named one son Treves and the other Turati, and the little twin girls, who were now sleeping together in the cradle, head to tail – it was already rather a crush – had been named Modigliana and Bissolata, so that everybody got a look in. Anyway, that evening at supper – of course they were all still small, and couldn't understand – every time that Mussolini got carried away, and he got carried away a lot, but he still kept trying to catch my grandmother's eye – well, every time he came out with: 'That bastard Turati this', or 'That dirty dog Turati that', my grandfather would give him a warning nudge.

And also shoot him a warning look – he'd better cut out that sheep's eye business – and carry on nudging, and gesturing towards the child in question: 'It's too late now, I've named him and that's that.'

And from that moment on – throughout the years that followed – whenever that uncle of mine had a tantrum or got into a fight, his brothers and sisters would gang up on him and taunt him with the chant: 'That bastard Turati this, that dirty dog Turati that.' And he would go mad and start throwing stones left, right and centre. But actually it wasn't our Turati who had the worst of it, because once he got over his tantrums and grew up we stopped teasing him, and anyway there was another Turati then, Augusto Turati, who became the secretary of the National Fascist Party, the PNF, so teasing was no longer in order, indeed, a bit of caution was called for. No, the one who really got it in the neck was one of the little twins, Aunt Bissolata, because when my grandfather came back from the registry office and told her the name he'd chosen, my grandmother flew into a towering rage : 'Bissolata? What brought that on? Who'd marry a woman with a name like that? Can't you see that everyone will call your daughter *Bissola*?' And indeed they did – in our dialect *Bissola* means little snake – and we called her that too, behind her back, because she was indeed a snake, and a poisonous one at that. Whereas Aunt Modigliana was an angel.

Anyway, from Nice Rossoni went on to Brazil, to Sao Paulo, where he met up with Alceste De Ambris, but a few months later he was kicked out yet again, for having organized the first ever general strike in a big glassworks at Agua Branca. The workers were cock-a-hoop, but the glassworks was owned by the prefect of Sao Paulo, so, as you can imagine, there wasn't room for both of them around those parts, and Rossoni was bundled on to the first steamer bound for Europe. When he arrived in France there were more strikes and a load of trouble – accusations, court cases, convictions – but somehow he managed to dodge arrest and make it to New York, where he immediately became the union boss and owner of the paper *Il Proletario*, and it was he who organized the first textile-workers' strike ever to be held in that city. But once the strike was over, and the reformists went off to sign the agreement about a pay rise with the bosses, Rossoni refused to sign, saying they'd been had: 'We should have got more, they've stitched you up,' meaning a bit of under-the-counter bribery had gone on. And that's how he became the Hero of Two Worlds. He'd pick a quarrel with anyone and everyone. And by now every emigrant – in North and South America alike – carried his photo in their wallet. He went to Canada as well, moving from country to country to dodge arrest, and it was quite some years before we saw him again.

But every so often he would send us newspapers, which might or might not reach us on our wanderings, because by now we too were always on the move, depending on how my grandmother, through her brothers, could find us better conditions for renting or sharecropping. So, we were on the open road, and one year we were at Mesola, the next at Argenta, and then at Taglio del Po, Ariano Polesine, Papozze, Polesella... And in one of those newspapers – in 1911, I think it was – we read about a demonstration in New York in honour of some descendant of Garibaldi's, and at the end of the meeting Rossoni had got up on to the soap box and had spat on the Italian flag 'in the midst of an adoring crowd'. Yes, it was in 1911, when Italy declared war on Turkey in an attempt to take Libya from her.

But I can't spend all day telling you every detail of Rossoni's career. What's that got to do with us? What interests you, if I've got this right, is the story of my family, and here Rossoni just happens to have a walk-on part as an accidental link in the chain of events which ultimately took us to the Pontine Marshes, no more no less. So, as I've already said, we didn't see him again for a number of years, but – if that had been all there was to it – my uncles would never even have taken it into their heads to get on their bikes and go down to

Rome to try and call on him in Palazzo Venezia. And we were no fools, either. By now it was 1932, and the Copparo business dated back to 1904; you can't pay a call on someone on the basis of an acquaintanceship dating back thirty years. And how likely is it that someone who's covered so much ground in the meanwhile will agree to see you just because he climbed on to your father's cart all those years ago at Copparo? If that's what you were counting on, you might as well have stayed at home. That was the beginning, of course, but there was quite a bit to follow.

Anyway, we were over here and he was over there, sending us those newspapers, which we read whenever they reached us. Otherwise, we carried on working and making a little headway in the world. In Codigoro we'd already been joined by my grandfather's brother and the whole brood he too was producing with his wife, who just happened to be a cousin of my grandmother's. So, we were quite a tribe. The kids were growing up, and soon there'd be enough of us to work the whole of the Po Valley on our own. Every so often – as I've said – we'd move on, depending on conditions; but always upwards, as you might say, always gaining the odd hectare here and there. The land wasn't ours, let's make that clear: we were sharecroppers, we were renting, there was always a boss; but now it was us who chose him. Sometimes we would go back to the same one, but under improved conditions. We'd leave at the end of the season with all our clobber – pots and pans, furniture and tools all piled up on our carts – and we'd amassed quite a lot clobber by now, all earned with the sweat of our brow, and even the seven-year-olds had work-worn hands. We always moved around the same region, of course – along both banks of the Po – and everybody knew us, because they lived the same sort of life as we did. A year here and a year there, always with an eye to the main chance – nothing very ambitious, just an extra hundred kilos or so of wheat – and for a few years things might go well and then, suddenly, the next year you'd make a loss and find yourself back where you'd started from, only with one or two fewer carts and one or two more debts. So people scraped by, and we scraped by fairly well, what with all those children and our good health. And whenever we arrived in some new place – after we'd looked around the house and followed my grandmother on a tour of inspection of the haylofts and the cowsheds – while she was already giving orders for the unloading of the carts, my grandfather would ask: 'What do you say, then, shall I go and have a look round?'

'Off you go,' she'd say, and he'd go off to inspect the local wine-shop too, to see how things were around these parts in terms of *briscola* and the local Farmworkers' Union.

So back to September 1911, with Italy declaring war on Turkey to have a stab at Libya.

Half a century ago we were still a country divided, a hundred or so separate little states – you needed a passport to go from one to the other – and all the foreigners who came to Italy lorded it over us once they'd got here. The laughing-stock of Europe, that's what we were. And then just fifty years later we were becoming a power which was marching off to defy Turkey and colonizing Africa: 'Libya!' the cry went up. Never mind that fifteen years before that – when we'd made a grab for Ethiopia first time round – the Abyssinians had sent us packing, after making mincemeat of us at Adowa in 1896, them with their arrows and lances, and us with our rifles and machine-guns. Six thousand dead. And now we were off to have another stab at Libya.

The Socialists of course had no time for this policy of colonial and imperialist aggression: 'What's all this?' they'd say. 'Until the other day you yourself were trampled on and jeered at by foreign powers, and now you're off to trample on and jeer at someone else?' And the most outraged of all was Mussolini himself, who had become something of a top dog among the Revolutionary Syndicalists in Italy, and who was also a big cheese in the Socialist Party. 'I always thought as much,' my grandfather would now say in the wine-shop when he read about him in *Avanti!* 'He's one in a million. If he takes it into his head to do something, there's no stopping him,' and indeed within a few years everyone was of this opinion, not just my grandfather – and more particularly my grandmother – even Treves and Turati, who tried to keep on friendly terms with him. Well, he kicked up an almighty kerfuffle about Libya. First he managed to win over the other Socialists – and the ones he failed to win over, like Bonomi and Bissolati, he had expelled from the party because they were 'too compliant, too much in cahoots with the crown' – and then he led the general strike against the war in Africa with revolutionary action amounting to out-and-out sabotage, with people blowing up bridges and removing railway sleepers so the troop trains couldn't get through. So the following year he was tried and sentenced and put inside. He said that the Italian generals were bloodthirsty and warmongering, and so was Giolitti, the head of state who had sent them there.

In 1911, he expressed these same opinions when he came around our way. By now he had settled in Milan, because that was where the money and the factories were, and also the best chance of a good rumpus. But for the strike against the war in Libya he put himself about a bit, and he also came to where we were living at the time, so my grandfather went along to the demonstration, together with his older children. Of course, before going off we'd milked our cows and cleaned out the cowsheds, because we were on strike too, and obviously to carry on working in the fields for our boss – with the risk that someone might have seen us – never even entered our heads. Indeed, my grandfather had been the first in the wine-shop to say: 'Everybody out!' But our cows were a different matter. We couldn't let them die of hunger, could we? Or leave them with bursting udders? We had to milk them, otherwise they'd have got mastitis. But once we'd milked them and cleaned out the cowshed, we too went off to the town square. There was no way we were going to be left behind.

Mussolini was on top form, he had them all eating out of his hand. The moment the secretary of the local Farmworkers' Union uttered the words: 'And now I'd like to introduce Comrade Mussolini,' he immediately started to lam into them. He didn't spit on the Italian flag, like Rossoni in America, but near as damn it, believe you me. You have no idea what he dared to say to those four scabs, particularly Giolitti, 'that shifty, mealy-mouthed man from Piedmont', the worst of the lot, in his opinion: 'With all the hunger there is around these parts, and all those poor devils who are being exploited and bled white by the priests and bosses, are we going to go and attack those poor Bantu out there to make slaves of them too? Shame on you!' said Mussolini, 'especially Giolitti and Bissolati.' As my grandfather used to say, when Mussolini said something, he didn't beat about the bush, out it all came, he wasn't one to mince words.

Once – in Lausanne, I think, in Switzerland, when he was there dodging some sentence or other – he came across a priest who was going around bad-mouthing the Socialists, and gave him a good kick up the backside in front of everyone. Then, from on top of his soap box – after taking his watch out of his breast pocket and hanging it from the handrail, where everyone could see it – he went on: 'But now it's time to have done with your boss, too: God doesn't exist, and I'm going to prove it. I'll put him to the test. If he exists, I give him three minutes to strike me dead right here in this square. If nothing happens, it means he doesn't exist. Three minutes, I said, and that's it,' and he stood there in silence for three minutes, with the watch hanging there in the air, and those three minutes seemed very long indeed. Put like that, of course, three minutes seems no time at all; but if no one says a word, and everyone's on tenterhooks, then it's another matter. And even saying 'I'm an atheist; God does not exist,' that doesn't sound like much either. But mark my words: that time in Lausanne there was a crowd of Socialists and rabid anti-clericals around that soap box, but the moment Mussolini said: 'I give him three minutes,' people started quietly drawing back, moving away; suddenly, he was on his own.

And he just stood there, cool as a cucumber, waiting for those three minutes to pass, and when they were over he put his watch calmly back into his breast pocket, rolled the chain around it, and said triumphantly: 'There, what did I tell you? I'm in the clear: there is no God.' You can't imagine the applause. But also a great sigh of relief: 'Aaaah.'

Anyway, after the meeting was over – the one in our town, in 1911, about Libya – when he came down from the soap box, people gathered round to greet him, and he went off with the hard core to have a glass or two, as you do on such occasions. My grandfather had been one of those who had gone up to greet him, even if he was a little nervous that he might not be recognized. But in fact, as soon as he saw him, he shouted: 'Peruzzi! What a shame, this time I won't be able to call round at your place to eat, I've got to be off right now. But there'll be other opportunities, don't you worry.'

Anyway, when he learned that this time Mussolini wasn't coming to supper, my grandfather heaved a sigh of relief almost as heartfelt as the one heaved by the crowd in Lausanne when they weren't struck down by God, and as they were driving home in the cart he turned to Uncle Pericles who was sitting beside him and said to him jokingly, but only half-jokingly: 'Who said anything about an invitation, anyway?'

But Pericles, who was cock-a-hoop because Mussolini had remembered him too – 'Ah, it's Pericles, isn't it, remember me to your mother and tell her that next time I'd like some more of those beans,' – was quite upset and gave his father a baffled look: 'How can you say that, pa? It would have been an honour.'

'An honour? He talks as though he owns the place. "This time I won't be able to call round." Whoever asked him to, clodhopper that he is?' and because he never lashed out at his children – he'd never laid a hand on them in all their lives – he gave his horse a whipping it wasn't going to forget in a hurry.

Anyway, one way or another three years went by, and now it was 1914, and we were in Cavarzere, near the sugar refinery. Uncle Pericles was now fifteen, with just the faintest hint of a beard, but he was a late developer, and at that time he was more of an overgrown boy. 1914 was the year of the so-called 'red week', that shambles that lasted seven days, from 7–14 June, and the old people remembered the exact dates because the next week the First World War broke out.

Salandra was now Prime Minister, but actually it was still Giolitti who was in the driving seat, and he was a chancer who could twist people round his little finger. One way or another, he headed the government for two decades. 'Today I head the government and tomorrow you can have a go, but only in name because it'll still be me who's in charge.' At first, in 1892, before the Socialists were in the government, because the party had only been founded two years earlier, anyway, that year – after the scandal of the Banca Romana, and here Giolitti too seems to have had a finger in the pie – to avoid prison he'd had to flee to Switzerland, together with the anarchists and revolutionaries. But after just a year or two he breezed back into government, jaunty as anything. So you can see what sort of hands we poor devils were in, and in fact it's not so different now, "he who rules the roost gets the roast", as my grandmother used to say, God rest her soul. Anyway, that great chancer also knew a thing or two, and he knew things had to change. Apparently the country had made considerable progress under him in economic terms, particularly the banks, and industry. He also had a certain care for the poor, it was him who passed the first law concerning accidents at work, and against child labour. And at some point it seems he went to the king and said: 'Dear king, we can't go on like this. If we carry on giving the workers and the poor such a hard time, the moment will come when they'll become well and truly fed up with us and throw us all out, bag and baggage.'

'All right, Giolitti, I take your point. What do you think we should do?'

'We need to give them a little sweetener,' and then he passed the laws I've just mentioned, and extended the vote to all males, not just the big cheeses. 'But I don't think that'll be enough, king.'

'Fine. What else do we need to do, in your opinion?'

'We're going to have to ask the Socialists to join the government,' because now, at the beginning of the twentieth century, Socialism was spreading like wild fire.

'The Socialists?' the king said. 'Are you mad? They want a republic, they want me out. Me, ask them to join the government?'

'King, a cobbler should stick to his last: you do your job and I'll do mine. You do the king bit and I'll do the politics. I'll set them up nicely, I'll bring them into government, I'll feed them one reform at a time. Time and straw make medlars ripe, and if you give them enough to be getting on with they'll become as decent as the next man,' which, you've studied history so you'd be the first to agree, is just what the reformists wanted.

'All right, Giolitti,' said the king, 'do as you think best, I'm in your hands.' So off Giolitti went to the Reformist Socialists – the big boys: Bonomi, Treves, Turati, Modigliani – and said to them them: 'D'you want to join the government?'

'No thanks; not for all the tea in China,' they said.

'But are you mad?' Giolitti asked them. 'So what's it all about? You're in parliament, you take part in the elections and when I ask you to join the government, you just say no, no dice?'

'Gioli, we just can't, no point in harping on.'

'What sort of talk is that, who says you can't, the doctor?'

'No, but if we join the government, what would the Revolutionary Syndicalists have to say? We'd never hear the end of it.'

'I take your point, but that lot are really mad, there's no reasoning with them, they want revolution. Um, er, that's not by any chance what your lot want, as well?'

'Certainly not, the very idea,' was what Treves, Turati and company came back with. 'We're reformists, we don't want revolution just like that, we want one reform at a time, step by little step, that's our watchword.'

'There you are then,' Giolitti said: 'That's exactly what I'm getting at. Join us in government and we'll bring in one reform at a time, step by little step.'

'Gioli, don't go on about it. We just can't do it! You'll have to bring in our reforms on your own.'

After that, Giolitti wouldn't have any more dealings with them. That was how he was – with you today and with someone else tomorrow – and he wasn't too fussy about who were his enemies and who his friends. When he needed a vote in parliament, he would buy it from the first person who came to hand; more or less like now, when it comes down to it, indeed people say that it was he who dreamt up what they call transformism. And collaborationism too, come to that: he beat the *camorra* at their own game by enlisting the support of the *camorristi*, and he'd have invented the centre-left, as well, if he'd had half a chance. And all this over a hundred years ago. But the reformists weren't having any, so he dreamt up Christian Democracy.

Now why are you laughing, don't you believe me? Just go and look it up. Until a few years ago the Catholics didn't even vote, they kept completely clear of politics because the pope had expressly forbidden them from meddling in such matters after the *Bersaglieri* had blasted their way in through Porta Pia in 1870 and Rome became the capital of Italy. The pope hadn't liked this breaching of his domain: 'How dare you? Rome belongs to me, or rather to Saint Peter, and you have committed a mortal sin by coming in to take it from me, so I'm excommunicating the House of Savoy and the whole Italian State; upstanding Christians must have nothing to do with all this. *Non possumus, not expedit.*' And that time they weren't joking, either.

In 1905, though, the pope began to ease up a bit – 'Well,

okay, it's no longer really a mortal sin,' – because by now the Socialists were preaching the glorious future on every street corner. 'Oh well, I'll have to make a move while the going's good.' And it was then, after Pius X let up a bit, and after the Socialists refused to join the government, that Giolitti began conniving with the Catholics and persuaded them to form an electoral body telling people – in the constituencies where they couldn't be sure of getting a candidate elected – to vote for the one he was supporting. And that's how Christian Democracy was born, another of Giolitti's cunning little inventions. But the fault lay with Turati, that's what my people said.

I'm in no position to tell you whether they were right or wrong. Of course, Turati too must have had his reasons, and looking at things all these years later – now that we can see how the revolution turned out in the USSR, with the gulags and all that business, when even they started to say: 'That's enough, let's go back to capitalism, it wasn't all that bad; we won't be getting justice and equality, but we will be getting freedom, and dishwashers and colour TV,' – you might reasonably say: 'Okay, Turati was right.' But you're saying that now; you have to think back to then. In those days, perhaps – if nobody had gone for out-and-out revolution, like in Russia – the capitalists would never have taken fright to the point of saying: 'Okay then, let's give them a few reforms, before they start the revolution here.' What do we know of what might have happened?

I don't want to have to speak badly of Turati. That was just what my people said. In my view he was a good man, and indeed it's not true that the draining of the Pontine Marshes was all Fascism's doing; Turati had already considered it, with Nitti, in 1919, after the Great War. He had a friend, an engineer called Omodeo, who wanted to create a lot of artificial lakes so they could build power-stations, and another friend – called Serpieri, an expert on land reclamation and agriculture – who had links with the *Banca Commerciale*. They'd been in contact with someone called Clerici, who wanted to reclaim the Pontine Marshes and had already come to an agreement with the princely Caetani family who were big local landowners. Turati gave them his support and helped them obtain state funding.

What did you say? That it's almost as though I didn't like the fact that Turati was cosying up to the *Banca Commerciale* and Clerici and the Caetani? But I'm not passing judgement, I'm just telling you what I've been told, and even I accept that sometimes you have to meet your opponents halfway. Didn't Agnelli say, of Moggi, that the head of the king's stables must be able to spot a horse-thief? He'd have been stymied, otherwise. As soon as his head was turned, they'd have filched the lot. So of course I'm not shocked at the idea of Turati going to dine at Villa Fogliano with Prince Caetani. What's it to me? What interests me is that he wanted to drain the marshes. But then everything went belly-up and we got the 'Pontine Marshes Scandal', as the papers called it. That is, they wanted to reclaim the land using state funds, and then sell it off plot by plot to the highest bidder. Indeed, they'd already started selling it off before they'd even reclaimed it, and used the proceeds to buy themselves palaces in Rome. Spondoolicks for all and sundry, including the journalists. Of course it wasn't Turati's fault. It was that Clerici. But the Caetani too would have stood to gain, while Omodeo – that friend of Turati's who was a specialist in lakes, who went on to rake it in, in the Soviet Union – wanted to make a lake here, between Doganella and Cisterna, not even a hundred metres above sea level. How much electricity would that give you, with so little head? Anyway, even if you dammed up the Teppia – which was all murky water from the Alban Hills – how long would it be before it got all silted up with volcanic debris? This attempt at land reclamation was rubbish from start to finish. Take the money and run, as they say nowadays.

Anyway, in 1914, at the beginning of June, there was this Red Week. Giolitti was no longer Prime Minister – Salandra had taken over, though of course he was one of Giolitti's placemen – and my Uncle Pericles had his first dealings with the priest.

At this point we were at Cavarzere, and there was a new young priest, with new ideas, who wanted to set up some sort of youth club, and in the meantime he was getting the kids to play football. They played barefoot in those days, you only put shoes on when you did military service, or had your first communion, and even then a whole family would use the same ones. In the countryside and in the streets you always went barefoot, so you played football barefoot too, using one of those very heavy old balls made out of leather. If you got it right on the big toe, you'd be limping for a week. Furthermore, unlike other priests, this one never got up into the pulpit to preach that you had to be obedient and submissive and never fight back, because it's God's will that you're poor; and anyway being poor is an advantage, because it isn't this life on earth that counts, or rather, the more wretched it is, nothing but pain and sacrifice, the more the Lord will reward you for it in the Kingdom of Heaven. It's almost a stroke of luck to be poor. But although he no longer preached that sort of thing, the priest at Cavarzere wasn't all that keen on the local Farmworkers' Union. He didn't like the reds, and he was already trying to organize a rival 'white' friendly society of his own, a Catholic association of day-labourers and peasants which would represent their interests with the bosses. Just like our Socialist equivalent, then, but without the violence and blaspheming against God and the Church: 'Where's the need for revolution? You've got the Church to protect you,' he said one afternoon – during Red Week, into the bargain – denouncing various red excesses and factory occupations and peasant strikes and thrashing of black-legs who wanted to go and milk the bosses' cows. And bear in mind that this was June, and soon the corn would be ready, and if you don't harvest it at the right time you can't just go back and harvest it a month later, or plant it again when the mood takes you. You plant it once a year, and if you miss the harvest, you miss it for the whole year. You're left without bread; the whole nation is left without bread.

My Uncle Pericles was fifteen at the time, but he was a late developer and he was still rather short – one metre sixty, if that – and he'd never had any truck with priests. The whole family had been on 'Good morning and good evening' terms with them, and nothing more. But then came this football business, and for some time now he and Uncle Iseo had been spending their afternoons kicking a ball around next to the church. Anyway, that's what they were doing when the priest had said what he had, and he was meddling in politics, speaking out against the reds, whose watchword was down with everything, who were 'nihilists', as he put it. And then my uncle said to him: 'Are you joking? We're desperate. Can't you see what the bosses have reduced us to?'

'Of course, fair's fair,' said the priest. 'The Church too is on the side of the poor, but without all the violence, which is an offence to God and achieves nothing. Whereas we want true justice, freedom and progress, because Christ was a worker, not a rich man, and it was he who said that it is easier for a

60

camel to get through the eye of a needle than for a rich man to enter the Kingdom of Heaven.'

'Well, you soon forgot about that,' said my Uncle Pericles.

But the priest took no notice of what he was saying, he just carried right on with his own patter: 'The Church has its own thinking on these matters! We've set up our own 'white' Workers' Associations and co-operatives, which fight against the abuses of the rich, but also against the violence and bullying of the reds.'

'But father,' my uncle asked him, 'how come you've waited two thousand years before starting to come up with this talk of social justice? If it weren't for the glorious future just around the corner, such talk probably wouldn't have crossed your minds. You'd have kept it to yourselves for another two thousand years. To hell with you, father, all your lot cares about is money, you're just carrion hovering over the corpses of the proletariat.' Sometimes, my Uncle Pericles could talk just like *Avanti!* But the priest wasn't best pleased; indeed, he responded by giving Pericles a slap.

Now the priest was an adult, and my uncle still looked like a small boy. But that slap – all right, it wasn't a hard one, but it was still a slap in the face, and everyone had seen it – caused him to see red. And no sooner had it been delivered than my uncle had pulled out a knife and thrown himself on the priest and pushed him roughly up against the wall, and now he was brandishing the knife under his nose – up against that wall, the priest was much taller than he was, he was still so small – and then pressing the point threateningly against his throat: 'That's the last time you'll do that to me.'

Everyone seemed frozen to the spot; nobody said a word, the priest and my uncle included. I don't know how long it lasted, seconds perhaps, maybe longer. Then my uncle withdrew the knife and snapped it shut, put it back in his pocket, turned round and started to walk away.

Don't pull that face. My uncle was no delinquent. Then why was he carrying a knife, you ask? Don't be ridiculous, things were different then. Everyone carried knives, a knife was a tool of everyday life, like a watch or a mobile nowadays. In those days you never saw anyone wearing a watch, only the nobs. What would the poor want with a watch? They didn't have to be anywhere on time. What they needed was knives. Just to get by: to cut off a piece of bread when they were in the fields, a bit of cheese, an apple, or to make themselves a walking-stick, or carve themselves a whistle, or to kill a snake or cut back brambles. They were always in the middle of nowhere, they weren't in a city, or on a train in the underground, and a knife could always come in handy, everyone had one, not just my uncle. I don't want to sound over-defensive. It was probably a misunderstanding. Years later, some people said that there was nothing mean or vindictive about that slap, that it was just his normal way of dealing with the boys in that youth club of his; every so often he would give them a playful box round the ears, and anyway in those days even infant school-teachers would deal out pretty sharp raps on the knuckles, so the priest might have meant nothing by it, my uncle might just have got it wrong. But he was fifteen, he did the work of a grown man; physically, he was small, but he regarded himself as an adult and he was having an adult conversation, and he felt that that slap in the face – however it was meant, whether it was just routine, or somehow more personal – was quite uncalled for. And that was that.

But I can also see why the priest too should have lost all sense of control when he felt himself being pinned against a wall by a mere boy, with a knife at his throat. You can never tell how these things will turn out, my uncle might really have made use of that knife and sent that priest to his maker, and in such cases you shouldn't be afraid, not if you're a priest, because you'll be going to Heaven, that is, to a better place, but we're all human, and it's reasonable enough to feel frightened when you've got a knife right up against your throat, and not only frightened, but also humiliated, because it was all so shamefully public. So I understand his reaction and I'm not blaming anyone, that's how things go, and I also know that when you begin something you never know how it will turn out, there's a chain reaction, the iron logic of events. But when what had happened had happened and my uncle had turned around and folded up the knife and put it back in his pocket, and even started to walk off in the direction of home – 'To hell with you and your football!' – there was no need for him to shout out 'Jailbird!' after him.

My uncle swung round and retraced those few steps in a single bound, and then he was at him again, pinning him up against the wall of the priest's house with the open knife against his throat and ordering him to hold his tongue; and the priest held his tongue and went white as a sheet.

Uncle Pericles turned on his heel again and walked off. He never went back to play football by the church, indeed he never went near the place again, not that he'd ever been a regular attender. And once he was passing by on his cart with a load of hay, and sitting on the box and whittling away at a stick to make a doll for one or other of his sisters, and the other boys – by now he scarcely even said hello to them – were kicking a ball around, and one of them kicked the ball on to his cart, probably by mistake, and he thought they'd done it on purpose, to annoy him. The knife was already in his hand – he was making that doll – and he caught the ball in midair and made a jab at it. Then he tossed it back to them, all floppy and deflated: 'All yours. Carry on with the game.'

But there's no need to go on about it, I accept that my uncle was at fault, and indeed his mother – my grandmother – went on about it every blessed day for a whole week, after someone had gone to tell her what had happened. The world is full of people who don't know how to mind their own business. There's always some busybody hanging around, ready to rush off and inform the family the minute something unpleasant happens, to make them feel bad too, and in this instance I think, but I wouldn't swear to it, that the busybody in question was my grandmother's older brother, the one who was still unmarried; in this he was like Uncle Adelchi – the one you say was such a decent sort, the peacemaker-policeman – he too was a telltale. Anyway – once the tale had been told – my grandmother wanted Uncle Pericles to go and apologize to the priest, because, she said, that was no way to carry on. First of all because the priest was older than Pericles, and boys should respect their elders, but above all because he was a priest, 'a man of God', as she put it, and whether or not you believe that this God exists, such men are working in a good cause and anyway you never know, was what she said. Such a lack of respect would bring bad luck. Sooner or later you'd pay for it: 'God is a sure paymaster.'

My grandfather, on the other hand, said nothing. Knowing what you know, you'll quite understand that if his wife was angry with their son and had decided to chide him from dawn to dusk, he wasn't going to get involved. To what end? To defend him? This time their son was absolutely in the wrong, because it's true that you must always keep your self-respect and not allow yourself to be insulted by the first comer, even if he is of superior rank or, as my grandmother put it, 'a man of God', but on the other hand your betters are always your betters and you'd do well not to forget it, even if it's a question of keeping up appearances, and anyway – before pulling a knife on someone – you'd be well-advised to think twice, not pull it out twice without having thought even once. But apart from the fact that this time their son was in the wrong, there was no point in coming to his defence. She was all too capable of rounding on him, and then it would turn out to be all his fault. Silence was golden.

What did you say? That he too could have given his son a ticking off? That would only have made things worse. You clearly haven't understood the kind of woman she was. 'What are you sticking your nose in for?' she would have said; and then she would have changed her tune, and started to say that her son was right and he was wrong, out of pure cussedness. It was better to mind your own business when she got going, and wait till the whole thing blew over.

But every so often, while he was in the cowshed forking up the dung, every time he heard my grandmother shrieking from inside the house, my grandfather would mutter 'Monti and Tognetti' under his breath.

'Monti and Tognetti!' he would repeat, piling the manure into the wheelbarrow to take it to the dung-heap. 'Monti and Tognetti' were the names of the two patriots who were executed on the pope's orders in 1867 after an attempt on his life, while Garibaldi and the Cairoli brothers were converging on Rome to make it part of a united Italy. Christ said to turn the other cheek, but Pope Pius IX had Monti and Tognetti's heads cut off. *Coram populo*. In the square. With the guillotine. Then, before throwing them into the basket, he lifted them up to display them to the ranks of Zouaves, the French soldiers he kept there specially to fire on the Italians: 'In Rome,' said the pope, 'it's me who's king, and woe betide anyone who breathes a word against me.' That was Pius IX for you. It wasn't much more than forty years ago, after all, it was still fresh in people's memories, and every time the subject of priests cropped up, in the wine-shop or in some argument, my grandfather would immediately say: 'Monti and Tognetti! That says it all.'

Anyway, the week after Red Week, the First World War broke out. Of course we didn't know that that was what it would become, we didn't go around saying 'Hey, the First World War's just broken out'; it was only later that we learned that was what it would be. We didn't think it would be much of a war – 'It'll be over by Christmas,' – because we were still thinking about Red Week. In our opinion, that was the big event. It had been a mighty struggle and we'd all been very caught up in it, but the results were nil: no revolution, no reforms and no reformism; all words and no deeds, as always. So, after a bit, we stopped talking about that and began to talk of this new and more important thing – the war – but not straight away. For a bit, we carried on living, working and cursing without batting an eyelid, all wrapped up in our own affairs: our bosses, the tenant farmers, the land, our contracts, sharecropping, our livestock, our cart, sons growing up and new daughters arriving on the scene.

But the really important new arrival was this World War. We weren't in it, though, we were staying neutral, and while everyone else had been butchering each other for months, in Italy all that was going on was an all-out dogfight between those who wanted to join in and those who didn't (though perhaps all-out dogfight isn't quite right, because the only ones involved were those few nobs and intellectuals who read the papers and were interested in politics, while the rest of us just went hungry and got on with our lives). At all events,

66

while the Socialists and the left were against the war and were all for peace, the most hard-bitten Revolutionary Syndicalists – Rossoni in America, and De Ambris and Corridoni, and Mussolini, who had become the editor of *Avanti!* – suddenly came on the scene saying that we too had to intervene and join the fray, but on the side of the Triple Entente, with France, Russia and Britain, against Austria and Germany, who were actually our allies, and with whom we'd made any number of treaties. But what meaning does the word treaty or ally have In Italy? So then they started laying into those reformists who didn't want war : 'Socialism means peace, we hate war,' was what the reformists said.

'Oh yes?' the others shot back. 'So why have the German Socialists entered the war alongside the Kaiser, to defend their own wellbeing, at the expense of those they're preparing to butcher?' In a word, a worse dogfight than ever.

At first, my grandfather wasn't all that convinced by his friends' sudden conversion to interventionism: 'In a war, it's not unknown for men to die,' he would say to my grandmother. But by now Mussolini had had to resign from *Avanti!* because he'd got the whole party against him, and he'd started a paper of his own, *Il Popolo d'Italia* , even though the words 'Socialist Daily' were still there below the title. So it wasn't as though the party had changed its spots, they were still Socialist but also interventionist, and they explained the reasons for this in his paper. Indeed, they also went around the place explaining them to anyone who cared to listen, and he, Mussolini, came round our way as well; or rather, he came to Adria, which is eight kilometres from Cavarzere, and my father and the older boys went to hear him speak. Actually, it was the boys who were the more insistent: 'Let's go and hear him, pa.'

'Why couldn't I have kept my lip buttoned?' was what he

said, because when he got back from the wine-shop, where by now they were reading not only *Avanti!* but also *Il Popolo d'Italia* he'd let slip: 'He's coming to Adria.'

So they piped up: 'Come on, let's go along.'

It was really quite simple: the Revolutionary Syndicalists said that Red Week had gone badly, just a week-long general strike with nothing gained. The men who'd occupied the factories had gone back to work under the same conditions as before; the reformists had got nowhere: unless some new element entered the equation, the revolution would never come about, because clearly what was required was violence –there was no way the bosses would give in otherwise – but the reformists and the proletariat which supported them were against violence, they wouldn't stoop to their enemies' tactics, they preferred to grin and bear it.

So this war was just what was needed, a stroke of unforeseen luck which would shake things up so much – said Comrade Mussolini – that they would never be the same again. Once the proletariat found itself all hugger mugger under arms, the World War would inevitably become a social war. After all, it had been triggered off by a conflict of interests between the capitalist bourgeoisie of the various countries of Europe. So, out on the battlefield, it could not fail to develop into a general war between the classes, with the proletariat of Europe pitched against the bosses.

Now I don't know whether this is clear, but that's how he explained it; and, as I've already said, it wasn't too clear even to my grandfather, because, that evening at supper – as soon as he caught sight of them in the crowd, 'that clodhopper' Mussolini had invited himself yet again: 'Ah, Peruzzi! This time I can make it,' as though he were doing us a favour – that

68

evening at supper my grandfather had said to him: 'We kicked up all that fuss about the war in Libya three years ago, you even went to prison over it, and now all of a sudden this one is all right. So what exactly happened in the meantime?'

Mussolini was about to answer, but then my Uncle Pericles piped up: 'Can I say something, too?'

My grandfather looked at him sharply, because it wasn't like nowadays, when everyone chips in at table and anyone can have a go. In those days children addressed their parents in the polite form and wouldn't have dreamt of contradicting them, or indeed even of agreeing with them, without their permission; the day you suddenly took it into your head to speak at table, or to interrupt without permission, well, that was the day you'd also taken it into your head to get up from table and go off to set up on your own. So my grandfather rolled his eyes: 'What's all this democracy all of a sudden? Where will it all end?'

But, almost before he'd finished speaking, my grandmother put her own oar in: 'Let the boy have his say.'

And Mussolini too – eyes on my grandmother, not for the first time – was nodding in agreement: 'Let's hear what the young folk have to say.'

'Very well then,' said my grandfather, though somewhat grudgingly: 'Now he's monkeying around with the younger generation as well,' was what he was thinking.

'Listen, pa,' was what Pericles finally came out with, once he had the chance: 'it's not the same thing at all. Libya was a war of aggression, and we were the rich ones...'

'Us, rich? Whenever were we rich?' my grandfather objected.

'Compared to them we were,' Uncle Pericles went on; 'we were attacking people poorer than ourselves. But now it's us who are poor, and we're attacking the rich.'

'He's got it in one,' said Mussolini, gazing in wonderment at Uncle Pericles as though he were Pico della Mirandola *Redivivus*; and he gave my grandfather – and even more so my grandmother, of course – a look which said 'Mary mother of God what a bright boy you've got there, congratulations,' and my grandmother looked all cock-a-hoop; my grandfather slightly less so, largely because of the looks. Then, later that evening, when they were alone in the bedroom and she was about to put out the light and turn towards her husband – they did it every night, at least until they came down here, according to my uncles who could hear the bedsprings creak – my grandmother said: 'He's quite something, that Mussolini.'

'Don't talk to me about that man, I've already warned you, you filthy bitch,' said my grandfather, between clenched teeth.

So we went to war anyway. For us it was to be a social war, but in order to convince people to go along with it they started drumming up interest in the Fatherland, and dragging in Trento and Trieste. Now, as we all know, the more something is talked about, the more people will go along with it, and ultimately we too were convinced by all this talk of the Fatherland, though before that we hadn't even known what the word meant – never heard of it – but now it was as though we'd always known it. But there were a lot of other people who didn't want to go to war, they couldn't have cared less about the Fatherland, or Trento or Trieste either for that matter, and there were deserters by the cartload, and when they were caught they were shot. My father's brother and his children – we all lived together in the same farmhouse but we'd started dividing up our possessions, even if we carried on giving one another a hand with the farm work – had stayed with the Reformist Socialists, the pacifists, and they wanted no truck with the war.

We on the other hand were on the side of the interventionists, with Mussolini, Rossoni and *Il Popolo d'Italia*. On a collision course with the party, which was now in the hands of the reformists, or at least the leadership was. They'd more or less driven Mussolini out, and things were getting heated; the leaders who had edged him out of *Avanti!* had already called him every name in the book, 'Turncoat' among them. Those who had always been closest to him now rejected him, including the Balabanoff woman who had been his lover and companion and had taught him not only the rudiments of Socialism, but also about literature, and even a smattering of half-decent manners. And it was then, when he was leaving, and he could see how truly furious they were, that he came out with the phrase: 'You hate me because you still love me.'

But my grandfather just said to my grandmother: 'Don't you be fretting about our boys, they're only young, too young to be called up. How long do you think this war can last?' But last it did, it seemed to be never-ending, it went on for years, and hundred of thousands died. Millions. And there were millions of wounded. And people coming and going all over the place. And finally they called up Uncle Themistocles. The postcard arrived and off he went. She didn't shed a tear when he left. The tears were all inside her. Same with my grandfather. Uncle Themistocles did seem a bit worried – Uncle Pericles on the other hand was almost envious – and when at last he was about to leave, my grandfather said to him, there on the road: 'Make sure you come back in one piece.'

But: 'Make sure you make it back,' was what my grand-mother said, 'never mind about in one piece, just be sure you make it home,' and that night, in bed, each turned to face their own way – 'Goodnight,' was all they said – to think, each on their own, about the son who'd gone to war. And my grandmother made the sign of the cross and began to pray, just as she'd done when he fell ill when he was little.

Then came Caporetto, as you know, with the German breakthrough and us all retreating as they advanced: some threw away their guns, some abandoned their cannon and some fired on their own officers as they tried to stop them in their tracks. Some officers killed themselves, out of pure shame. For the most part, though, the high-ranking staff officers were the first to scarper; but in the end – when the end finally came, that is – they said it was all the soldiers' fault, and the officers all got off scot-free, now they were jauntier and more self-important than ever, and made good careers for themselves, like Badoglio, who bore particular responsibility for Caporetto. Whereas the soldiers who had retreated were all rounded up and shot. Or rather, the divisions which had taken to their heels en masse – by the platoon, the company, the battalion – were lined up by the *carabinieri*, who then counted 'One, two, three, four, five: you're for it,' and that one went to the wall. The others were spared. Decimation, they called it.

At some point, Uncle Themistocles too panicked at Caporetto, because fear is infectious. The more frightened people you see around you, the more frightened you yourself become. At first, you might simply have had your doubts: 'Just how bad are things around these parts?' But you didn't say anything – you kept it to yourself – partly because you weren't yet sure how matters stood. But as soon as you saw that the others were frightened too, then you'd say to yourself: 'Hey, things are bad,' and you took to your heels and made a dash for it. And everyone else did the same. Including Uncle Themistocles – seeing the Germans advancing like fiends, and our boys retreating like so many hares and throwing down their rifles so as to be able to run faster still, at a certain point he too turned tail and ran off like the rest, though he couldn't bring himself to throw away his rifle, 'you never know,' was what he thought to himself. And how right he was, because later on he came upon a group of men who were saying: 'Where are you off to, cowards,' and those without rifles were shot dead on the spot.

But that word 'coward' had put him on his mettle, and he stayed where he was and put up a fight – 'I've had it, either way' – and they set themselves to organizing an orderly retreat. And that's when they gave him the bronze medal, though he couldn't say he felt he'd earned it, because he hadn't performed any particularly heroic acts on that occasion. He'd simply stayed rooted to the spot, no more than that. It required far more courage to get yourself out of the trenches – as he had done so many times before, and indeed after – and engage in hand-to-hand fighting, butchering Germans with your knife. Whereas there – at Caporetto – it was our own side who did the butchering, of Italian deserters, on this occasion, and he too was forced to join the execution squads, and he couldn't get it out of his head that it was only by a whisker that he'd avoided being stood up against that wall himself.

After three years of war, Italy was on her knees. I'm not just talking about hunger, food shortages and so on. I mean that by now there was hardly anyone left to be sent into battle. So they had to call up mere boys, the last class, the class of 1899, including my Uncle Pericles, who was eighteen: 'Just a lad,' my grandmother would say, 'still wet behind the ears.'

He had grown a bit taller, but not much. He was skinny and spindly, with a mop of blond hair, and piercing blue eyes which were never still, and he was as jumpy and nervous as an eel. Now he too had to go. My grandfather's heart bled for him: 'To hell with this darned war, and with me who was in favour of it.'

But he – my Uncle Pericles – was cock-a-hoop, because he'd often imagined scenes of derring-do and putting the enemy to rout while he was in the fields with the oxen, ploughing. Deep down, of course, he must have felt a pang of fear, but he didn't let it show, he played the braggart. He went off as cheerful as could be – at least so it seemed – and his brothers and sisters went with him down to the main road at the end of the farm-track. They all went, except Uncle Alelchi, who stayed at home – 'There's work to be done around these parts' – the older ones and the little ones, with the little ones shrieking to be carried or given a piggyback or a shoulder-ride, just one last time. And when they got to the main road, one of the carts which went to Adria and then to Rovigo every day with the milk-churns happened to go by, and Uncle Pericles lifted his thumb and the driver said: 'Jump up.'

Then he kissed his brothers and sisters one by one, starting with the littlest and ending with the oldest, and then he hugged his mother, my grandmother, who said: 'Come back, son. Come back in one piece,' and her voice was breaking. She wasn't crying but her voice was breaking, now she had two sons at the front and she didn't know if she'd got enough prayers to go round, and there was still that worry about the priest, because priests must always be shown respect, and sooner or later you'd pay for your lack of it, some things are bound to bring trouble in their wake – 'All I can do is pray' – and what she felt was not so much a sense of foreboding as a virtual certainty of impending disaster.

He on the other hand was laughing, hugging her and laughing: 'Don't worry, ma, I'm off, I'll win the war and I'll be back.' But perhaps that laughter was just a sham. Last of

74

all he hugged my grandfather, while the carter was saying: 'Jump on, my horse wants to be on its way,' and father and son exchanged not one word, just hugged each other tight, and didn't even look one another in the eye, each knowing what they'd see there. Then he jumped up on to the box and the cart set off and he shouted: 'Don't worry, ma, ill weeds grow apace. I'll come back triumphant.' And indeed he did.

He and those like him – the class of '99 – went off to war and won it. Well, I know they didn't win it on their own, they had some help, but that was what they said in those days: 'It was the boys of '99 who won it.' Mere boys of eighteen, lined up along the Piave, then going on the attack, amidst all those bombs and shrapnel and that gas. That's what made them grow up.

When he came home on leave, at Easter 1918, we were no longer at Cavarzere, because what with Caporetto and the front having moved down almost as far as the Piave, my grandmother wanted us to move down too, because you never knew, they might break through there as well, and reach the Adige and then we'd lose crops and livestock, the lot; all right, her sons might be at the front, but not the crops and the livestock. So we went back to Codigoro – and it certainly wasn't the best moment to be drawing up a contract, with people coming and going all over the place and crowds of evacuees going south too – and so my grandmother's brothers took what work they could find by way of sharecropping, in the place they'd been before, but under less favourable terms this time: 'Anyway, we'd been at Cavarzere too long for my liking,' my grandfather said to her by way of consolation.

When he came back on leave that Easter and we were back in Codigoro, Uncle Pericles had shot up and was suddenly taller than my grandfather. Tall and fair and broad-shouldered with muscles like iron – a rock – with all his veins and tendons rippling and standing out as though they were cast in bronze.

In the end we won that war on 4 November 1918. But in June another baby girl had come into the world and my grandfather was fed up with the war and all that scrimping and saving, because food too was rationed. Uncle Pericles said that he'd managed to shoot up because when you're in the army they give you at least two square meals a day – though everyone complained because they were wartime rations and would sometimes arrive cold, after hours of sitting around in cooking pots on the backs of mules which had taken shelter in some mountain gorge, waiting for a lull in the fighting; and when they arrived they were just a gluey mess – but at least you got them regularly twice a day, and my Uncle Pericles hadn't turned his nose up at them: 'If you don't choke on it, you'll thrive on it,' and they had served to oil his muscles and put flesh on his chest. But my grandfather was fed up with all that scrimping and saving and worrying about his sons and whether they'd come safely home. So they called the June baby Santapace, which means heavenly peace (or 'a bit of peace and quiet', if you like) – which was a way of entreating the gods to grant them precisely that – and when his brother's wife had a baby girl the following month they called her Santapace the second, as a sort of back-up, and my grandfather's brother said to him: 'So, you're not quite so much of an interventionist nowadays?'

Anyway, the war was over and all's well that ends well. My uncles came home safe and sound, and so did my grandfather's brother's sons, and no family had such a good war as ours. Everyone else we knew lost a son, but not us. We'd led a charmed life. All we'd done in that war was kill: 'Rather them than us,' was what my uncles said. But they didn't shout it from the rooftops – it was just an expression, a way of warding off bad luck – and when my grandfather was wandering around the village or in the wine-shop and came to hear of someone's son who'd been killed, or who'd lost his legs and had to go round on crutches, or was now one-eyed or one-armed, young men of twenty or so whose lives had now been ruined, he would feel a great sense of pity, and he stopped talking about politics, and he laughed less than he had before. Or so my grandmother said.

Uncle Themistocles came straight back, at the beginning of '19. Uncle Pericles on the other hand was kept on for another year and not demobilized until '20. In fact, when a war is over – even if you've won it – it's not as though you send everyone straight back home, otherwise you'd find yourselves without any army at all, and then anyone could snap you up. You have to keep the army on standby for all eventualities, so you demobilize bit by bit and organize reserves, even though it's peacetime.

So Uncle Pericles stayed on in the army. Until mid 1919 he was quartered in Milan. He did field practice and drill and suchlike things, and when he was off-duty he went to variety shows or to the cinema, or walked around or went to brothels: 'This is the life,' he'd say, because all he'd seen until then was Cavarzere and Codigoro, and the battlefields. And who should he bump into, wandering around Milan, but Rossoni.

Actually, he'd come across him once before, behind the lines, shortly before the final push from around Arcade. He'd seen this officer with a little notebook and a pencil, taking notes in the middle of a group of ambulances – Rossoni was working for the propaganda and intelligence services at the time – and he'd said to his friends: 'Hey, I know him,' and then he'd shouted out: 'Rossoni!'

Rossoni had wheeled round quick as a flash, riled that some common little private should have addressed him as 'Rossoni,' without a rank, as though he were his closest friend. All right, he was a Socialist and a Revolutionary Syndicalist, but rank was rank, and things were different now, we were at war, the Fatherland was the Fatherland and an officer was an officer. So he gave him a nasty look as though to say: 'How dare you? Who do you think you are?' partly because – to give him his due – the last time he'd seen Uncle Pericles had been in 1908, when he was just a little boy of nine, so how could he have been expected to recognize him now? Uncle Pericles on the other hand, ever since the age of nine – or earlier, in fact, since the age of six, when he and his father had been in prison together – had had Rossoni's features lodged in his mind as though he were Our Lord himself. Whereas to Rossoni he was a nobody. And that was why he shouted out: 'Rossoni!' as though to say: 'Look over here! I'm a soldier too, and it's you I'm serving.' So when Rossoni gave him a blank look – or, actually, a slightly irritated look – my uncle lost heart and was rather hurt. But by now the die was cast, so he persisted, trying not to lose face: 'Excuse me, captain,' and he snapped to attention: 'I'm Pericles, Peruzzi's son, I don't know if you remember.'

'Well now,' said Rossoni, throwing his arms around him: 'As if I could forget! I was in prison with your father,' and then they talked for a bit. But then they had to part company, because my uncle's division had begun to move off, and Rossoni gave him a packet of cigarettes and also some cash – 'Buy a drink for your mates' – and then Uncle Pericles went round saying: 'That's Rossoni, he's a great man, my father was in prison with him.'

In 1919, after the war, he met him wandering around Milan,

and this time it was Rossoni who saw him first: 'Peruzzi!' My uncle and some friends had just come out of a brothel and were laughing together on the pavement on one of those little streets around Piazza Duomo, bragging to one another about their recent exploits. Rossoni was on the other side of the street, in civilian dress, he'd already been demobilized and gone back into full-time politics.

That time in the war, my Uncle Pericles had written home about this meeting: 'I saw Rossoni and he sends you all his very best,' but we hadn't seen him for over ten years, not since 1908. He'd wandered the world in the meantime, pursued by warrants for his arrest. But as soon as Italy entered the war and, more to the point, as soon as they'd annulled his various sentences, he came back and enrolled as a volunteer like all the other Revolutionary Syndicalists, including Mussolini and Corridoni, who later died in combat. Rossoni had had better luck, and now he was on leave, wandering round Milan, planning further mayhem and all kinds of dodgy dealings.

At one point Rossoni – who always kept his eyes peeled, like the hunted man he often was – caught sight of that group of sniggering soldiers, and Pericles among them, and called out: 'Hey, Peruzzi.'

On that occasion, my uncle hadn't noticed him. In fact, when he and his mates went wandering round Milan – on leave – they tended to take little notice of civilians, indeed they positively ignored them and tried to stay among their own: 'Let's steer clear.'

Because not everyone was best pleased with those in uniform; in fact they often spat in their faces. Above all because there were still a lot of pacifists around, people who had refused to fight and now found themselves with dead sons and relatives, and then of course there were the crippled and disabled. The truth is, though, that after the war people weren't better off than before, that is, than when the war was still raging. There wasn't more work, or more amusements, or more prosperity. Indeed, during the war the factories had been working flat out producing armaments, but with peace came the recession, factories were closing down and things were worse, rather than better. And everything had changed. People who'd run their own little businesses before the war now found themselves unable to keep their heads above water, or noticed that some neighbour, who'd never done an honest day's work in their lives but always got by with some shady racketeering, had now actually become rich through their wartime double-dealing – 'sharks', they called them. And then, as I've said, there were all those cripples, who'd never be able to earn their living. 'And what was it all for?' people wondered: 'For Trento and Trieste?' And they put the blame on the soldiers.

Not on the king or the politicians, oh dear no, but on the soldiers. Perhaps it was the uniforms. Perhaps they'd seen so many uniforms around the place that they'd got well and truly fed up with them, so the moment they saw one they began to insult the wearer – indeed, even attack him – particularly if you were on your own. Small boys would throw stones at you; it was the military's fault there'd been a war, their fault that there was all this mess and all this hunger. Partly – you don't need me to tell you – because when the war was over we weren't actually all that pleased. Everyone started yelling: 'We've won, but we've been done!' because all that they gave us was Trento, Trieste and Istria. Goodness knows what we were hoping for. So then d'Annunzio went off on his own – or rather, with his myrmidons – to go and take Fiume, in defiance of the peace treaty. His ideologist at Fiume was none other than De Ambris, who drew up the 'Carnaro Charter' and made provision for factory councils, soviets, management committees and a corporate state. Fiume was practically Leninist Russia, and all that baggage – a corporate state and so on – then went straight into Fascism. Indeed, Fiume was a sort of dress rehearsal for Fascism, even if he himself – Alceste De Ambris, who had been father confessor to the lot of them, from Rossoni to Mussolini – went over to the other side when the going got tough, and made himself head of the Anti-Fascist Concentration in 1927. 'I don't know what that was all about,' my grandfather would say. 'Perhaps they just couldn't agree upon who should take command.'

Be that as it may, people were fed up: 'All those men who died for nothing, and we won, but we've been done,' because the real thing was, it seemed as though we'd won that war single-handed. People in Italy have always been loudmouths, you don't need me to tell you that: we'd won it all ourselves, England and France had done sweet nothing and then walked off with the spoils. And the soldiers were to blame. Soldiers who of course were fed up to the back teeth themselves, because until yesterday they'd been on the battlefield risking their skin and seeing their best friends die and just thinking 'Oh well, they'll make it up to us once this is over.' Indeed, they hadn't kept you in the trenches – amidst the dead, and the severed limbs of the wounded – for all those years with mere talk about the glorious destiny of the Fatherland. At a certain point – to keep you there, rifle in hand – they also promised you that when the war was over and the enemy thrashed, you'd be given your own land: 'Land for the peasants,' they said. And that was the only reason you stayed there, risking death in others' stead. Because of that promise. And lo and behold, once the war was over not only did they not give you that land

– 'When did we ever promise you that?' – but they even said it was all your fault: 'To hell with you soldier-boys.'

So you can see why my Uncle Pericles – strolling about Milan on leave with his friends, after they'd been to the brothel – might have regarded passing civilians with some caution. But as soon as he heard someone shouting his name – 'Peruzzi!' – he turned round and recognized him and eagerly called out: 'Sir!'

'Sir nothing, Rossoni to you, come over here.'

'Ah,' said my uncle, as though to say: 'Make up your mind,' and he went over to him and they threw their arms around each other.

'How's your father?' and all that, and then – as they were taking leave of each other to go their own way – Rossoni said: 'I'll see you tomorrow in Piazza San Sepolcro. In fact,' and now he was addressing my uncle's friends, 'why don't you come along too?' And the next day my Uncle Pericles went to Piazza San Sepolcro in Milan and it was 23 March 1919 and Mussolini was there too, and some other fine folk, and together they founded the Fascist Party. And my Uncle Pericles was there as well, and he was particularly drawn to the programme Mussolini was putting forward because it defended the soldiers' honour, and the Fatherland had better start to express a bit of gratitude and above all give the peasants their land, because it was they who worked it, and they who had won the war.

'See?' Rossoni said to him as they were coming away from Piazza San Sepolcro: 'We're just the same as we ever were.'

As to Mussolini, Pericles had only seen him from some way off, or rather, he'd also seen him from close to but he was surrounded by an excited group of people, all with medals and decorations, even on civilian greatcoats, and now he too –

Mussolini, that is – gave the impression of being someone who was going places, who knew a thing or two and was pulling important strings. My uncle felt too intimidated to say to him: 'I'm Peruzzi.' 'Why should he give a damn about the Peruzzi family, nowadays?' he thought. 'The main thing is, he's got our interests at heart,' and so he became a Fascist. A founder member of the party. He'd been there when the thing had been invented.

But now my uncle was in the army, in Milan, he wasn't at home and he couldn't come and go as he pleased. He was under orders, he went out when they let him out and at that time it wasn't as if he could do much for the Fascist cause; he went to hear a bit of speechifying, when he could, and that was all. Once, though, he got caught up in a spot of bother fighting off a group of reds. By now we and the Socialists had nothing in common. Now we were enemies – us on one side and them on the other – because they'd been against the war and now they were against the soldiers and they carried on doing what they'd always done, namely nattering, all talk and no action. Or at least that's what my people said. And if they were red, we by definition had to be black, even if it wasn't as though we sided with the capitalist bourgeoisie while the reds were for the proletariat. We didn't side with different classes, at least not at first. If you look at the programme which was proposed at San Sepolcro, you'll see that we were simply two rival groups from the same class of working people, and it was just a question of seeing who got the upper hand. Perhaps that's why we hated each other so much, because we were brothers who had fallen out. People never hate a long-standing enemy as much as they hate their brothers. Romulus and Remus. Cain and Abel. Anyway, that time – it was the middle of April – a procession of reds was coming up Via Paolo da Cannobbio, where *Il Popolo d'Italia* had its offices.

These offices were known as 'the lair', and it looked as if they might be going to attack them. My uncle happened to be passing with his friends, on the way to the brothel; but seeing what was going on, they joined in the fray and had a punch-up with the reds. With sticks, and clubs. But there were also people shooting, on both sides, and after the reds had gone off, our boys went into the offices of *Avanti!* and wrecked the place. My uncle and his friends went back to barracks with their uniforms all dishevelled, and their superiors soon realized what had happened, because in the meantime news of the attack had spread like wildfire, and everyone was saying that there'd been soldiers involved. But the authorities said nothing, and all the lieutenant said was: 'You've had your fun, now leave off,' but actually they were far from displeased, because the Fascists were on the side of the ex-combattants, indeed they were ex-combattants, whereas the others, the reds, were on the other side. So they turned a blind eye, although they said 'That'll do now,' and Uncle Pericles was transferred.

He was sent off to Rome to join a division of the military engineers, whose job it was to acquire horses for the army. At that time, the army was still using mules and horses for transporting almost everything, including artillery and all the other arms, and even for ambulances. He had to come and go between Cisterna and Rome, together with the horses. They would be loaded forcibly on to goods trains, and he knew about such things, being a carter's son. Then they would be sent all over Italy, wherever they were needed by the various units, and sometimes he would go with them, sleeping with them in the wagons, stretched out on hay and straw, and he would feed them, and water them when the train stopped at a station, filling the drinking troughs with water, and calming them down when they took fright and became restive and started to kick, when the train jolted, or went over the points. Sometimes, though, you had to be firm and hit them on the muzzle with your fists, or take a stick to them, because in this world you have to use both fair means and foul, as my grandmother always used to say. That went on until the late spring of 1920, when they discharged him, and Uncle Pericles came home: 'That's goodbye to the good life,' he thought, half regretfully, 'but at least I'll have a bit of peace and quiet; so now it's back to plodding up and down the fields.'

All in all, he'd only been involved with the Fascist Party because of Rossoni. All right, he'd gone to the 'lair' on Via Paolo da Cannobio a few times, and he'd also been in on the attack on *Avanti!*, but only because of what the reds had just done at the offices of *Il Popolo d'Italia*, and to please Rossoni – who was a family friend – and above all because he had nothing else to do, poor little soldier boy that he was, all adrift in the big city. You couldn't just strike up a random conversation or get into discussion with some little skivvy. You might as well have been invisible. You had to stick to your own kind. And once you'd been to the cinema, or the brothel, even with the reduced rates for the military, you'd have run through your ten days' pay and then you really didn't know which way to turn. So they used to go to the Fascist Headquarters. It took their mind off things. It passed the time. And when they sent him to Cisterna he was pleased rather than anything else. He was dealing with horses, he was in the open air and time passed in a flash. On the few occasions they'd gone back to Rome, the accumulated ten days' pay had been enough to allow him to spend a lot of time in the brothel. So in Rome he'd never felt the need to go to the Fascist Headquarters; only to the brothel.

In point of fact, the Fascist Party didn't seem to be catching on in Rome. In Milan, yes, with all those gents and shopkeepers going round saying: 'Aha, at last this Fascist Party is bringing us a bit of discipline, we've had about enough of the reds and all their strikes and general commotion.' But even in Rome, and in Cisterna, they'd come to hear what a damp squib 16 November 1919 had proved to be, with the Fascist Party standing for election in Milan and in Milan alone, hoping to cut a dash. And everyone, Rossoni included, had said: 'But why just in Milan? Let's go for it everywhere.'

Not Mussolini, though: 'We haven't got enough support elsewhere, we're not much known, and if we don't get many votes people will say what's this then, the Pensioners' Party? Count me out. And that way we'll lose them for good and all. Better to make a go of it here in Milan, and get ourselves a good clutch of deputies, and then people elsewhere will start to take notice and see how well we're doing, and think of voting for us next time round.'

Except that – as you know – they scarcely got any votes even there. A pathetic showing. All those gents and shopkeepers who'd said: 'Yes, you've got my vote,' when it came to it, none of them voted for him. They voted for Giolitti's Liberals, for the Christian Democrats and, of course, for the Socialists. Not even one Fascist deputy got in. And the Socialists were going round Milan with a coffin on their backs, saying it contained the corpse of Benito Mussolini. Indeed, at *Avanti!* they even said that the body of a man who'd drowned in the *Naviglio* turned out to be none other than that of the late lamented Benito Mussolini. So it all seemed to have been a very damp squib indeed: 'If they couldn't make a breakthrough in Milan, which was their stronghold,' people said, 'how do you think they'll ever make headway anywhere else? It was just a flash in the pan.'

Nor did my uncle give the Fascist Party another thought as he took those horses up and down from Cisterna; he confined it to oblivion: 'I'm sorry for them, poor devils, but at this point Giolitti will have to take care of the politics and I'll take care of the whores.' After all, he was only twenty, why should he care? Whores were a wonderful new discovery, not like politics which he'd been chewing over ever since he was a boy, without gaining much profit from it, either, since both he and his family had always been on the losing side.

So, all in all, Uncle Pericles was well pleased to be back at home, leading a quiet life in the fields, among his animals: 'There must be the odd whore around these parts, too,' he told himself.

But when he got home he found himself plunged into politics whether he liked it or not. Indeed, there at Codigoro things weren't going any better than they were in the rest of the country, everything was in a pretty pickle there as well. My grandfather, as I've said, had always talked politics. Someone who's been in prison as a young man – and for his politics, rather than for petty crime – is surely going to carry on talking politics in the wine-shop for the rest of his days. Otherwise, what was the point of having gone to prison? And if you hear your father talking politics, the chances are you'll do the same. Indeed, right from when they'd been quite small, he and his brothers couldn't wait to go to prison like their father. Before the war, though, my grandfather and his sons were talking politics in the wine-shop with people who were their friends, because the whole village thought the way they did, siding against the rich and the gentry. The enemy wasn't present when they spoke ill of him, they were all friends together. Reds, Socialists, losers, every man-jack of them.

But now things were different. They were still poor and penniless all right, but otherwise things had changed. There were some people with whom they'd hadn't been on speaking terms since the time of interventionism. And other people gave them nasty looks, particularly those who had lost a son in battle. And even if now – after the war, that is – my grandfather would go into the wine-shop saying: 'Let's just talk about *briscola*,' and no one would talk politics, some people thought he'd talked quite enough politics already, and every time he left the wine-shop people would mutter behind his back, and say: 'He was for the war and his sons came back. I wasn't, and mine's dead,' as though it was all his fault. Well it was his fault, his sons should have died. When someone loses a son you no longer know what to say, you come out with all kinds of nonsense: 'But I wanted the war for social justice, for the revolution, so that we'd all be better off.'

'I lost a son,' those others would say. What can you say to that?

But now that the war was over, things were even worse. Politics had entered the mainstream. The enemy was in the wine-shop. Reds and Socialists on one side and Fascists on the other. No more united front. We could hardly even get on with my grandfather's brother and his children, who shared the same farm buildings. Fields, land, livestock, tools, supplies, everything was separate: mine over here and yours over there. We helped each other out, just as we'd always done, and if you needed a cart you just took it, as though it were your own. But we all knew what was ours and what was theirs, even if we did all get together in the barn of an evening and tell stories and talk about this and that before going to bed. But no more politics. We'd stopped discussing politics with our relatives by tacit agreement. They were red and we were black, better

88

to let things lie. Except that it wasn't enough just to avoid the subject, now everything seemed to be political, and even if my Uncle Pericles would have liked to spend his whole time whoring, the minute he was back he had to get between the shafts again, just like a donkey.

By the time he got back, they'd already set fire to our straw-stack. In fact, they'd set fire to two. And, once, to the haystack, but we managed to save that. It was Aunt Bissola who got wind of things – one of the little twins, the one whose real name was Bissolata. She wasn't like the rest. If she woke up at night and wanted a piss, she wouldn't do it in the pot, like the rest of mankind. In those days in the country the privy was outside, next to the dung-hill. At night you'd use a pot, which was kept under the bed, and they were still made of earthenware, not iron, or white enamel; they might be decorated with flowers, but they were all a bit chipped. Not Aunt Bissola, though. Even as a little girl she refused to put her little bottom where everyone else's had been – 'the princess and the pee' was what Uncle Adelchi called her, they'd never got on – and then she'd call her sister: 'Modiliana! Come outside with me, I've got to piss.'

'Piss in the pot, damn you.'

'Come with me – I'm scared,' and then that little angel Modigliana would get up and go out with her, even on winter nights when there was ice or snow on the ground. And that was how it came about that Aunt Bissola – going out at night to piss so as not to have to do it in the pot – happened to see the flames, or the beginnings of them, by the haystack. She screamed and rushed up to it, and heard steps running away and then her own brothers and sisters arriving, some jumping straight out of the windows and others with buckets and blankets and brooms. So the haystack was saved; but not the straw-stack.

When my Uncle Pericles came back they'd already burned the straw-stack down for the first time. It can't have taken any time at all: you set fire to it and run off, and while you're running off the fire has already caught all the way up and you can't go anywhere near it, the blast would strip the skin off your face from a distance of fifty metres.

What's that you said? It might have been spontaneous combustion? That those steps were a figment of the child's imagination? For goodness sake, that child was twelve years old. She knew how to run a house, how to turn a sheet, and the cows in the cowshed positively quaked when they heard her coming, a snake, that's what she was, a poisonous snake. And you think she might have got the wrong end of the stick? Anyway, you don't get much spontaneous combustion at night. They set fire to it out of spite, and that's that.

Sorry, what's that you said? Losing a straw-stack isn't the end of the world? But we were peasants, we weren't blacksmiths. Straw was meat and drink to us, it was our wealth, not just a by-product. We used it as litter for the animals, so they'd be warm and comfortable, but also for manure. The cows did their business on the straw, and when the two were mixed together they became manure, which is like golddust for the earth, because, over time, the earth too becomes sterile and needs a tonic.

Straw is meat and drink for a peasant, and they'd already burnt down one of our straw-stacks and tried to burn down our haystack. Luckily, my grandmother knew that straw-stacks are a hazard. She'd learned this from her brothers and she'd told my grandfather as much soon after they were married, because he was a carter, not a peasant. And she drummed this into her children every year at threshing-time, when the moment came to start the straw-stack: 'First you plant a tall, straight pole in the ground, and then you put layers of straw round it, and gradually the stack gets taller and taller.' The first layer had to be carefully laid, though, and completely even. You didn't just chuck the straw on with your pitchfork any old how, or the straw-stack would be all crooked, and collapse; the pole wouldn't be able to support it, and it would be lopsided and finally topple over. That was why you had to spread the straw evenly with the pitchfork, not just bung it down; in layers of equal thickness, so that it would grow evenly, and reach the top of the pole, and the men would pass it up from below, from hand to hand, standing on the hay carts: one pitchforkful from the ground to the cart and then another from the cart to the top of the straw-stack. At a certain point it would reach its full height – and tall it was – and over the following days it would get lower, as its weight caused it to settle and drove out the air. If you've done it badly it will collapse, as I've said, but if you've done it properly it will stand for the whole year, becoming gradually lower as you take the straw from it to the cowshed, until the middle of June, by which time you'll have used up all the straw, and hence the straw-stack, and there's not a single stalk to feed your livestock. Then you harvest the new corn, and thresh it, and another straw-stack starts growing – is born anew, if you like – to serve for the coming year.

Well, every year at threshing-time when my uncles drove in that post to make the straw-stack, my grandmother would shriek: 'Over there, put it further over there,' because she knew, so we all knew, that a straw-stack is a potential hazard. The least thing can set it ablaze – it's straw, after all, it's more flammable than petrol – and once it catches fire it will go up in a flash. Just in one single, mighty blast. And the least thing will cause the fire to spread. You have no idea how often the fire from a straw-stack has gone on to burn down the nearby house and cowshed, with livestock and even children burned to a cinder in their charred cradles, trapped in the house beneath the eaves. So imagine how Uncle Pericles must have felt when he heard what had happened. 'But who did it?' was all he said.

'Who knows?' came the answer. The people from the local Farmworkers' Union had come round – the reds and the Socialists from the Workers' Association – to tell us that every sharecropper had to take on his quota of day-labourers, 'compulsory labour quota', was what they called it. There was so much unemployment and hunger, so it made sense: 'For every so many hectares there must be so many day-labourers, and every sharecropper must take on their quota.'

Put like that, I can see that it sounds perfectly fair; like you, I believe that work, and wealth, should be shared out evenly. But on our land, we didn't need all those labourers. Who would pay them? All right, we were sharecroppers: the boss rented us the land, we worked it and we shared out the spoils. But we also shared the expenses: the seed, the supplies and any outside labour we might employ – the day-labourers. Here too we shared the expenses. But where was this money going to come from? Of course, when we did need a few day-labourers because there was too much to do, or we had to work fast, we too would take some on, we weren't idiots. If you have to get in a harvest and you're pressed for time, you don't just sit there scratching your head, you call people in from outside and off you go. But it's one thing for me – or my grandmother – to decide when you really need them, and quite another to have someone else roll up and say: 'From now on you've got to have Tom, Dick and Harry working in the fields.' What if I don't need them? What if I call you in to work – and it's me who has to pay you, because that's what the Farmworkers' Union says – and meanwhile my own sons are hanging around twiddling their thumbs? Why did I bother having them in the first place? Where am I supposed to send them to work? What can I give them to eat, if I'm giving it to those outsiders, namely you? I know you've got to share and share alike, but you can only share what you've got, you can't share what you haven't. 'We haven't even got enough for ourselves,' was what Themistocles said to the people from the Farmworkers' Union, after exchanging glances with his mother and brothers.

At that time Themistocles had two children of his own, even though we all still lived together and he was only twenty-two or twenty-three. The first time he'd come back from the war on leave – in 1917, when he was twenty – he'd clapped eyes on this girl my grandmother had taken in to help out.

Not that we were rich enough to have a servant. True, we weren't badly off, we had enough work, and good health too, and we didn't go hungry, but we were still sharecroppers, working land that was not our own. Though it's also true that there were plenty who were worse off than us. You have no idea of the poverty at the time. Some people didn't even have a roof over their heads, I don't mean they didn't own a house, I mean they couldn't even rent one, because they hadn't got a lira to their name. They'd do a day's work when they could find it, and when the work dried up they'd go and poach eels from the canals, but they'd be in trouble if the country gamekeeper caught them at it, because round those parts even the canals belonged to the nobs. There was nothing that didn't have an owner, and that owner wouldn't be best pleased if he caught you fishing for 'his' eels. They paid those gamekeepers just to spend the livelong day tramping about their property – fields, canals, rice-fields – with their rifles slung over their shoulders, all decked out in caps and uniforms with the owner's coat-of-arms, and riding boots and breeches. And they didn't have those rifles just for show; they'd use them.

And the eel-pilferers didn't even have a home to go to. There were lots of people like that, not just in the lower part of the Po Valley but throughout the Veneto, believe you me. They lived all hugger mugger – one family on top of another – in dreadful huts made of nothing but dry branches and reeds, which were known as *casoni*, which means 'big houses', but which were in fact nothing but big huts without any dividing walls, and a hearth in the middle, and men and women all slept together in the same space, not to mention their animals, dogs, cats, pigs and hens. But some were even more destitute, they hadn't got anywhere to sleep at all, so night after night they and their whole families would go to sleep in someone's cowshed, in the mangers. Obviously, all these people were worse off than us, so whenever someone would say to her: 'Do me a favour, take this girl off my hands,' my grandmother would do so. She'd give the girl bed and board, and clothe her, and the girl, of course, would work like all the others, without pay. Then, when she grew up and found someone to marry her – some other poor wretch like herself – then that girl would go off and my grandmother would take a new one on. And then as time went by – after they'd married and had children of their own – every so often they'd come back to visit her, and show off their children, and they were already washed out and bloated by hunger and hardship generally, because their husbands hadn't fared much better than their own fathers. Anyway, when they called round at my grandmother's they'd say: 'Ah, how good things were when I was here with you! I wish I'd never left.' And my grandmother would always give them a few eggs and a hen when they went on their way.

In short, when he came back on leave, Themistocles found this great big girl wandering around the house. And he took a shine to her. Uncle Themistocles, really, was just a boy. He was tall, and strong, and dark-skinned like his mother, not fair like his father. He had a high forehead and big dark eyes. He was quiet and reserved, not much of a talker, but a good listener; he felt no need to offer his opinion, but when he was driven to it, he did so in few, precise words, with never a second thought. People who didn't know him well might find him unsociable, but he wasn't, he was just reserved, he had nothing to prove, he didn't look for opportunities to make his point, he knew his own worth and that was enough for him. He was the first-born, and the first-born knows that their mother loves them, for that very reason. For her, everything – a cry, a step, a word – is a first, a new excitement, and the child senses it. But with the second child it's like water off a duck's back, she's seen it all before; she's got other things to be getting on with, she can't sit around gawping in wonderment at every silly thing he does. And, at that age, silly things are what you want to do; indeed, you do more and more of them, you climb up mirrors to grab her attention, to get a smile out of her, just a moment's notice and a little scrap of leftover love. That's life. 'Some people just have it made,' as a prostitute in Rome used to say to my Uncle Pericles. She wasn't particularly beautiful – or at least not in an obvious way – and she wasn't much in demand, even though she made a better job of things than the rest, which was why my Uncle Pericles was a loyal client. There was another one, who was prettier, but a bit of a show-off, who simpered and gave herself airs, and the madam was in awe of her and would grant her every whim; the more she answered back, the more the madam would smile at her, whereas this other one – the one favoured by my Uncle Pericles, who was less attractive but who did her job well, she could bring the dead to life, was what he said – the more she did, even tidying up

95

the rooms like an ordinary maid, the worse the madam treated her. So that poor Cinderella found consolation with my Uncle Pericles: 'Some people just have it made.' 'That's life,' he would agree, and then climb back on top of her.

But the odd thing is that those first-born don't even know their luck. They're jealous of the newcomer, they say: 'You're always taking sides, you always give him more' – talking about that poor second-best who's already busy climbing up mirrors himself. She was right, that prostitute favoured by my Uncle Pericles, because they too – the first-born – don't act that way out of devilment, they really feel hard done by. Poor things, when they came into the world they were the apple of their mother's eye. Then this intruder comes along – the second-born – and their mother has to take her adoring eyes off him and find a brief moment for this new one too; but it's nothing in comparison with what she's lavished on the first. Yet even that brief moment is a moment purloined from the first: 'You're always taking sides.'

Anyway, this wasn't the case with my Uncle Themistocles, who always got along with all of his brothers; he didn't have much time for chat, but they got along, even if he was never there to play with the youngest ones and dandle them on his knee. Nor his own, come to that. He had work to do, and he just looked at them and that was that, with that look of his that made it hard to know whether he was pleased or annoyed. My Uncle Themistocles was reserved by nature, and he hadn't gone to brothels even while he was on service during the war. The others would ask him, as they were setting off: 'Are you coming?'

'No,' he'd say.

'But tomorrow we might be dead.'

'Then we'll be dead,' he'd say. But then he came home on

leave and saw that nice-looking young girl, who'd flashed him a smile, and that was how they carried on – throughout his leave – scarcely exchanging a word. And on the last evening – when he was leaving the next day, and there was no knowing when he'd be back – he never took his eyes off her while she was bringing the food to the table. Without once raising her own, she came and went, around the kitchen and around the table; because women – even those who were members of the family – would eat after the men, and standing up, like my grandmother did. It was only the menfolk who sat down at table, and my grandfather was always seated at its head. My grandmother would serve him first, and he would be the first to eat. No one touched a mouthful until he did. And after that the older boys, from Uncle Themistocles who sat at his right, to Uncle Pericles at his left, and then the others, downwards in terms of age, Iseo, Adelchi and then the smaller ones – boys and girls alike – and then the littlest of all, who'd be crawling around on the floor, under the tables, fighting over the scraps with the dog and the cats. The women would sit down only at the end, when the menfolk had finished and my grandfather had lit his cigar and the brothers, from Uncle Themistocles to Pericles, had begun to fill the cigarette papers with shag. And my grandmother would be leaning up against the kneading-trough or the kitchen sink, eating where she stood and overseeing proceedings purely by a series of meaningful looks.

But that girl – who was later to become my Aunt Clelia – kept her eyes lowered as she brought the food to table. At one point she raised them for just an instant, and it was then that Uncle Themistocles made a sign to her – just with his eyes, though, like his mother – looking towards the hayloft, and she blushed and lowered her gaze. But she made a sign that she had understood, and when everyone had gone to bed and put out the lights, the pair of them sneaked out and ran up to the hayloft without a word, except, on her part: 'It wouldn't be right, not before I'm married.'

'But I might die,' he said, and that was all they said that night. And when it was drawing to a close, and the first glimmer of dawn was coming up over the sea, he went into his mother's bedroom and woke her up: 'I've made a decision, ma, I'm getting married.'

My grandmother began to shriek. She wouldn't hear of it: 'Are you mad?' because that girl was even lower than us in the pecking order. 'She's from those huts, she doesn't even know who her father is. She can't even read or write.'

'So what, ma, does my father know where he comes from?' and meanwhile he, my grandfather, had woken up as well.

And when his son said what he said, my grandfather pulled a face as though to say: 'Yes! Where do I come from?' but without saying anything, just that face, because otherwise she would have flown into a rage. But she flew into a rage anyway, just imagining that face behind her back, while she was standing up to her son, and then she said: 'I'm sending her packing, right away. I'm throwing her into the street. And that's the last you'll see of her.'

'Horse, stable door,' Themistocles hissed at her, so that only the two of them could hear. Not even my grandfather caught what he said. All he saw was his son's glaring eyes and he guessed that he'd said something she didn't want to hear. But he didn't understand. He hadn't heard the words. 'What did he say?' he asked.

'Nothing, nothing at all,' was my grandmother's answer, and she stuck to it. And off he went again the next day, back to slaughtering Germans with cold steel, at night, or with a knife when he was on patrol, because he was in the *Arditi*. He went back to slaughter in order to avoid being slaughtered – *mors tua* etc – and he was given his first leave after exactly nine months, when the baby had just been born and christened Paris, you know, that Ancient Greek who was the fairest among men and all the goddesses of Olympus were in love with him and he set off the Trojan War and all the trouble that brought with it. Yet there in Northern Italy – where we lived – people called their sons 'Paris' convinced that it would bring them good luck. My uncles included. And ever since he was a child he was always handsome, strong, good, just, generous and brave. Not that it brought him any luck. Any more than it did Troy.

But we didn't know any of this then, when my Uncle Themistocles came back on leave the second time in the spring of 1918 and met his baby son. He was delighted, and off they went to get married, he and his radiant bride. Radiant because she was all set up, said my grandmother, she couldn't believe that she who had been a servant was now a mistress, who could ever have believed that someone from those huts would find herself a sharecropper? Radiant with love, thought my Uncle Themistocles, but so did all those who saw her as she came before the priest, with her husband, and her baby in her arms. Baptism and marriage service rolled into one. And my grandfather wanted to be the only one to hold that baby, and all the brothers and sisters were there, from the oldest to the youngest. The only one missing was Uncle Pericles, and he was away at the war. Actually, my grandmother wasn't there either. She hadn't been able to go to the church because she wasn't well, was what she said. She herself was pregnant yet again, and having trouble with her stomach. 'Twinges!' she said. 'I'm having twinges,' and that was something she'd never had with any of her previous pregnancies. That was the only time she'd ever had any trouble, and a couple of months later Santapace was born, the one my father had named A Bit Of Peace And Quiet because he was fed up with the war, and in this case the grandson was older than the aunt, though only by two months, and they too grew up and played together like twins, just like Modigliana and Bissolata. Friends for life.

Anyway, the people from the local Farmworkers' Union told my Uncle Themistocles that we too had to take on a certain number of day-labourers because we were sharecroppers – rich, Fascist sharecroppers – and my uncle said to them: 'What's all this Fascist sharecroppers business, we're just poor people like the rest, and if we take on your people where will we all find work – in the great cornfield in the sky? To hell with you.' So off they went, and that same evening the straw-stack caught fire, and if it hadn't been for Aunt Bissola the haystack would have caught fire too. In order to get by – just up to July, to threshing-time and more new straw – we had to buy some straw on tick; we had to have a bit of straw, what would the cows do for bedding?

So that was how things stood when my Uncle Pericles came back from the war. He'd looked around, been told the story and then simply asked Uncle Themistocles: 'Who did it?'

'How should I know?'

'You don't want to know!' was what his brother said.

'What's so wrong with that? Sometimes it's better not to know,' and that was all he said. Themistocles was his older brother and, all in all, he might even be right. What could you do, anyway, start a war? 'Let's just hope that's the end of it,' my Uncle Themistocles said mildly.

At this juncture I'd like to make one thing clear: I don't take my uncles' part just as a matter of course. Indeed, I can see that the people from the union had reasons of their own.

There were so many unemployed, so much hunger, such poverty, there were the people living in those huts, men and women and animals, all together. Of course they needed work, and they came to ask my uncles because my uncles lived in a house with rooms with beds, and they had livestock, they had food, and work. For people like that, my uncles were rich. But my uncles felt that they were poor, and they had to work every hour God sent them just to keep their heads above water. It wasn't as if they got handouts. So when those people said: 'But we've got nothing,' my uncles said: 'Why don't you go straight to the man who owns the land? Go and see the count, if you've got the guts. Why come to me, who's hardly got a brass farthing more than you?'

But the count wasn't as easy to track down as we were. He wasn't right there, to hand. What was to hand was you, who had more to eat than them, and it was you that they came to, to try to take from you such little as you had. What else could they do? They came to you, just as our immigrants nowadays come to us. But do you think they don't know that nine times out of ten their boat will capsize and they will drown? It's all very well saying to them: 'You've got a nine out of ten chance of drowning.' They'll say: 'I know, but a ten out of ten chance of dying if I stay at home.' That's life, everyone climbs up mirrors to try and keep going, or get ahead. They climb up other people, what do you expect them to do? The Africans see the hunger all around them and know that they have to come over here, where else is there to go? So, to avoid being overrun, we find ourselves having to sink their rotten boats. What else can we do? Give up some of our prosperity in order to ease their hunger? We're not that foolish. Everyone looks after number one, that's how it goes.

In any case, our relatives who lived in the same farm

buildings as we did – my grandfather's brother and his children, Peruzzis like ourselves, who still live in the north – and who had their own haystacks and straw-stack quite separate from ours, on the other side of the house, well, nothing ever happened to them. They had remained Socialists and carried on attending Farmworkers' Union meetings, they were friendly with the people from the union, and these people had gone to see them as well, but they were friends, comrades, if you like; they wanted to find a solution; they'd been asked to take on ten hands, and in the end they settled on two, and that way everyone was satisfied.

When July came, and the harvest-time, the men from the union showed up again, looking as if they meant business and telling us we'd have to take on some hands. 'It's the law.'

'Get out of here!' said Uncle Pericles, because this time it was him they spoke to, in the middle of the threshing-floor with a pitchfork in his hand. 'Out! I'm not having you in my house,' and he waved the pitchfork in their faces.

So off they went as they had come, without any sign of surprise or irritation. It was what they'd expected. The whole purpose of their visit must have been to be able to say, when the time came: 'Look, we did our best.' And when they went off along the road, laughing and joking, it was only Pellegrini – someone they'd known since they were boys and had never got on with, and this alone would be enough to prove that it was a put-up job, because if they'd really wanted to come to some agreement Pellegrini was not the man to send – only Pellegrini turned round and said to my Uncle Pericles: 'You'd better get off your high horse, Peruzzi, before we throw you off!'

'Just try it then, if you've got the guts!' But they just carried on on their way, and he just walked back to the threshing-floor.

Later, in the wine-shop, my grandfather and my Uncle Themistocles tried to talk to someone from the union they were still friendly with, and see if there was some middle way: 'Let's have a bit of give and take, give me a reduction, we'll take on two and that'll solve the matter.'

Nothing doing. 'It's all or nothing,' they said: 'You're Fascists and you're asking for a reduction?'

We were the only sharecroppers in the district who didn't go along with that labour quota. Or rather, in the end my grandfather and uncles would have gone along with it, but with this reduction. And in the end we didn't take on anyone at all. We brought the harvest in on our own – just as we'd always done – and we even helped the other part of the family, and they helped us. We did the threshing together, put our sheaves and theirs to either side of the threshing-machine. It was one of those steam ones, with a tall smoke-stack, and it had been pulled there by oxen together with the cartload of coal. So we had first to harvest the corn by hand, with a reaping-hook – all strung out in a row – and then everyone would make a bundle of ears of corn and tie them into a sheaf. Then you went by with the big ox-cart, loaded up the sheaves and took them to the threshing-floor – a great big pile of them, bigger than the straw-stack. Then the threshing-machine would arrive, with the steam engine in front, to power it, and the boiler, and all the belts and pulleys which set the threshing-machine and all its sifters into motion. Those belts put the fear of God into you. If you got caught up in them, you were done for. Sometimes they would break and whip around like giant snakes, lashing over twenty metres into the air, and many people got hurt, even killed. And you needed a lot of people for the threshing. It was the high point of the farming year, you'd have worked the whole year long just for that day. Some people tended to the machine, some to the pile of sheaves, passing them up towards it with pitchforks, while some fed them in from above. Below, someone would hold the gradually filling sacks, and someone else would take the sacks into the barn. They weighed a hundred kilos each. Others would number them and count them – and the factor would be there, so there would be no funny business – and others would remove the straw from under the threshing-machine with a pitchfork and take it to the straw-stack.

Meanwhile the gleaners would go around the fields, the women from the huts, or poor devils with young children who were allowed – not by law, but by common consent – to go round after the harvest, field by field, furrow by furrow, picking up the ears of corn which had got scattered or somehow left lying on the ground, though around our parts theirs wasn't much of a harvest, because my grandmother was like a general, with all her children out gleaning as long as there was a glimmer of light left in the sky: 'Keep your eyes peeled, every ear' means bread.' And if she saw the women from the huts going off looking gleeful at an unexpectedly bountiful harvest, she would administer hearty slaps all round to her own brood. 'That's what you get for work poorly done,' she'd say.

That year too we did the threshing with the other branch of the family, first our wheat and then theirs. We made our straw-stacks together, too, and ate and drank into the night together with the other workers on the threshing-floor, and danced to the sound of the accordion.

Then, for a month, my uncles took it in turns to sleep beside the straw-stack, you never knew what might happen. And they carried on like that, in relays, throughout August and until the beginning of September, because anyway it was good to sleep out there beneath the stars, good and cool, even if you were in all that straw. Meanwhile, in the village all seemed well. My uncles had even started to nod to the people from the union again. Not all of them, of course – not my Uncle Pericles – but Uncle Themistocles did, even to that Pellegrini who had been Uncle Pericles' childhood enemy. And Uncle Iseo. And of course Uncle Adelchi, in the wine-shop with my grandfather: 'Let bygones be bygones, we're all in this together,' he'd say, before a glass of wine. Until one evening when the weather was turning cooler and it was Uncle Adelchi's turn, and he said: 'I'm not going to sleep out, they'd never try that one on again.'

His brothers agreed: 'We don't need to sleep outside any more.'

But Uncle Pericles stood his ground: 'I'll sleep out anyway,' and he slept out there for a whole week, and the others mocked him for it, and at last even he had had enough. 'You're right, they won't try that one on again,' and then he stayed indoors to sleep.

And that same evening, on the stroke of midnight, when the church bell rang at Codigoro, while they were all asleep and even the animals were silent – not a cricket chirping, not a dog barking, not a donkey braying – my Aunt Bissola was woken by a noise. It was the crackling that roused her – she was like a snake, she could hear the grass grow – though it wasn't proper crackling yet, just the early stages, because when it really catches it's like a blast, a real explosion. So what she heard was as it were an idea of crackling, she immediately called out: 'Fire, fire!'

Then everybody was instantly awake, and from their beds they saw the walls of the room lit up by glowing flames, coming from beyond the windows. And they all leapt out of bed, and now all the dogs around were barking fit to burst, right as far away as Codigoro. And all the cats were mewing, too, and the cattle in the byre were lowing with alarm, while calves, donkeys, mules, horses, chickens and turkeys mooed and brayed and neighed and clucked and gobbled. Even the rabbits squeaked.

Now all my uncles, young and old alike, had jumped out of the windows, and the other branch of the family were giving them a hand. Not at putting out the fire, it was too late for that, the straw-stack had gone up in flames. What they had to try and do now was save the rest. So some were rushing into the cowshed, to unchain the cows and get them out into the open, into the pen, which was quite far away, should the fire spread to the cowshed. And others were already on the roof – the women, mostly, dousing the wind-borne brands with their nightclothes, and others were all around the haystack with their buckets, doing their best to stop the fire from spreading from below. And while they were all rushing around, each one already at their post and my grandmother in the middle of the threshing-floor directing operations – and less than a minute had gone by since Aunt Bissola had shouted 'Fire,' and Uncle Pericles had realized that the straw-stack had gone but that the rest was safe – well, even then Uncle Pericles was already ablaze with fury. And when he saw Antaeus in the midst of all those relatives – his 'comrade' cousin as we called him, that is, the one in his own class, his opposite number in his father's brother's family, the second son, just like himself, his 'comrade', as I've said, which here means his 'equal', the same age as himself, who had fought in the war with him, and they'd been very close, they too were almost like twins, they'd always played together and as boys they'd gone looking for frogs together and he too had been at Cavarzere on that occasion with the priest and the knife – well, my uncle went up to him and grabbed him by his undershirt: 'Who was it? You know who it was!' and the fire from the straw-stack lit up his face, which was all contorted, like that of the devil himself.

'I know nothing about it,' said Antaeus mildly.

'Who was it? Tell me who it was,' Uncle Pericles insisted in a lordly fashion, twisting his undershirt and prodding him in the chest.

'I know nothing about it!' said Antaeus, and even he was riled by now, prodding him back: 'And take your hands off me, Pericles, or there'll be trouble.'

'There's trouble now,' and he pushed him backwards with all his bull-like strength, just as he had with the priest. And then my grandmother stopped giving orders to the others and turned to him imploringly: 'Pericles, Pericles,' almost whimpering. But he just carried on shoving and snarling, and he'd already taken one hand off Antaeus' undershirt and was clenching his fist, about to strike.

It was the affair of a moment: 'Pericles!' my grandmother barked.

And my uncle paused, lowered his fist and let his cousin go. He carried on looking at him threateningly, though, and muttering: 'You and me...' but without finishing his sentence, just making a curt gesture with his hands, as though he were wielding a sickle, as if to say: 'That's it, you and me won't be sharing anything any more,' and then he turned away.

'I forgive you,' was what Antaeus said.

'Forgive me, but keep clear of me.' Then Uncle Pericles joined the others in doing what had to be done. But as soon as he realized that what could be saved had been saved, and that now all that was burning in the straw-stack was the central pole, and there was no more straw, burnt or otherwise, he turned to his younger brother: 'Dirty dog Turati, get harnessing that cart,' and Turati – who was fourteen by now – went to get the horse and put it between the shafts.

'Into the house, the lot of you,' my grandmother said, though without much hope of being obeyed.

'What are we waiting for then, for the third one to go up in smoke?' my Uncle Pericles said to her, and my uncles all trooped back into the house to put on their breeches and pick up their weapons, which consisted of two double-barrelled shotguns, because we would all go hunting together and take it in turns – 'my go', 'no, it's mine' – but my uncles had a stock of cartridges like you've never seen, because they were fanatical about hunting and spent all their summer evenings in the kitchen after supper, with the oil lamp on the big table, filling them with lead pellets and gunpowder. Besides, game was the only meat we ever ate at home, except for a bit of pork in November and a turkey at Easter and Christmas, because my grandmother would sell all the poultry. It wasn't like now, when you eat meat every day. And so my uncles – the older ones – set off on the cart, all except Uncle Adelchi who stayed at home, because 'someone had to', as he solemnly put it, looking almost envious.

'You look as if you wouldn't mind coming too,' Dirty Dog Turati said to him.

So, there were five of them: Uncle Pericles, Uncle Themistocles, and Uncles Iseo, Treves and Turati. Five.

'That'll do,' said Uncle Pericles, and he wouldn't let the younger ones go too. Uncle Turati was only fourteen, as I've said, and my grandmother shrieked: 'At least leave me Turati,' and Uncle Themistocles too was beginning to think she had a point.

But he – Turati – wouldn't take no for an answer. 'Me too,

me too. Don't leave me behind, Pericles,' and he jumped up beside him on the box. Uncle Pericles began to laugh, and moved over to make room for him.

Aunt Bissola too was shrieking: 'I want to come too, I want to come too, goddam you all.'

'Shut up, you silly goose, what are you thinking of, do you think this is women's work?' Aunt Modigliana, her twin sister, tried to reason with her.

'Why? What have they got that I haven't?'

'A brain,' wallop, 'a brain's what you haven't got,' said my grandmother, and slapped her round the head.

Now my uncle was geeing up the horse, and they were gone with the wind. Uncle Treves was clinging to the side panel, because the cart was lurching over potholes and stones: 'But how will we manage with just two shotguns?'

'Two?' said Uncle Themistocles, and pulled a third out from a sack, because he'd forced his 'comrade' cousin to give it to him. All he'd said was: 'Hand it over.'

'But Themistocles,' objected his cousin, another man of few words, a twin soul, in fact.

'Hand over,' he said again, as baldly as before.

And he had. Who was he to quibble over details? 'All I want is to see the back of them, they can get into trouble on their own.'

And so the two shotguns had become three, plus a pistol which Uncle Pericles had conjured up out of thin air. No one had even known of its existence, he must have smuggled it back with him after the war – perhaps it was an Austrian pistol – he'd never shown it to anyone, except possibly to my Uncle Iseo. Anyway, with their three shotguns and one pistol, my uncles rode into Codigoro, at one o'clock in the morning, firing wildly all around the village. Or rather, first at the house belonging to the school-teacher, which stood some hundred metres outside the village if you were coming from our place. He was the local school-teacher, but also the head of the local Socialist branch office and Farmworkers' Union. He'd walk around sporting a red bow tie, just like Rossoni in Copparo in 1904. My uncles pulled up in front of the house and my Uncle Pericles said 'whoa' to the horse and then: 'Hey you there, mister schoolmaster!'

Nothing.

So Dirty Dog Turati got down from the cart and went to knock on the door, while Uncle Pericles carried on shouting 'Hey you there, mister schoolmaster,' from the cart.

At last there was the sound of a window opening on the first floor, and the schoolmaster's head appeared: 'Who is it?'

'Peruzzi! Bang,' and then the sound of gunfire.

'Holy Mary!' they heard his wife saying, inside the house.

And him: 'They've got me, they've got me.'

'Holy Mary, Holy Mary,' she said again.

Then my uncles went 'Bang-bang' again with their shotguns, and Uncle Turati went back to get on to the cart, laughing the while.

My uncles carried on with their 'Bang-banging' until at last Uncle Pericles said: 'Don't let's waste cartridges, we've got plenty of others on our list,' and he let the horse have its head and dealt a slap to Turati, who was still laughing: 'What are you laughing about, you dolt, they've just burned down our straw-stack,' and then another bang.

'Go to hell,' said Turati, covering his head with his arm.

And so they went on through the whole village, with the sound of 'Holy Mary' in the background by way of a refrain.

And him, the schoolmaster, with his: 'They've got me, they've got me.'

And my uncles laughing, because it was clear they couldn't have killed him, and not just because he was still shouting, either, but also and above all because those were shotguns, and the window must have been some thirty metres away from the cart and the shot would have been bound to scatter. How many pellets could have hit their target? Yes, he'd have a bloody nose, but he'd been the one who'd given the orders. He was the leader of the Workers' Association and the Socialist Party – with his red bow tie and his white breeches, and his way of speaking as though he was holier than the priest himself, and at school he would whack the little ones with his cane – and it must have been him who'd said: 'Set fire to that straw-stack.'

Now my uncles weren't completely sure who'd started the fire. If they had been, they'd have gone straight for whoever it was. But they did have an idea, even if rather a vague one, as to whom it might have been – a group of suspects, let's say – and so, to hedge their bets, they'd taken a potshot at all of them. First in the square – where the Workers' Association was – then hell for leather up and down the main street, with the cart going clickety-clack over the cobbles like a train and people woken by the firing standing at their windows and wondering what on earth was going on.

Then Uncle Treves started bang-banging too, a couple of rifle-shots along the row of windows – now people had started slamming the shutters closed again – and they were back in the square.

'Whoa,' said Uncle Pericles, pulling on the reins, and the horse had barely stopped than they all jumped down from the cart like so many infantry shock troops coming down from the back of their tanks.

The Workers' Association was housed in the ground floor of one of the houses on the square, and its glassed-in main doors overlooked the street. It was a big room, which also served as headquarters for the local Socialist Party and the Farmworkers' Union. I think they were already calling it the *casa del popolo* – which was what they called their Socialist Cultural Centres – and at that time of night, of course, it was all shut up and dark. But various families were living above it. So my uncles – down from the cart – began shouting: 'Everybody out,' to those above.

They took a bit of time opening up – 'Shall we or shan't we?' – talking it over with their wives, because they too must certainly have heard the gunfire.

'Don't even think of it.'

So my uncles started up again, 'Everybody out!' and then they did come to the windows and, as they did so, my uncles shouted to them again: 'We'll count up to three, and then we'll set the place on fire... One, two, three: fire!' and they broke down the doors, knocked over a couple of oil lamps and set the room on fire while the people who lived on the upper floor were still streaming down the stairs with their babies in their arms.

Now the Farmworkers' Union wasn't a straw-stack and it didn't burst into flame all in one fell swoop; setting things on fire requires a certain skill, you don't just breeze in, set fire to something and hope that things will take their course. As I've said, it wasn't a straw-stack, there are fires and fires. So they had to keep at it because it wouldn't catch. They had to feed the fire from the oil lamps with newspapers and posters, and break up some tables and chairs, and by that time everyone had come downstairs. Except for one girl, who was shouting down: 'Help, my brothers and sisters!'

'Throw them out of the window,' Pericles called to her, from below. And she threw the littlest ones out, one after another, and he caught them and put them in the middle of the square, while his own brothers carried on feeding the fire. Then, opening his arms, he called to her: 'Now it's your turn,' and it was then that he saw that she was fair-haired, and beautiful.

'Go to hell, you murderer,' was her reply, and then she began clambering out on to the windowsill so as to climb down on her own – she must have been about fifteen or sixteen – while her mother and father, from down below, were screaming at her: 'No no, come down the stairs.'

But she was already out of the window, she didn't jump but came out on to the windowsill and started lowering herself down, supporting herself with her hands, kicking her feet around to find a place to rest them, a cornice or string-course, while the wind and flames lifted her nightdress and you could see her calves. Lovely fair calves, and a bit of leg. And my Uncle Pericles shouted, again: 'Dirty Dog Turati!'

And he came under the window with the cart and my Uncle Pericles jumped on to it and put up his hands, trying to catch hold of that golden-haired she-devil, but she, as soon as she felt his hands brushing her feet, started to lash out like a mule: 'Get your hands off me, you murderer,' kicking out and hanging on to the windowsill.

Then at one point she let go, and Uncle Pericles caught her as she fell and put her in the cart, brushing her breasts with his hands as he did so. But as soon as she felt the cart beneath her feet – instead of turning round and thanking him – she turned round and slapped him roundly on the cheek: 'Hands off, you murderer!'

Meanwhile, though – at the end of the village street – a little group had formed, muttering together and spurring each other on, apparently about to move towards them. Uncle Iseo

113

and Uncle Themistocles didn't waste any time; they started shooting again, and the ones in the group didn't waste any time either, and turned tail and went off.

Then – to regain his dignity, after that slap – Uncle Pericles got down from the cart with his pistol in his hand, and he too started to shoot, into the air. But he carried on looking at her.

'Who do you think you're scaring?' was what she said, waving her hands in his face, while he carried on staring at her, and now her mother came forward to shield her – to protect her – but she rounded on her, too: 'I would have done a better job than this lot here,' and she pointed towards her father, and the neighbours. Then, by way of challenge, shrieking at my uncle: 'And you should be ashamed of yourself!'

My uncle fired into the air again. He was lost for words. Then he said to his brothers: 'Let's be off,' because they'd done what they had to do, the Farmworkers' Union building had been set on fire and now the people who lived there could put it out themselves and save their houses, together with that witch. And also because by now – better late than never – even the *carabinieri* were aware that something was afoot, and opening the odd shutter in their barracks: 'I thought I heard a strange noise,' the sergeant said to his wife.

So off they trooped, making one last tour of the village. Going by the houses where the suspects lived, all five or six of them. They drew up in front of those houses with the cart, 'Whoa there,' and some would get down from the cart and others would stay on it and take potshots at the windows.

'What's going on?' people would shout from time to time.

'It's us, the Peruzzi boys! Bang-bang!' all around the village.

The thing was, my uncles couldn't get their own back by setting fire to anyone else's straw-stack. The people who'd set ours ablaze didn't have straw-stacks, they were poor people – day-labourers, poor devils from the huts, or schoolmasters, barbers or blacksmiths – so what kind of a straw-stack were they going to have? They had even less land than we did, and they lived in a village. What could we do, set fire to the village? So we went looking for them house by house, taking potshots at their windows, making it quite clear to them that they had to call it a day. Anyway, no one had been killed, just a few hurt. And after all it was only the Farmworkers' Union offices that had gone up in smoke, not the houses above it. Come to that, it hadn't really been burnt at all, just the walls blackened, and some sticks of furniture and the windows broken, and the next day it wasn't even smoking and – had they wanted to – they could have patched it up and got it back into shape. In fact they did try to, and it was us – bang-bang, more rifle-shots – who made them think again, and it stayed as it was for several months, with the doors smashed in and the walls blackened, until such time as we took it over and turned it into the local Fascist Headquarters.

Anyway, at some point that evening Uncle Themistocles wasn't sure how many of them there were on the cart – it was quite dark, of course – but there seemed to be less room now, and he started to count his brothers: 'One... two... three... four ... five?' and he saw he'd got one too many. The extra one turned out to be my Aunt Bissola: 'What are you doing here?'

She'd run behind the cart on foot – he hadn't noticed – and got on it only in the square, shortly before they left. So, 'Let's go home,' said Uncle Themistocles.

'What about Pellegrini?' said Uncle Pericles.

'Pellegrini! Quite right,' said Uncle Themistocles. So they went the long way home, past the huts, because that was where he lived. But Pellegrini was waiting for them outside, there on the road, and when he heard the cart it was him who fired first.

But he was some way off, and there was no way he was going to score a direct hit. They heard the odd pellet whizz by near the horse. My uncles jumped down from the cart and then fanned out, firing at random, running through the field and ditches towards the huts. Meanwhile Pellegrini must have stopped shooting. Now it was only us, and Aunt Bissola was running along the ditch, bent double, clinging like a leech to Uncle Pericles' arm and pulling at it violently: 'I want a gun too.'

'You shut your trap, you little sow,' snarled Turati, kicking her.

When we got to the huts there wasn't a soul there, neither outside nor in – they'd all gone into the fields – and no lights, either. My uncle lifted his lighter to the branches covering the roof and set fire to them. Everything went up instantly in one great 'whoosh', just like our straw-stack.

A great rending shriek of 'No!' went up from all the surrounding countryside – women's voices. 'Murderers,' they shouted at my uncles.

'It's fire for fire, in my book,' answered Uncle Pericles: 'One bad turn deserves another, ask Pellegrini,' and off they went home.

At home, though, my grandmother was waiting for them, and she'd noticed that Bissolata was missing. She threw herself at the cart before it had even stopped on the threshing-floor, grabbed her with one hand and dealt her an almighty slap with the other. On the nape of the neck: 'I told you not to go!'

She didn't turn a hair – no shrieks or tears – just waited quietly for the fit to pass.

And the more she didn't shriek or cry, the more furious my grandmother became: 'You impudent little brat, you guttersnipe! Show a bit of respect for your mother,' followed by more walloping.

Until Uncle Pericles said: 'Ma, what's all this about?'

Then she rounded on him too – 'Do you want some more of the same?' – and Aunt Bissola ran inside, rubbing her head, and Aunt Modigliana asked her what had happened. And she spent the whole night saying: 'Holy Mary, holy Mary. They've got me, they've got me,' as though it was a sort of refrain, laughing and whispering, with her other sisters clustering around the bed.

Now no one seemed to care about our straw-stack any more; we'd taken our revenge. 'We'll buy some straw on tick, and we'll pay for it,' my grandfather would say. Anyway, after that there was no more straw-stack burning. In fact, it was us who did the burning, Workers' Associations were going up in smoke left right and centre. By now we'd got the knack.

Next day, my uncles all had black shirts made for themselves. They sent the womenfolk to buy a whole bolt of black cloth at the market and the trader said to my grandmother: 'My sympathies. But, if you'll forgive the question, how many people died?' partly because in those days you only wore black if you were in mourning, and he'd never sold so much black cloth all in one go before. And then the sisters sewed the shirts, and when they all tried them on together, Aunt Bissola said: 'You look like a gang of undertakers.'

What they were now, in fact, was a Fascist action squad – *squadristi*, they were known as – and they went round all the villages, together with other *squadristi* who were friends of theirs. And now, at home, those two shotguns were joined by carbines, pistols, machine-guns and hand grenades. In our houses, even the youngest children – those who were still crawling around on their hands and knees, Uncle Themistocles'

Paris, and our own Santapace – moved around under the table with knives between their teeth.

My uncles were now in contact with the Fascist Party in Ferrara, and things were hotting up. At the end of August – 30 August 1920, to be precise, even if my uncles didn't yet know what this date would come to mean to them – the workers in Turin, and then in Milan, had started occupying the factories. The FIOM – the Mechanics' and Metalworkers' Union – had set up factory councils like the soviets. There'd just been a revolution in Russia, and they wanted their own version over here in Italy. So they'd used these occupations to try to take over the factories and become their owners – them, the proletariat – and set the bosses working. That was roughly what us syndicalists too had been aiming for during the red week of 1914, and that time they'd said: 'No dice. We'll have to call it a day,' and so we lost the fight.

Now on the other hand it was them saying: 'Let's have a revolution, let's occupy the factories,' and you'll have seen this period – from 1919 to the beginning of 1921 – referred to in books as the 'red years'. Every day there were strikes, sit-ins, demonstrations and assorted violence. Nothing like that had ever been seen before in Italy, and Senator Agnelli himself – after they'd occupied Fiat, but also Ansaldo and Pirelli, the cream of Italian industry and capitalism – was resigned to such goings-on; he was working towards an agreement with his close associates and he said: 'All right then, there's nothing more that we can do, we're in deep water. Call them in and we'll come to an agreement: I'll hand the factory over to them and we'll own it jointly, me and them, and from now on we'll run it together too, them and me.'

But his associates came back to him and said beseechingly: 'Agnel, please, give it a few more days.'

'All right, we'll give it a few more days,' because every so often you have to keep your associates sweet, even if he himself – after a month of sit-ins – had resigned himself to the worst and was ready to negotiate: 'At least then it'll be over and done with, and we can get back to work, all in all it'll be better if I hand the factory over to them than if they take it from me with a kick up the backside; after all, they'll always need someone to run the show.' But this time too – just like in red week in 1914 – it was all talk and no action. Some revolution. Indeed, after less than a month – at the end of September – they lowered the red flags with the hammer and sickle put up by the factory councils, the new soviets, and the workers went back to work for the very same bosses, mild as milk. Nothing had changed. And not only had they not had their revolution or taken power into their own hands, but they were working in the very same conditions as before. If anything, the bosses were haughtier than ever, and Agnelli's associates never stopped reminding him: 'If it hadn't been for us, you'd have lost the lot!' So much so that in the end he found himself saying: 'That'll do now! The next person to say that will be out on his ear.'

But even a child knows that if you keep on urging people to fight without ever getting tangible results, in the end they'll lose faith in you: wolf wolf. Indeed, the more you make them fight fruitless battles, the less eager they'll be to join the fray: 'I must be mad. Am I going to take another beating just for the fun of it?'

Anyway, one way and another, those red years lasted all through 1920 – they'd started in 1919 – but by 1921 things had cooled down a bit, what with the 'waning of the struggle', as Lenin called it (I don't know if you know this, but Lenin and Mussolini had met in Switzerland before the war –

penniless exiles, the pair of them – in 1903 or 1904. They met in Lausanne, which was full of revolutionaries wandering the streets and constantly asking each other: 'Can you lend me a franc?' I don't know if Lenin was there when Mussolini, watch in hand, had issued his challenge to God. At all events, in 1917 Lenin saw to it that Russia had her revolution which put him in power, and when Mussolini read about it in the papers, he said: 'Good old Lenin, I'm really pleased for you.' And when in 1922 he organized his march on Rome and rose to power himself, Lenin said to Stalin, no less: 'Good old Mussolini! I always said he was the only revolutionary in Italy.' And he wasn't best pleased with our Italian left, which had allowed him to slip through its fingers).

So the reds had that 'warning' of theirs, but for us things were hotting up: now the knives were really out, with shoot-outs and fires and dead and wounded. Reds on one side and blacks on the other. And we were with the blacks – indeed, we were the blacks – and once my uncles too came home with Uncle Pericles stretched out flat on the floor of the cart. Dirty Dog Turati was driving, and when my grandmother saw from a distance that it was him and not Uncle Pericles on the box, she thrust her hands into her hair – but without saying a word, or drawing a breath; just waiting for the cart to stop, hands in her hair – and Dirty Dog Turati started shouting: 'Don't worry, ma, it's nothing.'

'I'm fine, just fine,' said Uncle Pericles in sepulcral tones, still from within the cart, while Uncle Themistocles was saying: 'Hold still,' to him, and preventing him from moving.

Anyway, that time they'd got him, a bullet in the side. It had gone in and come out, gone right through him, and when he came that evening the doctor said: 'All we can hope is that it'll heal of its own accord.' And he bandaged him up and off he went.

My uncle stayed in bed for a month and was plied with chicken broth, but he just felt more and more weary; so everyone began to think that there was no more to be done, and my grandmother would say: 'It's because of that priest. I always said no good would come of failing to show respect to one of his kind,' and finally one evening she lit a candle and began to pray. And the next night he got up, groped his way down to the kitchen, hugging the walls, lit the oil lamp, saw the saucepan by the hearth with the remains of the beans, and the plate with slices of polenta on the sideboard, carefully covered with a damp cloth, and ate the lot. And the next morning he said: 'I'm better,' and went off into the cowshed to do the milking.

Anyway, in 1920 my uncles had joined the local Fascist branch in Ferrara and they'd gone round all the villages in the Ferrarese drainage area with lorries, the 18BLs left over from the war; and between November and December they set fire to the lot, burned down the Workers' Associations and the local Socialist branch offices.

But it wasn't as if the other lot – the reds – just stood by twiddling their thumbs. They reacted all right. Bang-bang. They defended themselves. But less each day. By now it was civil war, me on this side and you on that. There was not as yet any bad blood between us and my grandfather's brother and his brood – no arguments, no ill-will. It was only Uncle Pericles who cold-shouldered them. He didn't even give them the time of day. It was as though they just weren't there. He did say good morning and good evening to his uncle, though, out of respect for his father. But that was it. Of course we didn't help each other any longer as we'd used to, and at seed-time – at the beginning of November – each sowed their own fields, and when anyone needed a donkey, or a horse, we took our own, not those belonging to the other lot, it was each for himself by now, though nothing was said in so many words; we carried on talking as before, as though all the surrounding bedlam hadn't seeped into our own house. But when we bumped into each other in the village, or at fairs, we pretended not to see each other, or know each other.

In the country at large, though, it was civil war, as I've already said, and war is war and you fight with what comes to hand – teeth and nails – but my uncles told me that it wasn't they who'd started that whole quarrel, that civil war, but them, the others. And not just by verbally insulting the returning soldiers, as though they'd betrayed their country and the proletariat, but by assaulting them physically as well, punching and shooting and all manner of rough stuff. 'It was you who burned down the straw-stacks and occupied the factories,' my uncles said, 'and that's what set off the gunfire and caused people to be killed and wounded.'

And that's how this quarrel became a war – a trial of strength – and quarrels aren't settled peacefully in this world of ours. When you start a quarrel, if you want to win it you have to go for broke, you can't say: 'Let's keep this clean, nothing below the belt.' And if it's you who starts it, I'll come back at you with no holds barred: I'll punch, I'll kick, I'll bite, I'll thrash. It's no holds barred, my life's at stake. That's the only way that I can hope to win.

First, though, the others – the reds – occupied the factories and burned down the straw-stacks, and then they had another think and started calling my uncles *squadristi*, or Fascist thugs. And the more we fired, the more they had another think, because, as I've said, they weren't united, they didn't have one acknowledged leader or one recognized aim. There was no way of bringing them together. Indeed, they were constantly calling each other traitors – just like the left today – and some were calling for revolution while others were saying: 'No, slow down: reform is what we need,' and in the end nothing got done. And in the end even the ones who wanted to put up resistance – the *Arditi del Popolo*, the red militia, for example – found themselves alone and said to themselves: 'Why do I bother? What am I, even more crack-brained than the rest? I'm going to hang around at home like everyone else, and see what happens.' And that's how the red years were lost.

Not even two months later – as early as November and December – the Socialist administrations in the area around Ferrara, and in Emilia, Puglia, Venezia Giulia and lower Lombardy were all falling apart. They were red, and they were falling apart because of resignations – at gunpoint, naturally – and replaced, when the elections came, by our lot. The Fascists. And whereas before there'd been any number of Workers' Associations and Farmworkers' Unions and Socialist branch offices, now people were changing their allegiances en masse and signing up with the Fascists, because they saw that they were powerful and determined, unlike the others, and single-minded: 'This lot will make it. In fact, they've already made it.' Just like on 25 July 1943: the day before, everyone had been a Fascist, and the day after there wasn't a Fascist to be found the length and breadth of the land; or in 1989–94, when first they were all Communists or Christian Democrats, and then all of a sudden they were for Berlusconi and the Northern League. The wind changes, my friend, and then the storm arrives.

But now we were with the Fascist branch at Ferrara, they were our local group. And in Ferrara it was Italo Balbo who called the shots. Rossoni on the other hand was in Milan, running the Fascist Unions, and he'd never been able to stand Balbo. Wherever Balbo was, he had to be in charge. Right to the end, he'd always said to Mussolini: 'You're the big boss, and I'll do your bidding. But in that small area where you've put me in charge, it's me who's boss, and you'll have to keep your nose right out of it.' And in fact he was never much taken with Mussolini, even after he became Duce. And in the end the Duce couldn't stand him either, because he was the only one in the Grand Council who addressed him in the familiar form.

That really needled him; it seemed to indicate a lack of respect. So he packed him off to Libya: 'Go and play the governor over there, that'll get you out from under my feet.' It was even said – though my uncles didn't believe it, and neither do I – that the orders for the anti-aircraft guns to open fire, that time when Balbo was coming back from a flight over Egypt, wasn't a mistake at all, but Mussolini's doing. The Second World War had just broken out, and seeing this aircraft approaching, the crew of the *San Giorgio* – a battleship which had been specially positioned to defend the stronghold of Tobruk – had thought that it was English and had opened fire, and carried on until they hit it, and brought it down. Then the whole crew started throwing their caps in the air from sheer joy: 'Spot on, this time we've got them,' and it seems that from that time on the *San Giorgio* never scored a hit on any single enemy plane. Neither before nor after, come to that. Planes came and went and not a thing happened to them – the reverse of the Bermuda triangle – and the British pilots used to say among themselves: 'Let's fly over the *San Giorgio*, they wouldn't get us if pigs could fly.' That was the only hit they had in their entire career. They couldn't believe their eyes. But, when they looked closer, they saw that what they'd got was

Balbo. And people in Italy said that it hadn't been a mistake, but a piece of skulduggery, because the Duce was jealous and afraid that Balbo would oust him from power.

All this was only tittle-tattle, obviously, according to my uncles, even if it is now known that on that same day the *Scire* – a submarine famous for its top-secret special operations – was also in the roads, and it too had opened fire without a word to anyone. It had arrived the evening before and gone off that same day, just an hour or so after Balbo's plane had been brought down. You can draw your own conclusions; though the fact remains that he, Balbo, was a great organizer, a ball of energy, and it was he, in 1924 – when Mussolini was in a spot of bother because of the Matteotti business – who gave him a shake and brought him back from the dead like Lazarus. Or Frankenstein.

By now, everyone was attacking him in parliament. He was out on a limb, and everyone said he'd have to resign, within hours, what was more, because the Matteotti case was one step too far and he had been the instigator. Though in fact he said that wasn't true, and so did my uncles: 'It was Dumini who masterminded that bungle.'

Now it may indeed be true that that was Dumini's bungle and that they didn't mean to kill him, just teach him a lesson, and all it may have taken was the fact that, on 30 May 1924, Matteotti had let fly at Mussolini in the chamber.

That had sent Mussolini into a mighty rage, and as soon as he left parliament – right there at the main door, red as a beetroot and fizzing with fury – he shouted at Cesarino Rossi, his private secretary, who knew him inside out, warts and all: 'So where's Dumini when he's needed?' and he looked black as thunder. That much is history. They kept Dumini on in Rome on purpose – hired and paid for by the Ministry of the Interior, with his whole Fascist action squad, the 'Black Cheka', as they called it – for just such eventualities.

So when Cesarino Rossi went to Dumini and said: 'Where are you when you're needed? Out eating and drinking at other people's expense? What are you waiting for? Where is Dumini when he's needed, that's what the Duce is asking,' he wasn't slow to catch on, and sent for a couple of his henchmen, and off they went in their car. They caught up with Matteotti on the Lungotevere. He didn't want to get in. He put up a fight. They started to beat him up. They bundled him in by sheer force. But he continued to put up a struggle even in the car. They turned the heat up. They'd started out wanting to teach him a lesson – at least that's what they said – but at a certain point they pulled out a knife and stabbed him to death. They'd brought the knives along for that very purpose. Then they hid him in some woodland. Matteotti, God rest his soul, wasn't found until two months later, on 16 August, and once more Mussolini wasn't best pleased: 'Now what have you done?'

'But I did what you told me to do,' said Cesarino Rossi: 'You know, "Where's Dumini when he's needed?" '

At that point – in 1924 – Mussolini was still answerable to parliament, and parliament set about crucifying him. All Italy regarded Mussolini as a murderer, a Prime Minister who, if challenged by a deputy, would send the heavy mob round to his door. The whole nation was scandalized: now he was on his own. In the papers it was all Matteotti this and Matteotti that. The whole parliamentary opposition were against him, of course, but quite a lot of Fascists too were now steering clear, people who'd been on his side but who – in view of this whole sorry business – were starting to turn elsewhere: 'Just a minute, that's no way to behave,' as though they hadn't already known that that was how he'd got where he was, with a lot of bang-banging, and that's how it's always been, power is a dirty business, that's what my grandmother said. If you want to keep your hands clean you try something else, not that particular greasy pole. It's the same nowadays. That's how power works; as long as you're in office, people will say that it's nothing to do with you, it's all a put-up job; all slander invented by your enemies to discredit you. But if you're fool enough to seem to be losing your grip, everyone who was pretending to take a lot of no notice will round on you and say: 'Wait a minute, that's no way to behave,' and they'll be the first to stab you in the back.

And so it was for Mussolini at the end of 1924. Now he was on his own. He spent those last days of December completely unhinged, prowling around the Prime Minister's suite like a madman. Traipsing along the corridors white as a sheet, and the caretakers expected to hear a pistol shot ring out from one moment to the next, when he was in his room alone.

And that was how it came about – between Christmas and New Year's Eve, while he was poised between political life and death, between flight and surrender – that Italo Balbo popped up out of the blue in those same rooms, together with a group of other *ras*, and said to him in no uncertain terms: 'Snap out of it, you're going to have to fight back. And if you don't – by fair means or foul, it's up to you – I'll do your fighting for you, and then it'll be me who'll be taking power.'

He was still dithering, and shrunken, both literally and physically: 'But the opposition...'

'Opposition my eye!' snapped back Balbo: 'Why did we bother to take power at all – to hand it back to them at the first opportunity?'

So at that point, he rallied. He puffed out his chest – if only to show the other *ras* he wasn't scared of Balbo – and a couple of days later, on 3 January 1925, he made that speech to the chamber where he said: 'That'll do now, I'm taking responsibility for the Matteotti business, but those who are in are in and those who are out are out: no more parties, no more newspapers, what we have now is emergency law. From now on democracy has had it in Italy, it's me who's in command. Just me. Dictatorship.'

But all this happened in 1924, and we're still back in 1920; I just brought it in so you could see what kind of a man Balbo was – afraid of nothing and no one. And he couldn't stand Rossoni. Balbo was from Ferrara, whereas Rossoni came from Tresigallo, and Balbo treated him like a country bumpkin. Balbo was a strapping young man – he'd been born in 1896, more or less like my uncles, and he was ten years younger than Rossoni – not very highly educated but from a good family. He'd been an officer in the war, he knew nothing about politics, let alone workers and peasants. Whereas Rossoni had read all of Marx's *Das Kapital*, and Cafiero and Bakhunin, the lot. Balbo was a man of deeds, but he was from Ferrara and – as we know – everyone from in and around Ferrara is a muckraker, even though they rake their muck as though they were the prince of Este in person. And that's hardly surprising – they're all his sons, because in those days there was the *ius primae noctis*, and when you got married the prince had the first go. So everyone from in and around Ferrara has their prince's blood in their veins, and his ways are in their DNA and they know how to behave in society and the world at large; they're all noblemen and merchants, even if they're poor as church mice, particularly if they're from the city itself. And Balbo was just that, and that was why Rossoni couldn't stand him. But by now Balbo was very much in command, and not just because he had been an officer, much loved by his men, and he knew all about tactics and strategy even though he'd never studied them – they were in his bloodstream, together with the Este princes' sperm – and he was personally very brave, which is just what you want of a commanding officer. But apart from his courage, and his military talents, he knew his way around Ferrara. He didn't know anything about workers and peasants and he wasn't there at San Sepolcro with my Uncle Pericles, that time they founded the Fascist Party. He hadn't heard that the Fascist Party was to the left, a rival to the Socialists but revolutionary and proletarian. He was an officer, he'd fought in the war and he was of good family – and from Ferrara into the bargain – and, understandably, he felt no great desire to work. It was only when he came back from the war – and saw that the reds were causing mayhem and riling the returning soldiers – that he became aware of the local Fascist group, which was the only one to put up resistance to the troublemakers. So then he said: 'This is the place for me. I'll set up a local Fascist branch here in Ferrara,' and – to finance it – he came to an agreement with the local bigwigs and landowners.

Apart from money, they also provided him with protection, in the form of the local judiciary, prefect, municipality and *carabinieri*. What he set up amounted to a veritable army. Where do you suppose they came from, the rifles and machine-guns and hand grenades lying around in my uncles' house? And the 18BLs haring about all over the place, burning down Workers' Associations left right and centre? Of course they had to offer the bigwigs something in return, but my uncles never had anything against Balbo. Not that they were on familiar terms or anything, he never ate at our house nor we at his. He was on one side of the fence – as leader – and we were on the other, as his troops. He mixed with his equals – lawyers, counts, landowners – not with people like us. That wouldn't have been to our liking either. We were different: we were peasants, and he had the blood of princes in his veins. But he certainly had charisma; he too had his magnetism, almost as much as Mussolini.

But, as I've said, there must have been something in it for the landowners as well, and this something didn't go down too well with my Uncle Pericles, and once, when Rossoni had come to see us from Milan, Pericles asked him: 'What's all this about an alliance with the landowners? Are you sure they won't cut up rough when the moment comes to give the land to the peasants? If it's to be given to us, it'll have to be taken from someone else, and it seems to me that that someone else has more or less got to be the landowners. And you say they won't cut up rough? It seems to me an odd alliance, because in the end one of the two is going to have to be hit where it hurts. Either us or them, Rossoni.' 'Now look, Peruzzi, the thing is...'

'Just tell me whether what was said at San Sepolcro still stands, or whether it's gone by the board.'

'I take your point,' said Rossoni, 'but the thing is, we've got to inch forwards slowly, one thing at a time. First we'll take power and then gradually we'll get it all sorted out. But in order to take power we need to form alliances, come to an agreement even with people who don't share our views. And if we don't, it'll be like all the other times: squabbles, bedlam and nothing gained.'

'Look, Rossoni, are you sure we haven't turned into reformists like everyone else?'

'Look, Peruzzi...' and now he turned to face us all, particularly my grandfather, not knowing that for many years – ever since the war, in fact – he'd stopped thinking and talking about politics, he left that to his sons. Anyway: 'Look, Peruzzi

130

... in order to take power, and change things, we have to make agreements with the very devil, even with the king. Even with the pope, if it serves our purposes. Then, once we're in power, we'll kick over the traces and get our hands on the land and launch a second series of attacks. But first we have to get into the room with the buttons.'

'The room with the buttons?' said Uncle Pericles, and the first thought that came into his head was when his sisters all got together and sewed the missing buttons back on to shirts and breeches. Then he thought about it a bit more carefully, and said: 'All right, Rossoni, I'll see you in the room with the buttons.'

Truth to tell, this room with the buttons wasn't our own idea, it didn't originate with the Fascists or with Mussolini. It came from a friend of his – Pietro Nenni, from Romagna like himself – and they'd known each other when they were young, and red. In fact, Mussolini had been red, Socialist and revolutionary. Whereas Nenni – when they'd got to know each other and gone to prison together for the first time – was still republican. Then they'd been interventionists together, and it was after the war, with the growth of the militant Fascist groups, that their ways had parted. In 1921 Pietro Nenni became a Socialist and then party secretary, and in 1963 – sixty years after Giolitti had foreseen as much – it was he who managed to bring the Socialists into the government with the Christian Democrats, and he was still saying: 'Now we really are in the room with the buttons.'

'Hey, Pierin, what's all this about the room with the buttons?' Mussolini would tease him when they were still in prison together. 'I could use a button or two,' he'd say, pointing to his grubby, tattered shirt.

For Nenni, power was the room with the buttons, and you

would go into that room – it was in the building where the government was housed, or perhaps the king – and there was a big table with all the buttons, and you pressed one of them, and orders were issued automatically. There was a button for banks, another for shops, one for the army, the air force, the navy, the power-stations. There was a button which said yes and no for everything, all you had to do was press it and the train that was the country would go this way or that. 'It's all about making your way into the room with the buttons,' Nenni would say, 'then you can press them and control them and everyone does what you say.' He made his way into it in 1963. But Mussolini got in there before him, in 1922. And what they found there – in that room with the buttons – is known to them alone.

Anyway, my uncles believed Rossoni – or allowed themselves to be convinced by him – because he himself was the first to be convinced that that was the royal road to deliverance and the social justice they'd always dreamed of: 'I just can't stomach Balbo, with all his landowners and that goatee beard.'

And so, at last, in 1922 – with the march on Rome – we got into the room with the buttons. 'Your Majesty,' said Mussolini to the king, 'I bring you the Italy of Vittorio Veneto,' which meant that he was bringing him the Italy of fighting men – the peasant proletariat who had fought and won the war – and they were all behind him. It was at Vittorio Veneto that the last battle before the armistice with the Austrians had been won, on 4 November 1918. 'The remnants of what was once one of the world's most powerful armies are now retreating, hopeless and in disarray, up those same valleys down which they came in prideful confidence. Signed Diaz,' was what was written on the victory bulletin which was now stuck up everywhere, and you have no idea how many people rushed off to the registry office when they'd had a baby boy and said: 'Signed! We'll name this one "Signed", after Diaz.' You couldn't move for baby boys called 'Signed'. Whereas my uncles – after they'd said something of note in the wine-shop, for example – would sometimes end it: 'Signed Peruzzi', and bang loudly on the table. But also when they played an ace. Particularly my grandfather: 'Signed Peruzzi!'

Anyway, that Italy of Vittorio Veneto – brought to the king by Mussolini – included my uncles. Mussolini had pressed the button and off they went. My grandmother was not so keen. It was the end of October, the rain had come and the fields were ready for sowing. The ploughing had been done in late summer, from August onwards. 'Ploughing first, then you can go on your jaunts,' my grandmother would say firmly every morning. And off they'd go in a line with the oxen, turning the earth which was still smoking from the burning of the stubble, because in those days stubble was still burned. Stubble is that bit of stem left in the earth after the ear of corn's been cut, and it's so stiff and spiky that from a distance you might think it was straw. But if you walk on it – barefooted, as we always were at the time – it's so stiff that it will pierce your skin, it's like a nail. And people used to set fire to it, and everywhere you'd see a pall of thick dark smoke rising from those stubble-fields. They don't do that nowadays. They plough straight after the harvest, with the stubble still stiff and dry on the ground and, as the plough turns the sod over, it sends this stubble down below the new layer of humus. Agronomists say that it serves as compost, and nowadays, if you set fire to it, before you know it you'll find the fire brigade's arrived to put it out and is reporting you as a pyromaniac, an arsonist, and they'll fine you for polluting the environment with the smoke. But in those days we used to burn the stubble to cleanse the earth. Burning was a form of cure, it would kill off weeds and germs and illnesses, because the earth too gets ill and needs treatment. Fire was a form of treatment. It gave the earth new life. It was therapy and preventive treatment rolled into one. And what you got from it was compost.

Anyway, after a couple of days of burning the stubble and the remains of the straw, straight after the harvest we'd be ploughing from dawn to dusk, under the blazing August sun – the earlier the better – so that the sun would dry up the earth, would cauterize it, if you like. Then we'd go over it with the harrow, to break up the clods of earth which the first rain had already softened, and the more often sunny days began to alternate with rainy ones, the more successful this process would be. By mid-October it would be finished, and by the beginning of November – on All Soul's Day, to be precise – you could start sowing. Not earlier, because the corn might sprout too soon and be killed off by the cold. But not much later either, or there'd be no time to cover it, and the seed would get soaked in all the water lying on the earth or, if it had been covered, it wouldn't have had time to sleep, ferment and ripen under the snow: 'Under the snow lies bread,' as the proverb has it. All Souls Day was the right time to sow. Neither sooner nor later.

So, towards the end of October, on 25 or 26 – the seed was ready in sacks in the small stable where we kept the horse, and it would have been cleaned out specially – when my grandmother saw everyone starting to pack their knapsacks and have their black shirts washed and ironed by their sisters, and oiling their weapons and saying to her: 'Please, ma, make some bread, we're off,' my grandmother flew into a rage: 'And where might you be off to?'

'To Rome.'

'To Rome? Why stop there? There's sowing to be done here, you bunch of idlers. And who's going to do it, if not you?'

But off they all went anyway – all the oldest male children, the usual lot – and this time too they nearly had Aunt Bissola trailing behind them. So it was Uncle Themistocles, Uncle Pericles, Uncles Iseo, Treves and Turati, who was now sixteen, and Uncle Adelchi too this time, and when they saw him getting ready no one could believe their eyes: 'Are you coming too? What on earth for? Surely someone should stay at home?'

'You stay then,' he said, spreading brilliantine on his hair.

So off they went, all six of them, and there are still photos of them – taken later, when they were in the Pontine Marshes, and all grown up – wearing the uniform of the militiaman, but also the Fascist scarf, worn over their black shirts, showing that all six had done the 'march on Rome'; it was something they'd earned, and there can't be many families in Italy who can boast of so many sons with that Fascist march-on-Rome scarf, and Uncle Turati, as I've said, was just sixteen and he had more weaponry than any of them, he was fairly bristling with knives and hand grenades, all hanging from his belt. And my grandmother was shrieking after them as they went off down the road in the middle of the night of 26 October, as the 18BL drove off: 'Shirkers, the lot of you. There's sowing to be done.'

'We'll sow, ma, don't worry, there's plenty of time.' And they were indeed back in time to sow, and even they themselves could hardly believe it had all gone so smoothly. They were indeed going off to another war, but even then they spared a thought for that threatened sowing: 'The women will do it.' But they left on the night of 26 October, and by the evening of the first of November, All Saints, they were already back,

135

dog-tired; and the following day, All Souls, she sent them out to sow.

They hadn't fired a shot. The only part of Rome where there'd been any action was around San Lorenzo. It was a working-class district – full of railway-workers, who were Communists and Socialists – and when they went through it on the morning of 31 October they felt a certain tension. That was the day the Fascists finally made it into Rome – they'd had their way with their march. The king had already summoned Mussolini and said: 'All right then, you can be the government.'

And Mussolini said: 'Your Majesty I'm bringing you the Italy of Vittorio Veneto,' and everything was over even before the first Fascist entered Rome. Not one of them had yet entered the city. We'd won. But before sending them all off home again it was only fair that they should at least be allowed to enter Rome, have a march past and let themselves think it was all their doing, that they'd won by force of arms, not just by backroom manoeuvrings; otherwise, what would have been the point? And when they went in on 31 October and had their march past, and the column which had come from the Abruzzi, on Bottai's orders, was going through the district of San Lorenzo and started to fire into the air, it was then that the local railway-workers started firing back on them out of their windows and there were dead and wounded. But only there. Everywhere else, nothing. Just a lot of hard slog.

Throughout 27 October, while the train was grinding slowly towards Terni – that was where everyone was going to meet up – the other brothers kept on saying to Uncle Adelchi: 'Why have you tagged along? There's going to be shooting.'

'I'll be shooting too,' he'd say.

But they weren't convinced, and kept on insisting: 'Are

you sure? It's going to be real shooting, you know.'

'And I'll be shooting too!' he kept on answering. 'Anything's better than staying at home. She'd have made me sow the lot all by myself.' In fact, though, not one of them fired a round throughout the whole march on Rome except for those in San Lorenzo, as I've said, after the march was over.

They'd spent two days hanging around Terni Station in the pouring rain. It never stopped. Night and day it poured. Every so often someone would say: 'Let's be off.'

'No, let's wait a bit.'

And so it went on for two whole days, in the pouring rain, and some people said that the army was putting up road-blocks and wouldn't let us through and it would be a bloodbath, while others were saying that the army was on our side: 'They'll let us through.'

Now I don't know what really happened. Some people say that Facta – now head of the government – had already made preparations for a state of siege, with orders to the army to open fire. But when he went to the king to have it signed, the king had said: 'Hang on, hand over, I need to think this through,' and he had him resign. Then he discussed matters with Giolitti, who was old by then but still thoroughly in charge.

'State of siege?' said Giolitti to the king. 'Hang on, king. Call in that Mussolini and put the reins of government in his hands, and then we'll come to terms and make him do what we want, just as we've always done. The important thing is to get him on our side and keep him there, so we can let him loose on those toads of Socialists,' because he'd never forgiven them.

The king agreed: 'Okay, Giolitti, you're right,' and he called in Mussolini and everything was fine.

'Your Majesty, I'm bringing you the Italy of Vittorio Veneto,' and the march on Rome was as good as in the bag. My

Uncle Adelchi shot a passing coot while they were camping out at Settebagni near Rome – in the middle of the countryside – on the afternoon of 29 October, when it had finally stopped raining. And they roasted it on a spit, together with a couple of chickens my Uncle Turati had produced from somewhere or other. No one ever knew whether he'd bought them or stolen them from a nearby hen run. But he'd been given some money by his brothers: 'I paid for them,' he said. The next day, the evening of 30 October, they went into Rome, and Uncle Pericles took his younger brothers to that brothel he'd always gone to when he was a soldier, when he was ferrying horses up and down from Cisterna. But Uncle Themistocles hadn't wanted to go: 'I'm a married man,' he said.

They hadn't wanted to let Uncle Turati in because he looked too young. 'But he's a Fascist,' said Uncle Pericles while Turati brandished his knife, 'and I'm a regular.' So they let them all in, but everyone wanted to go with the one who was a bit of a show-off – the one called Mimi – while Uncle Pericles persisted on singing the praises of his own favourite: 'Really, she's a better deal, there's no comparison in terms of what you get.' But they weren't having any.

So she repeated her usual wistful refrain to Uncle Pericles: 'In this world, some people just have it made...'

The next day they paraded through Rome, all forty thousand of them, after having seized power armed with nothing but rifles – 'Look, that's the Colosseum; that's Saint Peter's' – and then they took the train back north. My uncles got out at Ferrara – it took a whole day – and then they went by lorry to Codigoro, where they threw themselves on to their beds without a word, just ate polenta and lashed out at Aunt Bissola who was insisting on a full account: 'Tell me about Rome, tell me everything.' But they just flopped down on to their beds and the next morning – All Souls Day, early, before daybreak and they could hardly believe that they were sleeping in their beds – my grandmother was on at them again: 'There's sowing to be done around these parts.' So the march on Rome had been a picnic. Hard work, but all in all a picnic. And they had taken power.

Whereas what really was no picnic – though that was why they felt they could go to Rome all those years later, in 1932, to knock on the door of Palazzo Venezia: 'Knock knock,' 'Who's there?' 'Peruzzi,' it was the only thing they could do, their last resort – was the following year, 1923.

So now we were in power. Mussolini was heading the government, but parliament still counted for something. There were parties, oppositions, democracy. Of course it was the sort of democracy that suited the king but it was still democracy, with the 1848 Constitution still in force, even if you were head of the government and the prefects and everyone had to do your bidding; to the point that Giolitti was already wondering: 'Could I have made a bad mistake? How are we ever going to get rid of him?'

But the king was cock-a-hoop: 'At last I've got someone in charge who does things for himself and doesn't keep badgering me.' The old power vacuum and the chaos it brought with it were things of the past – now you knew who was in charge and there was no more mayhem and shooting. Nor were there many Workers' Associations around, either, because either we'd burned them down or they'd become Fascist Associations and people were flocking to apply for membership. We had to send them packing, none too kindly at that: 'No room for any more. We're full up.'

My uncles were now working, and not so much involved in

politics. Uncle Pericles would go into Codigoro of an evening – to the ex-Workers' Association that was now the Fascist Association – just to chew the fat, play cards, drink a glass or two at the wine-shop and, more to the point, if he could sneak a glance at the floor above, to catch a glimpse of that famous blonde she-devil who'd been hanging from the windowsill by her fingertips and lashing out with her feet on the night of the burning of the straw-stack and our own counter-attack. But there was never any sign of her. Or rather, the few times he did glimpse her she would spit on the ground and mutter: 'Murderer.'

So, all was quiet on the politics front, there was a bit of opposition in parliament but otherwise all was quiet: 'Mussolini is on the case,' according to *Il Popolo d'Italia*.

But in one village near us – somewhere near Comacchio – there was a priest who was far from quiet. You remember the priest at Cavarzere? Well, this one was worth ten of him. He'd also been a chaplain in the war and once, when his unit had been on the verge of surrendering to the Germans – during the rout at Caporetto – he'd suddenly felt himself not so much a priest as an Italian. A soldier among soldiers and an Italian among Italians. He threw down his crucifix and started firing along with the rest. He'd grabbed a machinegun whose gunner had just been killed. And the sight of him had given his men back the courage that was failing them, and they fought on, and he got the medal for military valour.

What did you say? That a priest shouldn't take up arms? Yes, that's the kind of thing they say today, but actually I can't see much difference between opening fire directly and blessing those who are opening fire on your behalf. That's the kind of hypocrisy you get nowadays. The further we advance, the more finicky we get. It wasn't like that then. The priest would give the blessing because that was what he was there for; when blessing was no longer enough, he too would open fire. Not just that priest, but all the others in all the other countries. Come to think of it, it wasn't that long ago that the pope too had armies of his own, and went round shooting and killing with his own hands. Julius II wasn't the only pope to don a breastplate. What about Pius IX: 'Monti and Tognetti,' as my grandfather used to say. Of course it is right and proper that Catholics today should all talk of non-violence. And non-violence is no bad thing – I'm not denying it for a moment – but it's a modern thing, because I don't think there was much sign of it even as recently as 1969, in Piazza Fontana.

Anyway, this priest from Comacchio was worth at least ten of the one from Cavarzere. He really did set up a boys' club, and it wasn't just so that the boys could play football either: he also had them study, with evening classes and some sort of professional training. He taught them carpentry and joinery, because there were boat-yards around those parts where they built boats and fishing-smacks and – at the time – there were still water mills on the Po. He'd even rigged up a cinema screen in a hay barn – this was in 1923, so what he showed were silent films, with the church organist playing the music on the harmonium. He also dabbled in politics. He'd set up a 'white' friendly society, and in his sermons he spoke out against the Fascists and the government. He was for freedom, and he said the Fascists were repressive, and since he couldn't go along with them, he preferred to go along with the reds. He always went along with the Socialists. And this alone was more than enough to enrage the blacks, because if news of this got around to the other villages, people would start to say: 'If the priest is in cahoots with the reds in Comacchio, why don't we follow suit?' and then it would be curtains for our lot.

And indeed this news was spreading throughout the region round Ferrara. Every Sunday morning – at High Mass, at noon, which was attended by all the better-off, the lawyers and the office workers – he'd climb up into the pulpit and repeat that it was this assault on freedom that was the real danger, not the demands of the proletariat, who also had inviolable rights of their own. That was what Our Lord said, too, when it came down to it, so our own lords and masters ought to examine their consciences and give the people what was theirs by right, and band together against those who were mounting attacks on everybody's freedom – 'not just with words, but with violence!' And word had spread throughout Emilia, and even beyond; and now this priest – apart from going along with the Socialist ringleaders and letting himself be seen with them at the wine-shop – had come up with the idea of setting up a boy-scout group.

At this point Balbo got hopping mad, and went to see the Bishop of Ferrara: 'Hey, what's going on here?'

And the bishop said: 'What can I do about it? I can't beat him around the head like you would. We're the Church, we talk and pray. But I'll try talking to him, don't you worry.' So off Balbo went, not worrying. But nothing happened. The priest from Comacchio continued on his track, just like a train, both in his Sunday sermons and at the wine-shop with the Socialists. And above all in his parish, with the boy scouts.

'What's all this to me?' the Bishop of Ferrara must have asked himself as he showed Balbo the door: 'We're the Holy Roman Church and we've always run with the hare and hunted with the hounds. You just wait, they might see the light one of these days. I'd need to be mad to say anything to that priest,' all the more so because he of all men – the Bishop of Ferrara – knew that Balbo wasn't exactly one of his own, and he was a mason to boot. Not only that, but he also had a lot of Jewish friends. In Ferrara, it was the Jews and masons who'd set up the local Fascist branch, it was they who were Balbo's strength, and anyway, by now – with the merging of March 1923 – the Fascists had joined up with the Nationalist Party, which had always consisted mainly of Jews and masons. Some Holy Roman Church. Furthermore, in the first Mussolini government there'd even been the odd Catholic minister from the PPI, the *Partito Popolare Italiano* – the Christian Democrats of the day, a party which Giolitti had dreamed up precisely in order to keep it separate from the Socialist reds – even if later Giolitti had regretted having had a part in this: 'I think we've made a bad mistake,' he told the king.

'You may have! Not me,' the king thought to himself. And he carried on thinking that way until April 1923, when Mussolini kicked the ministers from the PPI – the Catholics – out of the government: 'Out with you, the lot of you.' Then, at the beginning of July – in agreement with the Vatican, because there too, like the bishop, they must have thought: 'You never know' – anyway, at the beginning of July Mussolini forced don Sturzo – the secretary of the PPI, which the Duce had always loathed, worse than Giolitti loathed the Socialists – to resign and go off and lock himself in a monastery somewhere abroad: 'Get praying then, why don't you.'

In a word, the screws were being tightened, except on this priest in Comacchio, who continued to do just as he pleased. 'Boy scouts too now, is it?' By now, Balbo could hardly sleep at night. 'How on earth am I going to sort this one out? That cur Mussolini is like a dog with a bone.'

Sorry, what did you say? What was the problem with those boy scouts? What was the trouble with those cubs? Well, in the first place, Mussolini and his lot had never liked competition.

143

Whatever game they were playing, they had to play and win it on their own. Were they likely to let the priests come muscling in on the act? The country's youth had to take instruction from them, not from the Church. They weren't going to allow the young to fall into the clutches of a bunch of priests, now were they? Just get on with your praying and saying mass, they'd say. Not satisfied with your boys' clubs, then? And now along come the boy scouts into the bargain, with their uniforms, their squads, their caps, their knives and their squad leaders. It's all looking a bit paramilitary round here. Want some little action squads of your own? Couldn't we make do with my blackshirts, the nationalist blue shirts, the red shirts and Parma's red militia, the *Arditi del Popolo*? No, apparently that wasn't enough – so now along come the pope's white shirts to join the gang. Where's it all going to end, they must have wondered at the Fascist Headquarters: 'As if Don Sturzo wasn't enough. Now we've got the priest from Comacchio, with his soldier boys.'

What did you say? That it was silly of them to have been so worried about little boys, the Mickey Mouse Club, the Wolf Cubs, environmentalism, non-violence, knots, woods and camping? No, you have to see it in context. Perhaps, even then, the young explorer was really nothing but a good Samaritan, all knots and jungle book. But, as it so happened, *The Jungle Book* had been written by Kipling, and he'd written it to glorify and immortalize the British Empire, not the Kingdom of Heaven. And the boy scouts, or scouting – with all their knots, songs, squads, rules, catch-phrases and oaths – had been invented by a friend of Kipling's, Lord Baden-Powell, an Englishman and a soldier. And he'd invented it during the Boer War in South Africa, so that he could turn boys and young children against the Boers – he had them act as couriers, sentries and scouts, as the need arose – and some of them paid for their involvement with their lives.

I don't mean that the Fascists were right. Far from it. Here we're clearly not talking about decent people – that was just how they were, if you spoke out against them in parliament they sent the heavy mob round to your place to do a bit of knifing, like they did with Matteotti – while the priest from Comacchio was clearly doing what he did from the best possible motives. He wanted peace, freedom, progress, the Kingdom of God and universal love. He was a man of God, and he set up his scouting group to give young people an education in just such love. They were only boys, and it was the Fascists who saw bad intentions where there were none. So it's beyond dispute that today the scouts are all for environmentalism and ecology, and are a force for peace. But, equally clearly, at the time when they came into being – not so long ago, that is, in my uncles' time – they came into being as a force for war.

Be that as it may, they got the Fascists worried. Everything else was ticking over nicely, the country seemed to be back on track, my uncles were busy hoeing and my grandmother was delighted that they seemed to have stopped wandering around all over the place. All they did now was work. But those in high places were worried, and one day, in Rome – just after a meeting of the Grand Council – Mussolini said to Balbo: 'So, just what is going on in Comacchio? Can't you even get a country curate to see sense?'

Balbo went red with shame and fury: 'I would have had a word the bishop, but...'

'Ah yes, the bishop...' said the Duce, and then repeated the words with a crooked little smile, specially designed to mock him and roast him gently on the spit: 'The bishop, eh?'

'Well, no, actually, I was also thinking of speaking to

someone else...'

'Think away, by all means!' said the Duce. 'And what have you come up with?'

'Well, I don't really know, I thought I'd bring in...'

'Perruzzi from Codigoro!' shouted out Rossoni, who was standing beside him and who couldn't believe his luck at being on the spot to solve the problem of who else to bring in, and showing everyone – first Balbo and then the Duce – that he too still had his own henchmen, around his own parts.

'Peruzzi? One of the Peruzzi boys?' queried the Duce, as though to say: 'Why? Why him?'

'He knows how to talk to priests,' explained Rossoni, and then, turning to Balbo: 'Tell him what I told you,' while pure rage was causing Balbo to swell up like a toad, because he was now well and truly caught up in Rossoni's web.

But the Duce was looking more and more sulky: 'What are you on about? I haven't a clue what you're getting at.'

'Cavarzere! The priest at Cavarzere,' Rossoni reminded him.

'Ah!' said the Duce.

And so – once back in Ferrara – Balbo reluctantly summoned one of his own men and had word sent to my Uncle Pericles: 'You ought to go and have a word with the parish priest at Comacchio, that's what Rossoni says,' and off my uncle went.

And that was why, almost ten years later, we felt able to go to the door of Palazzo Venezia and say: 'Knock knock!' to the doorman.

'Who's there?'

'Peruzzi! We want to see Rossoni,' and they couldn't turn us away.

Ten years had gone by since our own personal march on

Rome, and by now we were no longer at Codigoro, but at Ca' Bragadin, working for Count Zorzi Vila, and things had been going swimmingly for our whole family, at least until that point, because we had plenty of land, good land at that, and plenty of hands to work it. We even had good working conditions. We'd never had such good conditions before, and they'd been negotiated for us by the local Fascist branch, because Count Zorzi Vila was one of Balbo's landowner friends. He thought the world of us – or so it seemed – and now everything was going our way: things had been getting better and better for almost ten years, though we'd had seen neither hair nor hide of Rossoni or Balbo, much less of Mussolini, or the Duce, as he now was; they were all in Rome.

We were just peasants, living our own quiet lives. It was all work and no play, but we were well satisfied. We were accumulating livestock, the girls were getting married, as were the boys. New children were being born, the family was growing. Until, out of the blue, disaster struck: in the form of that new exchange rate, quota 90.

It was now 1927 and, as you know, at that time foreign trade was carried out not on the basis of the dollar, but on that of gold and the English pound, which in September 1926 had climbed to 149, almost 150 lire to the pound. The export-import balance of payments was in dire straits. Italian industry was in a state of crisis. Corn too was feeling the pinch – feeding the people was a problem, because Italy was not yet producing enough grain, and indeed a few years later they coined the phrase 'the battle for grain' – and when you purchased it from abroad you now had to fork out no fewer than 150 lire to one pound sterling.

So one day, out of the blue, the Duce announced: 'I'm revaluing the lira, from today onwards the rate stands at 90, never more than 90 lire to one pound sterling,' and soon the exchange rate went down to less than 86 lire to the pound. How he wangled that one I do not know, but you can imagine how Italian industrialists must have been rubbing their hands, because everything they'd bought abroad – coal, iron, copper and so on – which, the day before, had cost them let's say 150 lire a kilo, now cost them 90. Then and there we Peruzzi too joined in the chorus of praise: 'By gum, that's some Duce we've got there.'

But it was only later – because in the meanwhile we carried on with Count Zorzi Vila as before, that is, sharing the harvest out in terms of each hundred kilos, and doing the same for expenses we'd paid out in lire: 'Sign here, but on trust, and then at the end we'll make out one single bill,' that damned count would always say – only after we realized that if our land continued to produce, let's say, its usual thousand kilos of grain a year, for which, until 1926, we'd got a market price of 1500 lire, lo and behold, from 1927 onwards we'd be getting just 900. So, as you can see, we were the losers by a long chalk: this new rate spelled ruin for the Italian peasantry.

Imagine what that meant for us sharecroppers. It did for us. The agreement was that we would share the harvest – go fifty-fifty with the landowner – but always in terms of each hundred kilos. And we also had to share expenses. And that damned Zorzi Vila reckoned those all in lire. We carried on signing for our debts for years, convinced that we were paying them off on a yearly basis with part of what we'd earned from our share of the harvest.

Count Zorzi Vila had other ideas. At a certain point he summoned his sharecroppers and announced: 'Time to pay up.' And what with this and that, so much for 1925, 1926 and 1927, up to 1932, each of us found we had to fork out a sum to make your hair stand on end.

'But what about those extra hundreds of kilos we've given you?' we all asked.

'What extra hundreds of kilos? Here we're talking hard cash. Let's see those receipts, if you've got them,' said the count.

'Receipts? But we always did things on trust.'

'On trust?' shrieked Count Zorzi Vila. 'Let's see that cash, or those receipts, or I'm calling the police.' Then he presented everyone with their bill and kicked us out and took all our livestock, in order to be quits – or so he said – and he didn't even value our livestock at a fair price, but at a lesser one based on that famous new rate, damn his eyes, and he even had the gall to say: 'Quits indeed, they're so thin there's no quits about it! I'd go further, but the Zorzi Vila have always been big-hearted, and you should thank them for that.' Thanks, count.

And that was that. We were up a gum tree. Now we were starvelings. And it was then that even my Uncle Adelchi went berserk and began to fire at the count and the factor, and the *carabinieri* came to take him away in chains.

That was why my other uncles had had to go to Rome, on that occasion when Rossoni had thrown his arms around them, hugging and kissing them and scolding the ushers and guards for not having shown them due respect and had them come in earlier. How sincere he was, I cannot say.

Anyway, Rossoni took them up to his office, had them sit down and asked them to tell him all about it in the greatest detail. He kept on nodding as they talked – 'I see' – and at the end he said: 'Come back tomorrow, in the meantime I'll look into matters and see what I can do.'

And the next day my uncles went back – taking the

opportunity to cast another dirty look in the direction of the porter's lodge – and when they got up to his office, Rossoni said to them: 'Cheer up! It's all solved,' and it wasn't long before they were positively dancing around in glee.

In fact, the only person whose problems were solved was Uncle Adechi: he'd been freed, on orders from above, after all he hadn't hurt anyone – 'A Peruzzi missing his mark,' said Rossoni teasingly, 'what was he firing at, a will-o'-the wisp?' – and the count had agreed to withdraw the charges. But he stood firm on the matter of the livestock: 'There's nothing to be done: it's quota 90, 90 lire to the pound, and the count is well within his rights.' He'd got them there. 'The only thing I can do is to get you a couple of holdings in the Pontine Marshes.'

'The Pontine Marshes?' said Uncle Pericles aghast, because he'd seen the Pontine Marshes when he was doing his military service, though only from afar, from Cisterna in fact. He saw them again in his mind's eye, the impenetrable forests, the endless pools, the swamps, and people with stomachs swollen like footballs – even boys as young as fifteen, their livers bloated like melons from malaria – not to mention the corpses thrown out on the roads and into the ditches. There was also talk of bandits, who'd killed men in their own villages, or indeed in Rome, and taken refuge in those same impenetrable forests, because no one would ever come looking for them there. They'd arrive in the Pontine Marshes, which were in a free zone, all you had to contend with was malaria, and one another – because such outcasts were the only ones to be found around those parts, you weren't likely to stumble upon a *carabiniere* or any relative of the victim in search of vendetta – and if you did venture into those foul regions, according to the people of Cisterna, you'd be set upon by those same bandits. Sometimes they'd venture out on to the roads and set upon the wayfarers, the country buses, the stagecoaches, in earlier times: 'Your money or your life.' The Pontine Marshes were the kiss of death. As my uncle knew, because he'd spent some time there in Cisterna, tending horses for the army: 'Are you mad, Rossoni? Excuse me, your Excellency? Do you want to kill off the entire Peruzzi clan? What did we ever do to you to deserve that?'

'No, no, Peruzzi, you're behind the times! We've turned the place into a paradise, we've drained the marshes, it's not like it used to be; we've turned it upside down,' and he held out his hand, palm up, then palm down: 'Upside down, we've turned it. It's become a garden, an Earthly Paradise, and we're giving the land to the peasants.'

'I don't want that land. That land is tainted. I want my own land back, and my livestock.'

'That I can't give you. But in the Pontine Marshes I can give you all the holdings that you want. And that land will become yours, Peruzzi, this time we're really giving the land to the peasants, after a few years sharecropping it'll be yours. You too will be a landowner, Peruzzi, a gentleman,' Rossoni's eyes were shining as he warmed to his theme. He might have been offering them the Promised Land.

'In the Pontine Marshes?' repeated Uncle Pericles suspiciously. 'Nooo, I know all about them.'

'But the land will become yours! You'll be a landowner! At least go and have a look at the place before saying no,' Rossoni insisted.

'Nooo,' repeated Uncle Pericles, so Rossoni found himself turning to Uncle Themistocles: 'What do you say, mister silence, damn your eyes?'

'Well...' was all Uncle Themistocles came out with, and then he pulled a face and made an imploring gesture, directed at his brother, as though to say: 'We've come all this way, we might as well go and have a look. What have we got to lose? In for a penny, in for a pound.'

Then Uncle Pericles said: 'All right, we've come this far, we might as well go and have a look, what have we got to lose?' and off they went.

Rossoni went out of the office with them, and while they were standing in the corridor, saying their last farewells, another door opened and out came the Duce. The ushers snapped smartly to attention – 'Duce!' they barked, and gave the Roman salute – and my uncles did likewise. Rossoni executed a more half-hearted version.

Then, after a rather stilted '*A noi,*' and a perfunctory wave of the arm, the Duce seemed on the point of going about his business. But as he was about to walk past my uncles, he stopped short for a moment and looked them in the eye: 'They look familiar.' He frowned, as though to concentrate his mind. After all, they'd been young boys when he'd last seen them, and now they were grown men, and goodness knows he'd seen a lot of people in his life over those years, with all those worries of his own into the bargain; but my uncles probably looked a bit like their parents, and he'd seen Uncle Pericles on occasions, if only from afar, wandering around in the lair on Via Paolo da Cannobbio in Milan in 1919. 'Perhaps at San Sepolcro... I wouldn't want to get this wrong... what the devil are they called?' The Duce carried on racking his brains. 'Ah...! Peruzzi! You're the Peruzzi brothers,' he said at last.

'Duce, Duce!' crowed my uncles.

'My regards to your mother,' said the Duce, cock-a-hoop at having remembered, and then he walked off and disappeared into another office, a positive ball of energy. But then, no sooner had he closed the door behind him, than he reopened it and poked his head into the corridor: 'How's the harrow? Still going strong? Tell your mother not to hesitate to let me know if she needs me. I'm still a dab-hand with the hammer. *A noi!*' and in he went again.

And off went my uncles, back to that place for travellers near the station, to take off their black shirts, their Fascist scarves and militiaman's uniform, which they then rolled up and tied to the back of their saddles. They put on their everyday clothes – old breeches and patched shirts – and got back on to their bikes. They took the Appian Way – the so-called Via dei Castelli – and after a lot of legwork they reached Velletri and then Cisterna, and then the Pontine Marshes, and had a good look round. My Uncle Pericles was able to note for himself that there were indeed no longer any marshes – they'd all been drained – and Uncle Themistocles for once broke his silence to comment: 'You see? Same old suspicious you.' So they turned their bikes around and after another week of legwork they were back up north, where they found Uncle Adelchi as free as a bird. Indeed, the moment he set eyes on them he asked them: 'What on earth did you trek all the way down there for? I managed all on my own, I've been here for days!'

Then they arranged to get their papers, did their packing, loaded the family on to the carts and brought the lot down here, to the Pontine Marshes. They'd had enough of the Po Valley, where we'd lost everything we'd ever had, all our livestock and the stores we'd built up over years of hard grind, and from which we'd been sent packing. And here, as luck would have it, we started again from scratch, and all because in 1923 – ten years earlier – one of Balbo's men had come up to my Uncle Pericles and said to him: 'You ought to go and have a word with that priest from Comacchio, that's what Rossoni says,' and my uncle had promptly done just that.

153

'Father!' he hailed him heartily. He wasn't wearing his black shirt when he went into the sacristy, he was wearing his Sunday best, a clean shirt and jacket and trousers, equally clean, but patched, because it wasn't every year you got a new suit; a jacket had to last you a lifetime, and even then it got handed down.

'Father, your business is with their souls,' he'd said, 'and we'll take care of their bodies.'

'What?' said the priest, who'd thought he'd come in connection with a wedding or something, and hadn't immediately understood what he was getting at.

'Politics!' my uncle added for extra clarity. 'Steer clear of politics,' and I don't know whether he sounded threatening, maybe not, maybe he just sounded polite but firm, and perhaps they chatted for a bit. Perhaps the priest from Comacchio too was polite but firm, and tried to interest my uncle in the Church's social thinking, and after a bit – still polite but firm – he said to him: 'All I do is God's bidding.'

'So, carry on doing as you've done for two thousand years; why change now?' barked Uncle Pericles, a little less politely but almost certainly firmly. 'A man forewarned...' were his last words, and the unfinished proverb carried a menace of its own.

But after Sunday mass, the priest from Comacchio climbed up into his pulpit and took the bull by the horns: 'The Fascists have threatened me, and by so doing they have threatened not just me, a poor worthless sinner, but more importantly the Church and the people of God. So, in defence of the Church and the people of God, and indeed of the freedom of all, even at the cost of his own life this poor sinner must continue to make his small voice heard; he cannot bow his head in the face of such a threat.'

At Comacchio, things moved fast. When they came out

of mass, everyone looked at the passing Fascists as though they had been stricken by the plague. At our house, on the other hand – at Codigoro – my uncles were still having their Sunday lunch – still all sitting round the table, some lighting up cigars and others roll-ups, looking forward to an afternoon nap, because, being mid-August, it was hot and close – when they heard the roar of a motorbike, the kind they'd used in the war, coming from the main road. Uncle Pericles sensed that it was for him, and went outside, with Paris, his brother's child, hot on his trail, shouting: 'Uncle, uncle, look at the bike!' and Pericles took him in his arms.

On the motorbike was someone from Comacchio – someone from the Fascist branch headquarters, one of Balbo's men – who said to him: 'See? Now look what you've done! Couldn't you have stayed home in Codigoro, you and your Rossoni,' and my uncle looked daggers at him, indeed he was angrier with that Fascist from Comacchio than he was with its priest. He turned round, took the child back into the house, put on a shirt, stuffed a jacket under his arm and went off on the motorbike, riding pillion behind the driver. They went to Massafiscaglia to pick up a third party – another grim-faced character, like the first – and arrived in Comacchio three to a bike.

They went into an isolated house outside the village, just off the road, waiting for night to fall. No one ever passed that way, not even the coots which were for ever flying to and fro between the pools with young eels in their mouths. Even the coots gave the place a wide berth, it was more sinister than Dracula's castle. And my uncle and his friend – the man from Massafiscaglia – spent the time playing *briscola*; but behind the house, not in front of it, so as not to be seen. And when they were bored of playing they stretched out on the grass with their jackets under their heads, and rolled themselves cigarettes until late evening, while the Fascist from Comacchio chatted to the man who owned the house and gave him a hand in the cowshed.

Then – when night had fallen – they had a bite to eat and got to work. They took a country lane that led to the outskirts of the village, and the man from Comacchio sent one of his henchmen to the priest's house, to tell him that his poor old grandfather was at death's door and in need of extreme unction, in that same house, just outside the village, he wouldn't need his cart – he could easily get there on foot – on that same road where Uncle Pericles and his friend from Massafiscaglia were waiting. The Fascist from Comacchio on the other hand had gone to the wine-shop on the square, to buy a round and make sure that he was seen.

My uncle and his friend were not actually on the road, they were on the other side of the ditch – behind an elm tree – and each of them was armed with a hefty stick they'd taken from a nearby woodpile. The wood wasn't even all that dry, in fact it was still green, the peasant to whom it belonged must have cut it quite recently.

There was a bit of a moon.

They saw the priest arriving with another man – the sacristan, perhaps, or one of the boys who attended his boys' club – and they were talking quietly to each other. The priest was holding a sort of pyx with little bottles of holy oil, and possibly also the Eucharist, though that's unlikely, because in those days they weren't so free with it. Nowadays you go to mass and you take communion – and the person involved may be a deacon or a layperson, even a woman – and they tell you to do so every day, not just on Sundays. But it wasn't like that then. In those days you didn't approach Christ in your own way, as the mood took you. Back then, if you wanted to take communion you practically had to hand in an official form, and even then only at Easter and Christmas – perhaps at Whitsun too, if you were really devout – but certainly not every day, so I don't think he would have been carrying the Eucharist. Just holy oil. At all events, he had his hands full with his priestly equipment, and he was wearing his black cassock and stole; and also a light coat, because the evening was quite cool, even though it was only the end of August, it had been muggy all day, but by evening it had cooled down, and even my uncle and his friend – under the elm tree, beyond the ditch, hidden by the leafy branches, with their sticks at their feet – had put their jackets on. So the priest was clutching his holy oil to his stomach, and the sacristan was walking beside him, and when they reached the place where the other two were hiding, they leapt out at them and barred their way, and the sacristan – or the young man from the boys' club, I'm not sure which – took fright and cried out, and took a step backwards.

And, just as he was crying out, my grandmother, in her bed in Codigoro, woke up with a start, unable to breathe. 'What is it?' asked my grandfather, awakened by his wife's sudden movement, to find her sitting up in bed beside him, gasping for breath, while outside an owl had started hooting. 'Goddam you!' said my grandfather to the owl, then, softly, to his wife, again: 'What is it?' 'I saw a figure, all dressed in black.' 'Hush, go back to sleep.' And, after a bit, she did.

At Comacchio, on the other hand, the sacristan was not so easily silenced, and carried on crying out as the others leapt out and barred his way.

'A man forewarned, that's what I said,' growled my Uncle Pericles, even more angry with the Fascist from Comacchio and with Balbo and Rossoni and indeed with Mussolini than with the priest. And he put out his arm, so that his stick became visible in the moonlight.

Unlike his companion, though, the priest had not taken a step backward. He had just stopped, and almost imperceptibly he'd raised his hands from his stomach to lift them to his chest, together with the holy oil: 'I am a man of God,' he'd said. And then: 'Be careful what you do.'

'Threaten away,' said Uncle Pericles' friend, lashing out and delivering a sideways blow to his left shoulder.

The priest had tried to dodge the blow, he'd moved sidewise to avoid it but – as he did so – the pyx with the holy oil almost slipped from his grasp, so he'd leant forward, as though to catch it as it fell. And the words: 'It wasn't a threat, it was a warning,' were hardly out of his mouth, when Uncle Pericles delivered his own blow.

He too had aimed at the priest's shoulders – full on, this time – but by the time the stick met its mark, the priest had already leant forwards to save his holy burden, and what the stick encountered, fairly and squarely, was his head, or rather the nape of his neck. My uncle heard a sudden 'splat', like the sound of a smashed melon, or rather he didn't hear it, he felt it, as though transmitted along the still green fibres of his elm stick. The priest collapsed in a sort of somersault, curled up around his holy bottles; he was already at his last gasp.

My uncle immediately realized what had happened. But his friend didn't, so while the priest was already on the ground, he dealt him another couple of blows, then took aim at the approaching sacristan.

'Come on now, that'll do,' my Uncle Pericles told him, 'we're in enough trouble as it is, I'd happily see the lot of them roast in Hell,' and he was thinking of Rossoni and Balbo and Mussolini, and of his father and mother and the day he'd come into the world, 'and me first among them, son of a bitch.' And they ran off down the road that runs from Comacchio towards Lagosanto, a dusty white road, strewn with big stones, over which they stumbled in the darkness. And my uncle kicked at them in his fury, thinking of the priest's face as he crumpled and fell, and how he said: 'It wasn't a threat, it was a warning,' there in the moonlight.

I don't know how far they walked, nor indeed what time it was when they were joined by the man from Comacchio with the motorbike, who'd come to take them home: 'Now what have you done?' He was agitated, and his tone was disapproving.

'Watch your tongue, or you'll be next!' snapped Uncle Pericles.

They got back on to the motorbike and went back home. To wait for the *carabinieri* to show up.

At the trial, they wanted the names of the ringleaders, and confirmation that it had been a political matter. But my uncle said: 'What do you mean, ringleaders? Politics didn't come into it. It was just a matter of women, your honour,' and the crowd behind him – in the courtroom – was shrieking and yelling fit to burst. The Catholic Action Group were there in force, and the judge ordered the courtroom to be cleared. Outside – under the arcades – the square was full of Fascists in full militia rig-out.

'That priest was fond of women,' my uncle insisted, to cover for Balbo and Rossoni, and he was given a stiff sentence, thirty years or so. But those in the know told him he needn't worry, and three years later – in 1926, by which time we had a dictatorship, and emergency law, and there was no longer any organized opposition in Italy – he was given a retrial, convicted of manslaughter and given just five or six years. He'd served most of his time already, and was given a suspended sentence.

When he came home, we were no longer in Codigoro. Every now and again my grandmother would be woken up at night by a figure all dressed in black, which left her gasping for breath, she said. But by that time we were at Ca' Bragadin – with Count Zorzi Vila – and we thought we were in clover. We had no inkling yet that this would be our hell, the end of our livestock and of such few possessions as we had.

But in fact it was precisely because of that same priest – that time in Comacchio, on the road to Lagosanto, just outside the town, in the light of a summer moon, who'd told my uncle that: 'It wasn't a threat, it was a warning' – that Uncle Pericles and Uncle Themistocles had felt that they could go to Palazzo Venezia, in Rome, and say: 'We want to speak to Rossoni.'

It was there that our story began: when we were forced to emigrate to the Pontine Marshes – with nothing but the clothes on our backs – to start again from scratch, our whole generation of Peruzzis and those to come.

That was why we came down here: because they drove us out. Because of quota 90, and because of Count Zorzi Vila. We came here because of a priest. A figure all dressed in black. And, come to think of it, because of a horse. That horse at Copparo.

II

It was a real exodus. Thirty thousand people in the space of three years – ten thousand a year – were taken from north to south: from the Veneto, Friuli and the region around Ferrara; driven by circumstances to live among foreigners who spoke another language; who called us 'polenta-guzzlers' or, what was worse, Vikings. Who gave us nasty looks. And prayed to God that malaria would do away with us.

A real exodus, then, and by the time we got there Piscinara had already been drained. *Tabula rasa.* A billiard table. No sign of a tree, even on the horizon – not a sign of those woods and forests Uncle Pericles claimed to have seen, teeming with animals and murderous brigands who had fled there from their towns and villages up in the mountains. Not a drop of water or a blade of grass, either, and thirty thousand of us helpless human ninepins who'd rushed southwards to populate that billiard table, that dead expanse, that waterless unending blank of virgin land. It looked like a desert, and indeed the moment they got her out of the lorry, Grandma Toson – a member of the family with whom we'd made the journey, and who still live on a holding two away from ours – burst into tears, and shrieked: 'It's nothing but a desert, here.'

The Toson family came from Zero Branco, a town midway between Venice and Treviso; flat as a pancake, just like the Polesine, where we came from, with the nearest mountains a hundred kilometres away. But at least there the horizon wasn't one endless blank. There were trees at Zero Branco, all over the place, running along the edges of fields and headlands: elms, acacias, poplars and huge ash trees, bordering roads and canals. And bell towers. Every village had its own – even if they were quite close together – and every village wanted to build the tallest. It was one endless competition, and every now and again one would fall down, because they were always adding to them – an extra metre or so a year – so as not to be outdone by the next village. And everyone was proud of their bell tower, and at Zero Branco they were proudest of all, because they'd just rebuilt theirs from scratch, and it was the tallest in the region – it still is. Grandma Toson even said as much on the train, to the people who'd come in to chat from other carriages: 'We're from Zero Branco, you know, the place with the tallest bell tower.' When you were out in the fields – under the blazing sun, hoeing your beets – it was a blessed relief to hear the hour being struck, and everyone would straighten up and mop their brow and look towards that bell tower. It served not just to give you a sense of direction – though that's already something, when you're out on the vast Po Plain – but it also exerted a strong spiritual pull, because it was thanks to a bell tower that you knew you weren't alone in that great flat landscape, and you could be sure that it would ring its bells in an emergency, and everyone would come running to help you, and each other.

But the moment old Grandma Toson got on the back of the lorry – when they were taking us all from the station at Littoria Scalo to our various holdings, and she was clutching two small children in her arms, there among the household linen and furniture and tools – she'd started peering around to left and right and already she'd turned quite pale, she couldn't believe her eyes: 'They can't be going to leave me here' – and when it was her turn to get down from the lorry she looked around her quickly once again, just long enough to see that strip of mountains some fifteen kilometres to the east, a long way away but looming large, because there was nothing between us and them, not a tree, nothing, just utter emptiness from here all the way to the horizon; only that blue strip to the east – the mountains – and then the banks of the Mussolini Canal. But those too were bare – not a single blade of grass on the earth they'd been made from – in fact they weren't really banks at all, but grave-mounds, newly-made tombs without even a cross. The other thing that caught her eye were the little blue houses – blue like the mountains, but empty, lifeless, no one in them, not even a tree beside them; strewn here and there across the plain, empty, and the plain itself was a sea of mud, of earth, transported from elsewhere, without a trace of greenery, not even a weed: a desert. A desert of mud.

'Where have they brought me to?' she began to shriek. 'Take me straight home again!' and she tried to climb back on the lorry, cursing herself for ever having got off it, and clinging to its side, tears running down her cheeks, while her sons, weeping themselves, tried to force her to release her grip.

'Take me back to Zero Branco,' wept Grandma Toson. And all her grandchildren wept along with her: 'Granny, Granny,' they wailed, all tugging at her skirts.

163

But the area as a whole wasn't in that state of readiness – like Piscinara, already drained – and when we arrived there was plenty more draining to be done. Even if we didn't know it, work had barely started. The only area that had been drained was between Cisterna and the so-called Quaternary Dune – where Latina is today – but from there on to the sea it was still the same old Pontine Marshes that Uncle Pericles had told us about, a hellhole which, a few years earlier, had stretched from the walls of Rome all the way to Terracina: over seven hundred square kilometres of marshes, swamps, impenetrable forests with snakes two metres long and swarms of anopheles mosquitoes which would lay you low with malaria if you so much as looked at them. If the quicksands didn't do for you first, that is.

The Ancient Romans had already had a go at draining these marshes, and so had the popes and Leonardo da Vinci, and Napoleon, and Garibaldi; so far, though, the marshes had had the upper hand. No traveller in the eighteenth and nineteenth-centuries – Goethe, Stendhal, Mme de Stael – returned home without telling all Europe of the death and desolation of the Pontine Marshes. Then along came the Duce and Rossoni and, where Julius Caesar, Pius VI and Napoleon had failed, they drained the lot in the twinkling of an eye.

It's the Mussolini Canal which gives life to the Pontine Marshes, and that explains why all previous attempts had failed. Because, just downstream from Rome – as you can see if you look at a map – a ninety-or-so kilometre deep rectangle of relatively level ground opens up below the Tiber, its long sides being the Tyrrhenian Sea to one side, and the Alban Hills and Lepini and Ausoni Mountains to the other. At its base – ninety miles from Rome – lie the promontory of Circeo and the cliffs of Terracina.

164

The upper part of this rectangle, though, some fifty kilometres deep – from the river Tiber to the Astura – is more accurately known as the *Agro Romano*, or Roman Plain. This area wasn't marshy, since in fact it wasn't really a plain, but a continuous succession of small rises, knolls and ups and downs. But it was no paradise, either, because the water was often stagnant, here and there forming marshes and swamps from which malaria spread. Life there was hard – no question about it – but not nearly as hard as in the Pontine Marshes, which began in the remaining part of the rectangle, now known as the *Agro Redento*, or 'Redeemed Plain', as Mussolini called it. And this is indeed all plain, all forty kilometres of it – *Hic sunt leones*, as the ancient Roman put it – as far as Terracina.

From the foot of the Lepini Mountains, the plain slopes down to the Tyrrhenian Sea, becoming ever more level as it goes. Before it reaches the sea, though, there's a slight puckering – some five or six kilometres in width – which cuts across it longitudinally like a backbone, parallel to the coast. This puckering is known as the 'quaternary dune', and it was here, some four or five hundred thousand years ago, that the waves broke. Then the coastline started receding and the sand-laden waves gradually gave rise to a new dune – the present-day coastline – a couple of kilometres from the older one. But, over time, a sort of level basin formed between the old dune – the quaternary one – and this new one, a couple of metres below sea level, and, since the rainwater never really drained off, a series of lakes and pools and coastal marshes came into being.

I'm sorry, what did you say? Were these the famous, or should I say infamous, Pontine Marshes?

No. Marshes doesn't mean that the whole area was under water. In Latin, *Palus* or *paludem* in the singular means a pool,

165

a backwater, land that is flooded, under water. *Paludes* in the plural means an area of pools and flooded land alternating with land above sea level, but covered by dense forests and ravines, with lots of brambles and animals and prickly vegetation. And in the forests there are other pools known as *piscine*, particularly on the quaternary dune because there – once they'd filled up with water in the winter months – even the slightest hollows, whose uppermost strata were of clay, stayed flooded, stagnant and putrid, the whole summer long.

But this wasn't the worst of it – the fact that on those parts of the land below sea level the rainwater never drained off or got absorbed. After all, here all they needed to do was to fill in the hollows – none of them were more than two metres below sea level – and get the water out with pumping engines. Indeed, the first private steam-pumping engine had already been installed at Forcellata as early as 1907. The Fascists installed electrical pumps all over the place – they installed a huge one at Mazzocchio, with six vertical screw pumps, the largest in Europe – and nowadays, as you're going down the Appian Way or along the coast, in the lee of the last dune, at the end of every canal you'll see those groups of yellow houses with big long rectangular windows, and that's where they keep the pumping engines which raise the water at the river mouth and empty it into the sea.

No, the worst of it was in that larger area of the plain called Piscinara, which runs from the foot of the mountains down to the quaternary dune. Up to that point the water would flow effortlessly downhill on its journey to the sea. But when it reached these last eight kilometres, when it arrived at that slight puckering, it had to stop – as we all know, water on its own can't flow uphill. So the only way it could get to the sea was by taking the longer route, by flowing lengthways towards

Terracina. Since this route was forty kilometres long, and all on the flat – the difference in level was barely two metres overall – you can see that that poor water never had any hope of making much headway, but had to resign itself to virtual stagnation.

And the rivers and mountain-streams from the Lepini Mountains were not the only ones to flow into this part of the plain, though that was already bad enough; there were also others that came from outside the marshes, brought by the River Teppia and the *Fosso di Cisterna*. All these water-courses come from higher up, from our mountains and the Alban Hills, and if their way had been clear they would have flowed straight into the sea. But as it was – blocked by the dune – by mid-autumn they would already be flooding the whole plain of Piscinara for kilometres on end. And there they would stay for over half the year.

In Roman times, someone – Nero, perhaps – had cut a canal through the quaternary dune, in the middle of the plain, linking the *Fiume Antico* to the coastal lakes and the sea. The truly astounding depth of this canal suggests that it could indeed have been Nero, who'd also started digging out the Corinth Canal. Nero would tackle anything. But then they murdered him, the Corinth Canal was left unfinished and ours, the one on the dune, which is called *Rio Martino*, got silted up, and it took Mussolini to dig it out and get it working again. But even that didn't really solve the problem, and in our time, whenever it rained, the whole plain would be flooded with muddy water from the tufaceous soil of the Alban Hills. When the current was strong, the *Fosso di Cisterna* and above all the Teppia would dislodge all the earth from the slopes and bring it here. Then on the plain, where the rivers flowed more slowly, the earth would settle, and other sediments and obstructions would build up, and Piscinara would become a marsh, and would be flooded until the August sun began to dry it out, amidst clouds of mosquitoes. Come November, though, we'd be back right where we'd started.

So the first thing the Fascists did was to dig out a large canal at the area's northern limits, into which the 'upper' waters would flow before they could get into the marsh – a sort of bastion, a frontier, telling the waters to stop right there. This is the so-called Mussolini Canal, which starts out running along the foot of the Lepini Mountains and then turns southwards, crossing the plain and receiving in turn the Teppia, the *Fosso di Cisterna* and all the other rivers from the Alban Hills. They all flow into the Mussolini Canal, which then cuts through the quaternary dune and takes all the waters straight to the sea. But don't forget that when we say *Fosso di Cisterna*, or indeed *Fosso di Femminamorta,* here the word *Fosso*, which usually means 'ditch', doesn't refer to the sort of ditch you might have on the road outside your house. These 'ditches' were real rivers, much bigger in winter but never actually dry – their water came from springs in the Alban Hills and Lepini Mountains – and in the winter they were the very devil. They turned the whole place into one great marsh, as I've already said, and that's why there were these marshes, and that's why we were there to tell the tale.

It's the Mussolini Canal which gives life to the whole area: if it weren't for the Mussolini Canal, we'd be under water all over again. Don't be misled by the six-metre trickle you see running under the bridge in summer. You should see it in winter, or in the spring and autumn floods, when it's one massive wall of cloudy reddish water from one bank to the other – a good eighty metres wide – whipping along fast and furious. Believe you me, it makes a sound like when the steam exhaust is let out of boilers in a factory. A thousand cubic metres of water a second, when it's in spate. Think of the speed, the quantity, the power. If you fell in, it would do for you on the spot with the punch of its sheer volume, even before it drowned you. In the bars in Latina they have a toast that goes: 'Here's to you and the Mussolini Canal, may it hit you head-on one of these days.'

It took us eight whole years – from 1928 till 1935 – to excavate the thirty-one kilometres of its course. My uncles worked on it, too. It hadn't yet been completed when we arrived, only the first part – from the Lepini Mountains to *Fosso Moscarello* – and even that was only half-dug, the left-hand part. My uncles – together with other workmen and sharecroppers, obviously – dug out the rest.

There were four Tosi diggers at work, as well as two Rustons and a Bucjrus. But at the Mussolini Canal most of the work was done by those four Tosi diggers, with buckets on a continuous belt. They were vast contraptions, and they looked like dragons – indeed, they were known as drags – or giant millipedes: essentially, they were a series of buckets, attached by a chain to a long slanted lattice-like structure which sent them circling around, one after the other, removing the earth from downstream and taking it upstream, so that they would dig out the channel and start to build up the banks beside it all in one go. The four Tosi diggers were powered by electricity – it was quite a feat to get the cables there from Cisterna – and each one worked on its own stretch. Every now and then they would meet up, like in tunnels, and when this happened the teams would do a lot of celebrating. Then they'd dismantle them and reassemble them somewhere else.

On our stretch, though – some six or seven kilometres long, between the Appian Way and the bridge at Babbaccio – under the top strata of earth there was a continuous series of

169

outcrops of *tufa*, deposits of travertine and bars of limestone, namely the Lepini Mountains. So here the diggers had to stop, because they could barely scratch the rocky surface. It had to be blasted open with explosives, with dynamite, and only once those rocky strata had been broken up could the Tosi carry on their work. Hearing all that crashing in the middle of the night – they worked at night, too, using searchlights – my grandmother would say to Uncle Pericles: 'When will you be done?' As though it was all his fault.

What with all that digging, every so often they'd come upon archaeological finds. There were archaeologists from Rome – important professors like Lugli and even as big a fish as Carlo Alberto Blanc – who would come along to see how things were going. At Torre Annibalda, towards the bridge known as Ponte Marchi, they found Roman mosaics of swimmers. They dismantled them and took away the lot, though no one can now remember which museum they ended up in. Near Borgo Santa Maria, on the other hand – only then it was known as Plick plock, because when you walked through the marsh there in your shoes, or even your bare feet, it made a squelching sound – just as the Tosi buckets were about to trundle it off, Blanc found the complete skeleton of a mammoth. More often, though – when they discovered walls or tombs or run-of-the-mill bits of pottery – being Romans, the archaeologists would say: 'Carry on, it's of no importance, go ahead.' What else was there to do? We couldn't stand around all day staring at bits of pottery. If we too had carried on like the people making the underground in Rome, 'We'd still all be under water,' as my Uncle Adelchi used to say.

Once the Tosi had done their work, we'd dig out the low water channel – deeper down, in the centre of the excavations – which is always full of water, even in the summer months;

170

we'd dig it out by hand, with shovels and pick-axes in the summer, and with heavy spades in winter. After this channel had been dug out – by hand, as I've said – it was then flagged with stone. Stone upon stone, all carefully fitted into the bed of the canal one after the other, with lime and cement, to prevent the water that filtered in from the banks or springs in periods of low water from seeping into the foundations and encouraging the growth of marshland plants. Every so often, though – all along the Mussolini Canal – you can also see whole stretches of canal which are made of stone, with the entire bed completely clad, not just the low-water channel, and a step one or two metres deep and, below it, a large basin and another stretch of paved canal. These are the so-called 'bridles', which are dykes, or reinforcements. We children called them 'little waterfalls', because the water did indeed come tumbling down them, and we would bathe and swim below them, in the basins. They served to make the water flow more slowly, because otherwise the banks would have been worn away.

But even though the calculations and measurements had been done by the regime's foremost hydraulic engineers, certain bits of work had to be done again – on two or even three occasions. Once wasn't enough. The flood of 1934, for example – 4 November 1934 – swept away the whole of the bridge known as Ponte Marchi, the one that crosses the Rome-Naples Railway to the north of the Appian Way, less than four kilometres from our holding. That night, my grandmother would say, the banks were making not just a great whooshing sound, like the steam exhaust being released from boilers in a factory, but a whole lot of boings, as well – the sound of the poles and bars and trees and carts and machinery that the Mussolini Canal was dragging along with it as it swelled and created havoc further upstream. We were awake all night, my

171

grandmother said, and we all went to the upper floor, with the stepladders at the ready to go on to the roof, if need be, while my uncles took it in turn to keep watch on the canal banks, to check the water level and give the alarm. As luck would have it, at daybreak the canal burst through the other bank and the level went down, after flooding the Right-Hand Parallel. That time, we got off lightly. What didn't get off lightly, though, was Ponte Marchi. At one point the whole span was blocked by tree trunks and stumps and brushwood brought down by the swollen Teppia, and all this acted as a sort of dyke. The waters rose, and the pressure increased, until the debris reached the roadway, and the railway, tearing up the tracks – bing-bong-boing, as my uncles put it, you could hear it even from our place – and the ballast with it, stone after stone. All that was left was the poles, still attached to the wires, wrenched this way and that way by the current. Then the canal burst its banks with a loud boom, and carried the whole bridge away. Luckily no trains were on it at the time, though a goods train did arrive shortly afterwards, tried to brake and almost succeeded. We've still got photographs of it at home, taken a couple of days later, with its steam engine – just the engine, though, because the rest of the train was unharmed – up-ended on the bank, wheels in the air, beside what remained of the bridge's piers.

We had to build Ponte Marchi again from scratch, stronger and sturdier than before. And we also set to work again on that whole stretch of the Mussolini Canal, making it wider: 'That'll put it in its place.'

That time, though, a couple of days later the flood was back again with a vengeance, carrying off the embankments – stone by stone – from Ponte Babbaccio as far as 'Plick plock', now known as Borgo Santa Maria, where Blanc had found the mammoth. There it created total havoc, tore everything up, swept it away, including the bridge – absolutely nothing was left of it – and perhaps that was the mammoth's doing, or that of its injured spirit, because, as my uncles used to say: 'You don't dig up the dead, even if they're just prehistoric animals.' There too everything had to be rebuilt from scratch and made stronger and wider and sturdier, in the hope that now the mammoth would be appeased. And indeed nothing like what happened in 1934 ever happened again, even though the Mussolini Canal does still sometimes overflow its banks, flooding the odd field.

Anyway, when we arrived the canal was still only half-finished. But the upper part of the Pontine Marshes – Piscinara – had already been thoroughly drained, the otherwise empty countryside was already dotted with newly-built farmhouses and the villages that served them, and in the distance you could see the building sites of the new town of Littoria, with the tower of the town hall already mostly built. It was a colossal undertaking, no two ways about it. Until 1926 there wasn't even a detailed map of the area, and there were places where no one had ever set foot before. Just marshes, mud and quicksands. If you got into any kind of trouble, that was where you'd breathe your last. My Uncle Benassi, the one who married my Aunt Santapace Peruzzi, said that while they were clearing the Pantani da Basso of trees, and he was working on the banks of the canal on a tractor – a Fowler, it was, one of those huge steam-driven things which could shift absolutely anything, using a windlass – at one point the Fowler went off the duck-boards they'd laid down on the mud so that it wouldn't sink. First it tilted slowly to one side, then it was sucked in completely and no one has ever been able to get it out. It's there to this very day. Like the lorry under the Fontana della Palla in Piazza del Popolo at Latina.

It was quite an exodus, as I've already said.

Over a period of three years, they loaded us on to trains and brought us down here. On troop trains. Divided into groups. One train a day. Ten thousand people a year. Sent us down all through Italy. They had us assemble at various starting points – the stations at Ferrara, Rovigo, Vicenza, Udine, Treviso and Padua – and in the evening we'd be off. We'd say goodbye to our houses and villages in the morning; then they collected us in lorries belonging to the Militia, helped us to load up our possessions, a few sticks of furniture, our tools, our livestock, if we had any. All tied up in bundles. All the farmyard animals were in osier cages we'd made during the previous days; there wasn't a single green branch left on any willow tree in the whole of the Po Plain. All that we'd done, while we were waiting, was to build cages for the animals we were taking with us to the Promised Land, and stripping those trees bare had been a way of helping us to loosen our grip on our old home, we tore them off furiously, heedless of the damage we were inflicting. No one – before – would have harmed a hair on a tree's head. But enough was enough: now you've driven me off my land, to hell with the lot of you, you and your trees as well.

The whole day had been one constant bustle of lorries going between our old houses in the smaller hamlets, and the nearest country station. The first exiles had arrived at dead of night. Then, after shedding their loads, the lorries had gone back again to pick up the rest, until the area outside the station was full to bursting. Over the previous months, the department for internal migration – the people who'd looked into the requests, checked on the qualifications, made the choices and stamped the documents: 'Thumbs up for you, thumbs down for you' –

had already allotted everyone their place outside the station, so that, when they got on to the train, they would be seated next to the people who would ultimately also be their neighbours in the south. But we didn't know that. We thought we were seated randomly next to people we'd never see again. No one had told us anything. But that was typical Fascist attention to detail. So we began to make friends with people as they arrived outside the station, though some of them were from our own village, and we'd already had to learn how to get along with them. Then at last we climbed on to the train, an endless troop train which arrived in the early afternoon, pulled by two steam engines, with passenger coaches dating from the First World War, third-class coaches without compartments, with wooden seats and luggage racks above them, and doors by every other seat.

At the head of the train – after the engine, and before our carriages – there was also a second-class carriage, with compartments and upholstered seats, and that was for the officials from the internal migration department, the staff of the Servicemen's Association, the provincial party secretary when he happened to be there, and the Militia Blackshirts. Sometimes there were also second-class carriages – though with wooden seats – for us or the militia, when they hadn't found us places in the third-class ones and had to fill up the train somehow. And they shoved our women and children into these second and third-class carriages until they were full to bursting, together with old men with bags of linen and household pots and pans and sieves for flour, which they hung from the luggage racks, together with the odd cat or rabbit in a cage that some child had refused to leave behind: 'I want my rabbit.' Its mother would administer a hearty slap – 'Go to blazes the pair of you, you and your blooming rabbit' – and then go off to find it some corner amongst the saucepans, and then, as soon as a bit of rabbit-shit fell on someone's head, as was bound to happen, she would administer another hearty slap: 'I'm throwing the dratted thing out the window.'

'Nooo,' the child would wail.

'Shut up, or I'll throw you out as well,' accompanied by another slap. But in the end a place was always found for the cage, even if was under the seat amidst other equipment, or hanging from a hook to the side of the seat.

The men travelled at the end of the train, in the goods wagons, seated according to the same system as had been used for the women and children and old men, that is, near those who would be their neighbours in the south. The department for internal migration – even before it put you on the departure list – had made a list of everything you had, or didn't have, and had planned everything down to the last detail, allotting people their various places in the carriage: 'A proper seat for you, a folding one for you.' And in that carriage was everything we owned, or rather all that was left to us: tools, dismantled carts, mattresses, kneading-troughs, sideboards, livestock. The men weren't short of work: they had to tend the animals, soothe them, give them water, or a kick in the ribs, and then have a quick smoke, lie down on the straw and pretend to sleep, after a last gulp or wine, or grappa.

The troop train would travel through the night, crossing almost the whole of Italy. From the Veneto – or Friuli, for those who came from around those parts – through Emilia-Romagna and the Apennines, endlessly in and out of tunnels. And you immediately knew when you were in one – a tunnel, that is – not so much because of the thunderous roar, or because your ears would suddenly be blocked, but because of the smoke from the smokestack which, after swirling around inside the

176

tunnel, would then seep into the train through every nook and cranny, sending us into paroxysms of coughing.

Our train left in the evening, at sunset; after a whole day spent unloading families and baggage and provisions from the lorries, then bundling them up one on top of another like sheaves on a haystack, then taking them down again and rearranging them, down to the last child, or rabbit, on the train, under the eagle eye of the men from the department for internal migration and the supervisors from the Servicemen's Association. Eager and conscientious, the black-shirted militiamen were sticklers for order; but they also behaved kindly towards children when they started running off, and towards the mothers who ran after them, delivering a hearty slap when the soldiers returned them to them; and they were even more solicitous and well-disposed toward their big sisters, with whom they would try to exchange a furtive look, or smile.

At midday there had been a queue in front of the counter run by the women from the local Fascist branch, as they ladled out food into the proffered mess tins, first and second course all jumbled up together, pasta – a bit overcooked, it's true, but good and hot, and free – with a bit of meat in a sauce and a glass of wine or grappa. In the evening – before the fateful departure – you'd get another meal, with soup and cups of hot milky coffee, and as much bread and polenta as you could manage. The serving women were all very gentle, indeed genteel, all from good families, the daughters of office workers or school-teachers, even of counts and marquises, all smiling at our womenfolk as they set out on their journey: 'Now make sure that you're a credit to yourselves in your new homes, and to your villages, and to the Duce.' The provincial party secretary from Rovigo – or Vicenza, or Udine, Padua, Treviso – had said the self-same thing when he'd been by in the afternoon. He'd arrived in a car with the party bigwigs and got up on a platform in front of the gathering: 'Make sure that you're a credit to the Duce and your Fatherland, never forget the places that gave you birth, be worthy of the trust that has been placed in you: one day you'll be landowners yourselves. Remember, for each one of you who's leaving there are at least a dozen left behind who would have given anything to go in your stead. You'll never be able to repay the gift the Duce's given you, not even with your lives. *A noi!*' Then he'd got down from the platform and gone around among the piles of luggage personally to check on every family – or at least giving the appearance of so doing – and to bless them. 'Peruzzi!' he'd called to us as soon as he caught sight of my Uncle Pericles: 'Out with those clubs, if you need them!' accompanied by a hearty slap on the shoulder.

The trains had gone off in the evening, while people were clutching mess tins still warm from barley coffee, with the band from the local Fascist Headquarters playing *Giovinezza*, and the provincial party secretary still saying '*A noi!*' from the platform. And everyone around him now joined in, arms raised – the black-shirted militia, the women who'd served the meals and all the railway-workers.

'*A noi!*' we shouted back – one arm stuck out of the window as the train moved off – our women from out of the third-class coaches and our men from the half-open windows of the cattle trucks. 'Moo,' went the odd cow, suspiciously, as the train picked up speed.

Now the only ones who stayed clustered by the windows were the young girls, tearfully contemplating the white handkerchiefs with which they'd just waved their sweethearts farewell: sweethearts they'd only glimpsed in church, some-times, or glanced at as they'd passed by on a hay-cart, or barely exchanged a word with in a crowd, or at most given a quick peck on the cheek – though not quick in the way we use the word today, there was nothing to be in a hurry about in those days; sometimes they hadn't even declared their love, just thought it, wordlessly, since they had their whole lives before them to share their every thought. And now there they were too – the abandoned sweethearts – lined up beside the tracks, waving a last goodbye to the sweethearts who were leaving them, sweethearts they'd never see again. Some exodus.

Iron on iron, the carriage wheels were going 'clickety-clack' at every join; now they were on their way. Trains don't make that sound any more, because the sections of track are longer, better made, and the joins are more accurate, laser-gauged. But in those days you heard it throughout the journey, and it was a lovely sound, comforting and regular, one endless 'clickety-clack', and you only had to close your eyes and lean back, allow yourself to be gently rocked and, if you were at all tired – and there was no shortage of tired people in those days – you'd fall asleep immediately, just like when your mother sang you a lullaby. After half-an-hour not one single child was still awake, and some grown-ups were asleep too. The girls, on the other hand, were still in a huddle, thinking about their sweethearts, while the women were sorting things out and exchanging gossip and courtesies: 'A bit of polenta? A little cheese?' and the men were doing the same in the goods wagons.

Every now and again, amidst much wheezing and clanking, the train would draw up in the pitch-darkness at the little stations, to give precedence to faster trains, or have the boilers filled up with water. Then it would chuff off again, but in the meantime, even before it had come to a complete halt, the men had got out to visit their women and children and exchange greetings and make new acquaintances all along the train. The children too would wake up at these stops, and there was a great deal of coming and going: 'I want to be with the animals.' So you'd take them along to be with the animals. Then it was: 'I want my ma,' so at the next station you'd take them back again, to squabble in the third-class carriage and play with the other children, the little boys and girls they'd met that morning at the station. And the grandmothers would take it in turns to try to calm them down, each one telling their own fairy-tales. Once they arrived down south, a lot of people who'd first met, as children, on that station – and quarrelled and made it up over the course of that long night – went on to grow up together, and fall in love and marry; and then to quarrel and make it up throughout their lives together, sometimes beyond the grave.

Bologna, the Apennines, Tuscany, Florence, Orvieto, Rome. When they got to Rome it was still dark – about half-past six, or seven, dawn was just coming up – and seeing the signs through the window one woman, who knew how to read, had said: 'We're in Rome!' 'Rome?' echoed the others, and went back to sleep amidst the chuffing and the clattering as the train shunted back and forth, jolting every so often with a change of engine or moving on a bit from one station to the next – Tiburtina, Termini, Casilino – or on to sidings, to let troop trains pass.

The train moved off again just as it was getting light, but everyone carried on dozing well beyond Torricola, Santa Palomba and Campoleone, because on every journey at first you just can't get there soon enough, you're eaten up with curiosity about the place you're going to, and in fact you're quite looking forward to a bit of peace and quiet. But then, after a bit, worry about what lies ahead of you sets in – the fear of the unknown, your aching limbs on the hard seats, nostalgia for all you've left behind, the people you'll never see again, and all you want is to go on sleeping – despite the fact that the sun is now pouring through the train windows and giving you a headache – and lo and behold, you find yourself wishing the journey would go on for ever. It doesn't, though: the train clanks to a halt. 'Everyone out!'

The train arrived at Littoria at half-past seven in the morning – every morning. End of exodus. We'd reached the Promised Land and the pharaoh's guards – lined up, in black shirt and fez, on platform one – were there to ease our landfall and help us take possession of our drained Red Sea. Moses had parted the waters only fleetingly, just long enough to ferry his people across, then closed them up again. The Duce and Rossoni, on the other hand, had banished the waters from those lands for good. They'd grabbed the Red Sea by its lapels and said: 'Off with you, we're making this a garden for all time.' And they'd brought us here – 'Littoria Station!' they bawled – and unloaded us all at half-past seven in the morning (although, in fact, the train on which the Peruzzi travelled was the only one ever not to arrive on time).

And, there in that country station in the Promised Land, we were met by a group of militiamen, their band belting out *Giovinezza*, and a throng of technicians and factors from the Servicemen's Association, their lorries parked outside the station, were ready to load us up, with our possessions, and take us, family by family, to the holdings that had been assigned to us. But best of all – right there, outside the station at Littoria – at the end of our exodus we once more found that regiment of women, awaiting us with tables laden with great saucepans of steaming white coffee, slices of toasted polenta, as much white bread as you could eat, and grappa for those who wanted it.

This regiment was made up of women from the local

Fascist women's branch, naturally, not from those of Rovigo or Ferrara: office workers and women from Roman High Society, but also the daughters of a lawyer from the Lepini Mountains and even the daughter of Prince Caetani, in a black blouse and veil, playing at being a good little Red Cross nurse. Smiling at the children. Queening it over our women. Saying: 'Would you like a little more?' And looking at us furtively, exchanging glances with her friends, who nudged each other as they saw our men – and the odd woman – who, after having gulped down the polenta and hot coffee, then galloped off towards the wine and grappa. 'What uncouth behaviour,' commented Princess Caetani to her little friends: 'Won't they get heartburn?'

Heartburn? We'd done that all our lives. And anyway, it was a cold morning, it was late October – they'd brought us down between September and October, ready to sow the corn at the beginning of November – and after all the knocks we'd taken on that long journey, surely we were entitled to a glass of grappa? Anyway, it wasn't just us. When they were working on the building sites, and it was so cold that the flesh of their fingertips stuck to the reinforced concrete rods, you've no idea how many people from those same mountains would start the day on the scaffolding on the fifth or sixth floor clutching a bottle of grappa. Not just us Vikings. Sorry, what did you say? Yes, us Vikings probably do drink a bit more than them, but so what? We drank in order to be able to work. Princess Caetani had never lifted a finger in her life.

Anyhow, there we were at last in Littoria, where all the trains ended up on the dot of half-past seven, because in those days – as we all know – trains ran on time. If they arrived late, the engine drivers would be sent into internal exile. So all the exiles arrived in Littoria on time – except for us, as I've already said, ours was the only train ever to be late – though actually it was Littoria-Goods Yard, not Littoria proper, which was going up some eight kilometres further down the track. The station itself wasn't the one you see today, but a smaller version, because when they'd founded Littoria the idea was that it would be just a small country town, so the station too would be just a small country station. They hadn't yet got everything planned in advance down to the smallest detail.

In 1928 – when the Piscinara Land Reclamation Consortium got to work – there was only one problem: getting rid of the water. That was the name of the game. But in order to get rid of the water, you had to have access to the land: 'How can we dig canals without the roads to get the machinery and the workers and the material where we need them?' But even to make roads, first you have to have the workers on the spot. You can't expect them to travel twenty or thirty kilometres a day, backwards and forwards across the marshes before they even set to work. They would have to sleep on the spot, near the building sites. Remember the one about the chicken and the egg? Well, there you have it. Here you didn't start with roads and canals: you started with urbanization, and land reclamation came second.

Work on the Mussolini Canal did indeed begin in 1928, but the buildings housing the consortium had been built two years earlier, at Cancello del Quadrato, on the site of what later was to be Littoria. Until 1914, all there was at Quadrato was a large cattle-pen, surrounded by a wooden fence and a gate, or *cancello*, whence its name, Cancello del Quadrato.

It was here, in 1926, that the consortium set up its first village, because Quadrato was right in the middle of the area to be reclaimed – midway between the Appian Way and the sea

– which made it the ideal place for the strategic running of operations. But most of the water comes from higher up, from the north, as I've already told you, and the following year – in order to be able to start work on the Mussolini Canal – they built the workers' village of Sessano, which is now known as Borgo Podgora.

There was nothing there at the time, just one single farmhouse and an old sixteenth-century tower belonging to the Caetani. But there was no road. All there was a rough track which was often impassable. So, in order to dig out the canal, they first had to make a road, and that's why they built the village. The earliest maps don't even show a crossroads, but meanwhile they started building houses, a small church, an infirmary, lodgings for the engineers and supervisors and – further from the centre – seven houses to serve as workers' dormitories. Before they could make the road, so as to be able to make the canal, what they built first was the village, and all the rest came later.

Throughout history, towns and villages have normally grown up along trade routes. If you travelled those routes often enough, you might find yourself pausing on your way – at a ford, perhaps, or at a point where your path crossed other paths – and setting up a little stall, and then other wayfarers might start stopping there too, and also do a bit of trading. Then word would spread, and more and more people would stop there and set up other stalls, and that's how a town is born. That's how Rome came into being: as a trading-place, a place where Etruscans, Sabines and Latins could exchange their wares. It's roads, and trade, that normally give birth to towns.

In the Pontine Marshes it was the other way around: it was the towns – that is, those villages – that gave birth to roads. And they didn't just spring up at random, one house here,

184

another there, but first a surveyor would come along, before there was anything at all, and say: 'We'll have a house here, and a church there, and that's where the wine-shop's going to be; the police station will be here, and the square there, and so on, and each subsequent house will be at such and such a distance from the road and from everything else.' And then they set to work, and up went the walls.

At first it was the Land Reclamation Consortium – an association of owners of the great landed estates who'd banded together – which went on the attack, draining the marshes and building the villages. But they started out without much idea of where they were going: they'd drain off the water, and then they'd see. They created large mechanized farms, run on capitalist lines, and they thought that the four or five villages they'd built to house the drainage-workers would come in handy as residential 'hamlets' for the few workmen or day-labourers who might occasionally be needed for work on those farms when they were in working order. That was as far as it went. In 1928, they hadn't the faintest inkling that their dreams were about to be blown sky-high by the bombshell of the Servicemen's Association, which was to dispossess them of their land, expropriate the lot.

This Servicemen's Association had come into being in 1917, during the First World War, before the Duce's time, and Fascism. It had been set up by Nitti – a left-wing liberal democrat – not just to give some form of assistance to ex-servicemen, but above all to honour the promises made after Caporetto, namely that now at last, after the war was over, 'The land would be given to the peasants.' This Servicemen's Association too had started reclaiming small areas of land throughout Italy, but by 1929 – when the Duce decided to have it headed by Count Cencelli – it was being wound down, it had a finger in every pie but was master of none. A very Italian set-up. More strings there than in a vat of pasta.

Cencelli went at it hammer and tongs, he sacked hundreds of people, took on hundreds of others and set the organization back on its feet: 'What we've got to do is reclaim the land and give it to the peasants.' That was the mission assigned him by the Duce and Rossoni when they sent him to the Pontine Marshes, like a latter-day proconsul, with full powers and carte blanche. No sooner had he got there than he began to inform them roundly that so far they'd been total slackers, they had no idea of how to go about their task and at that rate the whole thing would take generations.

His meddling really rubbed the members of the consortium up the wrong way because, although the actual process of reclamation was indeed still formally their responsibility, the Servicemen's Association, for its part, was responsible only for the organization, management and overseeing of the agricultural and human side of things. But all that compulsory purchasing had made the association the largest landowner around, and now it was also the main shareholder in the consortium, with Cencelli as the *ras*. In point of fact, it wasn't true that the seventy thousand hectares portioned out into holdings in the Pontine Marshes had all come into their possession through compulsory purchase, by being brutally seized from their original owners. Parts of them had, it's true, but other parts – to avoid red tape and legal appeals and wrangling – had been purchased straight from the owners themselves, albeit at rock-bottom prices: 'Either you accept my offer, or I'll slap on a compulsory-purchase order.' So private landowners weren't stripped of everything, and Prince Caetani, for example, was allowed to keep the great estates he owned the other side of the Appian Way, between that and

186

the mountains, but on condition that he too would do a certain amount of reclamation and divide the land up into individual holdings – and build cowsheds and farms, of course, and put sharecroppers in them – otherwise Cencelli would expropriate the lot. And Prince Caetani – who'd never lifted a finger in those marshes for seven hundred years, never reclaimed so much as a foot of land – instantly set about reclaiming them and settling whole families of sharecroppers on them, families who'd come from Umbria and the Marches.

So, right from the start, Cencelli had trodden on corns – he was like a tank, that was why Rossoni and the Duce had chosen him – and before you could say Jack Robinson he was on bad terms with everyone. It's true that they were all Fascists, all under orders from the Duce, but, as you know, there's Fascism and Fascism, and above all we were in Italy, all sons of Rome and Romulus and Remus. And if those two fell out, twin-brothers as they were, you can imagine how things worked out with this lot, who weren't even cousins. At official events, in public, all together on the platform, it was all smiles and cordial handshakes with Cencelli, a chorus of: 'All power to Fascism and land reclamation; ever onwards, as one single body, in the cause of the Fatherland and the Duce.' But as soon as they got down from that platform, they were so busy stabbing each other in the back that there was no time left for anything else. Just like now, in fact. On both right and left.

Until then, all in all, the members of the consortium had ruled the place with a rod of iron. They'd wandered around the marshes as though they were monarchs of all they surveyed. Indeed, the consortium's surveyors thought that they were God on high, their assistants regarded themselves as just one rung down the ladder, and even the man in charge of the horses thought he was the Archangel Michael. Then suddenly

Cencelli breezes in and everyone has to jump to attention: 'Put one foot wrong, and you're out; and I don't want any backchat, either.' Obviously, that got their backs up. But it wasn't just some personal power struggle, a matter of clashing ambitions: 'Who are you to speak to me like that?' Behind it all lay two different ways of understanding both Fascism and land reclamation. Right and left, yet again.

Indeed, reclamation wasn't something dreamt up by Mussolini, but a problem which a unified Italy set itself soon after the *Risorgimento*. All the plains in Central and Southern Italy had been completely abandoned for centuries, and people had gone up into the mountains, first to take refuge from invaders, barbarians and Saracens, and later on to flee the great landed estates, and malaria. Those plains were a desert. So, at the end of the nineteenth century – but always and above all in the Po Valley – they'd passed the first laws for the reclamation of the area, and set up the first large-scale enterprises, privately-funded undertakings aimed at increasing crop output and earnings. There was nothing philanthropic about them.

In central and Southern Italy, on the other hand – which were the parts most in need of attention, being poorer and more malaria-ridden – the problem had been totally overlooked, because there was no real entrepreneurial class, and the rich landowners made do with harvesting what they could and enjoying the fruits of their labours in their great city houses. So then – to modernize the south – the likes of Nitti and the *Banca Commerciale* had the bright idea of dragging it, kicking and screaming, into the world of capitalism: 'If the rich southerners can't do the job, we northerners will go and do it for them.' But with state funding, obviously.

And that's what they did in the Pontine Marshes, with the

help of the financier Clerici and the Caetani and Omodeo families. But that ended with a series of scandals. In the meantime the rich southern landowners had got fed up, Nitti had fallen from power, the 'old Italy' was no more and the Duce had arrived on the scene; but he had no ruling class to back him up, and every evening – before he went to sleep – even he would say to himself: 'Something tells me that a country can't be ruled with clubs and guns alone. Something tells me you also need a few technicians around the place.' So Nitti's technocrats were converted to Fascism, the Duce welcomed them because he needed them and off they went again, adjusting their sights as they did so. They apologized to the southern landowners and went into reverse: 'All right, let's do all this reclaiming business together, in partnership with the landowners.' Economically speaking, they were of the liberal persuasion, they'd rather have been working with the modern bosses from the north, but as it was they'd have to rub along with the more backward-looking southern variety. *Tertium non datur.* There was no other way, and a private boss had to be involved one way or another, because without capitalism you'll never get anything done. But they knew their job, and at last – after centuries and centuries of negligence on the part of the landowners – in 1928 the draining of the Pontine Marshes got under way. In partnership with the landowners. But who was going to be Mr. Moneybags, in your view?

This was how it worked: the cost of the drainage programme, with the digging of ditches and canals and other water-courses, was borne entirely by the state. For all the other work – everything to do with roads and buildings, the planting of trees, the reinforcing of the dunes, the draining of lakes, the provision of drinking water and electricity – the state paid only ninety-two percent, leaving the poor landowners to come up

189

with the other eight. Are you with me?

You had a bit of land – well, several thousand hectares – which was under water, all it produced was frogs, and if you wanted to sell it you'd have found no buyers, not even if you gave it away. Suddenly you find it's all been nicely drained, with roads and bridges and rows of trees and electricity poles. How much more is it now worth, I hear you asking. Well, you haven't forked out a penny, the state financed the lot. You coughed up your eight percent, which would just about have covered the gravel for the roads. Furthermore, if you then decided to build on that piece of land – which used to be under water, but which is now all dry and sunny, and you can even drive through it in a carriage – to put up a house and cowsheds and barns and whatever else you felt like, well, the state would pay for thirty-eight percent of that as well. And then, if you don't mind, in 1931 the Duce says: 'To hell with all this, what are you, soft in the head?' A dictator Mussolini may have been, what with his emergency laws, and wars, and persecution of the Jews – he spelled catastrophe, no doubt about it – but as a young man he'd been a Socialist, like my grandfather, and he was still taking a left-wing line at San Sepolcro, when he founded the Fascist Party. So at this point he said: 'I know what I'll do. I'm getting a bit fed up with all this forking out, and the landowners getting all the benefit. Damn it all, I'm going to give the land to the peasants.' He summoned Cencelli, and said: 'Get your helmet on.'

Cencelli did just that. As it happened, the association's newspaper was called *The Conquest of the Land*. Now what do you think that meant? Just what it said: conquest. With cold steel. And it was a hard fight. With steel; with knives.

Mussolini, understandably, kept a low profile, he put Rossoni and Cencelli in the firing-line. But the fact is, they weren't quarrelling because of personal dislike, they were attacking each other because this was a class struggle, this was the revolution that Rossoni and Mussolini had always spoken about to my grandfather, and the Servicemen's Association was its 'red guard' – a blend of Fascism and Communism, if you like. After all, taking the land from the rich and giving it to the poor isn't exactly at the heart of right-wing thinking – just take a look at the sacred texts by Marx, Lenin, Mao Tse Tung and their ilk. So far, it's been the province of the revolutionary left.

If the consortium had come out on top, the Pontine Marshes would have had a completely different look, both physically and socially. There would only have been some two or three thousand inhabitants – instead of half a million – and we'd still be up there in our little native villages, dining on thin air. It would have been goodbye to villages, let alone Latina-Littoria. And that's why the villages in the Pontine Marshes built by the consortium all changed their names, with the Servicemen's Association – while claiming simply that it wanted to immortalize the bloody battles in which their 'servicemen' had given their lives in the Great War – now renaming them once and for all, in memory of those same bloody battles.

Littoria – the present-day Latina – was built on the very spot where the village of Quadrato had been. But we knocked the whole place down, razed it to the ground. Stone by stone. The consortium had put up the buildings just four years earlier. That village had everything: a cinema, a Workingmen's Club, warehouses, repair-shops, a narrow-gauge railway. But it had to be razed to the ground *a fundamentis*: '*Delenda est Quadrato.*' Why did it have to be knocked down? We could have reused at least some of the materials, or built Littoria even just one hundred metres away and the whole thing could have been

191

saved. But you can't make an omelette without breaking eggs, far less a revolution. In France, too – at the Restoration – the first thing they did was to rush off and uproot the 'trees of liberty', and in Italy, on 25 July, they couldn't get the marble fasces off the walls quickly enough. And you expect Cencelli to have left Quadrato standing, when it had been the den of the consortium's 'white guards', the very symbol of counter-revolution? It was the first thing we flattened: *Vae victis*.

So, back to 1931 and the Duce summoning Cencelli and putting the Pontine Marshes into the hands of the Servicemen's Association. From then on it was all noses to the grindstone: morning and evening, three uninterrupted shifts on the Mussolini Canal, at night, too, with searchlights, come rain or shine. Now they'd down tools only when the work was done, whereas before they'd excavated only by day, from November to April, and in the summer months work would come to a halt, to avoid malarial infection. The consortium had given itself seven years to drain Piscinara alone – 1936 was the year they had their eye on, and that was just for the drainage, excluding settlement and cultivation – and even then they felt they were establishing some sort of record. Then along came the Servicemen's Association, which moved faster than Eddy Merckx, and before 1935 was out the entire Pontine Marshes had not only been drained, but also dotted with houses, villages and towns.

As early as February 1931 – the moment the Duce and Rossoni had given him their orders, while the members of the consortium were still deep in the undergrowth, rolling around in the mud with the buffalo and wild boar – Cencelli had let loose his technicians, set them to making on-the-spot inspections, measuring and planning. And in November 1931 – when he came into possession of the first fifteen thousand compulsorily-purchased hectares – he'd roared ahead like a tank: roads, bridges, deforestation, farmhouses, storehouses, the lot. At first, they'd thought that the peasants would make do with just farmhouses: 'What more do they need?' But the people from the association were quick to learn from their mistakes, and as they went around and realized what they were doing – creating a forest of holdings which sprang up from the mud like so many mushrooms – they also realized that something was amiss.

And, at the beginning of November 1932, the first sharecroppers were beginning to arrive, including the Peruzzi: big, patriarchal families they were. But it was one thing to imagine them as you sat there in your Servicemen's Association office – all cheery and nicely brushed and combed – and quite another to see them in the flesh, with all their children, swarming around the holdings. They couldn't spend their whole lives working. The people from the association hadn't thought of that. On Saturdays and Sundays, whenever they could, the sharecroppers would grab their bicycles and go off to Sessano, because that's where the wine-shop was, and the cinema and the dance-hall. The roads were alive with bicycles, and Sessano became known as 'little Paris'.

The people from the association got the message: 'Here we're going to have to come up with amenities,' that is, small towns incorporated into the network of holdings – one for every two hundred, on average – equipped with all the necessary utilities: a church, a school, the local Fascist Headquarters, a post office, a police station, a cinema, a sports ground, a Workingmen's Club and so on. And when the second and larger wave of sharecroppers arrived at the beginning of the new farming year – just before seed-time, in autumn 1934 – they found these places ready and waiting for them.

Cencelli himself had been even more farsighted: 'It's flat as a pancake around these parts, worse than Holland, one endless wilderness, what'll they do, all these people we're bringing here? Won't they be needing a registry office, or a cemetery?' And between February and March 1932 – within just three months – apart from the smaller places with the amenities, he'd had the idea of making something a little bit grander: 'Guess what? We're going to have a town,' (he came from Magliano Sabina, which is near Rieti, and they make them tough round there), and he got a couple of engineers from his technical department on to the job. The Duce and Rossoni went down on a tour of inspection on 5 April 1932, and when they arrived at the Quadrato he took them out on to a farmhouse terrace and pointed around him, in all directions, drawings in hand: 'I'm having the church there, the town hall there and the cemetery there'.

'But Cencelli, have you taken leave of your senses?' said the Duce, not best pleased. 'This here is a town, goddam you.'

At first, you understand, the Duce had no use for towns. He couldn't stand them. He was all for the country life and people leaving the towns. City growth was enemy number one, the source of all evil; people were leaving the countryside, where they'd toiled for centuries without bothering a soul, and flocking into town to organize strikes and be unemployed, going and getting drunk in the wine-shops and then discussing politics. 'City growth can go hang,' he'd said, 'I want the Italians in the countryside, every man-jack of them,' and he'd even shut down twenty-five thousand wine-shops the length and breadth of Italy, just to be on the safe side. In those few he'd left open, he'd had placards hung, all plastered with official stamps: 'No talk of politics allowed.' He'd stuck with this anti-town obsession for ten years or so, from 1922, when he'd come to power, until 5 April 1932, when he'd gone out on to that farmhouse terrace at Quadrato with Rossoni and Cencelli: 'Out of the towns with you, into the countryside,' he'd carried on saying throughout those years, 'that's what Fascism is all about.' And in the countryside the local Fascist Headquarters did indeed try to keep people there by force, even if they kept on worming their way out of its clutches and rushing back to those same pesky towns. His ambition had been to forge a new man – a countryman and a soldier – and he was having to do it by fair means or foul. Anyway, when Cencelli had the temerity to utter the word 'town', that had really got under the Duce's skin: 'How dare you? Expect a thorough walloping.'

'No, no, Duce, you've got me wrong. It's not a real town, not by any stretch of the imagination. It's a – a convenience-town. After all, these people will be needing a registry office, a cemetery. Certain amenities they've got to have, however basic. I can't deny them a few offices. There are going to be thousands of them, I can't leave them all stranded in the middle of nowhere, having to travel thirty or forty kilometres to Cisterna or Terracina whenever they want a birth certificate or a funeral. I'm sorry, Duce, but there are going to have to be a few perfunctory municipal trappings around these parts.'

'All right then,' said the Duce grudgingly, 'as long as it's a convenience-town, Cench! Just don't talk to me about town towns, that really sets me off.'

'Don't you worry, Duce. I'm not stupid! It'll be a convenience-town; all it'll have is a registry office.'

'You'd better watch your step!' Rossoni said to him again as they were about to leave.

'What, you too? What do you take me for, a nincompoop?' said Cencelli, now thoroughly piqued. But you already know what he was like: a tank with a helmet. And from near Rieti into the bargain. Tough mountain-folk they are, and used to sheep.

When he was alone, he started looking at the drawings his technical staff had done for him, and suddenly he wasn't quite so pleased with them: 'What do this lot know about such things? They know about canals and marshes, but for a town I think you need a proper architect.' So he had one come from Rome – Oriolo Frezzotti he was called – and he said to him: 'I want a completely new set of plans within forty-eight hours, or I'm not paying you.' And Frezzotti did as he'd been told, and he landed the commission. He'd first been summoned on 6 or 7 April, and by 30 June the site was all staked out, work had already begun and digging had started on the foundations for the tower on the town hall.

In the meantime, though – he was from Rieti, as I've said – Cencelli had contacted the papers: 'Now we're building a brand-new town,' and he'd sent invitations round to the bigwigs in and around Rome, asking them to attend the official ceremony of the laying of the first stone. The papers in their turn came out with banner headlines: Birth of Littoria – a brand-new town. *Il Messaggero*, unfortunately, hit on the phrase: 'One day, it will be a metropolis.'

Well, as I hardly need to tell you, Mussolini was hopping mad when he saw those papers. He was spitting bile all over Piazza Venezia. 'Just bring him here, I'll throttle him with my bare hands.'

Rossoni – as soon as he saw the Duce's reaction – got straight on the phone to warn Cencelli: 'I'd make a run for it if I were you, give Piazza Venezia a wide berth, say you're out of sorts and lie low for a day or two, otherwise there'll be trouble,' And lie low he did.

Meanwhile Rossoni was trying to placate the Duce: 'Come

on Duce, it's just a convenience-town, not a town town; anyway, why are you suddenly taking so much notice of the papers?'

'Damn the lot of you, what do you take me for, a numbskull? Don't you start too, Rossoni,' and it's true – I mean this – he may have been a dictator, he may have been evil incarnate, but he wasn't actually stupid. From the start – as he now saw from the plans – Littoria was to have three large separate squares, which were to serve as the hubs of the three respective centres of the future town. You felt like telling him: 'It's not a town town, it's just a convenience-town,' but each time you did so he'd get furious. Anyway, the building contracts had already been signed, there was no turning back. Cencelli had even tried to cancel the celebration for the laying of the first stone. But the invitations had gone out, and the following day a whole crowd of people came down from Rome. The Bishop of Terracina himself was there for the blessing of that blessed stone. The only one conspicuous by his absence was the Duce. He refused to attend. 'You're not going, either,' he barked at Rossoni. And, from that day onwards, not a peep about the subject in the papers. He'd sent a personal note to all the editors, which read: '*Littoria is most emphatically an administrative entity and not a town. Press comment flies in the face of the regime's entire thinking about urbanism. The ceremony for the laying of the first stone is another relic from bygone days. The subject will not to be referred to again. Mussolini.*' So none of the newspapers could so much as mention the topic, and now Cencelli found himself having to tell the officials from the Servicemen's Association that any journalist who showed up in the marshes should be shot on sight. By now Littoria couldn't not be built, but it had to be built on the QT. 'Careless talk costs lives.'

Unfortunately – as you know – there's very little point in crying over spilt milk, and precious little purpose is served by shutting the stable door after the horse has bolted. By now the news had got into the foreign press, and newspapers throughout the world began to scream: 'They're building towns!'And everyone was full of admiration. Slack-jawed with wonderment. From every corner of the globe – from America to Russia, from Thailand to Hungary – they were clamouring to be allowed to come and take a look, in person. Even the Soviet ministers and chairmen of the *kolkhozes*. To see how it was done. So then the Duce changed his tune and developed a sudden taste for the whole undertaking, and started to visit the site at least once a week, to see how work was going, and he'd always have some foreign ambassador in tow.

At this point, though, understandably, he also wanted to take the credit – 'It was all my idea,' he'd tell the above-mentioned ambassadors – and on 18 December 1932, not even six months after the laying of the first stone, which he'd refused to attend, it was he who declared Littoria officially open, amidst much pomp and ceremony. And after that he couldn't stop, he started founding towns galore – by the time the game was up, they'd founded over a hundred and fifty new towns of various sizes throughout Italy – he'd found a new town every day. 'Stone-sickness,' it's called, where I come from.

Anyway, one morning in 1934 – just two years after having declared Littoria officially open – he woke up suddenly and summoned Rossoni: 'D'you know what? I've had another thought, we're making Littoria into a province.' A province. Rossoni spread the word. Now everything had to be bigger and better, as befitting Littoria's new role, and in 1934 the station – which, in 1932, they'd naturally built as a small country station, with an upstairs flat for the station-master and his wife, who would hang her washing out of the window so that it dripped on to the heads of the passengers who were waiting for their train – had to be knocked down and rebuilt from scratch, bigger and better and Fascist, as you see it now, with its concave roofing, and a bar and waiting-room, and a four-storey building to house the railway-workers and their children and above all their wives, who'd now have to hang out their washing over the terrace, thank you very much. But it was at that earlier country station – the one where you'd get dripped on, not the one you see today – that all the trains with the exodus arrived at half-past seven in the morning, all except ours, that is. Unfortunately, we arrived late, so Princess Caetani had already been standing there for a good two hours, drumming on her grappa ladle with her noble fingers: 'When will today's batch be arriving, for goodness sake?'

'Any minute now,' replied the station-master, but they kept on not arriving. Then she put down her ladle and told her subordinates to reheat the coffee, while the militia were stamping their feet on the platform with the cold, and the people from the Servicemen's Association – with their lorries drawn up in readiness outside the station, engines running – were turning the air blue: 'How are we going to get this lot sorted before nightfall?'

We kept on not arriving.

Ours was the only train ever to arrive late, even though we too had started out dead on time. We'd set off from our village, Ca' Bragadin, well before dawn, because it was almost forty kilometres from there to Rovigo. We'd been taken to the station by our Peruzzi cousins, the ones we'd been close to in Codigoro and become increasingly estranged from, in terms of work, property and politics. But we still felt a sense of kinship, and indeed affection, albeit guardedly. By now they were no longer Socialists – by now no one was, they'd all come round to Fascism, because with this Duce of ours at least the country was feeling the smack of firm government, as they say, and you could relax because at last someone was there to keep an eye on things – but they weren't ardent Fascists either; you never heard them saying a word against the Duce or the Fascist Party, and if there were meetings in the village square they'd go along, but somehow you could see what they were thinking: 'All right then, we'll hitch the donkey where the boss says; but should things start to go wrong for him, you won't find me tearing my hair.'

But our cousins didn't come down to the Pontine Marshes. They too had been sent packing by the Zorzi Vila, and my Uncle Pericles suggested they come along. But they didn't want to: 'We're staying put. Something will turn up.'

I'm sorry, what did you say? You want to know why they didn't want to come?

I don't know. My Uncle Pericles would have brought the whole village down with him if he'd been able. He was quite a big wheel in the local Fascist Headquarters – I won't go into details – and he even managed to get a holding for his brother-in-law, my Uncle Dolfin who'd married his older sister; he was a loyal Socialist, one of the few who remained so. My Uncle Pericles was so insistent – 'I'll vouch for him!' – that they gave Dolfin a holding at Borgo Hermada, even if at first they'd said: 'Now, Peruzzi, are you really sure? Ourselves, we'd rather have your brother-in-law sent to Ponza,' which meant internal exile.

One by one, my Uncle Pericles managed to take everyone with him who wanted to go; given half a chance, he'd have ripped out the bell tower at Codigoro so as not to leave that behind as well: 'To hell with the lot of them, Northern Italy and the Zorzi Vila along with it.' So you can imagine how he felt when his own cousins wouldn't go with him, his own father's brother's children. But perhaps that's the very reason they didn't want to go: 'Here we're poor, but at least we're our own masters; that's better than a lifetime down there having to owe everything to Pericles.'

At all events, it was those same Peruzzi cousins – with their own carts, and others which they'd borrowed – who drove us by night to Rovigo, bag and baggage. And some of them even stayed on until evening, to keep us company, waving us off from the platform at dusk when the train set off amidst the first fat drops of rain.

The train had only taken a couple of chuffs out of the station when it began to bucket down, but the crowd of sweethearts – lined up on the ballast along the track – carried on undeterred, waving their handkerchiefs serenely in the deluge. Some rather sheepishly used them as headgear, but they soon got sopping wet and were promptly once more pressed into service for waving purposes, in the direction of my slowly receding aunts, who were all leaning out of the windows and gesticulating with handkerchiefs of their own. Then they collapsed on to their seats to have a good cry – all of them, married or otherwise; those with bastard children on their knee cried hardest of all.

My grandmother was weeping, too, but you'd never have known it: hers were inner tears.

It rained all the way to Ferrara, and then on to Bologna. It was raining all over the Po Plain. Only after they'd crossed the Apennines – when they got into Tuscany, and it was still pitch-dark – did it stop raining. And, all the way to Bologna, with the rain streaming down the windows – sleeping or dozing fitfully, waking up every now and then – my aunts had kept up

201

a permanent refrain: 'Just take a look at that madwoman,' was what they said to one another.

The object of their disobliging comments was their sister-in-law, the wife of Uncle Pericles, who hadn't got into the passenger coaches but had said she was going to travel in the goods wagon, with the luggage, and the livestock – to be with her man, or so she said, but in fact it was to be with her bees. Or rather, at first she'd tried to take them with her in the passenger coaches – 'They won't do you any harm' – with the hive covered by a net, to stop them getting out, and by a dark piece of cloth so they wouldn't be in a draught. She'd hung the hive from a hook in the luggage-rack. But the railwayman, and all the other women – from the other families – had said she couldn't: 'Bees are dangerous.'

'What do you mean, dangerous?' she'd said. 'I'll keep an eye on them'.

'Dangerous, that's what they are,' the other women would chorus every time they heard the slightest buzz; and, as is well-known, the more bees are kept covered, the more they're in the warm, the more they buzz, because there are special fanner bees which beat their wings to keep the air circulating inside the hive. One member of the Mambrin family – who was five or six months pregnant – wanted to call in the militia, even though she was a distant relative of ours.

Our women, on the other hand – the sisters-in-law – said nothing, in theory they were on her side; but secretly they thought the others were in the right. To be honest, our family had never had anything to do with bees, we were livestock people, what we dealt in mainly was big animals like donkeys and horses and cows. Not insects. When we saw an insect we'd swat it without a second thought, and if a bee or wasp so much as came into the room all hell would be unleashed.

It was she who'd brought the bees into our house, we'd never had anything to do with bees – well, we knew what they were, of course, but we'd never been in such close contact with them – it was she who brought them into the house, and we just had to put up with them. Don't look a gift horse in the mouth, and all that. But she had been a gift horse which was particularly hard to swallow, particularly for the women of the household. They paid her lip service, they listened to her respectfully. But the moment her back was turned, they'd say: 'Just look what Pericles brought in.' And not just because of the bees. The bees were the least of it.

They said she was by way of being a bit of a witch, and that she'd cast a spell on their brother: 'How else can you explain that he's gone so soft in the head?' But she was beautiful, and she was Pericles' wife, and quite honestly there wasn't a woman in this world who was good enough for Pericles Peruzzi in their opinion, not even the king's daughter. Where would you find anyone worthy of our Pericles? Only a woman from the Peruzzi family itself would have filled the bill. Had it been possible.

So Pericles' wife had picked up the hive, and the little boy she was still nursing – she left her older child, her daughter, with our grandmother – and made her way, with difficulty, along the train to the goods wagon.

The moment he saw her, my Uncle Pericles burst out laughing. He jumped down from his bunk, and while she was putting the hive down on the floor and handing the child to my Uncle Themistocles, he grabbed her from behind and lifted her up on to it, unable to resist a bit of husbandly groping as he did so.

'Hands off, you pig,' she'd said, freeing herself from his grip. But he carried on laughing.

I'm sorry, what did you say? Who was this woman, where had she blown in from all of a sudden?

Well, now I'll tell you.

You remember that time in 1919 at Codigoro, when they burnt down the straw-stack and my uncles went into the village to see that justice was done, let's put it that way. And you'll also remember that at a certain point the Workers' Association also went up in smoke (what did you say? It didn't catch fire without a bit of help from my uncles? That's true, but don't let's quibble about details) and my Uncle Pericles took his life into his hands and rescued the people living on the first floor.

What did you say? That it had been him who set fire to it in the first place? We've been through all this, there's no point in stirring things up again.

Anyway, you remember that fair-haired girl who was hanging on to the windowsill and lashing out so as to stop him saving her; but he saved her anyway, and she gave him a slap in the face for his pains, and called him a murderer?

And you'll also remember that other evening – years later – when my uncle had a... well, a mishap with that poor priest from Comacchio. Sorry, what did you say? That it wasn't a mishap? I know, I know, but we'll never get anywhere if we carry on like this. Just let me tell my story, will you?

Well, that evening when he got back from Comacchio, my uncle knew he'd made a big mistake, and that he'd have to pay for it in some way or another: 'I wonder how long I'll be getting.' But what weighed on him most heavily wasn't so much that he'd be doing time – 'That'll pass' – but what he'd done, or rather, as he would put it, what he'd been made to do. And, riding pillion on the motorbike – clinging to that hulk of a friend of his from Massafiscaglia, who in turn was clinging to that louse of a driver from Comacchio who was giving them a lift home – lurching around as the bike bounced over the potholes, with the wind whistling down his neck, he felt doubly tormented, on the one hand wondering how long he'd be inside, and on the other thinking back to the death-rattle of that poor dying priest.

Once they'd arrived in Massafiscaglia, and dropped that hulk of a friend of his off in the square, and there were only two of them on the motorbike, him clinging on to that louse of a Fascist from Comacchio – 'Touching him with my bare hands, for heaven's sake' – my uncle was really at a loss. He certainly didn't feel like going home – 'Where am I going to go? What am I going to do?' and he'd even thought of knocking the driver senseless and throwing the three of them – himself, the driver and the bike – into the Po di Volano: 'Put an end to things. No more worries.' But my Uncle Pericles wasn't that sort of man. He would have been all too capable of knocking his louse of a friend senseless and drowning him in the Po with his own hands, of that there's no doubt – holding him under water for hours if need be, making him thrash around until he begged for mercy, perhaps after having gulped down the whole river with his own mouth: 'Okay, I'll die, I'll croak, to hell with you.' My uncle would still be there to this day, holding his friend's head under water. But he'd never have killed himself. Suicide isn't in the Peruzzi DNA; your own life was sacred. In one way or the other the cosmos will treat you mercifully, even if you kill someone: there'll be a price to pay, but ultimately some door will open even for the worst murderer. The only thing the cosmos won't forgive is suicide. That is the only act for which there is no redress.

Anyway, once he'd decided not to kill that louse of a friend – 'One's plenty for one day,' – once they were near Codigoro he said to him: 'Don't take me home, take me into town,' and had himself dropped on the outskirts.

Jacket under his arm, grim-faced and lost in his own worries, he walked down the main street, came to the square and knocked at the door of her house. Of that girl's house, I mean.

Now this may strike you as odd, but since the burning of the straw-stack and the spontaneous combustion of the Workers' Association – four years earlier, that is, and please don't start butting in again – they hadn't exchanged a word. The last word spoken between them had been that 'murderer' she'd yelled just before she'd slapped him, while he was firing into the air so as not to lose face. Since then, not a word. And four years had gone by.

Not that they hadn't seen each other, of course, or had the opportunity to meet. You meet people by chance in Milan, how could you fail to do so in Codigoro? The thing was, every time she saw him she cut him dead. Even if they were nose to nose. You don't exist. I never saw you. And the more he tried to bump into her, the more she took no notice. She didn't see him. He didn't exist.

That girl had made my uncle lose his head. He dreamt about her every night. He dreamt about those calves he'd tried to lay hold of while he was saving her, and she was lashing out.

With his cronies from the local Fascist Headquarters, and his other chums, he'd always play the strong man and the braggart when they went to the brothel in Ferrara of a Sunday. When they were at the Fascist Headquarters in Codigoro – which, as I've said, was the old Workers' Association, and she lived above it – whenever she came down into the street he'd raise his voice, so that she'd notice him. And the more he raised his voice, the less she'd think of him. Her loathing was written on her face – she'd be looking away from him,

206

obviously, in the direction of her friends – as though to say: 'Look what the cat's brought in.'

My uncle, though, was like a dog with a bone. Particularly on Sundays, strolling along after mass – or at dances in the square on the local saint's day – when he would see her laughing and joking and dancing with, of all people, Pellegrini, his sworn enemy from the Socialist Farmworkers Union who, according to my uncle, had set fire to the straw-stack, and who my uncles had then gone after with their guns before setting fire to the huts. My aunts confirmed that it was him she was carrying on with: 'We saw her out with Pellegrini the other evening, out there in the drainage ditch, can't think what they were up to.' My uncle would go red in the face, but he wouldn't say a word. He was convinced that no one had noticed his interest – and who'd pay heed to anything those poisonous she-snakes said? – he never mentioned her or showed any sign of having seen her. But every time he met him on his own – Pellegrini, that is – he'd hiss at him: 'I'd watch your step, if I were you.'

'What do you mean?' Pellegrini would say, all injured innocence. Still, he avoided him, and their paths rarely crossed. Pellegrini gave him a wide berth.

My uncle, on the other hand, would seek him out, and of course her too, alone or in company. And she met him head on. She was no Pellegrini: bump into me as often as you like, for me you're so much thin air. Indeed, bump into me as often as you can: you're just not there.

He ate his heart out.

Sorry, what did you say? Why didn't he approach her, try to have a word with her?

Well, if you can ask me that, you clearly haven't understood my drift. He would cheerfully have throttled every man, woman and child in Codigoro with his own hands, he would have put the whole place to fire and sword, he was afraid of nothing and nobody in this world. But when he was faced with her, he didn't even dare to breathe. If she'd said 'Drop dead,' he'd have dropped dead on the spot. And so he dropped dead in silence, and on tenterhooks, further tormented by his sisters' endless oblique digs – 'Guess who we saw by the canal with Pellegrini' – for four long years, without managing to address a single word in her direction.

Then – riding pillion on that motorbike, clinging to that good-for-nothing who was taking him home, and thinking back on what he'd just done and mulling over his immediate future, which did not look especially rosy – at that point he said to himself: 'What with sheep and lambs and all that, I might as well go to her place; after all, things can't get any worse.'

It must have been eleven o'clock, or perhaps almost midnight. The main street was deserted, of course, and not very well-lit. That was before the days of television, or the cinema, and bars and discos and rock music. There wasn't even the wireless, and people went to bed early because the next day – at cock-crow, when it was just getting light – they'd have to be off to the fields, working their fingers to the bone. It wasn't like nowadays, when no one's got anything to do all day, although there's plenty going on all night. In those days night was for sleep, and there wasn't a soul around, except for ne'er-do-wells.

And so my Uncle Pericles, a ne'er-do-well himself, on this occasion, walked briskly down the dimly-lit main street – the moon itself shone brighter than those streetlamps – all on his own, without even stopping to work out a course of action. Except: 'We'll just have to see what happens.'

The last thing he would have expected – emerging from

the gloom and silence of the square – was to find that the lights were still on, on the upper floor, where she lived, and a group of people in the street, chatting outside the Fascist Headquarters, at the foot of the flight of stairs leading to the back of the building and the landing off which the doors to the first-floor flats opened: on this side the one where she and her family lived, on the other side those of their neighbours.

'What's going on here? Surely it can't be me they're waiting up for?' thought Uncle Pericles in alarm, struck now by the unlikely thought that everyone already knew what had happened at Comacchio and that they'd gathered here to teach the murderer a lesson.

That wasn't it. But here too a dead man came into the story. It was a wake. A neighbour, somewhere in his thirties, had had a stroke that afternoon while drinking in the wine-shop opposite – on the other side of the square – while he was playing *briscola* with his friends, with his little boy on his knee. '*Briscola!*' he'd said, about to thump his fist, and card, down on the table; but it wasn't only his fist that had thumped down on the table; he'd thumped down with it, forehead first. His little boy had fallen off his knee, and his friends thought he was joking. But he wasn't, not at all. After they'd taken him home and called the doctor, and the priest, all that was left was to call the undertaker; then they washed him, dressed him, laid him out on the bed, lit two candles and began to pray.

As you may know, around these parts, when someone dies, it's the neighbours who run the show, or at least it used to be. It's them who make the food, prepare the coffee and offer a glass of wine to the people who've come to offer their condolences, and share the grief. And wakes go on till late. Indeed they used to last all night, with the old women taking it in turns to say the rosary and litanies.

My uncle, though, didn't even stop to ask what was going on. He just went straight ahead, it didn't even occur to him to change his plans, along the lines of: 'Oh, they're having a wake, I think I'd better be off.' Not him: 'I'm here for one thing only, wake or no wake, I know what I've got to do.'

The group on the stairs weren't remotely surprised to see him – 'He's here to offer his condolences' – and they let him through. 'How did it happen?' he asked, and they told him. He heaved a sigh of relief – 'Thank goodness it's not one of her relations,' which would have made things even trickier – and he went straight up. The door was open, and in he went. After a nod in the direction of the assembled company, he went into the room where the dead man was lying. He stood by the head of the bed for a moment, as a mark of respect. He crossed himself. No one seemed surprised to see him. And then she came in – tray in hand – and she looked at him with loathing, as though to say: 'What are you doing here? Get out, and quick!'

At first she hadn't noticed him, she'd been in the kitchen making coffee when he'd arrived, but as soon as she saw him in the room with the dead man she said to herself: 'That man means nothing to him; he's here for me, goddam him.'

My uncle didn't say a word. He waited calmly for her to hand the coffee round, and when she came up to him, to offer him a cup as well – 'Please, help yourself' – although she'd rather have been offering him poison – he said to her, almost in a whisper: 'I need to talk to you.'

She turned round and went back into the kitchen.

He waited for a bit, then followed her.

There was no one else in the kitchen.

She'd spent the afternoon helping the dead man's family. At lunchtime – when he was still alive – her mother had sent her over to his house to take them a bit of salt cod. He'd even

210

engaged in a bit of banter – 'She's turned out a bit of all right, hasn't she though?' – he'd known her since she was a little girl, indeed he'd dandled her on his knee. But that same afternoon she'd found herself washing his hands, there on the bed – armed with a brush and basin – trying to get the dirt out from under his finger nails, but she couldn't make much headway, they were ingrained with grime from years of working on the land. And she'd had the dead man's children come and play with her own little brothers and sisters and had them sleep at her place, in her father and mother's bed. Now she was waiting for the crowd to thin out a bit, so that she too could go to bed: 'All I want to do is lie down.' Instead, though – it was after midnight, and there would be a lot to do tomorrow – who should come trailing after her but that same old thorn in her side. 'He's going to get more than he bargained for,' and she'd already picked up the big bread knife.

From his side of the table – she was on the other side, in front of the curtain that hung over the entrance to the larder – he repeated what he'd said, but quietly, so no one in the other rooms would hear them: 'I need to talk to you.'

'Well, I don't need to talk to you!' she hissed back, just as quietly.

'But I have to talk to you,' said Uncle Pericles insistently, almost beseechingly, and meanwhile he came around the table to be nearer her.

'Get out of here,' she said, more loudly this time, threatening him with the knife.

He put one hand over her mouth – to shut her up – and with the other he seized her by the arm and pulled her towards him: 'Today I killed a man – a priest, so help me God!' and when he'd finished saying 'So help me God,' he burst into tears. And hid his face in his hands.

211

And just while this was happening – alerted by her stifled scream – a relative of the dead man, a cousin, appeared in the doorway, and seeing my uncle's heaving shoulders, from behind, he'd thought: 'I'd no idea Pericles was so fond of my cousin. Who'd have thought it?' She gestured to him with her hand, as though to say: 'It's all right, I'll deal with this,' and he went out again.

They didn't even think to close the door. She just touched his hands, as though to tell him to stop covering his face, to stop him crying. But as soon as they'd touched, it was like an electric shock. They were both dumbfounded. For a moment my uncle saw the priest again, heard the dull splat of his skull as it split open beneath his stick, and his death rattle and that sudden foul smell as the priest lost control of his sphincter. Armida too had smelt the stench of her own dead man, had felt his lifeless head lolling to and fro as she'd dressed him, had felt the warmth gradually draining from him until he was stone-cold, that man who, that very lunchtime, had been so hale and hearty, and teasing her. And, while the strains of the prayers were drifting in faintly from the corridor:

> *Santa Maria. Ora pro nobis.*
> *Santa Dei Genetrix. Ora pro nobis.*
> *Santa Virgo Virginum. Ora pro nobis.*

those two had thrown themselves as one through the curtain in front of the larder. She'd made at least a nod in the direction of modesty, reaching out a hand to check that the curtain – which was all ragged, and had been patched up, by her, on more than one occasion – hadn't caught on the bread bin and hence not closed properly. Then they went at it as though they were possessed, there where they stood, propped up against the wall next to the jars of bottled tomatoes:

Mater Divinae Gratiae. Ora pro nobis.
Mater Purissima. Ora pro nobis.
Mater castissima. Ora pro nobis.

the mourners carried on, the women's high plaintive voices mingling with the men's low, powerful ones:

Turris Eburnea. Ora pro nobis.
Ianua Coeli. Ora pro nobis.

and Uncle Pericles was saying: 'Wait for me,' thinking of all those years he'd be putting in in prison: 'Wait for me, Armida, I can't live without you.'

'I'll wait for you all right,' she'd answered breathlessly, pushing herself more urgently towards him at every thrust: 'I'll wait for you forever, fool that I am.'

And when it was over – and the chorus were saying the 'Amen' – my uncle felt all the life drain out of him, and into her, and then return to him, all fresh and cleansed. And then he thought: 'Today, in you, I've given life to all my sons, and my sons' sons.' But he didn't say so aloud, because he was afraid of what she might think.

But she too – when she'd felt the life drain out of him, and into her – she too had felt that his sons, and his sons' sons, had entered her like a sacred stream: 'Today, just like my bees, I have conceived within me all your sons, and I shall guard them jealously, and put them into the world one by one, when the time comes, just like my bees.'

Then Uncle Pericles had said: 'Wait for me by the bridge;' he'd taken leave of the living and the dead alike, and gone off

213

to their meeting place, and from then onwards – throughout their life – when she would turn away from him to sleep, after they'd made love, she'd ask him hesitantly: 'What if I'd said no that time, what would you have done?' And he, invariably as hard as nails, would say: 'I'd have had you anyway.' And she'd jump back on to him, and they'd make love again.

That time, though, she'd been the first to reach the bridge. To the people at the wake, she'd said: 'I've got to go to my bees, I've got a feeling something's up,' and no one had given it a second thought. Her mother and father were used to it. At any moment of the day or night she might go running off like lighting: 'They're calling me. My bees are calling me.'

'That girl's mad,' her mother would say. But smiling, almost boastfully.

It was her grandmother who'd taught her about bees. There weren't many beekeepers around our parts. Her grandmother had left her this wooden hive, and every now and then she'd replace the odd board on it. It looked like a little house with a very big roof. She'd move it around – one day it would be in one field, and the next day it would be somewhere else – in search of the best position, where there were the most flowers for the bees to suck the pollen from. But where we lived, as I've said, there weren't many plants with good pollen. Only poplars, the occasional elm and the odd acacia. Acacia honey is very good, but there weren't many acacia trees: just fields of corn, lucerne, maize and beets. And even the lucerne – or purple medick, as it's also known – was mowed before it came into flower, which is when it would have had the most pollen, and then left on the ground to dry in the sun. So what was in it for the bees? That's why there weren't many of them – just hers – and why she moved the hive from place to place.

But anyway, people would flock to buy her honey – and

214

the priest would buy the wax – even when cash was short, because it always came in handy, not so much as a sweetener, but for the children. It was the only medicine around, and it was good for both coughs and for women who'd just given birth, and if there was no money at all they'd do a bit of barter, and she was the one who called the tune: she was quite capable of asking you for a calf in exchange for just one little pot of honey. Oddly enough, though, all those people who queued to purchase her wares were not best pleased when she parked her hive on their land. They would all try to drive her off: 'They scare me; get your bees out of here.' Then she'd go through the motions of removing it, and put it down again on the road, just off their land: 'Do you own the road, too?' – or on the banks of the canal, carrying on a mumbled conversion with the bees while people crossed themselves.

She'd be black with them – or yellow and black, to be more precise – with all those bees on her bare skin, all jam-packed one against the other, swarming over her hands, her arms, her neck, her face, even in her mouth and between her breasts. They'd make the sign of the cross. 'You little witch,' they'd say, convinced that she really was talking with her bees. Now – as you well know – such a thing just isn't possible. Neither on earth nor in heaven. All science rules it out. Men can talk with certain animals, perhaps even understand them. But they've got to be big ones, a bit nearer us on the evolutionary ladder.

My uncles and my other relatives talked to their animals. My grandfather, for instance, talked to his horse. When he got angry with my grandmother, and there was no hope of getting any satisfaction because she always had to have the last word, my grandfather would leave the house and call to his horse: 'Come over here, you're the only one in this world who understands me.' And of course we talked to our

215

dogs, and cows. Cows are highly intelligent, and my uncles always got along well with them. Each one had her own name in our cowshed in the Pontine Marshes – that's something I remember from when I was little. We arrived there – as I've told you – with hardly any livestock. They'd all been filched by the Zorzi Vila. But almost as soon as we'd got here – one or two days after we'd arrived – the Servicemen's Association took us to Doganella, to a place where they'd assembled I don't know how many thousand head of cattle, in an enclosure which was one great heaving 'Moo'. You could hear it from miles away, from as far off as the Appian Way, and once you got there it looked like a great dirty sea of white, with waves of rumps and horns rippling endlessly to and fro. Thousands and thousands of Maremma cows, all penned in together. We'd never seen that kind before. Where we came from, there were other breeds, raised for their milk or meat, with ordinary horns, not those great long sharp curved ones. At first, they rather frightened us. Then we got used to them, and they became like members of the family. They're not much good as milch-cows, they don't yield very much. Nor can you get much meat off them, they're always skin and bone even if you stuff the feed down their throats. But for draft purposes, God help us! They're unrivalled. There's no holding them: ploughs, carts, harrows, at it from dawn to dusk, they never jib – it's all go with them. Tractors, forget it. They should have monuments. And the Servicemen's Association told us all: 'Go right in, get yourselves six animals and then go home.' And my uncles went into the enclosure, a bit hesitant at first, shoulder to shoulder, eyes peeled, pinching each other from time to time to prove that it wasn't just a dream, but knowing that things were bound to turn out all right, because – even in the midst of that riotous herd of Maremma cows – the Peruzzi, as always, had the situation well in hand.

My uncles began running their hands over the cows' bodies, one by one, whispering sweet nothings into their ears, inspecting their teeth, lifting up their legs to look at their hooves; then, when one met with their approval, they'd signal to my Uncle Turati, who'd take it off and tie it up outside the stockade. Then they'd call him back: 'Here, Turati, this one,' and back he'd go. Then, when we'd got our ration, off we all went with our six new cows, clip-clop all the way home, and pleased as punch, and when we got back home what a scene it was, the whole family, women and children included, all in the cowshed making merry, and now it was like our old one, heaving with cows. But above all it was brand new, and when the first cowpat flopped on to the floor we all shouted: 'Here's to us!' and it all seemed like a dream. 'We did well to come here,' said my grandmother. 'The Zorzi Vila and the rest of them up there can go to hell.'

But not everyone at Doganella that day was as well-pleased as we were. Indeed, the factors from the Servicemen's Association were tearing their hair, because – and this they weren't expecting – a lot of the people who'd come down from the Veneto to work on the Pontine Marshes had never laid a hand on an animal in their lives. Once they were inside the enclosure, they were panic-stricken; some refused to go in at all. Others clung desperately to the stockade, and shrieked with fear if a Maremma cow went anywhere near them – and they were fearsome-looking creatures, as I've said, with those great horns.

'Get a move on, we haven't got all day,' shrieked back the factors in return. 'Take your animals and get out.'

The bravest among them set about their task. But, having no idea which end to start – and the front end , as I've said, didn't

217

look encouraging, what with those horns – they grabbed their tails and tried to drag them out backwards. It was complete pandemonium, with those poor devils knocked down like ninepins the moment the animal took a sidestep, and some of them got trampled under foot and were quite badly hurt.

'They've never laid eyes on an animal in their life,' the factors thought. 'What kind of sharecroppers are these? Who's bright idea was this?'

It had been the Fascist Party's bright idea, of course, who else's would it have been, some plot cooked up by the mighty Jews and masons? Or perhaps it was an act of 'sabotage', as Cencelli claimed? The association had asked for sharecroppers, not day-labourers, because a day-labourer is good for just one thing: hoeing or harvesting or shovelling or tending livestock, and that's all he ever does. He works by the day – when he's called for, that is – and goes back to his village or reed and straw hut in the evening. The sharecropper, on the other hand, is on the land that's been apportioned to him day and night, and he knows how to do all kinds of work and is a fully-rounded peasant. He knows the moment every kind of crop should be sown, and how the ground should be prepared for it. He knows what has to be done with every crop before it's harvested – thinning out, pruning, spreading manure – he's known it all ever since he was a child, harvesting according to the full moon and the seasons: from wheat to lucerne, from onions to fruit trees. He knows how to plant, transplant and graft, and above all how to tend livestock, he knows – just by looking at her belly – when to spend the night in the cowshed because the cow will be giving birth and there might be complications. But here there were people who'd never put a yoke on a pair of oxen in their lives, who'd have killed their mother and father rather than kneel down under a mule's belly to strap on the

218

packsaddle.

Sorry, what did you say? Why did they come here then? Because they were starving, that's why. It's hunger that drives people to get false papers, and that's what they did to have themselves passed off as sharecroppers, so they could move down here. In earlier times they'd emigrated to America to make their fortune. Then America pulled up the drawbridge, and in the Thirties the Pontine Marshes became the new America – 'America's in Piscinara' – and everyone started to get themselves false papers in order to lay hands on a holding – day-labourers, barbers, knife-grinders, cobblers, even town clerks. They went to the mayor or to the Fascist Headquarters for testimonials, to have themselves put on the lists drawn up by the department of internal migration. But you only need to look through the parish registers, or the civil status certificates in the registry office at Latina-Littoria, to see what a bungle they made of it. In fact, the rule was that you had not only to be a sharecropper or a peasant – that is, that you had to know how to turn your hand to anything – but you also had to have fought in the 1915–1918 War, otherwise why call it a Servicemen's Association? And the families had to be large ones, because you needed hands to work the land.

Each family had to have at least ten members, you had to have a whole gaggle of children and – once you got down here – you had to be able to produce more. So even if you were an experienced sharecropper, and had polished off more Germans or Austrians in the war than you could shake a stick at, if you didn't have many children – if you had just a few, like nowadays – you had to fiddle cards and documents, and you have no idea how many bogus family record books there were around, with the addition of any number of relatives who'd never set a foot outside of Northern Italy. And above all the fake marriages, arranged with the collusion of the parish priest or bishop, between young girls of thirteen or fourteen – so that there'd seem to be more of them – and every widow or elderly bachelor around, or even with the first halfwit who happened to amble on to the scene, and there was no need for these marriages to be consummated, all that was needed was for a bit of money to change hands. Just like the bogus marriages contracted nowadays to enable some non-EU immigrant to gain Italian citizenship. And then – when they arrived down south – those girls would find themselves real sweethearts and have children, but since in those days there was no divorce, those children remained illegitimate all their lives, and no one knew whether the names they bore were those of their real fathers or of those who'd stayed up north, who might now be dead and buried, and whom they'd never seen or known. But here honesty demands that I tell you the truth and the whole truth, at least as far as I know it, or as it's been told to me by my uncles. So here I have to admit that we too were not above a bit of fancy footwork.

My Uncle Dolfin for example – the one my Uncle Pericles wangled a holding for at Borgo Hermada, on the right bank of the River Sisto, just before you come to the lock – had been an ardent Socialist, and this alone would have debarred him from having a holding, though in fact once he arrived down here he too donned a black shirt. But he had fought in the war, no two ways about it, he'd gone on the attack with my Uncle Themistocles when they were in the *Arditi*, he'd fought with just his bare fists and hand grenades. But he'd never seen a pitchfork in his life, nor ever worked as a day-labourer. He'd never known what farm work was and later on, when he was older, he always complained that he had a bad back, and would curse the day he'd come down south. 'The earth's too low, couldn't they move it up a bit?'

My Uncle Dolfin was a barber and a shoemaker. Some of his shoes made you feel as though you were walking on air. He'd feel your feet, look at them, feel them again, measure them with his rule and make you two shoes that fitted like a glove, so perfect were his measurements. But how many new shoes were the down-and-outs in our village ever going to need? And even when they did have a new pair made, who do you think was going to have the gall actually to wear them, so that after a time they'd need new soles? In the north, we all walked barefoot, just as we did later in the Pontine Marshes until 1960, that is, when affluence arrived. Let alone the fact that the only time you ever wore those shoes was on the day of your wedding, and your funeral – so when your son got married, he'd have to buy a new pair; but here the catch was that in the Basso-Rovigotto, where we came from, there was a hallowed tradition that the dead were buried without shoes. Nowhere in Ferrara or Codigoro would you see a dead man in his coffin with his shoes on, and the same went for Pontinina and Borgo Hermada, down here in the Pontine Marshes. Never a shoe in sight. He'd be wearing brand new socks, and possibly a tie, he'd have been given a shave and his hair would be neatly combed, and he'd have a bit of money in his pocket – though of course you couldn't see that – and cigarettes and a lighter if he was a smoker, and, before closing the coffin lid, his wife and children would slip in a little bottle of grappa and a bite to eat. That was the way we did things round our way. Of course they'd always place a rosary in his hand as well: that was how it had been done for centuries, and there was no reason to change things now.

Sorry, what did you say? Why the money?

That was the way we did things, as I've said, it was a sop

to Cerberus. What do we know about how they do things on the other side? Why should our dead be forced to run any risks in the next world? Better to play it safe, that's what people said. I'll pay his ticket for him in the way we've always done – first class, at that – and if I've paid for one station more than I needed to, so be it; I can't send him off without all the trimmings, one station short. What would he say to the conductor? For the same reason, even today, when you're building a house, before you lay the foundations you throw in a handful of coins. They're to placate the gods, to ask for their permission for you to do violence to the earth, our mother. In the olden days they'd wall a human being into the foundations – a human sacrifice – then as time went by it was just coins, a sop to Cerberus, a substitute for the human offering. And even now, when you pass by a fountain – Trevi in Rome for instance, and the fountain of the Palla in Latina – you throw in a coin because, unconsciously, you're thinking: 'If I do that it's as though I'm dead already, and I won't die at least until the next time I'm here.'

At all events, where we come from the dead leave this world barefoot, even if they've got a bit of loose change in their pockets. Barefoot you came into this world and barefoot you went out. So you can imagine what a roaring trade a skilled cobbler could hope for around these parts, even a true artist like my Uncle Dolfin. And you couldn't hope for much as a barber, either – poor old Dolfin. Starvelings as they were, were the villagers going to stroll down to the barber's for a shave? They'd rather have gnawed off their beards with their own teeth. They'd only call in a barber when someone had died. Otherwise, they managed on their own. And my aunt – now she really knew how to work the land, she was the second oldest, the oldest girl, born a year after Uncle Themistocles

222

and one year before Uncle Pericles– my aunt had married him for love, because he had a lovely singing voice and knew a thousand stories, each more preposterous than the last, but the way he told them, she always believed them to be true.

But another thing that was true around those parts was hunger, and between one story and the next they'd spawned a goodly brood, and before we came down south she'd asked her brothers: 'But what will my boys do down there? Will they be so many starving cobblers like their father?'

It was then that Uncle Pericles went off to the Fascist Headquarters, where they objected that Dolfin was a Socialist, and told him: 'It's Ponza we should be sending him to, Peruzzi.' Then they asked whether he had ever worked as a sharecropper.

'Of course. I'll vouch for that.'

'What about livestock? Does he know how to care for livestock?'

'Does he ever! Has them eating out of his hand. I'll vouch for that.'

'All right. If that's the way things are, thanks for the suggestion, Peruzzi, that's one more holding well-allotted.'

'Now I'm in a pickle,' thought Uncle Pericles as he went home, and he said to his mother: 'How will he manage, he's never laid hands on a pitchfork in his life?'

'He'll learn. That's what his brothers-in-law are here for,' and throughout the first few years, taking it in turns, one member of the Peruzzi family was always on that holding on the River Sisto, at Borgo Hermada, teaching my Uncle Dolfin how to work the land, and how to tend the livestock and talk to them in his lovely singing voice, just the way he talked to his own wife. But even after he'd learned all they could teach him – wiping the sweat from his forehead as he did so – day after day, he never stopped saying to his brothers-in-law: 'The earth's too low, couldn't they move it up a bit?' Poor Uncle Dolfin, it wasn't really the trade he was cut out for.

And there were lots like him. Not all of them, of course, the great majority were genuine sharecroppers like ourselves. But the association had asked for sharecroppers, and sharecroppers was what they expected to get. So when they saw that bunch of incompetents scuttling about among the cattle, they didn't know what had hit them. They phoned Cencelli immediately, and played the whole thing up a bit. Cencelli leapt into his car – or on to his horse, perhaps, because there was nothing he liked better than wandering around the marshes on horseback, with his Borsalino on his head and his pistol in his belt – and when he arrived, he did indeed see two or three of them hanging on to a cow's tail and being dragged around. 'That's nothing, you should have been here this morning,' his factors promptly told him, because that's how it goes, some people don't feel that they've really had a hand in things unless they play them up a bit.

You can imagine how Cencelli reacted. It was a veritable hail of: 'You pack of deadbeat good-for-nothings,' left right and centre – he came from Rieti, remember. He wanted to send them all straight home again: 'To hell with the lot of them, and their Veneto into the bargain. Put them right back on to those ruddy trains!' But that wasn't an option. They were here now, whether he liked it or not. 'But we asked for sharecroppers,' he howled to Rossoni on the phone. 'What the hell am I to do with this lot?'

'Keep a civil tongue in your head, Cencelli, remember who you're speaking to. These are the Duce's orders, we can't set ourselves up against the department for internal migration and have them sent back home. Teach them their trade, and you too can go to blazes, while we're about it.' And the Servicemen's Association arranged courses, village by village, and taught the lot of them – who'd never seen a spade in all their lives – how you run a farm, how to hoe and plough, how to kill a pig, sow corn, yoke your oxen, sit on a stool in front of a cow's udders, and help her to give birth to a calf. And the women had always lived in villages, and bought their bread from the baker's, on tick, of course, paying much later, so they'd had to teach them how to knead their dough and make their bread as well, because that was something they'd never done before.

That is the truth, and it would be wrong to hide it, even if it didn't apply to everyone – us Peruzzi, for example, knew not only how to make bread but all the rest as well. We'd been competent peasants in the north, and on our mother's side we'd even been landowners, in days gone by. It had taken the Zorzi Vila – and that new 90 exchange rate – to reduce us to such dire need.

At all events, as I was telling you, my relatives always talked to their animals, indeed they almost got on better with them than they did with their fellow humans. As a young man, my grandfather had been a carter, and his horse was like a brother to him. As for their hunting-dogs – well, they treated them like their own children. But it was the cows that were our real love. There wasn't a single Peruzzi who didn't love his cows more than his wife. Or at least their cows were always more biddable than their wives – after all, the cows were in no position to answer back. But they could never get their wives completely under their thumb. That was the Peruzzi family's luck. It was the wives who were the real brutes, while my uncles had their cows eating out of their hands. Each cow had her own name – not just in our family, but in every cowshed up and down the land. Ours had the names of cities. I don't know how this custom came about; perhaps in the distant past – maybe one of my grandmother's relatives, or whoever it was who'd been in Russia with Napoleon – when the first cow arrived, someone had just returned from military service, having seen the world, as the saying goes, and started to name his cows after the cities he'd been to. And those names stuck – from cow to cow and from cowshed to cowshed, wherever we were, just as in some noble families there's always a Francesco or an Emanuele or a Vittorio or what have you, from generation unto generation – and so it was as long as we had cows. And, as long as the Peruzzi family had cows, and cowsheds, there were always one or two bulls called Saint Petersburg, or a cow or calf called Moscow, and I still remember my Uncle Iseo bringing the stools and pails into the pen when it was milking-time – they grazed freely, in those days – and calling out 'Venice!' and up she'd lumber in and stop beside him, neatly avoiding the stool, with her udders right above the pail. Uncle Iseo would massage her udders for a moment – if they were dirty, he'd wash them – and then he'd start to milk her crosswise, as it were, two udders at a time, first one pair and then the other. And if the pail was empty you'd hear the sound of the first milk hissing on to the aluminium base. When I was little, every so often he'd direct the jet of milk in my direction and I'd get a faceful – 'Drink that, you little monkey!' – as I stood there beside him, watching him, enraptured. He was my favourite uncle. Then, when he'd finished with Venice, he'd give her a pat on the flank and she'd lumber off and he'd call out: 'Toorin', 'Floorence', 'Mila-an', until they'd all been milked.

So for us, as you can imagine, people talking to animals was nothing new – indeed, it was what we'd spent our whole lives doing – but we talked to big animals, the kind with proper brains; not to insects, what sort of a conversation would that be? Whoever heard of anyone talking to an insect? Well, think again. She talked to her bees, and not just to vent her feelings, or out of desperation – like people who talk to walls, or to a doll, because there's no one else around, and it's as though they're talking to themselves, but aloud, because you can hear yourself better that way – no, she was convinced that the bees not only understood her, but also answered her, in their own way: that there was a genuine exchange of views. She claimed she understood them from the way they buzzed, and more particularly from the way they flew, when they were swarming. And that time she arrived at the bridge at Po di Volano – where she'd placed the hive under an arch a few days earlier – she'd said to them, all cock-a-hoop: 'We're going to have company. Behave yourselves.' But then, unable to contain herself, she shouted: 'I've found myself a sweetheart, bees!'

Now it wasn't that they didn't already know, or that she didn't know that they knew. They'd told her as much that morning, it was she who hadn't wanted to believe them. Or who'd failed to understand them.

The previous evening she'd already heard the queen bee starting on her love song, a song which became ever clearer, ever more high-pitched, one long pressing crescendo. She'd spent almost the whole night beside the hive, listening, imagining the drones as they fizzed round at each new piercing sound the queen bee made. After all, that was their purpose in this world, it wasn't as if they had anything else to do. They'd never lifted a finger in their lives, and it had always and only been the female bees who'd ever cared for them, it was they who'd kept those spongers in clover with honey until this crucial moment. This was the sporting event of their lives: *Hic Rhodus, hic salta*. Their most important hundred metres – their

Olympics – and there they all were, fizzing around and waiting for this din to cease, to hear the sound of the starting pistol and to see the traps being opened. And then at last they'd be off and out, and up, and on her trail, risking their all to save their souls, their lives, their progeny. Nor was there any knowing how many of them might already have died there in the hive during the night – thought Armida to herself – done to death just by that same relentless sound, brought to such climax by it that their hearts had burst.

Then, at day-break, the swarm had left the hive. Out sailed the queen bee, and they, the thousands and thousands of drones, went out after her. But, before they made to go upwards, towards the sun – strangely – the swarm had swept around her, twice, something which Armida saw as a bad omen, and she felt a pang for the drones which would not be coming back.

The queen bee flew ever higher, while the swarm behind her gradually thinned out. She is the strongest of them all, because she feeds exclusively on royal jelly, whereas all that the drones get is left-over honey. But none of them drops behind or turns around – or rather, those few who do so find the hive closed, barred by the guardian bees, so they stay around outside for a few days, until they die of hunger – and, in their burst of upward flight, one after another, the drones' hearts burst: it's been good knowing you, remember me in your prayers. Only the strongest make it to the top, and the last six or seven who do so are at last rewarded by being allowed to discharge that last drop of life that's left to them, that final gene, into her sacred womb – a prize much coveted, the high point of a cruel race. Once that's done, the male's copulatory organs break off – that was the only purpose they were designed ever to serve – and it's bye-bye drone. But his progeny live on for ever, because what counts is the hive – the community – not the individual, and even the warrior bee has only one sting, and when she injects her poison that sting breaks off, and the bee dies. But if anyone appears to threaten the hive, she won't have a moment's hesitation, she'll set off on her mission, because that's her be-all-and-end-all, it's what she came into the world to do: *Dulce et decorum est pro patria mori*. Then the queen takes all the drones' seed into a sac – hundreds of thousands or even millions of gametes – and over the course of the rest of her life, which is five years on average, whenever bees are needed in the hive, she fertilizes her eggs with the gametes she's kept in her sac. Whenever the need arises. Not all at once.

I'm sorry, what was that you said? That Krishna, or the god Vishnu – I didn't quite catch the name – does the same thing the first time he impregnates his wife Satyabhama, making her pregnant, at one fell swoop, with all the progeny she will then give birth to over the course of the ages?

What would I know about this Satyabhama of yours, or Krishna or Vishnu either? They're over there in India, while I'm in the Pontine Marshes, and I'm just telling you what I know about, or at least what my uncles told me. And at the end of that nuptial flight – that same morning – laden with her millions of gametes, the queen bee hadn't come back to the hive all cool and collected, as she usually did. Well, it's true, a queen bee never comes back from her nuptial flight exactly cool and collected. When do you imagine she'll have another day like that? It's the biggest day of their lives for the girls of my village, too – or at least it used to be – and they'll spend a fortune on a wedding dress, and the wedding breakfast, and new furniture and a photographer, and now on a video and a dvd as well. Put yourself in the place of the queen bee. The girls in my village got married just that once – well, maybe more than once, as things are now – but at least they can go for it every night, should the mood take them. The queen bee on the other hand has just that one chance, poor thing. You can understand that she might feel, how can I put this, a bit unladylike, a bit revved up. When's that likely to come her way again? So all queen bees come back from their nuptial flights a bit the worse for wear, as though drunk. Lurching and reeling. And that was why Armida hadn't worried when she'd caught sight of her own queen bee from a distance, doing just that. But hers – instead of making a beeline for the hive, or at least summoning her fellow bees for help – had started to whirl around her head like a mad thing, buzzing and humming and seeming to say: 'And now you're at it, too.'

Armida warded her off with her hand: 'Get off with you, just keep your distance, damn you, let me alone.' But the queen bee persisted, flying round in ever closer circles, then homing in on her left ear and buzzing: 'And now you're at it, too.'

'Be off with you, you pesky insect,' Armida snapped, 'did I or did I not tell you to give me a wide berth?' Then the queen bee had said: 'To hell with you,' and had flown back into the hive, clearly in something of a huff, still making a strange buzzing sound which, had you wanted to, you could easily have interpreted as: 'So, now you're at it too, you clown.'

Obviously, I can't tell you whether the queen bee really did say that, any more than I can tell you how bees think in general. You'd have to become one to find out. But Armida knew. Or thought she did. And now she saw that when the bees had swept around her, twice – the bad omen – that had been for the neighbour who'd dandled her on his knee as a child, and yelled '*Briscola*' in the wine-shop, and fallen down dead upon the table; whereas when the queen bee started buzzing gleefully around her ear, that had been for her, for when her

230

womb had opened up to receive the vital stream from Pericles, late at night, in the neighbours' larder. When she – like the queen to the drone – had said to that stream: 'Today, just like my bees, I have conceived within me all your sons, and I shall guard them jealously, and bring them into the world one by one, when the time comes, just like my bees.'

Then Uncle Pericles arrived at the bridge. They'd said all that they had to say to each other, and more besides, and carried on talking and doing until dawn. Then – out of respect for the dead man – my uncle had gone back with her to the village. Outside the Fascist Headquarters – after the last kiss, with her foot already on the bottom step of the stairs – Armida had caressed her stomach rapturously and said to him: 'I think I can feel it moving already, Pericles. The first will be a girl, we'll call her Adria.'

'Steady on,' said my uncle, laughing, and it was the first and last time that he laughed that day: 'Let's wait a bit; I want to be there when she's born too, you know.'

'All right then, I'll wait; I'll put her off,' and up she went. He laughed again, then went home and said to my grandmother: 'Ma, either today or tomorrow Armida will be coming, and I won't be here. Take her in, because now she's my wife.'

'I'll take her in like my own daughter, son.'

Not long afterwards, the *carabinieri* arrived.

Armida waited for another couple of days, then bundled up her few possessions, picked up the hive, walked out of the village and into the countryside, where the Peruzzi lived.

My Aunt Bissola saw her coming down the road – that road we'd always seen everyone coming down – with her bundle in one hand and her hive in the other. 'Now what does she want?' because she was dressed in her Sunday best, not in the sort of clothes she wore to go about her business with the hive.

231

'Surely she can't be thinking of foisting herself on us?'

'You be quiet,' my grandmother said to her, and welcomed Armida with open arms. 'This is your room,' she said, showing her into a room that was small, but all her own, not the one where all the other sisters-in-law slept together, 'and when Pericles gets back, we'll see.' And, together, they set themselves to waiting for him and, when he finally returned, my grandmother helped her to give birth, and bring Adria into the world at last.

My grandmother was very fond of Armida. She accepted her unquestioningly. It wasn't like with my Uncle Themistocles' wife, who'd come from the huts, after all, and had been our maid-of-all-work. She liked Armida, not just because she was very beautiful, as fair as fair, tall, blue-eyed, with good firm breasts and sturdy hips but a narrow waist and a proud bearing – she held herself erect, shoulders back, chest thrust out, she might have been the queen of Savoy in person – but because she was also proud by nature, very gentle with children, even those who weren't her own, and with all animals, plants and humans who were less strong than she was; but hard as iron, and haughty, with anyone she regarded as stronger and haughtier than herself: 'Just right for Pericles.'

But, for these very reasons, Armida never got on well with her husband's sisters. She got on all right with her other sisters-in-law, with the wives of his brothers, she was like a sister and a friend to them: Uncle Themistocles' wife, and above all Uncle Iseo's. The three wives were as close as the three brothers. They were like sisters, but there was something more – they were like friends, because even sisters can have their problems. We formed a team – a crew – but we weren't all bound together in the same way. We'd close up like a fist – men, women, children and animals – at the slightest hint of any threat from the outside world. But – on that occasion – my aunts must have thought that Armida constituted just such a threat: 'Her, in our house? Pellegrini's girl?'

Now I don't know if the things they said about her and Pellegrini were true. They also said that she'd had a baby when she was very young, and abandoned it at the foundling hospital. As you know, such things weren't unusual in those days. After all, we were no plaster saints. We came from the Veneto, indeed from round Ferrara, a region that's never been known for its lily-white morality. Of course we weren't heathens, but only the more respectable among us went to Sunday mass. Otherwise, we were easy-going, it was live and let live. With all that poverty around, who was going to be a stickler for convention and propriety? We had our flings. We let rip, and did our thinking later. And when a girl got pregnant, if she was too poor, or too young, she'd look for someone to pierce her uterus with a knitting needle, or – if she didn't find that someone – she'd take the newborn child to the nearest convent. She'd put it through the revolving door by the main gate, which was there for just this purpose, and then she'd turn around and walk away; someone would take care of it. The sharecroppers used to take on quite a few farm-hands who had been sent to them by the nuns, because of the allowance the state paid to foundlings, and they'd have them work for free. A bit like an internship, nowadays.

But there were also lots of girls who were neither too poor nor too young, and who'd maybe had an ill-judged fling with the wrong boy – who, because he was too poor, had then suddenly gone off to America, or France, or been called up, or died, or who perhaps was just a ne'er-do-well, good for a fling but not to spend a life with, and then it would be the family itself which would say to her: 'Just let it drop, girl, you

233

stay here, we'll take you in, bag and baggage'. There were lots of girls who found themselves pregnant but had no intention either of doing away with the child or abandoning it. So they'd stay with their families, waiting for Mr. Right to roll up – and sooner or later roll up he always did – and he would take her on, bag and baggage, or 'cow and calf', as the phrase went around our parts.

As I've already said, I don't know whether all the things my Uncle Pericles' sisters said about his wife were true. But what I do know is that we were from around Ferrara, and that like all or almost all the families from the Veneto and Friuli and Ferrara who came down here, when we arrived in the Pontine Marshes we too – what with my aunts – had one or two extra calves to cater for.

At all events, it was an exodus, and we too – despite that deluge – had left on time. But ours was the only train ever to arrive late, with all those black-shirted militia and Princess Caetani on the platform to welcome us, cursing the while. Our journey too had gone well as far as Rome, and even beyond, dead on time, just like the rest: same little stations, same grappa, same white coffee and women from the local Fascist branches at Bologna and Florence, same flood of men and little boys at every stop, however brief, rushing from one carriage to the other, same squabbles, same fairy stories told by grandmothers. Then all the shunting to and fro at the main station in Rome, the endless dozing while waiting to be off again, then deeper sleep, rocked by the clickety-clack, and on down through Torricola, Santa Palomba and Cisterna. We were almost there, in fact, and at that point we were still on time. But then we began to run late because of a moment's inattention on the part of one of the Mambrin children; the Mambrin were distant relatives on my grandmother's side, and we found ourselves in the same carriage. But lots of other people must have found themselves seated with their distant relatives on those troop trains. After all, the poor have so many children, they're all interrelated. It's not like that with the rich. But if you don't have any children you won't have any relatives.

Anyway, this child was about six or seven, and he was called Benito, but everyone called him by the diminutive, Benitin, because he was so small. Naturally, in those days, every family had at least one Benito to its name. My grandparents too had had one of their own – the last whelp of the litter – in 1926 or 1927. He'd arrived unexpectedly, because my grandmother thought she'd done her bit – 'Let's call it a day' – and for the first two or three months, when she failed to get her period, she didn't give it a second thought: 'I'm old, that's all it is.' But that wasn't all it was, not by any means, and when my grandfather noticed her stomach getting bigger, and her breasts becoming harder, and saw her starting to knit again, and she told him that she could feel the child moving and kicking, he came over all cock-a-hoop: 'There's life in the old man yet,' he thought proudly. We were still at Ca' Bragadin with the Zorzi Vila, and my grandparents were by now somewhat over the hill in terms of such matters, and the lifeblood they passed on to this new son was not what it had been. Just after his third birthday he'd come down with a serious fever on the first day of carnival – and my grandmother had been making him pancakes with raisons and other seasonal goodies – and by Ash Wednesday he was dead. He's still up there, in the cemetery at Ca' Foscari. 'My poor little Benito' had been my grandmother's last words on the platform at Rovigo Station, just before getting on the troop train: 'Now who'll think to bring him a flower?' Well, we do – me and my cousins – every once in a while when we're up that way on holiday.

Anyway, ever since we'd set off, this Benito Mambrin had been causing pandemonium with his rabbit. He'd talk to it as though it were a human being, and as if the rabbit understood him back, you take my word for it. According to his mother, he would call it, even from a distance, if it was out on the threshing-floor, for instance, and it would come running to him like a dog. 'Jacky, give us your paw,' he'd say, and it would do just that. Or 'Jacky, jump,' he'd say, and jump it did.

'We'll send you off to join the circus,' everyone had said to him, and throughout the whole journey that was all he'd done, raise merry hell with his wretched rabbit – the only child on the train who hadn't had a proper sleep, not even between Bologna and Rome – because every so often he'd wake up and prod the creature into action again, and in doing so he'd wake up every woman in the carriage: his mother, his grandmother, his aunts and even other people's. Goodness knows how many times my grandmother had to tell him the story about the devil at Pontelungo. Then he'd be off again – the moment it was over – worming his way under the seats like a tick. They were at their wits' end. And during one stop – just after Florence, I think, when the men had come up the train to pay a call – they put him in the care of an older cousin, together with the rabbit, and the cage: 'You take him. We wish you joy.'

When his father had seen him coming, he'd not been best pleased – 'It's draughty here, and there's too much smoke' – but anyway he'd played with him and had him on his knee, even if he'd have preferred to be left on his own, so he could drink his grappa and chat and play cards with my uncles to his heart's content. Now, though, he had to make sure that his son was kept well clear of Armida's bees. 'What's under there?' the boy kept saying, his little hands tugging at the cloth, only to receive a resounding slap for his pains.

At the next stop they delivered him back to the womenfolk, and it even seems that at some point – oddly enough, not lulled by the clickety-clack, but by the eerie silence of Rome Station, during the long stop the train had made there – he too had finally fallen asleep. 'At long last!' the women had chorused in relief.

Then the troop train had set off again, and everyone slept on more or less undisturbed – except perhaps by dreams of what they'd left behind – until beyond Cisterna, that is, well into the Pontine Marshes.

But after Cisterna this same little boy, Benito Mambrin, woke up again, still gripped by the mad urge to poke around in the rabbit's little cage.

The train was actually running slightly ahead of time. The sun had just come out from behind the Lepini Mountains, which were lightly veiled in black cloud – it was November, don't forget. The train rattled loudly over Ponte Marchi, the bridge which takes the railway from the other side of the Appian Way across the Mussolini Canal. Everyone in the carriage was asleep – women, old men, even Benito's older cousin, the one who was supposed to be in charge of him. We were already in the Pontine Marshes. Just six more kilometres to go, and we'd be in Littoria.

Before we'd arrived in Rome, the rabbit's cage had been stowed away again under the seat where his grandmother was sitting, and at this juncture he suddenly felt the need to pull it out again – half-asleep, she parted her legs to let him carry on with his meddling unimpeded – and to hang it up in midair. His eye alighted upon something which, in his view, would serve the purpose – the door handle – and that's where he hung it. But it wasn't an easy fit, so he had to use force.

My grandmother – who was sitting opposite his grand-mother, after all they were relatives and had been chatting throughout the journey – always said that just at that moment, while the train was rattling over Ponte Marchi with its dozing occupants, a black-cloaked figure had appeared to her in a dream. She'd felt a sudden pain shoot through her stomach, followed immediately by a slap of freezing air which hit her full in the face, coming through the now open door. She'd woken up and the child was no longer there. The door was banging to and fro against the outer side of the carriage.

At the same moment – actually, a split-second before my grandmother – the child's mother had woken up as well. She was five or six months pregnant, and was sitting on a seat on the other side of the corridor, and now she threw herself forward to grab hold of him. She was already half out of the train, both shoulders and one leg.

My grandmother seized her by the arm, clutching at the layers of woollen garments in which she was swathed. And pulled her back. With her other hand she pulled the lever bearing the stark words 'Emergency brake' – she'd done no-thing but stare at it ever since they'd left Rovigo. Benito's grandmother, old as she was, joined in the fray.

The train had started to slow down. But a train can't stop just like that, it screeches on for a time even after the brakes have been put on. Now the child's mother was screaming: 'My child, my son,' and the grandmother followed suit, their hopes diminishing with every metre as the train screeched on. The other women looked around for their own children, counting them nervously and, finding them all present and correct, heaved a huge sigh of relief: 'Holy Mary Mother of God.'

Now people were getting out and the railway officials came rushing up, together with the militia from the front carriage and the men from the goods wagons, curious as to what had happened, including the male members of the Mambrin family, sickened to find that they were the ones who had been singled out for such disaster: 'Why does it have to be us?'

Then everyone walked down along the tracks, in search of the little boy. They found him some hundred metres further back, at the bottom of the stony embankment running down to the Mussolini Canal, just before the beginning of the bridge. Lying there in a heap. Not a peep out of him. With the back of his head and one small arm smashed to bits. Dead. But his face was that of a sleeping child.

His father gathered him into his arms, all bleeding as he was, and showed him to his wife, who had come running up: 'Benitin!' she was shrieking. 'You and that damned rabbit.'

'That damned new exchange rate, more like,' said his father, still cradling his lifeless treasure in his arms. 'Those damned Zorzi Vila, more to the point,' thought my Uncle Pericles, who was standing beside them, but the railway official told the man to put him down: 'We've got to wait for the authorities. Go and get something to cover him up with, please.'

'What do you mean, authorities?' bellowed the chief of the railway militia. 'I'm the authorities round here! Take that child in and get the train started, orders are orders.'

They wrangled for a bit: 'I'm the guard,' objected the railway official. 'And I'm the militia,' the militia chief snapped back.

Meanwhile the child's father had got back on to the train, in search of something to cover him with. But, as he approached the carriage, he saw the cage still hanging from the open door, with the squeaking rabbit still inside it. He snatched it off, shattering it as he did so, then grabbed the rabbit, dashed its head against the door and threw the dead body into the scrub

239

beside the railway line.

When at last two *carabinieri* arrived on foot from the station at Littoria, the guard and the militia had everyone get back on to the train and off it clattered. Two hours late. Then all was silence, just the faint swish of the water under the spans of Ponte Marchi as it flowed into the already swollen waters of the Mussolini Canal. Two years later – as I've already mentioned – the flood of 4 November 1934 swept the whole bridge away. They had to rebuild it from scratch – bigger and stronger – where it is today. And they also had to re-dig and widen that stretch of the canal. My Uncle Iseo – who worked on it – said that this time he too had thrown fifty cents into the new foundations, in memory of that poor child.

After the train set off, the only people left on the embankment were the child's parents. 'You'll have to see to everything,' his father had said to his brothers, putting his livestock and his other children into their care.

'Don't you worry,' they'd said to him.

He and his wife stayed sitting there – together with the *carabinieri*, at a respectful distance – keeping watch over the little body, covered now with a white tablecloth from the woman's trousseau. Its edges were all embroidered. And two small bloodstains, at the height of the little arm and head. She was crying, her arms folded over her swollen stomach. He had his arm around her shoulders.

Before the train had set off, though, my grandmother had gone into the scrub to look for the dead rabbit; when she had found it, and climbed back on to the train, the guard was shouting: 'Come on, let's go! Don't you start, too!' She'd given it to Benito's grandmother – her own relative, don't forget – saying to her gently: 'At least you can have it for supper this evening.'

One of my aunts said quietly to one of her sisters: 'It was her doing,' referring to Armida, her sister-in-law. 'Don't you remember how she looked at the child's mother when we set off, when she was carrying on about the hive? She put a curse on her.'

Benito's parents arrived at the holding the following day in a one-horse carriage, together with a factor from the Servicemen's Association. 'That's the one,' he told them, and had them get down on to the road, in front of the bridge.

The whole family came out to meet them, and the old woman – the Mambrin grandmother – hugged them and said: 'I've saved you a few bits of rabbit.'

'Thanks, ma.'

They buried Benito the next morning in the cemetery at Sermoneta – on land belonging to the Caetani, because the cemetery at Littoria wasn't ready yet – after having kept silent vigil for him in the little church throughout the night. Now he was dead and buried, and all of them – and all of us too, relatives and neighbours living on that same country road, because every family went to offer their condolences – walked around with solemn expressions and long faces for a time, but shortly afterwards we had to get our noses back to the grindstone, to busy ourselves with the new demands of the Promised Land. Here we were – we'd come a long way to get here – and now we had to get on with making a new life for ourselves. We couldn't sit around on our hands, pondering on death. Benito Mambrin was under the sod. He wouldn't suffer any more. Indeed, he was in Paradise because God took in children to be his angels: 'Now he can take care of the lot of us,' my grandmother would say.

We had arrived at our holding the day before, as I've already told you, and while we could hear old Grandmother Toson shrieking: 'Take me back to Zero Branco,' from four holdings away, in stark contrast with the mute Mambrin family who were thinking about their Benitino, my grandmother had been the first to climb down from the cart and start issuing orders: 'Come on, boys, we're here now, and we're here to stay, so let's get on with it,' and she assigned everyone their battle-stations.

'Suits us,' they said, and then they all jumped to it, some unloading the stuff from the cart, others taking it inside and putting it wherever she told them to. One lorry hadn't been enough for us, we'd needed two ox-carts, drawn by those Maremma cattle, and as soon as Aunt Bissola laid eyes on them, with their great grey-white horns, she'd shrieked in horror: 'What kind of things are they, when they're at home?'

The holdings were all identical. In point of fact, the word 'holding' referred to the whole plot which had been allotted to each family of sharecroppers, and that varied from ten to fifteen or even twenty hectares, depending on its fertility and irrigation possibilities. But we immediately started using the word 'holding' to refer to the farmhouse where we lived; not to the cowshed – although it was attached to it – or to the haylofts or storerooms, but to the house. That was the holding, because on it – on the side facing the road – on one corner on the first floor there was a sign, carved with large stone lettering, which read: "O.N.C. – Holding N. 517 – Year X F.E."

O.N.C stood for *Opera Nazionale Combattenti* – the Servicemen's Association – and Year X of the Fascist Era meant 1932, ten years after the march on Rome, the beginning of a thousand-year era which was never to end. First there'd been the world before, with all its chaos and injustice, and Italy being laughed to scorn by all and sundry; now a new age was upon us, during which the name of Rome would be triumphant and impose its peace throughout the world. Or at least that was what we proudly told ourselves. The farmhouse bore the word 'Holding' in large white stone lettering – standing out smartly against the sky-blue plaster – so, from that moment onwards and for ever after, we referred to those farmhouses as 'holdings'.

Our holding stood – still stands – on the Left-Hand Parallel, the road which runs parallel to the Mussolini Canal. Or, to be more precise, at the point where it goes over Ponte Marchi, to cross first the Appian Way and then the smaller provincial road. Our land – some four hundred metres square – lay between the Left-Hand Parallel and the banks of the canal, and our two holdings stood on the road, three hundred metres one from the other. Bordering one another. We were given two because our family included two men who'd fought in the First World War, Uncle Themistocles and Uncle Pericles. Uncle Themistocles had a big family – he'd already got a brood of seven or eight – but all the rest were under the care of Uncle Pericles: father, mother, brothers, sisters-in-law, sisters and assorted 'calves'. But right from the start we'd always worked together – just as we had up north – sharing our livestock, tools and working days, and doing everything as one big family. Right from the start, though, my grandmother said to Themistocles: 'This is your holding, and all that comes with it is yours. That's only fair.'

The holdings – that is, the farmhouses – were all sky-blue. On two floors, with pitched, pantile roofs and wooden rafters, and eaves and down-spouts. Every roof had a big, round, identical chimney in prefabricated concrete. The windows had been painted green; instead of shutters, on the outside they had mosquito nets with very fine metal mesh, to stop the insects

243

getting in, with glass behind that, and, inside, internal wooden shutters painted in some light shade which, when they were closed, shut out every last chink of light.

On the ground floor, overlooking the courtyard, there was a *tirabasso* – what we'd now call a bow window, or veranda – a covered area, also with a pantile roof, all closed in with mosquito nets, with an internal system of strings and pulleys and counterweights so that the door would close automatically straight after it had been opened. Then came the real main door, with this intermediate space – this sort of veranda – serving to keep out the mosquitoes, making sure they didn't get anywhere near the inside of the house. That covered space was the furthest they could hope to go, and on the few occasions when one did manage to slip through the net, the cry 'Mosquito!' would go up and everyone would be on the warpath. The worst sin in the book – and here the worst offenders were the little ones – was to be in such a hurry to open or close the door that you caused the string to come out of the pulley. Then everyone would be on to you as though you'd committed an abomination. But mosquitoes were our number one enemy, as the people from the Servicemen's Association and our school-teachers were always dinning into us: if they bit you, you'd get malaria.

Sorry, what did you say? No, no, they weren't the ordinary mosquitoes you still have around nowadays. They were anopheles mosquitoes, a bit bigger than the ordinary kind, but they weren't born with the malaria bacillus. They were just its bearers, and they got it by sucking the blood of humans who were already suffering from the disease. Then, when they went on to bite healthy people, those people too would become infected. And there was no shortage of people with malaria in the Pontine Marshes. There was also a bit of malaria up in the Po Plain, but not like down here, here it was a veritable scourge, and there were all types of malaria, not just the more endemic or normal kind, and these other types would kill you off bit by bit with intermittent bursts of heavy fever and poisoning of the liver, or hepatitis. Your liver would gradually swell up, and you'd see lots of people – shepherds from the Ciociaria and the Abruzzi, and the herdsmen from Cisterna – with great bloated stomachs, and you'd know that their days were numbered.

Malaria was treated with quinine. Couriers from the Red Cross would come round on horseback distributing quinine tablets, which were also taken as a preventive measure. Every hamlet had its dispensary, where they 'dispensed' quinine, and where they also sold salt and tobacco, because in those days quinine, salt and tobacco were all state monopolies. Then the people who ran them also had the bright idea of selling foodstuffs, pasta, seed oil and, later, wine by the glass – they became wine-shops – and you could play a game of bowls, and even now grocer's shops are still called 'dispensaries', despite the fact that fifty years have passed since the last known case of malaria, and no one's seen a quinine tablet in half a century.

But there were also more dangerous forms of malaria – the pernicious or tertian kind – which could kill you within forty-eight hours, with sudden outbursts of raging fever of over forty-two degrees.

There was no DDT in those days, there was nothing. All you could do was rush around after the little devils with a fly-swat. At best, there were man-made bats' roosting posts – tall wooden towers with rows of round holes in them, which were put up all over the marshes while they were in the process of being drained. They'd brought bats in from all over Italy, because bats are gluttons for mosquitoes, and take them out on the wing better than any fighter plane. Web-footed F-16s. The women found them eerie – bats aren't actually all that appealing, to be frank, and if they get into your hair, that's where they stay – but as soon as they started to make their nests, of their own accord, under the eaves of our holdings and the beams in the cowsheds, people virtually put up altars to them, laid down red carpets for them, treated them better than babes in arms. The women practically brought them milk and biscuits, and if you were so much as seen outside the cowshed with a catapult – in the afternoon, when they'd be sleeping in a row in the darkest corner, upside-down – you'd be walloped worse than a mosquito. The bat is a sacred creature in the Pontine Marshes, and even now, if you've got any sense at all, you'll leave it well alone.

But bats weren't the answer to prayer in that inferno of anopheles mosquitoes. The only way to beat them was to destroy their eggs in the marshy ground before they hatched. That was the linchpin in the fateful three-part phrase 'anopheles mosquito – marshy ground – malaria', because the anopheles mosquito lays its eggs just below the surface of stagnant water, never in running water or they'd all get carried away and then it would be bye-bye little 'uns. That's where the little egg spends its whole life as a larva; then, when the time is ripe, it breaks out of its sac, rises to the surface, gives its little wings a shake and buzzes off in search of prey; and sets about biting the first human being it comes upon – whether they've got malaria or not – sucking their blood and mingling it with its own.

That was why the whole area had to be drained in the first place – every swamp, every pool, every last puddle had to go. What was needed was canals. What was needed was flowing water, not still water – you couldn't leave out a glass with even a drop of water in it. When we arrived, it was a mortal sin to leave a bucket or a basin with a bit of water in it outside overnight. They'd send you packing – the association was all eyes, the factors would be stalking around at all hours of the day and night, ours even expected us to sweep out the drainage canals that ran beside the road – back where you came from, with your whole family. Forget all that blather about ecocide, according to which the marsh is an ecosystem which must be protected at all costs. Were we supposed to start protecting mosquitoes, and malaria?

I'm sorry, what's that you said? Buzzards and other migratory birds will stop coming here? To hell with buzzards, and with you too, if you don't mind my saying so. Do buzzards have a greater right to life than I do, all of a sudden? I'd like to see you in our place, there in the Pontine Marshes, along with malaria. Why don't you rear mosquitoes in your own backyard?

At all events, it wasn't as if the marshes were drained in the course of a single day. It took ten years for everywhere to be drained and organized, from Cisterna to Terracina and from the hills to the sea. We drained the land a bit at a time, and we went about it at a fair lick. And while sharecroppers had already settled in the holdings on the reclaimed areas, there was still marshland at a lower level, and there was always the danger that the workmen digging out the new canals might die of malaria because of the mosquitoes which were still alive and kicking in the remaining swamps. No one knows with any certainty how many people died of malaria during the whole undertaking, and even less how many – having been infected with malaria down here in the south – went home to die in Tuscany, for instance, where they had started from, or indeed anywhere else in Italy for that matter.

Between them, the Servicemen's Association and the

consortium employed over a hundred and fifty thousand men, and no fewer than ten percent of them – fifteen or twenty thousand – must have died of malaria. They worked in relays and then rushed off home with their paltry earnings in their pockets, their fates in the hands of the Almighty. Whereas those who were to die so suddenly of tertian fever, after having spent the morning shivering on their beds with raging fevers, would then be carted off on a stretcher to hospital in Velletri, so that no one could say that anyone had ever died of malaria in the marshes. Then they'd write 'Meningitis' or 'Heart attack' on the death certificate, because the Fascist Party had 'wiped out malaria'. But what kind of wiping out was that, if people carried on dying of it?

So off they went to die in Velletri, while down here on the marshes the local Fascist Headquarters would spread the swampy land with layers of carbide mixed with sand and dust from the roads. This mixture would float on the surface for a time, and the anopheles mosquito couldn't get through it when it tried to lay its eggs – something it found extremely galling – because the eggs would dry out in the dust, and then it would be bye-bye little 'uns. But no one was ever going to wipe out malaria with a bit of road dust. It wasn't much of a weapon, it worked for a day or two, and that was all. In America they used oil. And that did work. But they had oil by the barrel-load, whereas we didn't, we didn't even have enough to light our lamps, let alone to pour on to a pond. So we fought back against mosquitoes and malaria with dust from the roads, man-made roosting posts and a bit of 'flit' – a sort of insecticide which we'd spray with a hand pump with a little tin of the stuff attached to the end of it; but that turned out to be quite a 'pick-me-up' for the mosquitoes, they were gluttons for it, it filled them out a treat – and above all flypapers, which we'd hang from the ceiling and which would soon be black with insects. And of course wire fly-swats and slippers, with which we'd crush the brutes against the wall whenever we happened to spot them.

Such were the weapons in the fight against malaria in the Pontine Marshes – until the coming of the Second World War, and the Americans. And then malaria really did take a thrashing. If, as is so often said, the Americans brought freedom and democracy to the rest of Italy, what they brought us – who hadn't had so much as a whiff of freedom even before Fascism, rather the reverse – was above all DDT. It was they who'd invented it, and they hadn't yet tried it out on a large scale. So, when they pitched up in Italy, they said: 'Let's give it a try there!' They loaded a pair of their Dakotas up with all these drums of DDT and flew up and down the Pontine Marshes until they'd drenched the place with the stuff. It worked – 'Gee, did it ever work!' as some general or other must have said to Truman – and there wasn't an anopheles mosquito to be had for love or money in all Latium, nor a malaria sufferer either, not for all the tea in China. So – after checking that it hadn't done any harm to us humans, because DDT may be as non-biodegradable as you like, but it didn't have any negative effects on humans; who knows, perhaps the reverse was true – the Americans then had no qualms about going on to use it to disinfect those marshes of their own: 'Tested in the Pontine Marshes,' as they said.

Now the use of DDT is banned throughout the world. Because it's not biodegradable. It lingers on in the food chain and never dissolves. It's even been found in the adipose tissue of seals at the North Pole. So then they said: 'That's it, we can't use DDT any more.' But it saved us from malaria and, were it not for DDT, there wouldn't now be five hundred thousand

249

of us living on this land. It would still be a marshy, malaria-ridden desert, and at some point or other we'd all have had to go back to where we'd come from, or rather been kicked out of. Now I'm sorry about the seals at the North Pole – after all, everything is worthy of respect, including seals – but, if you don't mind my saying so, isn't it better for a seal to die at the North Pole than for me or my children to die here?

Anyway, each holding was entered over a little bridge spanning the ditch at the side of the road – each with its own parapet and little walls in living stone, cemented over, on which we all used to sit in a row on summer evenings, chatting – leading into the courtyard, or threshing-floor.

Then came the holding proper – the farmhouse. Immediately beyond the anti-mosquito veranda-like space were two small flights of stairs, the entrance door, the entrance hall itself and the stairwell with the stairs to the upper floor. The small flights of stairs were made of a mixture of crushed cement and marble – as was the kitchen sink – and at first they were quite light in colour, but time, and use, and constant scouring with water, mixed with soap and ashes, caused them to turn dark-grey, with the pieces of crushed stone and marble winking like diamonds. Like granite from the Dolomites.

To the left, immediately beyond the entrance, was the door to the kitchen, which was always open. The kitchen was a huge room – it had to be, to house that brood – with the range at the far end. This was the heart of the holding, where everybody ate, some sitting, some standing – and talked, when there were serious matters to discuss. Two windows were set into one of the long sides, looking out on to the threshing-floor and the road, while on the other long side were the doors into the stable where the horse would have been, and the small storeroom where we kept the grain.

In fact, though, we no longer had a horse when we were here – the Zorzi Vila had taken our last one – and my grandfather couldn't quite resign himself to the fact. Every so often he would say: 'How can we go on like this? There's never been a Peruzzi on God's earth who hasn't had a horse between his legs.'

'If that's how you feel, then you can go and talk to the Zorzi Vila about it, and damn the lot of you,' my grandmother would say in order to put paid to any such lofty ideas. Here all we ever had was mules and donkeys, for pulling carts and gigs, or harrows and mowers, sometimes even ploughs. And they always slept in the cowshed with the other animals – cheek by jowl with the cows – while we smartened up the little stable as best we could with a bed and a bedside table and used it as sleeping accommodation for a member of the family, and we did the same with the storeroom. On summer afternoons – when there was still a great pile of threshed corn lying around – my cousins and I would sleep directly on that sea of grain, and there's no better bed in all the world, I can assure you. It's stretched out on such a bed, when my time comes, that I would like to die.

To the side of the holding – just beyond the large round portico where we kept the carts – was the one-storey cowshed, which had concrete mangers, hay-racks, litter, a central corridor and transom windows. On the upper floor of the holding – which was larger than the ground floor, because it also included the roofing of the portico – there were four large bedrooms and one smaller one. Each bedroom had a painted iron wash-stand, with a basin on a shelf, a mirror, little containers for the soap and a jug and chamber pot. That was where you washed yourself, in the basin, and by it was a bucket where you could put the dirty water when you didn't just throw it out of the window – and if you did that, you'd shout 'Watch out,' in case someone happened to be going by, only it wasn't a perfect system, because the water would almost always arrive before the warning, and you'd be advised to take yourself off to a certain very hot place, and fast. The smaller bedroom was originally intended to be a bathroom. But we always had our baths, on Saturdays – there was no escaping it, once we were down here you had to have at least one bath a week, otherwise my grandmother would skin you alive – in the wooden tub in the middle of the threshing-floor, when it was fine, or in the kitchen, if it was raining. And in that bathroom we put beds, a bedside table, a chamber pot and a washstand, so that it too could house one or two of our brood.

Our holding was brand new, and it had a lot of bedrooms. The walls still smelled of whitewash and the doors of paint, and we'd never seen such a beautiful and spacious building in our lives. But there were an awful lot of us – too many, as I've said – and there was no such thing as too much space. Whenever you moved, you bumped into someone. In those days, people were certainly more comfortable in their coffins than in their homes, along with all those relatives. My grandfather – when he wanted a bit of peace and quiet – would go and smoke a cigar along with the animals.

In front of the farmhouse – on the threshing-floor – there was a round brick-faced well. Each holding had one, dug by hand, five or six metres deep and one metre wide. On the holdings on the quaternary dune – where the soil was drier, and the water table deeper – the wells might even be as much as thirty metres deep, and they were dug out with percussive drills, and held less water, and when they ran dry they would

252

take longer to refill, so every holding had a wind pump, a creaking structure with a paddle wheel which would gradually draw up the water and refill the tank. But around our parts – in Piscinara generally and on our own holding in particular – all you had to do was to dig a metre-deep hole in the evening, and by the morning you'd find it full of water. Because there was a spring. The veins of the water table were almost on the surface, so you had as much water as you wanted. And that was why our land – the Promised Land, indeed – was so productive, and the wells never ran dry.

To draw the water, though, all we had was a hand pump – or a bucket – because there was no electricity in the countryside in the Pontine Marshes in 1932. The only places with electric power – and telegraph offices and telephones and sewers – were the villages and towns, and there people also had inside lavatories and electric lighting. But on the holdings belonging to the Servicemen's Association you used oil lamps or carbide lamps, and there was an iron pump for the well, too, in the form of a bound sheaf, with a beautifully-shaped lever, which made a glugging sound when you used it, and the water fell into the drinking trough beside it, which was a square basin made of stone and waterproof cement. This drinking trough was the centre of our lives, there was always someone there, using the pump or doing some other chore. But my uncles wouldn't allow you to wash there, and they'd be furious if they caught you at it. First you had to pump the water into your bucket, and then you had to go off somewhere else to wash. And woe betide you if you used or dirtied the water in the drinking trough, which, according to them, always had to be full, and the water spotless. And every day there'd be trouble finding someone to refill it – it would be 'glug glug,' until your arms were numb – even though all the other chores were carefully allotted, and you always knew exactly who would be doing what. My grandmother would assign you your lot practically the moment you were born – 'You'll be doing this, and you'll be doing that' – and the drinking trough was the boys' responsibility. But every day off they'd all run, and every day there'd be new problems, particularly if – when it was time to water the cattle – my uncles found even so much as a speck of dirt in the water, an oily patch, any foreign body at all. They'd have you take out the bung from underneath it and empty the whole thing out – more glugging – lashing out at your legs the while: 'That water has to be absolutely clean for the animals,' they'd bellow.

Then, two by two, they'd loosen the chains that bound the cows to the mangers, and they'd come lumbering out of the cowshed on to the cobbled area in front, all in their own good time, delivering the odd cowpat here and there; then they'd turn left, past the corner of the house, and then, twenty metres on, they'd lower their heads into the drinking trough and drink. Of course someone would be standing on the path with a pitchfork at the ready, in case they took it into their heads to amble around the fields. Uncle Iseo would be there at the trough, whistling, and they would drink and drink, stocking up till the next day. Nowadays all cowsheds have drinking troughs at the mangers, and a cow can have a drink whenever the fancy takes her. In those days, though, they drank once a day, and then they drank their fill; and the more lovingly Uncle Iseo whistled, the more they responded by carrying on drinking. No one ever loved animals like my Uncle Iseo. Can you imagine anyone whistling for cows nowadays, as they stand at their automatic drinking trough?

We on the other hand drank from a pail, in the kitchen, using an iron or aluminium ladle. We didn't have automatic taps either, the kind you just turn and out comes the water. You had to work the pump by hand – yet more glugglng – and the water would flow into the pail you'd attached to the hook on the pump. Then you'd take it into the house, and there it stayed – in the pail, in the sink – next to the window. The ladle – which was rectangular in shape – hung from a nail in the wall. If you were thirsty you'd take the ladle, dip it in the water and drink it, right there where you stood. Then you'd hang the ladle up again, and when the water had got too warm, or the bucket was empty, my grandmother would order the first child who came her way to fill it up again at the pump. The ladle – like all the other pots and pans – would be washed twice a day, at the drinking trough if the weather was good, or in the sink, with water from that same bucket; and, in her view, the less water and buckets you got through, the better. If you wanted water that was really cold, and fresh, you'd go to the well, pump it up – glug – and drink it on the spot.

What did you say? Surely it wasn't very hygienic all drinking from the same ladle without even rinsing it?

I know, but that was how it was. We weren't at the Grand Hotel. In those days, pots and pans were washed with water, soap and ashes. Not much soap, because Tide and Ola hadn't yet come on to the scene, and it was home-made soap at that, made by boiling up fat and animal bones. And not much water, because the buckets were heavy and you washed all the pots and pans with the same water. That's how it was. Why don't you have a stab at draining the Pontine Marshes next time round?

Behind the house – some thirty or forty metres off – was the lavatory, or latrine, a sort of sentry-box built out of brick, a solid structure with a base of just over one square metre, a couple of metres high, with a pitched roof and pantiles, once again. When we first arrived – and she hadn't even got down from the cart, she still had one foot in the air, poised to jump down – my Aunt Bissola shrieked out to all and sundry that she must be the one who christened it: 'Me first! I've got to have the first go,' and off she streaked behind the holding. Back on the threshing-floor, all radiant, she announced: 'Wonderful, you can shit really nicely there.'

So the lavatory was some way from the house, and the Americans – the New Deal ones, not the ones after the war, with the DDT – said that this was what they called a 'privy', and they had them too, in the countryside around their way, some way off from their houses like you see nowadays in Westerns, like in *The Unforgiven*, and when they have to kill a man they wait for him outside it. It was Rossoni who'd brought them to our house – 'Look, Peruzzi, I'm bringing along some of our American Comrades' – when they'd been on a round of visits. They were old friends of his, from the old Socialist days, and now they too had become Fascists – well, New Deal Fascists. Indeed, Rossoni and the Duce always talked about 'Comrade Roosevelt' to each other, because after the crash of 1929, with him – Roosevelt – rising to power, from 1932 onwards America too was turning Fascist. Up to that point, state interference in the economy had been regarded as sacrilege – it still is – because that was the domain of the private capitalist. But the 1929 crisis was bigger than any of them – they had to get out of it pronto – so he too gagged parliament, rushed out some emergency laws, nationalized things all over the show and started reclaiming marshes, just like us, Soviet Russia and Nazi Germany. And it was the American papers – *The New York Times* in 1933, not just the Duce and Rossoni – who declared: 'This is Fascism, if not National Socialism.' 'If that's the case, I'm proud of it,' said Roosevelt, and went right

256

ahead. He was thick as thieves with us: 'Stalin, Mussolini and I are blood brothers,' he'd say, even in public, and he'd send his experts here – to the Pontine Marshes – to see how the New Deal was done. Later, though, things turned sour – rather as they had for Alceste De Ambris – and it was the parting of the ways: we became evil incarnate and Roosevelt was the champion of democracy. Talk about the world turned upside down. Who would ever have believed it, straight out of *The New York Times'* building in 1933? 'Some people just have it made,' as that old friend of my Uncle Pericles used to say.

Anyway, on that occasion at one point these Americans started saying: 'That's the privy,' and we didn't know what they were talking about. But, as you know, America was Rossoni's second home, so he piped up: 'The privy's the bog,' and from that moment onwards we too started calling it the 'privy', and we still do, even if there aren't any 'privies' any more, but inside lavatories. Once, when we had a visitor – I can't remember who it was, perhaps the doctor, or the priest – Aunt Bissola felt the call of nature and thought she would dignify her absence by announcing to the assembled company: 'I'm going to the privy.'

'You're going where?' everyone asked.

'To the privy.'

'Where?'

'To have a shit!' she screeched in exasperation.

And from that moment on – at first by way of a joke, and then in earnest – for the Peruzzi the bog was always the privy, and it stood on its own, detached from the farmhouse, as was the custom in the countryside. Not just in the Pontine Marshes, either. All over the world. For reasons of hygiene. There was no running water in the houses – there was no electricity – so the refuse couldn't be disposed of with pipes or sewers.

The only solution was cesspits – dug out directly under the latrine – with the sewage emptied out once or twice a year. So it obviously wasn't a good idea for people to live permanently right above their cesspits – to eat and sleep there, I mean. So the cesspit would be dug some way from the house, even if in the poorer and more backward areas – in the huts in the north, for instance – there were no privies, or latrines, or cesspits either, and people would just go off into the fields. On our holding it was near the dungheap, and when we first arrived it was all new and neat and clean, a concrete container which we started filling up with the solid refuse from the cowshed. As time went by, the straw from the litter, mixed with dung, would ferment and form a single whole, and the liquids would drain off, sink to the bottom and be carried away to the cesspit. The solid manure – sheer gold to the farmer, as I've said – would stay on in the dungheap, to be spread over the fields once or twice a year. The liquids, on the other hand – the human waste from the privy and the cow piss from the cowshed, known as urea, another form of farmer's gold – would go into the cesspit. When it was full, it would be emptied with a hand pump, the piss would be put into barrels and we'd parade through the fields and spread it over them like so much holy water. Nothing was wasted in the Pontine Marshes: 'Not even your own piss,' as my Uncle Iseo used to say.

So, the privy stood above the cesspit, some forty metres away from the farmhouse, because it had to be no less than sixty metres from the other well, the one on the threshing-floor, in the front courtyard, the one which provided water for washing, drinking and cooking, for men and animals alike. On almost all the holdings in the Pontine Marshes – not just on ours – the privy stood exactly sixty metres from the other well, not a metre less and not a metre more. Not a metre less, because that was the minimum distance ensuring that leaks from the cesspit would not pollute the water table which provided the clean water. But not a metre more, either, because the greater the distance, the more effort was required to carry the buckets of water.

Not that we made much use of water in the privy, because the buckets weighed so much. Our privy consisted of a pan without a seat, in the so-called 'Turkish-style'. You'd go there, squat down, do your business and go off again. You'd wipe yourself with a tuft of grass or a vine-leaf – not a fig-leaf, they're scratchy – or a bit of newspaper, when you could find one. As a child, I remember my older girl-cousins' photo-novels: *Bolero*, and *Grand Hotel*. They were printed on stiff paper, and it hurt. But we didn't know what we were missing – the first time I ever laid eyes on lavatory paper was in 1960. If by some stroke of luck the nearby bucket was full, you threw a bit of water into the pan to clean it and get rid of the refuse. If it was empty, too bad: you'd just leave it at that and to hell with the next-comer. Who'd be mad enough to go all the way to the well, load himself up with a heavy bucket when no one had asked him to, and struggle back with it to the privy, sixty metres off? Thinking of the next occupant, who'd find a nice bucket of clean water, thanks to you, and set about rinsing and re-rinsing and generally carrying on like Lady Muck? No thanks, he could get the bucket himself.

So, carrying buckets of water to the privy was always one of the most hated duties in the division of labour established by my grandmother within our so-called patriarchal family, and hence the most neglected. In theory it was the boys who were responsible, which meant that the bucket was almost always empty. But at least once a week – there was no getting out of it – a series of heavy thwacks on the back

259

with a kitchen spoon from my grandmother would send one of the girls scurrying off to give the place a thorough clean: buckets galore, transported by one of the menfolk in the big wheelbarrow from the cowshed, and then cresol and bleach, even on the walls. Clean as a new pin. But the next day it would be as filthy as ever. As I've said, there were an awful lot of us. What with one thing and another, it doesn't take much to mess up a privy.

What's that you said? Did we wash ourselves down there after we'd done our business? No we did not, what kind of talk is that? The bidet arrived in Italy in 1960 – as you may know, it still hasn't made it to America – and you expect us to have been using bidets during the draining of the Pontine Marshes? Can you imagine us saying: 'Hang on a minute', all mud-bespattered as we were from digging out the Mussolini Canal with our shovels and spades: 'Hang on a minute, I'm just going to use the bidet.'

Anyway, there in the Pontine Marshes it wasn't until after 1960, when affluence and electricity were within everybody's grasp, even ours, that the privy, or the bog, call it what you will, came into our houses – into any house, whether in the town or in the depths of the countryside. And then we did have an endless supply of water, because by now there were electric pumps and tanks and pipes to carry off our refuse, and there was no more need for any traipsing back and forth with heavy buckets. And ever since we'd met those New Deal Americans, the whole Peruzzi family had always referred to the place as the privy. All except one, that is: after that first occasion, Aunt Bissola never called it the privy again. My aunt was extremely prickly, you have no idea. As quick to strike as any snake, and she never uttered the word privy again in her whole life, to avoid being made fun of; and even quite recently, at her first grandchild's wedding, during the meal in the restaurant – as you know, around here wedding breakfasts go on for ever, even if we're not as famished now as we were then, when you'd eat your fill only at Easter and Christmas, and at weddings – she suddenly got up from the table, as people do between the twentieth course and the twenty-first. But she's got arthritis in her legs, and when she's been sitting for a time she has trouble getting up, and she staggers a bit at first. The bride noticed what was happening, and was somewhat concerned – she was an American cultural anthropologist, as it happened, who was almost more enamoured of the grandmother than of the grandson – and she said to the groom, Aunt Bissola's favourite: 'Look at your grandmother, poor old thing! See if she needs any help.'

'Grandma,' her grandson boomed out, the picture of consideration: 'Where are you off to then?'

'To have a shit,' Aunt Bissola thundered back, there in the middle of the restaurant, but then – sensing she'd struck quite the wrong note, and hoping somehow to put things to rights – she promptly added: 'Now go and have a shit yourself, and take that cow of an American wife of yours along with you!'

The bread oven was on the other side of the house – on the short side, facing the stable. There's someone called Gadda, who claims that no man-made heat engine is more absurd and irrational and wasteful than the so-called hearth or fireplace. He says that the ratio between the calories consumed and those which actually serve any purpose, whether for heating a room or for boiling a kettle, is quite ridiculous. Almost all the calories produced fly straight up the chimney and out into the open air. Hardly any of them do what you want them to. With their ovens, on the other hand, the Servicemen's Association had come up with a heat engine of the greatest possible efficiency

– albeit still only in relation to that woefully inadequate model already mentioned by Gadda – namely the bread oven, which was used once a week, or even every two weeks.

My grandmother would start work the evening before – and all the other women would be at work beside her, kneading and stirring – until the kitchen was full of hunks of raw dough, set out to rise. And the men would stack the wood. Then, the next morning, they'd light the oven and bake bread throughout the morning. After they'd finished with the loaves, they also cooked a bit of pizza, and biscuits and sweet things for us children. Then they'd put the lot into the chest where the bread was kept, and for the first few days it would be all fresh and crunchy. By the end it was hard as nails, but you'd eat it anyway, and carry on doing so until the cupboard was bare. It wasn't only Gadda who knew that that heat engine was wasteful; my grandmother knew it too, and she used it as little as possible. Had you been able to keep bread for years, my grandmother would have had us eating it years after it had been baked.

Anyway, the oven was painted sky-blue, like the house, and had the regulation pitched pantiled roof, with another flat roof infront of it, so that you could do your baking and your other chores come rain or shine. On top of the oven – to make use of the heat – there was a dovecote, and underneath it there was a place for storing wood and kindling, so that it would dry out and burn better. Behind it – also to make the best possible use of the heat – were the hen run and the pigsty. That way, everyone was in the warm and dry.

What did you say? It doesn't strike you as particularly hygienic to have the pigs and chickens in the place where you bake the bread?

Well, firstly, they were behind the oven, not actually in contact with it. And secondly, heat is heat, and you have to make the most of what you've got. Thirdly and most important, though, as the hen run began to fill up – not just with hens, but with turkeys, geese, ducks, peacocks and guinea fowl as well, and in such quantities that you'd have had trouble fitting them into that great pen at Doganella – we moved it, and built a whole series of new enclosures. We did the same for the pigs, because they too had started to multiply. We had a sow which produced piglets by the cartload, and each year, in November, there'd be a massacre worse than the 1915–18 War, with all my uncles with their knives between their teeth, killing pigs left right and centre, and making strings of *cotechino* and salami and other sausages, and hanging them up from every available hook on the ceiling to drain and dry.

Every room was full of them – we had to put them somewhere, there were an awful lot of us and we needed an awful lot of sausages to keep us going – and throughout November and December, and into January and February, too, all our ceilings were bristling with sausages, and sometimes at night, when you were asleep, you'd feel a drop of fat falling on to your face. And the place would be abuzz with flies, dodging the strips of flypaper we'd hang up between the sausages like scarecrows to keep them off. But don't imagine that we gorged ourselves on fancy meats to our hearts' content. There were an awful lot of us, as I've said, and however many chickens and pigs we exterminated, there were always more of us than of them, there was always a shortfall, and my grandmother would measure everything out with her tape measure, and whenever she cooked a salami or a *cotechino*, which was once or twice a week, one single one had to do for the lot of us. You'd get one slice per head, just enough to wave over your polenta to lend it a bit of flavour. But even with my grandmother's skinflint reckoning – as she calculated the minimum amount of protein required to keep us alive – come April-May the ceilings would be bare. All that remained was the strips of flypaper so expertly avoided by the flies, and the hooks, of course, poor empty iron barbs, stranded in the great white expanse of ceiling, without a single salami or *cotechino* to appease our raging hunger.

Anyway, that should give you an idea of what our holding was like. The Servicemen's Association had three thousand and fifty of them built in the Pontine Marshes, and filled them up with thirty thousand five hundred other unfortunates like ourselves, from Northern Italy, swept up to be transplanted to the south in a round-up of Biblical proportions; to become, at long last, the owners of the land we worked.

They brought us down here on their *Mayflower*, then loaded family after family on to lorries and carts with all our household goods. Then they unloaded us, one by one, into buildings which were so brand new that the whitewash was still damp, and – this beggars belief – we found that the fields had not only already been divided up, headland by headland, with the right incline, what's more, higher in the middle and lower at the sides, with drainage ditches already in place, but that they'd actually had them ploughed up by Fowlers and Favole, standing to either side of the whole length of the field, with cables attached to a winch, taking it in turns to pull a gigantic plough which broke up the earth, up to a metre deep.

And every one of those thirty thousand say that the first thing they did – after they'd unloaded their household goods, and peered into every nook and cranny of their houses, and arranged the furniture – was to rush from one farmhouse to another to see how all the other Pilgrim Fathers – whose exodus they'd shared on those troop trains, and whose lives and labours would be inextricably intertwined with their own from that day on – had arranged their own.

The holdings were arranged in pairs, just off the road – one this side, one that – every two hundred and fifty metres, on average. So that within a radius of just five hundred metres there would be at least six families, and not families like you get today – as I've already told you – but with between fifteen and twenty members each. An anthill, compared with what it had been before – even if, almost the moment she'd left Littoria, amidst the stream of carts and lorries which were unloading us one by one on the Left-Hand Parallel, old Grandmother Toson had been screaming: 'It's a desert here' – without a tree anywhere in sight for kilometres on end. Just the water tank and the scattering of houses that made up Sessano on one side, and the big building at Borgo Carso on the other, and the building site with the tower at Littoria in the background. And little eucalyptus trees, not even a metre high, on both sides of the road. We didn't even know what they were. 'What are they?' we all asked each other.

'Those'll be trees,' my Uncle Adelchi had rightly stated from where he was seated on the cart. He'd got his primary leaving certificate during his army service, and knew more than the rest of us.

'Eucalyptus,' said the supervisor from the association, who was sitting in front of him on the box, turning round as he did so.

'What?' said Uncle Adelchi.

'Eucalyptus trees.'

'Ah,' my uncle said approvingly, then turned round to face the others on the cart, confirming, once and for all, that they were: 'Cliptas. Cliptas is what they're called.'

'Ah,' chorused the rest of the Peruzzi clan. 'Cliptas!'

Not only did we find ourselves presented with ploughed and harrowed fields, and freshly whitewashed holdings, but – in the fireplaces inside them, on the end wall in the kitchen – we also found piles of ready-chopped wood, just waiting to be used. There were even matches, in boxes, on the shelf on the chimney piece. All you had to do was open the box, strike the match and put the copper pot on to the fire. The moment they arrived – thanks to the Fascist Party, and the Servicemen's Association too, it must be said – even before the men had begun to unload the household goods, all our grandmothers, my own included, were immediately able to light the fire and give life to the house. Fire was sacred, it was what they called 'Vestal', as we knew from the song:

> *Like Vestal fire, which from the temple blazes,*
> *Youth, too, with wings and flames, goes on its way.*
> *Like burning torches on our tombs and altars,*
> *We are the lifeblood of the dawning day.*
>
> *Our lives for you we gladly offer up,*
> *Duce, our oaths will never be foresworn.*
> *Our swords we'll bare at your august command.*
> *Rugged, if young, for you we are reborn.*
>
> *Weapons and flags from old heroic days,*
> *For Italy, for you, we'll wield – and sing your praise.*

We too felt the blood of the ancient heroes coursing through our veins as we began the conquest of the Promised Land: 'Here we shall build the Garden of Eden, brimming with fruit and flowers. Our name will be known throughout the world.

266

We shall tame the waters and every force of nature. Milk and honey will run in our canals, and the tower we see on the horizon, already rising skyward, will be our ivory tower. *Turris Eburnea*. From its top, we shall touch the sky'.

On that fire – and in that copper pot – my grandmother cooked us the first great lunchtime family polenta. This was the start of a new life for the Peruzzi clan, in the big kitchen of holding 517 on the Mussolini Canal, and we ate standing up, because we hadn't yet unpacked the chairs, just the big table, which we'd put in the middle of the room, and the polenta on it. And everyone took a bit, and ate, and laughed, though once in a while someone would say: 'Poor little Benito Mambrin, God rest his soul.'

At nightfall – about six or seven o'clock, after we'd eaten by the feeble light of an oil lamp, and the women and children were already starting to yawn – we saw Uncle Adelchi coming down the stairs, his hair all glistening with brilliantine: 'I'm off to see the bright lights of Littoria.'

'Steady on there, we're coming too!' said Uncle Pericles and Uncle Iseo, quick as a flash, while their wives gave them a nasty look.

'Well, I'm off. You can catch up with me.'

My grandmother gestured towards Armida, as though to say: 'Let him go,' and Uncle Pericles and Uncle Iseo positively flew upstairs. Then my Uncle Turati and the other male members of the family followed suit: 'We're coming too.'

'Stay where you are, boys,' bellowed my grandmother, with a face of thunder. 'We've got work to do, damn you. You can go tomorrow, or the next day. Right now, no one is going anywhere,' and everyone sat down again. Even Uncle Pericles and Uncle Iseo stopped in their tracks, crestfallen, and she looked daggers at them, but then said: 'All right then, off you go,' and off they shot, picking up the bicycles they'd just put down.

'I'm just going out to smoke a cigar on the bridge out on the road,' said my grandfather.

The road too was brand new, a smooth layer of white dust, and a bicycle would skim along it effortlessly – noiselessly, with just a faint whirring sound as the wind whipped through the spokes – and you didn't even need to pedal. I don't know whether you have any idea what roads used to be like. Nowadays the foundations are dug out with mechanised earth movers. Then they lay layers of *pozzolana*, mixed with crushed limestone, using steamrollers, then ballast, and then the bitumen surface – as smooth as smooth, and almost completely level – laid with those great big automatic machines, so that when you're driving along in the rain the water doesn't have anywhere to go, it just stays put, and the moment you brake you start to skid, and go off the road, and die. Or at the very least ram into the car in front.

Once, roads were built by hand. They dug out the foundations until they came to something solid, like you do with houses. Obviously, if the land in question was low-lying and the steady incline of the road had to be higher, then they'd bring in backfill, as it's called, to raise it to the right level, and off they'd go.

What did you say? What's a steady incline? Well, it's just what you'd expect, a stretch of road with a steady incline, or gradient. The land over which a road runs – or a railway, come to that, because a railway is a sort of road, except that it's got rails on it, hence its name – is never completely flat, it's always got rises and dips and hollows, even on a plain. First of all, the engineer traces the road's route out on a map. Then he makes a survey of it – a cross-section – showing the lie of the land at every point, with all its ups and downs, and the height above sea level. When that's been done, he draws a nice straight line from one place to another, and that's the steady incline. All the ground that lies above it will have to be dug out and removed, and all the land that lies below it will have to be filled in with earth or backfill. That's the whole secret: you map out these steady incline lines, you link them up according to the changes in gradient, curves and straight stretches, and there's your road.

But in the Pontine Marshes you can see this steady incline business best on the coastal strip, on the Litoranea, the coast road which runs from Sabotino to Sabaudia, which is sometimes as much as five or six metres above the surrounding countryside, because it's all hollows and ditches and swamps and pools round there, and they had to bring in goodness knows how many wagonloads of earth and ballast and build the road well above the rest. In fact, they had to do that with all the roads round here, so that they wouldn't flood; but you can see this at its clearest on the coast road.

Roads, or rather streets, are so-called because even in Roman times they were made from strata, that is, layers of stones, big ones at the bottom, then gradually smaller and smaller, to fill in the interstices, with the top layer paved with great slabs of stone, or with cement. The roads in the Pontine Marshes have macadam surfaces, so-called after the Scottish engineer McAdam who invented the system at the beginning of the nineteenth century. First you have to dig down till you hit solid rock, otherwise – what with the weight of its own materials, and the passing traffic – the road will sink and buckle. Then you lay the foundations – maybe tossing in a coin or two for good luck, otherwise people will be dying like flies – with a careful arrangement of big stones. Then comes another layer of medium-sized stones, then a layer of smaller ones – rammed into place by hand, using big tampers – and any amount of pit sand and gravel. Layers of coarse white sand, shovelled out of wheelbarrows, tamped down with rollers and generously watered – no need to stint on this, there was plenty of water, and indeed the whole system is known as 'water macadam' – because the water sends the sand down into the lower layers, filling up all the gaps between one stone and another, and between the layers, causing the whole thing to become one compact whole. The outcome was the so-called 'dirt roads' that used to run all over Italy, and this was how they made them in the Pontine Marshes.

If on the other hand you want an asphalt road, which makes driving easier, and sends up less dust, then you lay a layer of asphalt over the sand and gravel. When I was little, this was still done by hand. There'd be a boiler, mounted on wheels and linked up to a steam-roller, which melted the blocks of asphalt, and the asphalter – who'd be all swathed in bits of cloth, and aprons, and high boots, and spattered black with boiling asphalt – would train the rose at the end of his long hose on to the layer of sand and gravel which had already been compacted by rollers and rammers. He'd spray the road ahead of him with a swaying motion – first one side, then the other – and the other workmen who followed him would take the metal from the wheelbarrows and spread it over the black layer of asphalt with their shovels. And as this layer became white – because of the metal – the asphalter would go over it, and it would be black again; and this zebra-like process would be repeated for quite some time. The air was hot as hell – they'd all be sweating like pigs – and there was a strong smell of asphalt which you might find unpleasant, but which those who were used to it actually liked.

There was a constant hustle and bustle of men with

wheelbarrows – you'd load yours up with metal, take it to the asphalt container, wait for another workman to empty it, shovel it down on to the asphalt, then you'd run back to refill your wheelbarrow – and another whole crowd of men with shovels, not to mention the man bringing the cold blocks of solid asphalt and the man with the petrol for the rammer, and the men between the shafts of the asphalt container, for when they needed to move it forwards. Meanwhile the rammer itself would trundle backwards and forwards, pressing the metal down into the asphalt, so that when it cooled every bit of metal would be glued to every other bit, forming one single body, and every so often the asphalter would pause – he really was a poor devil, making all the other poor devils around those parts seem almost lucky in comparison – and fumble through layers of protective aprons, to fish a big asphalt-blackened handkerchief out of his pocket and mop his brow, and then set off again.

Almost all the asphalters were blind in one eye. Sooner or later, a spurt of boiling asphalt would always manage to hit the spot. One who still had both his eyes was Vullo, and he worked as an asphalter all the year round except at Christmas. I remember him cycling to my Uncle Benassi's for the Christmas novena with his bagpipes lying all half-deflated on the crossbar, and everyone would gather round the crib, grown-ups and children alike, and they'd all be standing, except for Vullo, who'd be sitting on a chair and pumping air into his wheezy bagpipes until at last they would be full, and firm, and then out would come the dirges of his native Abruzzi. He knew all of us children by name, and would greet each one of us – more of us by the year – and talk to us all there in front of the crib, or as he was coming into the house with his bagpipes half deflated, and he'd pat us on the head. He'd be back with more dirges on

Twelfth Night, when the Three Kings came, and then my Aunt Santapace and my Uncle Adelchi would pay him, and the next day he'd go back to his asphalting. But if you happened to meet him on the road, among all those shovels and wheelbarrows, clutching the handle of his steaming asphalt-container and all dripping with asphalt himself, and sweating like a pig, and you started shouting: '*Vullo! Vullo!*' he'd never answer you. Indeed, perhaps he hadn't even recognized you, just as his own beloved Abruzzi sheep might not have recognized him, all asphalt-black, among all those shovels and wheelbarrows.

When I was little, though, the dirt roads in the Pontine Marshes weren't what they had been. There'd been a war, and bombs, and those roads had been neglected. A road needs maintenance like a man needs bread, it's a living organism, people use it, lorries and carts and cars grind over it. It suffers wear and tear. What with all that use, it gets worn out. And then it's in the open, poor old thing, exposed to the elements: the cold, the rain, the sun, the frost. Every component, every molecule is forced constantly to expand and contract. With frost, the molecules of water which have got into the interstices will freeze and then expand, with the ice cutting into the fibres of the surrounding materials. But when the ice melts again and runs off, those surrounding materials are no longer as compact as they were before, they've been fatally weakened and don't really fill up all those spaces as they should, so the bonds holding the whole structure together are loosened and everything starts to crumble and fall apart, and that's the beginning of the end. Things which have been built need maintenance and restoration – whether they're houses or roads or indeed emotions – they need to be shored up against wear and tear and erosion by wind and weather, otherwise they fall apart. When I was little, when you were

272

cycling along our Left-Hand Parallel, by the Mussolini Canal, you had to be careful where you rode, that is, you had to avoid the middle, because by now that part of the road was all big stones. It wasn't too good for carts, either, but they'd jolt along somehow, whereas for bicycles it was a no-go area. And such little metal and coarse sand as still remained was now piled up at the sides, and had been trampled down into a sort of channel, which had a smooth, even surface that meant it was still all right for bicycles.

Now they've asphalted the lot. Those hundreds and hundreds of kilometres of dirt road have now all been covered with firm, smooth macadam, like a velvet cloak; and they used to be all nicely cambered, high in the middle and sloping down towards the sides, so that every drop of water could find its way down into the ditch. But now they make all the roads as flat as pancakes and every time there's a cloudburst the new town of Latina gets flooded – and if you're on the Via Pontina when it rains, you'll get wetter than you would if you were in the Mussolini Canal itself – and the old town gets flooded too, because they never clean out the trapdoors in the drains. No one ever comes round – after the contracts have been awarded – to check that the firms have done what they said they would, with the right gradients and layering. Perhaps what's needed is a bit of roughing up. The Servicemen's Association didn't pull their punches when it came to dealing with the firms in question. They were always breathing down their necks, and Cencelli was endlessly complaining about the standard of the work they'd done and threatening not to pay them: 'Sue me. Or rather, I'll sue you,' and forcing them to do the same work twice. He wiped the floor with them. He drove some firms to bankruptcy: 'If you're no good at your work' – he was from Rieti, remember – 'you're better off dead.'

Anyway, on that occasion my two uncles set off on their bikes in the dark – it was seven o'clock or thereabouts, but it was November, and the streets weren't lit in those days like they are now, even in the countryside – and after two or three kilometres they caught up with Uncle Adelchi who was waiting for them outside the wine-shop at Sessano. Then they rode on to Borgo Piave and then Littoria. Ten kilometres in all.

They didn't stop at Sessano because – with various excuses – they'd already been there that afternoon. Actually, the first to skulk off had been my grandfather: 'I'm out of cigars,' he'd started saying to my grandmother the minute he got down from the cart, patting his jacket and trouser pockets over and over, as though hoping one might appear by magic. She gave him one of her wily looks – she knew what was going on, but she wasn't going to let him off the hook: 'Come on then, at least have the courage to spit it out.' Then – seeing that she wasn't going to make it easy for him – he was obliged to spell it out: 'What would you say if I nipped out to get a cigar?'

'All right, off you go then,' she'd said. 'Couldn't you have got one at the station?' So off he'd gone to have a look at Sessano, which is now Borgo Podgora, he'd even gone to have a look at the church; but the main thing was the wine-shops, and he'd already chosen which one he'd be frequenting, and sampled the wine – which was *vino dei Castelli*: 'It's good' – and even made some friends: 'I'll see you later for a game of *briscola*.'

So it was dark when my uncles arrived at Littoria. Or rather, it wasn't yet really Littoria, just Littoria-under-construction. You could already see the lights from Borgo Piave – which was still called Passo Barabino, and there were a lot of stalls there too, selling wine, and there was scaffolding in the middle of the building site where they were putting up the water-tower for the aqueduct – but my uncles had set their sights on the bright lights of Littoria, so on they pedalled: 'Come on boys, let's see who makes it first,' and on they sprinted for another four kilometres.

Littoria was one big building site, with lamps and searchlights and as much hustle and bustle as if it had been daytime. Thousands of people at work on the streets and drainage trenches.

But it can't be said that my uncles were all that impressed, that night. Everyone seemed frantically busy all right, an awful lot of men were rushing around the place – and there was a lot of noise and shouting and hammering, even at that late hour, and whirling of cement-mixers – the first they'd ever seen – and beams of light from the building sites and people shouting to one another, and distant sounds of drunken singing. They couldn't fail to be amazed. But it put my Uncle Pericles in mind of the chaotic, indeed anarchic carry-on behind the lines just before the last great push at Vittorio Veneto: 'It's like the war, only more so,' he said to his brothers, laughing.

But Uncle Adelchi said: 'This is the place for me.'

'Come on,' objected the other two, because – as I've just said – they weren't all that impressed by what they were seeing. 'With all that mud?'

'With all that mud,' insisted Uncle Adelchi. 'To tell the truth, I'm not all that keen on working the land.'

'That's a new one! You could have fooled us,' said the other two, because in fact he did always manage to wangle himself a place behind the lines, coordinating things, doing the logistics, as it were, rather than getting his hands dirty. Uncle Pericles and Uncle Iseo, on the other hand, were only too happy to be told to get their hands dirty, they wallowed in it. Uncle Adelchi

275

was the only member of the Peruzzi clan – at least after he came back from military service – not to have black-rimmed nails. Before that, yes. But once he was back they stopped trying to get him into the thick of things, and if he really did find himself having to pick up a pitchfork or yoke the oxen – at harvest-time, say, or ploughing-time – he would always be careful not to get his nails too dirty, and then he'd brush away at them in the evening.

Anyway – apart from all that frantic late-night flurry and teeming activity – Littoria was certainly not beautiful, at least not yet. There was mud everywhere, and white clay – it stood on the edge of the quaternary dune – which was quite unlike the soil around the Mussolini Canal, which was very dark, or sometimes reddish, because of the sediment brought there over the course of the millennia by the Teppia and the *Fiume Antico* and the *Fosso di Cisterna*. Any amount of rain could fall on our land at holding 517; the more God chucked it down, the more our land would guzzle it up; half an hour after it had rained for weeks on end, we could go out into our fields with our cattle and plough. There, on the other hand, around Littoria – just ten kilometres away, where it was all clay – one drop of rain and you couldn't go into your fields for a week, either with cattle or with tractors. The water stayed on the surface, or at most it would seep through to the upper layers, so what you had was soapy china clay, which would stick to your skin like a limpet; and the more it rained, the deeper this layer of slime would become, until there were whole marshes and quicksands of the stuff. And now the Servicemen's Association was building a town on it.

They'd told us that it would be ready – completed, officially open for business – by the middle of December. My uncles cast a practised eye over the building sites: the walls of all the buildings were already in place, up to the second floor, and some had been roofed over, but most of them still had no floors or fittings or windows, or plaster. They were just bare walls, flanked by scaffolding. The square itself – what is now Piazza del Popolo – was an utter shambles, like something out of Dante's *Inferno*, a sea of mud, criss-crossed by the rails of the little narrow-gauge railway, with the odd wagon lying on its side, and just behind the town hall – or rather, the place where the town hall was being built – were the engine sheds, and here too there were overturned wagons and carriages, with twisted axles, waiting for the day when someone would bestir themselves to come and mend them. So my uncles said: 'How could this possibly be ready by December? It won't be ready by December next year, not even if the Duce comes down in person and lays every brick himself with his own hands.'

And while they were standing in front of the searchlights which lit up the scaffolding of the tower of the town hall – my Uncle Pericles remembered such searchlights from the war, scanning no-man's-land from the trenches, on the lookout for Austrian assault troops in the barbed wire entanglements – they saw some workmen bumbling about on it, rather like assault troops, in fact, and Uncle Iseo said: 'To me, that tower looks a bit low, in comparison with its base, that is.'

'It's not finished,' a passing workman explained. 'We haven't got to the top yet, we're still in the middle.'

'I think the people from the association have got it wrong,' said my Uncle Pericles. 'They must have meant December next year.'

Then they turned back – and now they really were starting to enjoy themselves – and wandered around the old hospital and the militia barracks, which were just being built, and found themselves more or less where Piazza Roma is now, behind the unfinished town hall and the old engine sheds belonging to the association, which served as a shunting-yard for the narrow-gauge railway. On both sides of the street there was a whole series of stalls where you could buy wine, with a great throng of what seemed like tens of thousands of workmen jostling in front of them – they'd been working day and night, ten or twelve hours at a stretch, it was only reasonable that they'd want to find somewhere to spend a bit of their hard-won earnings. At some stalls there were also prostitutes, but you had to queue for them. And makeshift tables and benches all over the place, made with planks filched from the building sites, with oil lamps on them and groups of drunkards – the people they'd heard earlier on – who were singing *Angioina, bela Angioina*, and also *Ta-pum*:

> *In the valley there's a graveyard.*
> *It's for us poor soldier-boys.*
> *Ta-pum, ta-pum, ta-pum.*
> *Ta-pum, ta-pum, ta-pum.*
>
> *It's for us poor soldier-boys,*
> *Perhaps I'll come and join you there.*
> *Ta-pum, ta-pum, ta-pum.*
> *Ta-pum, ta-pum, ta-pum.*
>
> *Soon we're going to attack.*
> *Soldier-boy, please make it back.*
> *Ta-pum, ta-pum, ta-pum.*
> *Ta-pum, ta-pum, ta-pum.*

My uncles too stopped at one of these stalls. They leaned their bikes against a wall, asked for a litre of wine and sat down on a bench, and the men already seated there made room for them.

278

Uncle Pericles – and Uncle Iseo too, come to that – wanted to join in the singing. 'Didn't you do enough singing on the train?' my Uncle Adelchi teased them.

There were people from all over Italy. Poor people from all over the world seemed to have made arrangements to meet up here. From Calabria, Tuscany, Piedmont, Sardinia, the Marches, Genoa, anywhere where there was no work – and that was most places – they'd all flocked to Littoria. They'd go off back home again in a few months – when the place was ready – and then every so often they'd have an attack of malaria; apart of course from those who, as I've already said, would never be going home, because they'd breathed their last down here, beneath some scaffolding or in the hospital in Velletri. All young, strong men, aged between twenty and thirty.

But mainly they were from the Lepini Mountains, and from Latium: from Sezze, Cori, Norma, Sermoneta, Bassiano, Priverno and Sonnino, and also from the Province of Rome, and the Ciociaria, from Alatri, Ceccano, Ferentino, Rieti and Viterbo. They'd all come here to work, but when at last after a bit of chat my uncles said where they were from, it was suddenly quite a different story. On learning that my uncles weren't working on the building sites or the canals, like they were, but were sharecroppers who'd come to live permanently on the land that they themselves had drained, on the holdings that they themselves had built, it wasn't long before they edged us unceremoniously off that same bench they'd previously welcomed us on to: 'You Vikings from out of the north, all ill comes forth!' they started saying.

At first, my uncles didn't know what they were talking about. My Uncle Iseo whispered into my Uncle Adelchi's ear, after all, he was the one with the education: 'What's that they're saying?'

'How should I know?' But not wishing to seem left out – because my Uncle Adelchi didn't like to be left out, nor, truth to tell, did any of the Peruzzi clan – and seeing that the phrase was clearly not intended as a compliment, he shot back: 'What's your problem, then, you dirty wogs?'

'The holdings... You've robbed us of our holdings!'

Now here it should be said that a few moments earlier – before things had started hotting up with this talk of Vikings, before they'd started to see us as having allegedly robbed them of their holdings – there had been talk of Littoria and how long it would take to build. And one of them, from the Lepini Mountains – from Sezze, to be precise – had said jeeringly, making it clear that he wasn't exactly a dyed-in-the-wool Fascist: 'It's all very well Mussolini saying he's going to be attending the official opening in December. What's he going to be declaring open? A swamp?'

Then Uncle Pericles had bridled, and had said: 'That's no way to talk. If the Duce says it will be ready by December, it will be ready by December. Signed, Pericles Peruzzi,' and he'd brought his fist down firmly on to the table.

'All right, no need to get so hot under the collar,' the others had said, and changed the subject – partly because at that same moment two *carabinieri* were passing by – while my Uncle Pericles was already saying to himself: 'What did I have to go and say that for?' Indeed, even his brothers – Adelchi and Iseo – had looked at him in astonishment, as though to say: 'Pericles, whatever are you thinking of?' They didn't say anything, of course, because Pericles was Pericles, and silence was the wisest course with him, but they did give him an odd look, and he knew why: 'I'd better keep quiet from now on, I've made enough of a fool of myself already.'

But when they started saying: 'Vikings,' and 'Out of the north,' and my uncle came back with his 'Wogs' dig, and they came back with the accusation that we'd robbed them of their holdings, let alone the business about the official opening, then my Uncle Pericles really saw red, and he stood up from the bench and shouted across at the man from Sezze: 'Take back what you said, you wog!'

'Take what back? I'm not taking anything back, you great polenta-guzzling Viking.'

Then my uncle landed him a hearty punch and dived over the table, promptly followed by Uncle Iseo. A group of men from Sezze fell on Uncle Adelchi, and a group of sharecroppers like ourselves – who'd also arrived here a few days earlier and who, like us, were paying a visit to the mysterious building site at Littoria – hearing all that bawling about Vikings and wogs and sensing that the whole business might somehow concern them too, now threw themselves into the fray. But then the people from Sezze were joined by some shepherds from Guarcino, who were on their side, and there was a general set-to.

'Cut it out!' shouted the stallholders. 'Cut it out, here comes the law,' that is, the *carabinieri*.

'Like hell we will,' shouted our new-found enemies, and all hell broke loose.

My Uncle Adelchi – who'd never been as good a hand-to-hand fighter as my Uncle Pericles, whenever they'd had a fight, he'd always come off worst – was oblivious to the punches which were raining down on him from all sides, he just batted them off feebly with the odd half-hearted cuff. His only thought during all this commotion was for his bike: 'My bike! What if they filch my bike while all this is going on?' And he made his way towards it with his crowd of assailants in leisurely pursuit, punching him as they sauntered after him.

But no sooner had he reached the place where he'd left it, and had the crossbar firmly in his hand – my uncles talked about it for years afterwards – than the Lion of Judah was suddenly unleashed. He was like Samson with the jawbone of the ass – Achilles beneath the walls of Troy, carried away by hubris – and he swung that bicycle around him as though it were a heavenly sword, massacring the enemy and further terrorizing them with his piercing shrieks: 'Me? Robbed you of your holdings? Get off with you, you load of shit-eating wogs, to hell with the lot of you!'

And they backed off. How they backed off. Such was his prowess with his bicycle that day – that night – that my Uncle Adelchi might have been wielding Durendal itself. To the point that my Uncle Pericles – seeing him from a distance as he kicked and punched and stabbed left, right and centre, as the need arose – said to himself: 'Just look at Adelchi!' And he felt a sudden pang, just like he had that time when he'd tried to shoot the Zorzi Vila's factor – 'I'll get you. I'll get you, wherever you are!' – a sudden stirring of love for that brother too: 'He's a real Peruzzi, a true brother!' And when at a certain point he dropped his knife and had to make do with his fists, he did what he'd seen his brother do, and wrenched half a plank from off a table and started flailing around with that as well, now that he'd lost his knife.

But then a stallholder started shouting: 'The law, the law!' and they saw two *carabinieri* coming over, and a few Blackshirts running towards them too.

The hubbub instantly subsided. My brothers acted as if nothing had happened, just tried to slink off, pushing their bikes. My Uncle Adelchi was wheezing and gasping. Every so often he continued to bellow: 'I'll show you wogs what's what!' still swinging his bike around his head.

'Shut up, you idiot,' Uncle Iseo said to him, laughing. 'Do you want to end up inside?' and he dragged him away, and made him put his bicycle down.

One of the men from Sezze went off along with them, and he said to Uncle Pericles, quietly though, so that the *carabinieri* wouldn't hear him: 'This isn't the last you'll be hearing from us.'

'Any time,' my uncle answered, quietly but clearly: 'Signed, Pericles Peruzzi, holding 517, Mussolini Canal. At your service.'

So, it had been a good bout, with not too much damage done. A few scratches and superficial knife-wounds. But when they were in bed later that night, making love, my Uncle Pericles had winced at her every touch: 'Not there; or there either, it hurts like hell.'

'Always the troublemaker, damn you,' she'd said, scratching his back even harder. But later, after she'd calmed down, just before going to sleep she'd added: 'Tomorrow I'll have to mend your damned coat again,' because it was his coat that had borne the brunt of the blows. And those dealt by Uncle Pericles can't have done much harm either, so the wogs too had got off lightly.

Sorry, what did you say? Why did they so dislike northerners, and above all why should the local Fascist branch have given the reclaimed land to us – who'd come down from the north – and not to them, who were already on the spot? Does that strike you as an injustice? Perhaps it was because down south they weren't Fascist enough, you say?

No, that's not the reason. They were as Fascist down here as everyone in the rest of Italy. There'd been local Fascist branches everywhere, right from the start, and they'd been as involved in the march on Rome as everybody else. Of course, before that here too they'd been Socialists, and had Workers' Associations. But here too, like everywhere else, at a certain point the wind had changed – today one thing's all the rage, tomorrow it'll be something else – and they'd all turned Fascist. It was the same old story as everywhere else. Don't you remember that a few years ago – all over the north of Italy – one day everyone was a Christian Democrat or a Communist, and the next day they were all for the Northern League or Berlusconi? If you went to see who was cooking steaks and sausages and beans at the get-togethers organized by the Northern League, most of them would be the same people who'd been doing the same thing at get-togethers organized by the Communist Party. That's just the way things are.

First and foremost, though, they told us that it was to compensate the three Venetias – us – for everything we'd suffered in the First World War. Secondly, ours was the poorest part of Italy, with the most hunger and unemployment, and people leaving by the boatload for America. Then that period of emigration came to an end – we were no longer welcome there, any more than non-EU immigrants are here today – and they had to send us somewhere else. So they sent us down here. We were the non-EU immigrants of the Pontine Marshes. But – as I've told you – what the Servicemen's Association needed was sharecroppers or tenant farmers, who knew how to do all kinds of work and would live on the holdings round the clock. Whereas the local people would go back to their villages every evening. With all the malaria there was around, why would they spend the night on their holdings, near their livestock? In Italy, sharecropping was practised in Tuscany, Umbria, the Marches and the Po Valley. But never in Latium – not in the Papal States. There they'd always followed the feudal system, and the first person to introduce sharecropping on his land in Latium, at Magliano Sabina, had been none other than Count Cencelli. Perhaps that's another reason why Rossoni suggested to the Duce that he should be put in charge of the Servicemen's Association.

But it's also true – as you quite rightly say – that the land wasn't completely empty before we arrived. The Pontine Marshes were hell on earth – a swampy, malaria-infested desert – but still there were people living there before we arrived, and that's a fact.

Mainly it was herdsmen, from Cisterna, who went around on horseback, like cowboys, tending the cattle belonging to Prince Caetani and other noble Roman families, the Borghese, the Colonna, the Annibaldi. They were the main occupants, and they worked for various noble families, first and foremost the Caetani. But there were also people from the Lepini Mountains living in the marshes. They grew most of their food up in the hills. The people from Cori grew their corn at Tirinzania and even as far away as Mount Lupone. The people from Sezze did the same: they grew their wheat up in the hills, at Casali and in the Valli di Suso, which means 'upland valleys', that is, valleys above the village. Not below. The only people who lived down in the marshes were the poorest-of-the-poor, not the rich – not even those who weren't actually rich, but not totally destitute – and they were engaged in a fight to the death against the marshes, and the malaria. But there were people in the marshes: hunting frogs, poaching fish in the fish ponds, trying to cultivate some little field tucked away where it wouldn't be seen. And gathering firewood and raising the odd pig.

The people from Bassiano had long-standing claims to collective ownership of various bits of land on the quaternary dune, around the present-day Borgo San Donato. Here, in the cooler months, various families – numbering some hundreds of individuals – would go and set up house in groups of huts more or less like our own huts in the Veneto, made of poles and branches and bits of wood and reeds and other marshland plants, and they'd plant maize. But the main source of income for the people of the Lepini Mountains – if you can call it income, because it wasn't exactly an oil well – was the shepherds who came down each year from the Ciociaria and the Abruzzi. In summer those shepherds would tend their flocks up in the hills, and in the middle of September they'd bring them down into the valleys.

Then, at the end of winter – when the anopheles mosquito came into its own down on the marshes, and the snow up on the hills started to melt, and the grass started to grow again on the pastures – shepherds and sheep would go back up into the hills. Indeed, there's still a road – running from the hills across the Pontine Marshes to the quaternary dune – known as the 'road of the Bassianesi', that is, the road taken by the people of Bassiano, and it's the one the shepherds took when they brought their flocks down here from the Ciociaria and the Apennines, and here the people of Bassiano mounted an armed guard and forced them all to pay entrance money, men and sheep alike, for the right to cross that land, and have their flocks graze on it.

So, at that time, throughout the winter period this whole endless plain – where some five hundred thousand people now live – was occupied by just two thousand, scattered here and there. In the summer months – when the air was black with mosquitoes – there was barely a soul; twenty at most, those brigands I've already mentioned who couldn't go back to their homes. It was a swampy, malaria-ridden desert, and when it was time for the people from Bassiano to harvest their maize, they'd go backwards and forwards from their villages each day. On foot or on muleback, those few who had mules; because, as I've told you, the only people who came here were those who were truly desperate. So, they'd go back to their villages each evening, the moment it started to get dark and the first squadrons of anopheles mosquitoes went on the warpath. What with one thing and another, the people from Sezze and Cori and Bassiano dropped dead of malaria like flies there in those marshes, and they wouldn't go there at all unless they had absolutely no other choice.

They'd been perched up there on those hills for centuries – millennia, even – dug into the limestone rock, looking down over the marshes from above. Those marshes spelt certain death. And for centuries – millennia, even – from the times of the Caesars down to those of the popes and beyond, they'd also seen people popping up out of the blue to have a shot at draining the place, digging a canal here, drying out a pool there. But after a bit – unfailingly – work would come to a standstill, the diggers would stop digging, and in the twinkling of an eye the marsh itself would have reclaimed the lot. Indeed, this time too – in 1928, when the consortium had started work on the drainage scheme – they shovelled away at all that endless mud and pushed wheelbarrows around and collected their pay, but they didn't have any grandiose illusions: 'It'll never last... the whole place will be under water again in no time at all, you'll see.'

In 1931, though, when they saw the Servicemen's Association get cracking on those marshes and settling the sharecroppers from the Veneto on those holdings, then the people from Sezze and the other villages began to get all hot under the collar: 'Why aren't you giving those holdings to us? Why are you bringing this lot in? We've been slaving our guts out here for ever, and now you're importing this lot from up there? They get nice well-drained land, and all we get is a chunk of stony mountain?'

Their only hope was that we'd all die: 'Don't worry, malaria will soon kill off those Vikings.' But one year went by, and then another, and people from the Veneto and Friuli and Ferrara kept on pouring in, settling on the holdings and surviving; or at least not dropping down dead in droves. And when they saw that we weren't dying, they were more outraged than ever. But it took time. At first, they weren't all that outraged; they called us 'polenta-guzzling Vikings', it's true, but they didn't actually go to the Fascist Headquarters and demand to be given our holdings. No, they were patiently biding their time until we died. And we didn't die, and we started breeding, and more of us kept on coming; and then they realized that there were no longer any marshes, and never would be, and that it was possible to live and prosper round these parts, and it was then that they started going to the Fascist Headquarters and bellowing: 'Why don't you give us those holdings? Why should they get all the rich pickings?' and from that moment onwards it was open warfare and undying hatred between us and them.

We never got on. Our ways of thinking were too different, let alone our ways of speaking and eating. For instance, they'd never even heard of *tortellini* or *cappelletti in brodo*, and my grandmother would tell a story about a gleaner from those hills who'd brought her some olives, to thank her for her generosity, and she'd taken them – 'Thank you so much, dear' – and thrown them into the ditch as soon as she was out of sight: 'What are they?' We'd never seen an olive in our lives. We must have thought they'd make us ill. We'd always flavoured our food with seed oil or lard.

The real trouble was, though, they thought all our women were whores. They'd never seen a bicycle in their lives, until we came along. For them, women were slaves, inferior beings. All muffled up in black, from head to toe. Our women wore garments that weren't exactly short, by today's standards, but at least they were comfortable, and colourful; and they went everywhere by bicycle, so inevitably you could see a bit of leg: 'Whores, that's what they are.' At village dances it was even worse. When it was threshing-time, we'd sometimes have joint get-togethers. For us, dancing was a totally innocent pursuit, a show of artistry, if you like. You had a dance, and that was that. For them, though – for the people of Sezze and the other hill villages – if you danced with a woman just once, you had to marry her. And when they saw our women dancing with all and sundry – first with you and then with somebody else – they'd go absolutely berserk, and there'd be all manner of misunderstandings and it would always end up with punch-ups and carve-ups, every Saturday when there was a dance, and at threshing-time and on market-days; particularly at Pontinia and the surrounding villages. Wogs, that's what they were. And that was what we called them, because they were behind the times, and once, at Doganella – I don't know whether it was at a dance or a cattle fair, or whether it was day or night – even my Uncle Pericles was forced to come to blows with one of them. But whoever it was gave as good as they got, and his brothers brought him back home on a cart. His mother – my grandmother – and his wife had to sew him all neatly up again. He hadn't been wearing a coat on that occasion – it was July.

Uncle Adelchi, on the other hand, had a story about when he was going by ship to Africa, to win us an empire in Abyssinia – we'd been down here two or three years, at the time – and one

289

night they'd got all the soldiers to go on deck and shown them a film. He was with the other Blackshirts from the 'Littoria' Company, who were almost all sharecroppers like himself.

The film they were showing was a Western, one of those American films in black and white, but with sound. The whites were always the good guys, who brought civilization and progress, and the redskins were the baddies who put a spoke in the wheel of progress and civilization with any number of atrocities. Anyway, at one point – they were already in the Red Sea, beyond Suez, all on deck, in the pitch-dark – the screen was suddenly filled by a close-up of the head of an Apache, on the lookout on some mountain, gazing at the pale faces as they advanced slowly towards him. His face was a mass of wrinkles, with spiteful eyes and a hooked nose, and he looked the spitting image of their own section leader – the equivalent of a sergeant – who was from Sezze. Now I don't know if you're familiar with the expression, but around these parts – that is, in the villages on the Lepini Mountains – there was and still is a saying which runs: 'Never give stripes to a man from Sezze, if you know what's good for you.'

Anyway, there on the equator, in all that darkness and silence – there on the deck, against that rousing background music, which seemed almost to stir up waves in the Red Sea, all glinting silver in the light of the full moon – my Uncle Adelchi said loudly into the darkness: 'That's our sergeant. Look, boys, it's him to a tee.'

The whole ship rocked with laughter. Believe me, everyone was guffawing. Even the officers.

Suddenly someone shouted out: 'Peruzzi.' It was him, the slighted sergeant. But by now everyone was bellowing: 'The man from Sezze! The man from Sezze!' and the noise was gathering momentum and becoming more and more loutish.

Then Uncle Adelchi went too far – there was nothing he liked better than being the centre of attention – and he carried on, even more loudly and more piercingly: 'We're the pale faces, and the men from Sezze are the Apaches,' and up went another roar of approval, so that the ship all but foundered. 'Men from Sezze wherever you look,' they all went on sniggering for hours.

What he got for his pains was ten days confinement to barracks, to be served when they disembarked at Massaua, though in the end his sentence was reduced by the company commander – a certain Barany, who was from Milan, but his family came from Hungary, and he worked for the Servicemen's Association as an agricultural adviser. The man from Sezze, on the other hand, got off less lightly. From then onwards, throughout the whole of the Abyssinian campaign, he was known as 'Sergeant Apache', and when the Ascaris started to use that name as well, it was too much for him. According to Uncle Adelchi, in the most risky situations – when it was a matter of life or death – he never hesitated for a moment, but always sent him, Adelchi, into the breach: 'Off you go, then,' he'd say to him, in front of everyone.

'Why is it always me?' Uncle Adelchi would ask.

'Because it is, you good-for-nothing Viking.' He wanted him dead. Or at least that's what my Uncle Adelchi used to say.

But when the other war was over – the Second World War, that is – and Fascism was over too, then the people from Sezze and the Lepini Mountains all went red, went Socialist and Communist, not just because that's exactly what happened in the rest of Italy, but above all because they said it was us who were the real Fascists, it was us who'd got most out of the movement. They were the only ones who'd had been Socialists earlier, and they'd suffered for it. We hadn't. So they occupied

291

the land. They started eyeing the holdings again. They wanted us out of the way, like the Israelis nowadays with the Arabs. The Christian Democrats sorted matters out, though in fact the Fascist Party had already started to patch things up, giving them a few holdings around Pontinia. Anyway, they took their cue from us and started staying on their holdings night and day, not traipsing up and down the hills for hours between their villages and their land. And those few who hadn't learned from our example got dealt with by the factors from the Servicemen's Association, and they were such *stakhanovites* that the *kolkhoz* undertaking in the Soviet Union seemed like a harmless picnic in comparison.

Indeed, for those who didn't toe the line, this place was like Siberia. As I've already said, we were looked upon quite kindly by the local Fascist branch, but nonetheless the factor was always breathing down our neck: 'Plant this and don't plant that, the drainage ditch needs cleaning out, I'll be reporting that, don't even think of taking on work as day-labourers somewhere else, you've got to stay right here on this holding.' To the point that my Uncle Pericles – despite the fact that he was an important figure in the Fascist Peasant Union – once had to take one of these factors aside. But not right there in the fields, in front of everyone. My uncle wasn't a monster, he knew that everyone has a right to their dignity. So he met him outside the association's headquarters in Littoria, as though by chance – wearing his city clothes – and said to him politely: 'Come on, factor, let's go and have a drink.' Then, as they were walking down the street, just the two of them, he turned to him, as calm and quiet as could be: 'Look, I'm as much a Fascist as you are, more so, in fact.'

'I know, I know, Peruzzi, but...'

'But me no buts. The Peruzzi aren't interested in buts.

Everyone has a job to do, and you have yours. But there are ways and ways of doing things. I'm a Fascist and I respect discipline, but...' and here his voice tailed off, though it now had a distinctly harsh edge to it.

'Are you suggesting I'm...?'

'No, no, of course not. I'm just making a general observation.' But that did the trick. At least as far as that factor was concerned.

Sorry, what did you say? What about those families who didn't have an Uncle Pericles?

The fact is, every family always had at least one Uncle Pericles, but if the worst came to the worst, when things got really bad they'd write a letter to the Duce. Rossoni still called round from time to time – you'd hear him hooting his horn as he approached, then he'd jump out of his car as soon as he was on the bridge, yelling: 'Peruzzi! Do you remember that time at Copparo, with the horse?' and once he told us about all the letters addressed to the Ducce, Palatzo Venetzia, Rome, ungrammatical and full of howlers, but perfectly comprehensible: '*Deerest Ducce, hear things aren't gowing at all well for one reeson or another,*' and he'd look into matters. Then, if you were seen to be in the right, things would be sorted out, and, if you weren't, you and your family would be sent packing – back up north – to starve to death again.

Anyway, believe it or not, by 18 December 1932 – just a month after we'd arrived – Littoria was well and truly finished and officially open for business.

Rossoni had called round a few days after we arrived – not just on us, but on all the new sharecroppers, though he did stay a few minutes longer on our holding – and my uncles had said: 'They'll never make it, there's much too much still to do.'

'Don't you worry. When the Duce says something will

293

happen, it happens.'

And by 18 December 1932 – a Sunday, the fourth Sunday in Advent, and the day before it had rained cats and dogs, all day – lo and behold, everything was finished. The buildings all freshly painted, spick and span – except for the church of San Marco, that is, they finished that later. But the town hall, with its big white travertine tower, and the barracks for the militia and the *carabinieri*, and the schools on Piazza Dante, the futurist post office on Piazza Mazzoni, the Servicemen's Association offices, the buildings on Piazza del Quadrato, the playing fields, the party offices, the Workingmen's Club, the cinema, the bars, the coach station, Hotel Littoria and the first blocks of flats, they were all finished, and my Uncle Adelchi – who'd somehow found a moment the previous day to cycle in and take a look before night fell, all swaddled in his waterproof and dripping wet – had felt the urge to run his fingers over all those marvels and take a peek behind the walls, to check that they were real, because at that point he thought they might be fake, put there to hoodwink the Duce. But no. Everything was well and truly finished. 'Such is the power of Fascism,' he said to my other uncles on his return. The only thing still unfinished was the square: 'They'll never finish that, there's much too much left to do.'

My Uncle Benassi, on the other hand – the one who'd married my Aunt Santapace – had been there throughout the whole of that Saturday night, because he worked for Motomeccanica, driving a Pavesi, one of those tractors they had at the time, with iron caterpillar wheels rather than rubber ones, which stopped them skidding. They were wonderful for ploughing, those Pavesi – apart from being strong, they were also very agile and responsive, and they could function in the muddiest conditions. My Uncle Benassi still worked

294

for Motomeccanica, a company which had been specially set up by the Servicemen's Association to run the earth-moving operations, with all its own machines, and depots, and staff. My Uncle Benassi would always tell us – when we were little – that Count Cencelli too had been there till ten o'clock at night, overseeing the works, and saying constantly: 'Now what on earth am I going to do? What on earth am I going to do now?' He'd sent out all the invitations, the Duce would be attending the official opening the next day – 18 December – and it was too late to fix another date. But, as I've told you, it was raining cats and dogs, and showed no sign of letting up. The drainage canals were all brimful, some were actually bursting their banks, and the square at Littoria itself was one big swamp.

The fortified farmhouse belonging to the Caetani, which stood in the middle, and the goods sheds belonging to the Servicemen's Association, to the side of it, with the water tower and all the rest of the old Quadrato, had been demolished a few days previously, but the 18BL lorries which were transporting the ballast for the macadam had all four wheels stuck in the mud, and couldn't move. So – in the early afternoon – Cencelli ordered all the tractors to be taken out of the depot and put to work towing the lorries, two per vehicle, if necessary. But at ten o'clock – all hope abandoned – Cencelli left the square and went home to bed. My Uncle Benassi even heard him saying: 'Bugger the lot of them' – he was from Rieti, remember – 'and the devil take the hindmost.' Only half the square had been paved over; the other half was something of a shambles. 'Do your damnedest,' a resigned Cencelli told engineers and workmen alike.

But when he went back at eight the next morning, 18 December 1932, and the sky was still overcast and it was still drizzling – the sun suddenly came out a couple of hours later, the moment the Duce's car edged its way into the square – he saw that everything was well and truly shipshape, the whole square had been levelled and asphalted, with the travertine borders in place along the pavements, and the pavements themselves finished, and lamps all round the square and saplings planted in the gardens in the middle. He couldn't believe his eyes. 'Well done! An extra half-day's pay all round!' Cencelli said.

But my Uncle Benassi also said that at another point during that same night – with all those lorries and tractors coming and going in the pouring rain – a chasm had opened up more or less in the middle of the square, just where the circular fountain with the big marble ball is nowadays, and that square is always known as Piazza della Palla, the Square of the Ball, rather than as Piazza del Popolo, or Square of the People. I don't know quite what happened – perhaps something gave way deep underground – Uncle Benassi never really explained it to us. Anyway, this chasm opened up, that's what he said, and lo and behold it sucked in all the surrounding mud and sludge and slime.

At all events, the 18BL which was standing by, about to dump its load of stones, also got caught up in this river of mud and was half-dragged into the abyss. Uncle Benassi said he just managed to hack through the rope by which his tractor was attached to it, otherwise he and his Pavesi would have met the same fate. They'd already been dragged along for a couple of metres before he managed to cut through the rope. Anyway, that 18BL lorry was stuck there in that chasm of mud and sludge, half in half out. They attached cables to it and used four Pavesi to try and pull it out, but nothing doing: 'The devil himself was holding it in place,' my Uncle Benassi used to say. And after a time, when they'd tried pulling it this way and that, somebody said: 'We haven't got all night.' They brought on other lorries, full of stones, detached the cables and let that 18BL slither down into the abyss with all the rest – 'To hell with you,' – and, as it sank, they covered it with stones. Then they laid the ballast and went over it with a steamroller, and bingo, the square was ready, just as dawn was breaking. Then they tidied things up a bit, and the official opening could proceed. The lorry is still there – beneath the fountain with the marble ball, there in the middle of the square, in front of the town hall – together with the kitten which the driver had had with him in his cab, and which he'd forgotten all about in his haste to get himself to safety. It had been mewing piteously while the lorry sank.

I do realize that this story doesn't sound all that likely. It was something that my Uncle Benassi used to tell us children. Maybe he exaggerated. Indeed, I'm sure he did. But it's a story you'll hear all over Latina. It wasn't just my Uncle Benassi who told it, all the old sharecroppers did the same, and there wasn't a grandfather in all Latina who wouldn't tell it to his grandchildren when they passed by that fountain, and he'd even give them coins to throw in for good luck. They'd throw them in together, grandchild and grandfather. And there are those who say that on winter nights, when you walk past the fountain – when it's pelting down with rain, and that's how it rains round here, when it does rain – every so often you can hear the mewing of that desperate kitten through the uproar, and the distant throbbing of the lorry's engine. Truth or legend? Superstition, certainly. Who can say how much truth and how much fantasy?

I'm sorry, what did you say? Why didn't we dig down and see if the lorry was there or not?

Forget it. Are you joking? A myth is a myth, and you don't

start scrabbling around in the ground to find out if a foundation myth is true or not. What counts is what it tells us. What if we dug down and the lorry wasn't there? Our myth would be blown to smithereens. What an idea! Myths must be treated with respect. And there was another saying which did the rounds in Latina and the Pontine Marshes – the old sharecroppers used to repeat it in the wine-shops, and I heard it from both my grandfather and my uncles: 'The day that ball topples over, or is removed, is the day that will spell disaster for Latina-Littoria and the Pontine Marshes. That will be the beginning of the end, and there won't be a thing anyone can do about it. Everything will topple. Death and destruction will ensue.' That ball is a stopper. It keeps the chthonic forces locked away. If you remove it for a single instant, it'll be Pandora's box all over again. The powers of the underworld will all burst out and get locked in mortal combat with the stellar-celestial forces. You'll have a cosmic short-circuit on your hands, and I wouldn't fancy being around the day it happens. Latina-Littoria confined to oblivion. Perhaps that's why certain politicians originally from Sermoneta – descended from the Caetani, wogs to a man – want to have an underground car-park built under Piazza della Palla. Woe betide anyone who lays a hand on that piazza, or that ball. Anathema.

Anyway, the next day, 18 December 1932, the Duce himself – who, just six months previously, had refused point-blank to come and officiate at the official opening: 'I wouldn't carry on calling it a town if you know what's good for you' – came to a sunlit Littoria to declare it open. Or rather, it was he himself who brought the sun, and he stood on the balcony of the town hall, with the tower soaring above him, and informed my uncles, and everybody else, all crammed into the square – and indeed the world at large, present in the form of the foreign press, all listening open-mouthed – '*This is the form of war that we prefer.*' Work. The land. 'Careful, though,' he seemed to want to warn them. 'Just watch your step with us.' Then, more directly to us locals: '*Peasants and country-dwellers, keep your eyes on this tall tower, for it is a symbol of Fascist power. Converging upon it, you will find help and justice in your hour of need. Mussolini,*' to quote the words still carved into the memorial tablet on that same balcony.

But then he went on to say that other towns would be built in the Pontine Marshes: Sabaudia, the very next year, and then Pontinia, Aprilia and Pomezia. The world would see what we were capable of: following the precepts of our forefathers, *Siccentur hodie Pomptinae Paludes*, 'Now is the time for the draining of the Pontine Marshes' – we would rebuild the 'vanished' cities mentioned by Pliny the Elder from scratch. Finally, within ten or fifteen years, the sharecroppers – ex-servicemen like Caesar's legionaries of old – would be able to redeem their holdings and become their owners.

This was greeted with deafening shrieks of joy and a hearty chorus of 'Du-ce! Du-ce! Du-ce!' and fanfares and the blaring of trumpets, and cannonades, and the roar of tractor engines, all switched on in unison; outbursts of song and assorted hubbub followed, and then it was over, the crowd broke up and every family – on carts or bicycles, or even on foot – set off back home again: 'Did you hear what the Duce said?'

'Yes, he's a Man all right,' but that didn't mean that he was just someone a little out of the ordinary. Once when I was a boy, my Uncle Iseo too had let drop: 'He was a Man,' and I'd objected: 'Yes, uncle, but I'm not a woman either' – and Uncle Iseo had said: 'What's that got to do with anything, you birdbrain? He wasn't a man like you or me, he was a Special Man, and you could go for centuries without seeing his like again.'

By now – and it was partly the Duce's doing, I'd be the first to admit it, because he and the Fascist Party were always harping on about the subject – all Italy seemed to be in the grip of an obsession with Ancient Rome and imperial display, and that was fair enough, such things were ours by right, because we were descended from the Ancient Romans, but there was something a bit unchristian about it, too, because it told us that not all men were, so to speak, equal. Or rather, there were us completely normal men – and also women – but we weren't exactly all equal, some were more intelligent and some less so, and it was only right that the more intelligent should be in command. Still, all in all we were normal men, and more or less equal. It was only once a century – sometimes only once a millennium – that a Man with a capital M would make an appearance here on earth, and he had human features, but within him he harboured the Spirit of a whole people and a whole age. He was a Man-God, a Demiurge, a cosmic power made flesh within one single man; not like an ordinary man at all. A sort of Messiah, like for the Jews, and anyway hadn't it been Pope Pius XI who'd called him 'the man whom providence has sent us?' What did that mean, in your opinion? It meant precisely this: that such amazing good fortune befalls a people only once every millennium or so, and on this occasion it was us who'd landed the great Man, and everyone else had better watch out. Maradona. Padre Pio. And if the pope believed it, who were we to doubt it? Every now and again, when somebody called round, my grandmother would say: 'And to think the great Man took a look at my harrow, on one occasion!' 'Yes, but that wasn't all he took a look at,' my grandfather would say when they were in bed that night, 'he also took a good look at your hindquarters, you slut, because you were wiggling them around right there in front of his nose.' The real trouble was that after a time he really began to believe everything they said – the Duce, that is, not my grandfather, obviously.

Anyway, that was one great day, not only for the new town of Littoria and the whole of the Pontine Marshes, but also for the Peruzzi clan, which – if it didn't find itself a Man like him, a sort of God – did at least find itself another normal man, something it sorely needed.

Because, when the inauguration ceremony was over, and the crowds were streaming back homewards, my Uncle Pericles stopped at a stall just off the square, opposite the militia barracks, where the registry office is now. There were similar stalls and stands all along the street, from all over the region. People throughout Latium – throughout all Italy, in fact – knew that it was the day Littoria was going to be declared officially open, and they'd thought: 'There'll be quite a crowd. Why don't I go along too, and see if I can pull one off on those polenta-guzzling Vikings?'

On this stall, they were selling underpants. And it was there that my Uncle Pericles got to know Lanzidei. Lanzidei wasn't an underpants-seller by trade, the stall didn't belong to him but to a friend of his from Rome – he himself came from Nettuno, a seaside town not far away – who'd asked him to come and help him out. He'd turn his hand to anything – labouring, building, fetching and carrying – and he was even more hard-up than we were. But he was likeable and quick-witted, and basically a decent sort. My uncles didn't think any more about it, then and there – my Uncle Adelchi too had stopped to look at those underpants – and I don't know whether they bought any, or just had a bit of a friendly chat, 'My name's Lanzidei, mine's Peruzzi,' and left it at that.

Anyway, the following year, when the Duce and Cencelli

went off to found Sabaudia, on 5 August 1933, even if it was August, it was cloudy, and raining. First it drizzled a bit, then it started pelting down. There was nowhere for anyone to take shelter, because there was nothing there, just holes in the ground, and wooden stakes marking out the area of the future foundations. But there was no shortage of people. We'd all been told to show up because – you've guessed it – the Duce was coming to found a new city, and he couldn't exactly cut a solitary figure, could he now? 'I wouldn't be in your shoes if you're not there,' was how the Servicemen's Association had put it. So along we'd all gone. Then, as you know – it's in all the history books – the moment his car arrived, it stopped raining, and everything was dry as a bone again within five minutes, and people were wilting in the heat. It was August, after all. But anyway, while it was still raining, my uncles too were looking for a bit of shelter, and at a certain point they heard someone shouting: 'Peruzzi!'

It was that same Lanzidei – with that same friend – who'd set up a stall on the road selling underpants, but this time it had a canvas awning. Actually, they brought it along to keep off the sun – 'It's August, after all!' – but it had turned out equally handy for the rain, and my uncles had gone to shelter under it, and Aunt Bissola was with them, and he introduced himself: 'I'm Lanzidei, pleased to meet you.' 'I'm Peruzzi Bissolata, pleased to meet you.' So they had a bit of a chat, there in the pouring rain. I don't know what they talked about. Anyway, the Duce rolled up and founded Sabaudia and then everyone went back to work.

A few days later, who should turn up on our holding – towards evening, at dusk – but this Lanzidei, on his bicycle, selling underpants. Then and there, obviously, no one had any objections, there were always lots of traders and pedlars calling at all the holdings, selling fish or fabrics or pots and pans or whatever, and even more famished than we were. None of them had a horse and cart. They were all on bicycles – with their wares tied up in packages on the handlebars and saddle-rack – or with a handcart, which they'd push by the shafts, for kilometres on end. They all called by here, why should Lanzidei be any exception? We greeted him, gave him a glass of wine and bought a pair of underpants (the great big sort made out of coarse woollen stuff, I don't know if you remember them?)

Then he came round again, and again, always at dusk. And Uncle Adelchi – who was suspicious by nature, and cunning as a weasel – finally smelt a rat, and took Uncle Pericles aside and said to him: 'How many bums does he think there are round here, anyway?'

'Eh?' said Uncle Pericles.

'It's Bissa he's after, damn you.'

'Well, he'd better watch his step,' said Uncle Pericles, clearly taken aback. 'He'll have me to reckon with,' and from then onwards they were on their guard. As soon as they heard him riding up along the road on that creaking bicycle of his – making a show of stopping on the other bridges saying: 'Need any underpants?' but just by way of something to say, because the moment they started saying: 'No, thanks, but...' he'd ride straight off without even hearing them out – Uncle Pericles and Uncle Adelchi went to lie in wait for him, pitchforks in hand, in a dip by the drainage ditch, just on the boundary between Uncle Themistocles' holding and our own: *hinc sunt leones*.

When he reached their holding, they popped up out of their hiding-place and blocked his way. Not threateningly though, just leaning on their pitchforks as though they'd been working and had suddenly seen him riding towards them: 'Let's say hello to him.'

He may have come from Nettuno, but he hadn't been born yesterday, and as soon as he saw them he got down from his bike and slipped a hand into his pocket, presumably in search of something that might be going to come in very handy, namely a knife. 'How's it going, Peruzzi? Always a pleasure to see you, need any underpants?'

'I won't mince my words,' said Uncle Pericles. 'Round these parts, you take the calves with the cow. Otherwise, you'll get something sharper than the sharp side of my tongue.'

'What's that?' said Lanzidei.

'You take the calves along with the cow. Otherwise, we bring out the knives.'

'No, I understand about the knives, it's the calves bit I'm not too sure about.' As I've said, he may have been from Nettuno, but he wasn't completely wet behind the ears, and even he – just to bring in the whole farmyard, at this point – had understood that the filly was no spring chicken, she was already twenty-five, and he'd already got some idea of her character; but he wasn't expecting this. Still, out of pure curiosity, he ventured to ask: 'How many of these calves are there, then?'

'Three,' said Pericles.

'Three? Then you can go and take a running jump, the lot of you,' and he started turning his bike around.

'Two of them are twins, though,' explained Pericles.

'That still makes three, in my book. What do you take me for, soft in the head? I'm off, and I shan't be back,' said Lanzidei, and he tried to pedal away, but the weight of the bundles of underpants caused his bike to sway this way and that, and Uncle Pericles and Uncle Adelchi had each taken hold of an arm and were trying to carry on with further negotiations.

'Leave go of me, or I'll report you,' Lanzidei was yelling.

'To hell with you,' said my Uncle Adelchi after a bit, ashamed of himself by now, and they let him go. But while he was creaking off, and had gone about thirty metres or so, suddenly a light went on in Uncle Pericles' head: 'Aren't you an ex-serviceman?'

'Yes,' he shouted back, and he carried on peddling, though he did turn his head round to look back at them. 'I was on the Piave, 21st Infantry.'

'Then we'll give you a holding, along with the cow and calves!' Uncle Pericles shouted in jubilation.

'A holding?' and at this point he got off his bike and turned it round, while my uncles went towards him, and together, one on this side of him and one on the other, with him in the middle – and now they were steadying the bundles and almost carrying him along, him, his bundles and the bike – they set off home again, discussing the terms of the agreement one by one: 'But I've never worked the land.'

'Don't worry about that, we'll teach you, and then she'll teach you.'

'But how many fathers are involved?'

'What's that to you – it's you who's the father now, it's you who's the owner of cow, calves and holding, the lot. How should I know how many fathers are involved? Just take that holding. We'll do our bit with the local Fascist branch.'

'But I'm no Fascist, Peruzzi, let's get this quite clear.'

'What the heck do I care what the heck you are? Take the cow and calves, and just get on with it.' And that's how Lanzidei married my Aunt Bissola and stopped going round selling underpants.

And once they'd got back home, the first person to jump with joy was Aunt Modigliana, Bissola's twin sister – 'I'm glad, I'm just so glad' – and they were very close, although they couldn't have been more different in character.

Armida – my Uncle Pericles' wife, the woman with the bees – clearly felt the same, and that night, when they were in bed, she couldn't stop saying: 'I'm glad, I'm just so glad he's getting her out from under our feet.'

'Hold your horses,' Pericles said to her, 'first we've got to get Dolfin and his wife settled, and ma's relatives married off,' and indeed for two or three years Aunt Bissola and Lanzidei stayed on at the holding on the Mussolini Canal with us – together, of course, with the new calves they produced along the way – and all my aunts and uncles were always fond of Lanzidei and taught him everything about working the land, and we all rubbed along quite well, partly because Aunt Bissola too had changed the moment he turned up. Not that she'd become another person – she was still a viper – but at times she was a bit more gentle, a little less disagreeable. And at last, in 1936 or 1937, when they founded Aprilia, my Uncle Pericles managed to find them a holding somewhere around those parts. 'Keep your hand in, Lanzidei, give her a good thrashing every now and again,' he'd say when he went to visit them, and she'd say: 'Just you try,' and my uncle would laugh, because he was fond of her.

Lanzidei was fond of her, too, and she of him: 'You damned wog,' she'd say to him twenty times a day, and he'd come back with 'Filthy Viking!' but with a laugh. All in all, if he'd called round so often with all those underpants, he must have had a reason. We hadn't promised him a holding at Sabaudia then and there. Clearly, the cow had appealed to him right from the start. The holding had come later. When they'd produced enough calves. And even with all these calves – the ones who were ready-made, and those who came later – they still got on well, and never had any real fallings-out. And the children who were closest to their new father, and who always had the most respect for him, were none other than those three calves who'd been there from the start. Anyway, as I've said, he was extremely likeable, and had a ready wit, even if he was a wog; his brothers-in-law too, my uncles, held him in high esteem. 'We've pulled off a good one here,' Uncle Pericles and Uncle Adelchi said to each other that famous evening, rubbing their hands after they'd introduced him to my grandmother: 'This is Bissola's intended, ma.'

'Heaven preserve us, he's one of them,' she'd said, turning distinctly pale.

'I know, but he's taking the calves as well,' chorused her sons.

'Oh well, in that case!' said my grandmother, nodding in assent.

'And a holding,' chipped in Lanzidei quickly, with just a hint of alarm.

'Yes, yes, don't you worry,' said my Uncle Adelchi, laughing and patting him on the shoulder.

After a time Uncle Lanzidei even caught our way of speaking, and whenever he had to go to the bathroom he'd say to his wife: 'I'm going to the privy,' and chuckle slyly to himself.

'Go to hell,' she'd shriek, because shrieking was one habit she never did cast off.

Only when he was dead, and lying in his coffin, silenced at last – even if he did appear still to be smiling just a little – did a weeping Aunt Bissolata point him out to those who passed by to pay their final respects, with the words: 'My handsome wog.'

'So long, polenta-guzzler,' he'd said to her smiling, just

before he died. With that same smile that had stayed with him in his coffin.

Sorry, what's that you said? That I haven't really explained why they referred to each other in this way?

I don't really know. They called us Vikings, or polenta-guzzlers, and we called them wogs, which meant Africans, or in this case of course people from the south of Italy, and you couldn't get more ignorant than that. But perhaps that use of 'Vikings' went back to the other time we'd been down here, at the beginning of the nineteenth century, with Napoleon, as they may have still remembered, and for them it more or less meant 'invaders'.

At that time this region was still part of the Papal States, and the pope ruled them with a rod of iron, worse than any king, and you'd better not step out of line. They'd hang you by the neck and chop off your head at the drop of a hat, as they had with Monti and Tognetti. Ignorance reigned supreme. You know who I mean by our lords and masters, the Counts Zorzi Vila? Well, they were enlightenment itself in comparison with the southern overlords, who were straight out of feudal times – feudal lords, they were – and they treated you like slaves. Prince Caetani – the man who had all Piscinara in his thrall, right from the mountains to the sea, the owner of each lake, marsh, swamp, field, forest – was also the owner of his subjects' very souls. In the Papal States, if you were a nobleman, you could do whatever you damned well liked, no one would lift a finger, and if some dispute did arise between noblemen, they'd sort it out, them and the pope together. But if they did the ordinary people wrong, no one could say a word: 'They're my people, they live on my lands, don't they? I'll treat them as I choose.' So it was thorough-going feudalism, and we from the north were gentlemen in comparison; starvelings, but gentlemen. But then along came the French Revolution, and Napoleon bought it down our way, too – to Northern Italy, that is – with equal laws for everyone, first in the so-called Cispadane Republic and then in the Cisalpine one. We northerners enrolled with him, all enthusiastic, and Napoleon said: 'Let's go and take a bit of this justice, equality and progress down to Southern Italy as well.' And we went with him, down to the Papal States and the Two Sicilies, and the pope got kicked out of Rome. Napoleon even took him prisoner and dragged him off to France, so that he couldn't carry on with any more of his double-dealing. And so – together with the French – we saw to it that liberty could take root everywhere in Italy, with equality and progress even for the people living in the hills around the Pontine Marshes.

But do you know what happened next? They didn't want liberty. They rejected it. And they rose up against their liberators. It was the priests – that's what my uncles said – who lit the fires of ignorance among their people: 'The Vikings offend against the Church and blaspheme against Christ. Plenary indulgence for those who slaughter them.' And the southerners said 'Go for it!' hoping to gain a place in Paradise, and earn the gratitude of Prince Caetani – or indeed Borghese – who, until that moment, had fleeced them to within an inch of their lives. They'd clean forgotten every wrong that had been done to them, and that enduring thorn in their flesh had now become their beloved prince, a prince of the Holy Roman Church; by defending him, you were defending Christ himself. Obscurantism could go no further.

The odd thing was, though, that same Pius VI – the pope who'd been held prisoner by Napoleon – had been progressive in his views. He'd taken it into his head to reclaim the Pontine Marshes, and he'd almost succeeded. He hadn't actually made the Mussolini Canal, but he'd dug out ditches and other canals,

309

mapped various roads, complete with milestones, dried out areas of stagnant water and put the Appian Way back into use. But he'd done all this work against the wishes of the Caetani – quite rightly, he expected them to pay for it all – and indeed against the wishes of those who lived in the surrounding hills, who didn't want it either. They wanted the marshes left just as they were. Prince Caetani wanted them left like that because he didn't want to fork out a lira, he was sitting pretty as it was. What did he care about reclamation? He was monarch of all he surveyed, he had his castle at Sermoneta and a ducal palace at Cisterna, but he spent all his time in Rome, in the even grander *palazzo* he owned on Via delle Botteghe Oscure. So he lived the high life in Rome, and had his property in the Pontine Marshes patrolled by an army of hired ruffians, factors, servants and soldiers, to check that people paid him for everything they took from the land, down to the last mushroom they found in the woods. Not so much as a single bundle of firewood came for free. He also rented out his lands to local profiteers, and they plundered everything they could lay hands on: timber, buffalo, game, horses and all the fish in the pools and lakes. So Pope Pius VI decided he'd reclaim the Pontine Marshes, and he set about digging out canals. But as soon as night fell, the locals fell over each other in their haste to knock down the banks and build dams in the middle of them – with posts and brushwood, like beavers – so that the water would cease to flow, and the whole place would be a swamp again: 'Reclaim the marshes? Over my dead body. If they do that, it'll be goodbye to any midnight poaching of the prince's eels and frogs.'

Poor Pius VI, they were the ones who ruined his health, Napoleon Bonaparte was nothing in comparison. The first time he saw the French bearing down on him from afar, he must have heaved a sigh of relief like no one has ever heaved before: 'Okay, now you can deal with this lot, and good luck to you,' and indeed he died soon afterwards. In the meantime, though – to carry on with the reclamation – he posted armed papal guards all along the canals, to take potshots at those savages who carried on their nightly activities of knocking down the banks. And once Napoleon got down here – together with us northerners – he had the Swiss Guards replaced by French and North Italian Militia, to keep an eye out for those local beavers. He wanted to carry on with the reclamation – 'It's a sacred task' – and he had engineers and experts sent down from France and Northern Italy to finish the job. But those wogs carried on with their sabotage – 'Come on, now's your chance,' Prince Caetani told them, through his priests – they started taking potshots at the French and North Italian guards, so that they could get on with wrecking the canals. But, as we know, Napoleon couldn't be satisfied with what he'd got, and off he went to export liberty and democracy from the Alps to the Pyramids, and we abandoned the dykes and went off after him, and in the meantime our wogs carried on putting his reclamation programme into reverse. And he said: 'All right, then, as soon as we've won we'll be right back, and do for those reactionary Apache savages in the Pontine Marshes.' But then he got a bee in his bonnet about taking progress and equality to Russia, too, and we went along as well, with that relative of ours – my grandfather's grandfather, I think it was – who was the only one of all his North Italian friends to make it back, the others were left there in their frozen ranks, ice statues on the great retreat. But he returned, with a nest egg he'd come by somehow or other, and spent the lot on water mills – floating mills, on the River Po – and the sons of his sons got through the lot, as I believe I've already told you, and once we'd got down to my grandfather we were even hungrier than when we'd started off.

Anyway, once he'd got back from Russia the game was up, and we each went our own way: Napoleon to Saint Helena and us back to Northern Italy. The pope went back to Rome – the new pope, that is, not Pius VI, who'd died in the meantime: 'To hell with you and the Pontine Marshes' – and Prince Caetani was in Sermoneta and the locals were back to splashing about among the frogs. So it was goodbye to reclamation, too: the marsh was lord of the manor again. No one could shift those wogs. Not even the Fascist Party. And when we arrived, it was us they had it in for.

I'm sorry, what's that you said? The fact remains that they were here before us?

Well, yes, that's beyond dispute. But it was us who brought them progress. Progress too must surely have its rights? Everyone in this world has their rights, and anyway I make no claim to be telling you God's own truth, the perfect and absolute truth which is known to Him alone. I'm telling you the truth according to the Peruzzi, as my uncles told it to me, as they themselves had lived it. To hear the other side of the story, and about other people's rights, you'll have to talk to them. From us, all you'll hear about are our own. According to my Uncle Adelchi, even the anopheles mosquito has its rights: 'It's got its rights. I'm a mosquito, it says to itself, and it's my right to bite. Even the Abyssinians had their rights.'

Obviously, Uncle Adelchi had said all this earlier – a long time ago – at the time when you remember him in the uniform of a traffic policeman at Latina, acting the peacemaker rather than the sheriff.

Before that, though – when he was still acting more the

sheriff – he hadn't thought that way and he said that it was us, like Napoleon, who'd brought civilization both here and to Africa, to Abyssinia, and that they ought to have felt nothing but gratitude towards us. He changed his mind – or at least he began to have his doubts – when my Cousin Manrico, one of my Uncle Benassi's children, who can't have been more than ten at the time, dared to put up a little resistance to his rantings.

We were at yet another family wedding – I can remember it as though it were yesterday – and Uncle Adelchi had been seated opposite one of the bridegroom's relatives who was some sort of school-teacher, or at least so he made out. They'd downed quite a few glasses of wine, and after a bit of discussion about Abyssinia, things had become somewhat heated.

At a certain point – quietly at first, but with the ghost of a sneer playing around his lips – Uncle Adelchi said to him in disbelief: 'I'm sorry, what's that you said? That we were the invaders, that we went out there to ransack the place? That's not it at all – we went out there to take them civilization. We didn't exploit them. Just go and see how they're getting on now, they've gone back two centuries. They're dying of hunger. Of disease, of plague. We took them civilization, and we paid for it, exploitation fiddlesticks. They had nothing. Gold, diamonds, oil? Nothing. We weren't like the English, who went to places where there was something to be had. They went to such places and took whatever it was away. They ransacked the place all right. Not like us, who came away with nothing. More to the point, we left them all manner of advantages. They didn't even have mule-tracks, and we left them roads and railways and bridges. What did you say? We built them because we needed them for our conquests? Well anyway, there're still there, we built them, and they're the only roads they've got. And do you know why we built them? To take them civilization. They were still in a state of enslavement. We took them liberty, we broke their chains and they're still grateful to us for it. You can't say as much of the French and English. They esteem and respect us, and wherever they are in the world, they say: "Italians good people." They still feel warmly towards us. I'm sorry, what's that you said? That it was conquest by mustard gas? What kind of talk is that? I go out to liberate you and you open fire on me? All's fair in love and war, if you don't mind. They even opened fire on Marshal Graziani, and that was truly treacherous. Seven killed by hand grenades, civilians included. What were we supposed to do? They gave us a free hand for three days, and that took the wind out of their sails. After that there wasn't a single black man to be seen around anywhere in Addis Ababa. They'd all gone to ground. We went from hut to hut, with petrol, setting fire to them, and then used hand grenades to deal with anyone trying to escape: men, women, children, you name it. A lot of them had to be beaten to death. I should know, I was there. We were taking them civilization. How else could we do it? If you have any suggestions I'd like to hear them. Signed, Adelchi Peruzzi, uncle of the bride.'

That's how my uncle wound up his homily – on his feet by now, his voice having risen almost to a screech – and he was mopping the sweat from his forehead with his napkin. But his face was wreathed in a radiant smile. A smile that was proud and satisfied.

My Cousin Manrico had gone to sit beside him as he talked, and it was then that he came out with the fateful words: 'But uncle, weren't they human beings too? And weren't you in their country?'

Uncle Adelchi was left speechless.

He suddenly looked thoughtful. Almost sad. He stared

314

around him for a moment – still panting from his exertions – and sat down, slowly, without a word, while his relations at the nearby tables started singing *Faccetta Nera*.

He stayed like that until the end of the meal – lost in thought, with Manrico sitting bolt upright beside him – amidst shouts of 'Long live the happy couple,' 'A kiss for the bride,' applause, dessert, fruit, sugared almonds, coffee and grappa. Then people started to drift away.

Only then did he rouse himself and stand up from his chair.

He downed a glass of grappa on the way out, forced his lips into a semblance of a smile, albeit a sad one, and laid his hand on Manrico's little shoulder. 'It was different then, son,' he said, and put his arms around him. Together they walked slowly towards the glass door of the restaurant. We were at the Fogolar Furlan. I remember it as though it were yesterday.

As soon as they were outside, though – on the gravel in the square – Uncle Adelchi leant down towards Manrico and said to him, quietly but with feeling: 'It's you who's right though, son. I'd never thought of it like that. Everyone has their rights. Them as much as us.'

III

What most struck Uncle Adelchi about Addis Ababa when he entered it for the first time at the head of the victorious troops, right behind Marshal Badoglio, were the eucalyptus trees. 'Look at those cliptas,' he said to his old friend Franchini from Cisterna, who was goose-stepping at his side, carbine shouldered, bringing up the rear of the platoon of honour of the Littoria Blackshirts Company, right behind the battalion flag: 'Look how well the cliptas grow around these parts!' It was 5 May 1936, and they were in the rear because they were the tallest.

'Shut up and get marching,' was Franchini's response, 'or we'll get it in the neck again.'

'Just look at the size of them, Franchin.' They stood forty metres high, and their trunks were so thick that two grown men couldn't have joined hands round them, as my uncle and Franchini could confirm from experience. Addis Ababa was one vast eucalyptus grove, one dark thicket with the dwellings hidden among the tree-trunks, and all you could see of them

317

was their roofs – among the leaves, and branches – and the sheet-metal tops of the larger ones and the public buildings.

We'd never seen anything like those eucalyptus trees. The ones we'd seen in the Pontine Marshes soon after we'd arrived were mere saplings, a metre high, they'd only just been planted. In the winter months my uncles would earn a bit of extra money from the Servicemen's Association – paid by the day – by going out to plant eucalyptus trees along all the roads and drainage ditches and canals. The first ones they planted were along the banks of the Mussolini Canal, and they were quite small, indeed you could hardly see them they were so straggly and frail, with rows of little leaves as spindly as fish-bones: 'Call these leaves? Call these trees?' they'd said. Then we bowl into Addis Ababa and find these titans. 'Blimey,' my Uncle Adelchi had said.

They'd been planted there on the orders of the Emperor Menelik II, Negus of Ethiopia – not long after he'd thrashed us at Adowa – because the junipers that had been there before had all withered away. 'Nothing will grow here any more,' our experts had apparently told him a few years earlier, when we were still thick as thieves. Then we had reconsidered being thick as thieves with him, and decided we wanted his empire all to ourselves. So then he thrashed us, and our experts were replaced by English ones: 'Try eucalyptus,' they'd said. 'We'll give it a try,' said Menelik, and those eucalyptus did better there than in their native home.

In the Pontine Marshes, by 1935 – when Uncle Adelchi left for East Africa – they'd reached a height of four metres, which wasn't a world record, but at least now you could call them trees and not just bushes, which was what they'd been the year before. And they were all covered with sweet-smelling leaves. Then when he came home two years later they were already taller than the holding: 'Look at those blooming cliptas,' he'd said to everyone, admiringly.

In fact, the only one who admired them as much as he did was Armida – Uncle Pericles' wife – and that was because of her bees, which were crazy about those eucalyptus trees. She'd never seen them so crazy about anything. The honey they produced had a scent that was out of this world. Their hormones were at boiling-point. Roses weren't good enough for them nowadays. Only cliptas. Armida had to get Uncle Iseo to make two new hives – he was the best carpenter among us – plus one for his own wife: 'I'll teach you,' Armida had said to her, because they got along like real friends rather than just sisters-in-law.

Anyway, once they came upon those eucalyptus trees, with their long leaves and flowers which looked like buckshot, the bees went mad with joy, and fucked from sunrise to sunset – 'Dirty beasts,' Armida would say – and within three years all the hives were producing new generations of young two or three times a year. Instead of just one, there were now four hives – with little roofs, each of a different colour – standing on the bank of the Mussolini Canal on the edge of holding 517. But, as anyone around will tell you, it wasn't just a matter of quantity – the fact is, there's no better honey than honey made from eucalyptus.

Today there are eucalyptus trees all over Italy, whole forests of them, or rows and windbreaks stretching far as the eye can see. But every eucalyptus in the land – even in the most desolate, lonely uplands in Sicily or Sardinia – is a permanent and tangible sign of what at the time was called the 'Fascist Era'. Some legacy, some *damnatio memoriae*. If you really wanted to root out all memory of that period, come 25 July 1943, you wouldn't just have gone round removing all the

Fascist symbols and inscriptions from the walls and towers. If you wanted to make a thorough-going job of things, you'd also have had to go and pull every eucalyptus tree up by the roots, *ab radicibus*, as Cato put it, to rid our native soil of them.

In Cato's time, though, there hadn't been any eucalyptus trees in Italy at all, only in Australia, where there are now six-hundred species. It was James Cook who brought them to Europe, after he'd discovered them down under in 1770: 'What ever kind of trees are those?' he was said to have asked his sailors when they went ashore, just as my Uncle Adelchi had done. It was Fascism which brought them here in a big way, and had them planted in areas where reclamation was under way, because eucalyptus trees just lap up water, and keep off the mosquitoes, and they're fast-growing, too. They can grow to a hundred and thirty metres in height, and can live for six or seven centuries, like cypresses.

We imported only two species, but the Forestry Corps planted them everywhere. By now, though, that was all that they planted, and those trees did indeed lap up water – too much of it, as it turned out. Worse than camels. Nothing else could grow around them. You might want to plant corn, or clover, which would need a lot of watering. Within a radius of fifteen or twenty metres from the eucalyptus, nothing would grow, not even a blade of grass. Attila would have been over the moon.

They grew fast, too, and by the time they were three years old they'd be about five metres high. But that didn't make the peasants feel any kindlier towards them: 'The more the wretched thing grows, the more it drinks,' they'd say. You can get useful things from them, of course – eucalyptol, for example – but mosquitoes flock to them like bees to honey, and in summer you can't walk underneath one without being dive-bombed by an army of bloodsuckers. I don't really know what to say about the quality of the wood. In Australia they used it to pave the roads; in the Pontine Marshes we just used it for its cellulose, or for fires, but they would just flare up briefly and then die down. The one thing eucalyptus trees were really good for was windbreaks.

Certain strips of land – between five and ten metres wide – to either side of every road, drainage ditch, canal and borderline between the holdings, were owned by the Servicemen's Association, and they were all planted with eucalyptus trees. This meant that the wind from the sea was no longer free to root around and work itself up into a whirlwind all over the plain and up into the hills. Now it was tamed by the obstacles it encountered in its path, and lost at least sixty percent of its force, down from an average of fifty kilometres an hour to fewer than eighteen. But now they've all gone. You won't see a single eucalyptus tree anywhere between Latina and Aprilia. The Servicemen's Association doesn't exist any more. It was a useless body, everyone said so – certainly it was a Fascist authority, that I wouldn't deny, or a blend of Fascism and Communism – anyway, they wound it up, and the thousands of hectares of windbreak strips became the property of the administrative region of Latium, and they're not there any more. Gone, though not with the wind. The land's still there, but the trees were sold off to various firms a few years ago, and sawn off at the roots, one by one, and loaded on to lorries. For cellulose. All that was left was the leaves, and as soon as the first wind swept in from the sea it carried them all away, together with a couple of calves and a roof or two, to dump them on the Lepini Mountains in the first slap-up tornado to have hit the place after a long a period of abstinence.

Now every year we are dealt at least three or four such

tornadoes, which scour the plain, whip the roofs off houses, rip up greenhouses and barns and uproot the magnolias and oleanders which city folk – but also peasants, nowadays – have planted in their gardens.

The odd eucalyptus tree has come to life again. But most of them are gone forever. People leapt on them as though they were the devil incarnate. Some drilled holes in their roots and poured in acid, or injected them with petrol; some would set fire to them each summer, while others used tractors to pull them out. They couldn't get rid of them fast enough. Originally, the Servicemen's Association would send round factors to check on things, and if you meddled with a eucalyptus you would be in serious trouble. Nowadays, though, the authorities don't give a fig about them. Indeed, in the commune of Latina – where they are busy casting off every last vestige of Fascist devotion – as soon as they see one they shoot it on sight. They can't stand the sight of them nowadays. Once the *monumentum perenne*, the undying monument to reclamation, the eucalyptus is now public enemy number one. They say it's not indigenous to the region, and that the only species which are truly native to these parts are oaks, ilexes and certain types of pine. That's biological racism: eucalyptus trees as non-EU immigrants. Nowadays, every flowerbed, every roundabout, every private and every public garden is planted not with the recently banished eucalyptus, but with palm trees, bougainvillea, hydrangeas, magnolias or bamboo. Which come from Africa, tropical America, Asia, Mexico and Japan. As do tomatoes, beans and potatoes, if you come to think of it; not to mention kiwis, of which the Pontine Marshes are currently the world's greatest producer, we produce more of them than New Zealand, their place of birth.

The truth is, all this talk of their not being native is just so

322

much hogwash, otherwise the first thing to be got rid of would be the gardens at Ninfa and Fogliano, the creation of a Princess Caetani, who had the most exotic species brought in from all over the world, and in the leaflets they boast of them as being the region's number one ecological attraction. At Fogliano she had an avenue of palm trees planted around the lake, so that she could ride in the shade while her herdsmen and the other marsh-dwellers were dying of hunger and malaria in the mud. Old Benassi – the father of my Uncle Benassi, who worked for the Caetani as a sharecropper – used to say that she wasn't satisfied with just riding about in the shade, but that she used to do a Lady Godiva. Ride there in the buff. And if she came upon some strong young herdsman, he used to say, you can imagine what would happen. Anyway, that's why they shot the film *Scipio Africanus* around this lake: not because of the naked princess, but because of the dunes, which could pass for the desert, and above all for the palms. When I was young they came here to shoot *Sandokan*, with Ray Danton and Franca Bettoia, and also *Bora Bora*. Are palms a native species, in your view? Palms yes and eucalyptus no? You can't imagine my glee when the red weevil came along. There is a bit of justice in this world. Nemesis, they call it.

The truth is, the eucalyptus had once been the very symbol of reclamation, and it reminds people of the poverty and wretchedness that had once been theirs. Everyone – not just us Peruzzi – came here because they were starving. Had we been making a decent living in our own parts, we'd have stayed put. We came here like the homeless, the poor, the huddled masses who had already gone to populate America and Australia. Everyone who's made it down here – as a politician, a lawyer or whatever – is ultimately just a *parvenu*, the child of some exile with patches on his trousers, and every time he sees a eucalyptus those patches come back to haunt him. So he takes it out on the eucalyptus tree. But what's there to be ashamed of, that's what I say? Everyone comes from nowhere, in the end.

Anyway, my Uncle Adelchi hadn't gone to Africa to gawp at eucalyptus trees, but to gain us an empire. Somebody had to go, and he drew the short straw. Obviously, the Duce wasn't the first to have had the idea of conquest – as soon as Italy was unified, everyone started saying: 'Now there's no knowing what we might lay our hands on.' We'd been estranged and disunited for so long, and now that we'd come together the world had better be our oyster: 'There's lots of us, and we're strong and poor: watch out, we're on our way.' It was Francesco Crispi – and the Left – who began the colonial adventure by making up for that rabbit punch we'd been dealt by Menelik II at Adowa. After a pasting like that, though, perhaps we should have thought again: 'Maybe that's not for us, maybe we should stay at home.' Just like the people of Latina – who only have to hear the word 'Eucalyptus' to think that you're insulting them – so the Italians only have to hear the word 'Adowa' to feel they've got to rush off and clear their good name. So far we'd held back, because we simply didn't have the brawn. But now at last the trains were running on time, Fascism had knocked things into shape, and we were a world power – and above all now we had this Man of Providence, the envy of the world, or at least that's what we told ourselves – well, now at last it was time to honour the word of our forefathers and go and settle that old Adowa score. And the Peruzzi had to be of the party. How could we not?

It wasn't exactly that we had nothing to do in the Pontine Marshes – we were working like galley slaves – but that was the music in the air at the time, and we sung along to it with

324

the rest: 'Everyone else in the world has got an empire: the French, the Germans, the English. We're the odd ones out. What's wrong with us?'

Now I know that France, Germany and England aren't the whole world, and that the rest of the world didn't only not have an empire, but that it didn't have one precisely because the French, Germans and English had got one at their expense; and anyway you don't just help yourself to things – or in this case places – that aren't yours. 'But if they're doing it,' my uncles said, 'then why can't we?' Answer me that.

What we Italians needed was land. Land and raw materials. All we had was manpower. Italians weren't in short supply. But we didn't have so much as a kilo of iron or a bucket of coal. We didn't even have enough land for everyone. Our people had to emigrate elsewhere. Lastly – this should cut short all discussion – there was the matter of *Imperium*.

Sorry, what did you say? What was this *Imperium*?

Well, I'm not really quite sure either, but I'll try and explain it to you as my uncles did to me, and as Rossoni had explained it to them. Empire, or *Imperium*, doesn't just boil down to the mere fact that there's stuff up for grabs out there, and you go and grab it. That would be barefaced robbery, or theft. *Imperium* is the hallowed right to go and get that stuff, and this right is dependent upon your actions being consistent with the more general will of the forces which rule the cosmos. Or at least that's what Rossoni said: if you're living in a land of plenty, with gold and oil and iron and coal, and plenty of fertile land, but you yourself don't know how to work it, or how to make use of those raw materials, then for the cosmos it's as though all that potential was being wasted. So it seems to be fair enough for it, the cosmos, to send someone out to teach you how it's done, that is, to send everyone marching off in the direction of those famous 'magnificent and forward-looking destinies of the human race'. That's what *Imperium* is – the right to take things over in accordance with more general wishes, ones which are extra-cosmic, extra-terrestrial.

'And how can you tell who's got this *Imperium* and who hasn't?' my uncles asked.

'It's very simple,' Rossoni told them: 'All you need to do is look in the history books.' For him, *Imperium* wasn't a dove which flittered about and then plonked itself down on the head of the first-comer. It didn't land just any old where. It's a cosmic force, and in the history books it's written that the first and only time that *Imperium* – the imperial eagle – left its celestial perch to land on earth, to give rise at last to an age of universal justice and progress, was in Ancient Rome, and there alone. Does that strike you as coincidence? No, nor me. If it landed in Rome, there must have been some extra-cosmic, extra-terrestrial reason for it, otherwise why would it have landed there and nowhere else? Rome is predestined to be *Imperium*'s abode.

Sorry, what did you say? Then how can you explain the English, French and German empires?

What's that to do with anything? Those empires were usurped. What right did they have to take what was not theirs? They hadn't got *Imperium*, they hadn't been chosen and predestined by the cosmos. They were usurpers. We were the chosen ones, the direct heirs of the Roman legionaries who, led by imperial eagles perching on their ensigns, had brought peace and civilization to the world at large. It was up to us – now that we had a Man at last – to raise those ensigns once more and bring the world a new order of peace and justice in the sacred name of Rome. Then everybody burst out singing:

326

O rising sun, o free and joyous star,
subdue your horses on this hill of ours:
Greater than Rome no thing will ever be,
No empire, for we have immortal powers.

Sorry, what did you say? You don't find this sort of talk all that convincing?

Look, I couldn't agree more. But let's face it, the idea of taking democracy to Iran, or to Afghanistan, or to the moon, for that matter – at any price, with tanks and drones – doesn't seem much more sensible. Indeed, put like that it sounds total rubbish. But we believed in it – that's the whole trouble – and what's even worse is that the Duce believed in it even more than we did: 'I am a Man and we've got *Imperium*: No one in this world is stronger than we are.' For instance, when Balbo came back from his transatlantic flight all smitten with America – after they'd given him a hero's welcome, shown him around, and he'd fallen in love with the place – the Duce told him not to worry, sooner or later we'd find ourselves tangling with them too. Balbo had blenched: 'But Benito' – he was the only one who still called him by his first name, and addressed him in the familiar form – 'have you any idea of their economic might? They can magic up an air force ten times the size of ours in the twinkling of an eye. They'd overwhelm us in a trice! We're pygmies, in comparison.'

'That'll do, Italo! What can the might of their gold do in the face of the power of our blood?'

'Well, yes, quite right,' said Balbo, but as he left the room he said quietly to Rossoni: 'Is he going off his head? Do something, boy.'

'He's a Man, Italo,' was all Rossoni said.

At all events, even the Cardinal of Milan – that is, the Catholic Church – said that it was quite right and proper for us to go off and get ourselves an empire in Abyssinia: 'They're heretics, and we are going to save them from themselves in the name of Christian Rome.' So off we set with the Church's blessing, and that of all her bishops. And a whole load of chaplains came along with us, too, and they not only fought alongside us, they distinguished themselves by their bravery and enthusiasm – their patriotism – winning gold medals for having 'broken the chains of slaves and prepared the way for Catholic missionaries,' as they put it, 'who will go and liberate millions of souls and bring them back into the fold of Jesus Christ and into the bosom of the Catholic Church.'

Now just how much Jesus Christ agreed with all this I do not know. But that was how it was, and that was what we believed, and in any case it's true that they were heretics. They weren't Muslims, like the Somalis or Libyans. The Ethiopians were Christians, but they were Copts – or Monophysites – that is, they acknowledged Christ's divine but not his human nature. And for centuries and centuries they'd had a civilization of their own, with writing, literature and works of art. They had priests, churches, bishops, seminaries and seminarians. They said mass and took communion. And before becoming Christians they'd been Jews, because the first Negus, Menelik I, had been none other than the son of Solomon and the Queen of Sheba, that is, Ethiopia, and all their descendants – the Falasha – had remained Jews until the other day, when they'd gone to Israel. So you can see for yourself whether this was indeed a people without a history, and if theirs was a land without a people. Anyway, we'd got this *Imperium*, which had started flittering about again above that fateful hill in Rome, and we couldn't just say to it: 'Okay, why don't you go and flitter somewhere else?' We heeded it, and went off after it. In search of an empire. And some of the Peruzzi clan had to be in on the act. We couldn't just stay sitting quietly at home, now could we?

Above all – let's be clear about this – we were all for it, we were ardent Fascists. If we didn't up sticks and go to Africa, then kindly tell me who would? When Fiat presented the Fascist Headquarters at Littoria with two tractors, to be given to two of the Pontine Marshes' most deserving sharecroppers, guess who was the lucky recipient of one of them? You're right: Uncle Pericles. And the first thing he did with it was sell it: 'What would I be doing with a tractor?' He used part of the proceeds to buy himself two or three good milch-cows – the first black and white Friesians to be seen around these parts – and put the rest into various investments. My Uncle Benassi couldn't contain himself: 'Are you mad, Pericles? Keep the tractor, you've no idea how useful it could be, what it could earn you.'

'But I know nothing about machines.'

'Well, I do. And I could teach you.'

'No, no, I'll stick to animals. Tractors can't produce milk.' The Peruzzi family were all for livestock. The Benassi family were machine men.

To go back to Africa for a moment: they'd given us a holding, or rather two. Or indeed three, or four, or five, if you count the Dolfin family, the Lanzidei and my grandmother's relations. How could we not return the favour by going to Africa? Some member of the Peruzzi clan had to go to war, and when he arrived at our holding, Barany was pushing at an open door.

This Barany worked for the Servicemen's Association, he was an agricultural expert and a half. He'd been born at Paullo, between Lodi and Milan, but he was Hungarian by birth. Actually, his surname was Hindart Barany: Camillo Hindart Barany, he was called. His grandfather had left Hungary to come to Italy and fight with Garibaldi. He took part in the expedition of the Thousand, when they went to Sicily. But then he stayed on here, and Camillo – his grandson – was a man after his own heart, and he too fought in Mexico and in the Argonne under one of Garibaldi's grandsons, or a son of Menotti or Ricciotti, I'm not sure. In Mexico I think he fought with Pancho Villa, or Zapata. Then he was taken prisoner in the 1915–18 war, escaped from an Austrian concentration camp and went back to fight. After the war he got involved in anti-guerrilla operations against the Libyans, then went as a legionary to Fiume, then joined the Fascist Action Squads and went on the march on Rome. He was a true patriot, and between one war and another he devoted himself to agronomy. He was involved in the reclaiming of Maccarese, then of Mussolinia in Sardinia – now called Arboria – and lastly of the Pontine Marshes. In a word, he spent his time either fighting or reclaiming. *Tertium non datur.* He was also a Jew. A Hungarian Jew. When they saw him, my uncles would say to each other: 'Just look at him. He doesn't even look like a Jew,' though goodness knows what they thought a Jew looked like.

In the Pontine Marshes, when he wasn't engaged in some agrarian pursuit, surveying some plot of land or other or perfecting some new farming technique, Barany and a few sharecroppers would organize activities at the Workingmen's Club – an amateur theatrical group putting on plays, usually by Goldoni, a group of Alpine folk singers – and above all the local fledgling company of Blackshirt Militia, the so-called 'Littoria'. My uncles were part of this company, and every Saturday afternoon – the Fascist Saturday, that is – they'd go marching and exercising in the local town, or even in Littoria. As he always put it to them: 'The smarter you are here, the smarter you'll be in the fields. Forward, comrades, *eia eia alala!*' The Fascist greeting.

'*Alalala!*' my uncles would shout back at him, firstly because they were ardent Fascists, but also because they were extremely fond of him – he knew how to make you fond of him – and last, though I won't say 'and not least', because he was the agricultural agent for the Servicemen's Association.

Anyway, as soon as the Abyssinian War broke out and he heard the voice of his country calling, that was the last we saw of him: 'My country's calling.' He threw down the tools of his various trades and rushed off to fight the good fight yet again, this time together with his whole Littoria Company. He did the rounds house by house, holding by holding: 'I'm off to conquer the empire, boys! Who's coming with me?'

'Your wish is our command,' we all piped up. Anyway, it didn't take much to find volunteers around Littoria. Some people were even sent home again: 'There's too many of us.' So, as I've said, they'd given us that land, and now that our country was calling us, you could hardly not volunteer. We gave them all the volunteers they wanted, enough to fill even the last RSI 'M' Battalion, even the X Mas, the Commando Frogman Unit. And don't start telling me – again – that Abyssinia was their country, and that it was us who were the invaders. That's not what we thought, no point in going on about it, and that's the whole tragedy of the human condition: you're doomed forever to be in the wrong, thinking you're in the right.

The one we sent was Uncle Adelchi: 'It's your turn now,' because he was the only one of the older brothers who was not yet married, with children. Indeed, he himself was the first

331

to say it: 'It's my turn now' – before his brothers even had a chance – because it was all work and no play around here, and he thought a bit of adventuring and world sight-seeing would be no bad thing. So when Barany came round that evening saying: 'Who's coming with me?' Uncle Pericles didn't even hear him out, but just said: 'Would Adelchi fit the bill?'

'Of course he would,' said Barany, because he'd always liked him. And anyway, truth to tell, Uncle Adelchi was cut out to wear a uniform. Livestock for the Peruzzi, tractors for the Benassi and chevrons for Adelchi.

Uncle Adelchi had always liked uniforms. Ever since he was a child, he'd always said to his mother, my grandmother: 'When I grow up I want to join the *carabinieri*.' Or perhaps it was she who'd said to him, when he was little: 'You'll have to join the *carabinieri* when you grow up.'

He was the apple of her eye, her favourite. You must remember him, he was so tall and dark. In our family dark and fair alternated, one every two years or so, first a boy and then a girl – one fair, one dark, and so on: my Uncle Pericles was fair and my Uncle Adelchi was dark. They didn't get on well together even as children, my Uncle Pericles would rough him up at every turn; he was much closer to my Uncle Iseo, the one who came straight after Uncle Adelchi.

But Uncle Adelchi was strong as a lion, with broad shoulders and a big smile revealing the whitest of white teeth, and a perfect face, and dark eye-lashes and thick black hair with one wavy tuft which always fell to one side – a positive mane of hair, always carefully combed and gleaming with Linetti Brilliantine – and a proud and happy look which told the world: 'Hello, World, I'm here to make you happy.' As my Aunt Bissola always said, that was the look with which he'd come into the world, the moment he left his mother's womb.

How could you fail to fall in love with him?

Naturally, Uncle Adelchi knew quite well that he was not the oldest, as of course did my grandmother. The oldest male child in our family – the one who, after my grandfather, held the greatest *potestas* – was my Uncle Themistocles, and the fact that my grandmother didn't like his wife was neither here nor there. She didn't like her but she put up with her, it was she – like it or not – who would ultimately take her place. Then, when we arrived down south and were given two holdings, and my Uncle Themistocles was given one of his own, my grandmother didn't hesitate to tell him: 'That one is yours, to do what you like with.' He'd tried to put up some objections: 'No, ma, we're one single family, there are an awful lot of us but we'll carry on being one family, just as we've always been.'

'No, son, it's right this way,' and secretly my grandmother had been in seventh heaven, because she'd always got on very well with Pericles' wife, as had all the brothers-in-law, though not their wives. So Uncle Themistocles had set up on his own, and at that point – as was only right – the *potestas* had passed to Uncle Pericles, without there ever being any need to say as much. Everyone already knew it.

So Uncle Adelchi too knew that he was only the third son, and it never crossed his mind to dispute the matter. Indeed, when Uncle Themistocles set up on his own, Uncle Pericles had said: 'Okay, ma, here we all are, time for a fresh start. From now on the younger ones will have to study, they'll have to make their way in the world, so that no one will ever be able to swindle the Peruzzi clan out of their livelihood again the way the Zorzi Vila did.' And Uncle Adelchi had immediately nodded in agreement. So had my grandfather. Only my grandmother had looked doubtful: 'What about the money?

333

How much will it cost? How will we manage?'

'We'll manage,' Uncle Adelchi had said, as though he was the one who'd had the idea in the first place.

'What if they're not up to it?'

'I'll make them up to it with my boots, if necessary.'

And so it was that my younger uncles were sent to school. When we were still up north, our family stayed on until the second or third years of elementary school. Down here, on the other hand – after finishing elementary school in the local town – we were sent off each day by bicycle to Littoria, children of ten or twelve like Uncle Cesio and Aunt Ondina, come rain or shine. And when they made a fuss, true to his word, Uncle Adelchi would indeed use his boots on them: 'It's for your own good, you dunderhead.'

'But I'm cold.'

'Get off with you,' and his voice would rise to a piercing shriek, because – I don't know if I've mentioned this – that's what would happen when he shouted.

But – and this I know I have mentioned – you didn't often see him with his breeches smeared with mud, or his shirt stained with sweat, or above all with a hoe or pitchfork in his hand. He always had some more important task to be getting on with – to everyone's advantage, naturally – he might need to pay a visit to the factor, or check on the seed stock, or take a tool to be repaired. In fact, it was almost as though he was the factor, and every morning – even when we were still up in the north – he'd be at them like a rabid dog. Already shaved, he'd charge into the room where the women slept, before it had even started getting light – at five o'clock, a quarter past at most, as soon as he glimpsed the faintest gleam of brightness through the mist – and then he'd give that piercing shriek of his: 'Wake up, girls, the sun's already up,' stalking up and

334

down between the camp-beds and pulling the covers off his sisters. 'Wake up! There's work to be done.' His sisters hated him. They adored Pericles, but it was him – Adelchi – who was the real family sheep-dog, the one who stood guard over everyone and kept a wary eye on things. Had Pericles been in charge, there'd have been a whole drove of illegitimate calves.

Anyway, Adelchi had always fancied uniforms – or was it really my grandmother who fancied them? at this point, we'll never know – and he didn't much fancy manual labour; he preferred to exert authority, or to do mental work, if you could call it that, but it was really the authority he liked, and he was already asking about joining the *carabinieri* from the age of fifteen or sixteen, when we were still up north.

In those days you started young, and they took him on. My grandmother was cock-a-hoop: 'My Delchin, in the *carabinieri*!' But when he'd been taken on – in some barracks in some distant town, I don't remember where, but it was a long way from home, and he was as big and strong as he is now, but inside he was just a sixteen-year-old boy who'd never seen anything but cowpats and the mists of the Polesine – he'd sob into his pillow every night, and after a time the commanding officer came to hear of it: 'What's up, then, son? Is someone giving you a hard time?'

'I want my ma,' Adelchi had said, and so they sent him home: 'Go to your ma then, you're no use to us here.'

His brothers teased him about it for years, and when he was called up for national service in the infantry, at the age of twenty, they were quite merciless: 'Whatever you do, don't start that blubbing,' and he was mortified. But he'd grown up in the meanwhile, and this time he didn't blub, and during his national service he'd also got his school-leaving certificate. He still missed his mother, but he didn't blub. So now at last – by this time he was thirty, and he was tall and strong, and was being told to go off to Africa with Barany and take Abyssinia – he could say firmly: 'Yes, now it's my turn.'

'All yours,' his brothers said to him, and off he went with the Littoria Company of Blackshirts: 'Conquering an empire – it's got to be chickenfeed.'

But, as you know, this conquest of Abyssinia wasn't exactly a walk-over. We had a modern army – or so we thought – with artillery, trucks, cannon, machineguns, armoured cars and above all an air force. After all, hadn't we just flown the Atlantic? They on the other hand had nothing more than a couple of planes in all, and though they did have some modern weaponry, machineguns and the odd cannon purchased from abroad, what they really had in abundance was lances and swords and men. Hordes of them. So it took us eight months to get from the Eritrean border to Addis Ababa. They made us suffer. In order to stem the flow, we had to resort to arsine and mustard gas, released in drums from aircraft or discharged with shells from cannon. Gas was manna from heaven, it left blisters all over your skin, and damaged your eyes and lungs. Depending on how much you inhaled, you could die within a couple of hours, or a week. I don't know which was better.

Uncle Adelchi – truth to tell – said that he'd never seen mustard gas. 'No, I never saw any gas.' But he did admit – such was the general mood of brutality – that if we'd had it, we'd have made use of it: 'If we had had the atom bomb, we'd have pitched that in too.' They fought us off tooth and nail. We had to wrest their empire from them inch by inch. They were remorseless. If you fell into their hands, they'd gouge your eyes out and put their swords and knives to work to relieve you of those jewels that you had between your legs.

We weren't all that gentle either, truth to tell. Once, in

Asmara, when they were off duty – after having paid a visit to the whorehouse – my Uncle Adelchi and his friend Franchini had walked as far as the air field and had caught sight of the Duce's son, Vittorio, who was an airman, and they'd gone up to him, together with some other soldiers. He'd started on some boastful rants: 'The Abyssinian is an animal and he knows how to lie low. This morning we saw one running southwards, with a gun. We let him have it, and that was that. A manhunt, nice and personal – all our aircraft rummaging through every hiding-place, after one single Abyssinian.' Best of all, though, were the incendiary bombs: 'They're really a lot of laughs. You get a bit of satisfaction out of them: at least you see fire, and flames. I was trying to hit a big zareba, surrounded by tall trees, but I was having trouble. What I needed to do was aim squarely for the straw roof, but I had to give it three goes. The wretches in there could see their roof on fire, and they were jumping around as though they'd got ants in their pants,' and he was laughing.

'Ah, he's the Man's Son all right,' said Franchini from Cisterna warmly.

'What's that you said, Franchin?' my uncle asked.

Anyway, the fact remains that on that night, the night of 12–13 February 1936 – five months after the start of the advance – the commander of Littoria Company, Camillo Hindart Barany, Jewish by religion and Jewish-Hungarian by descent, reclaimer of Maccarese, Mussolinia in Sardinia and the Pontine Marshes, died there in Abyssinia during the conquest of Amba Aradam. He was forty-six years old, and in Ancient Rome legionaries were discharged from military service at the age of forty-five.

In fact, Barany had already been wounded at Abbi-Addi, but as soon as his wound had healed and he'd been released from hospital, he had refused the leave that was his due. He wanted to get back into action, even though his arm was in plaster, in a sling. That's how he died, and that's why they gave him a gold medal, and that's why we immediately renamed the local Recruiting Centre and the local Fascist Headquarters near the council houses after him. 'Camillo Baranj Barracks' it said on the pediment of the Recruiting Centre, but with a j, not with a y. After the fall of Fascism the name was changed – purged, I suppose you could say – and replaced by 'G. Mameli Barracks', which is a bit shorter than 'Camillo Baranj Barracks'; and when I was a child, every time I walked past I'd wonder why the inscription was off-centre. Now they've removed Mameli, too, and no one gives a hoot. The Recruiting Centre isn't there either, come to that, now it's the university, and there's no inscription at all left on that pediment.

The 'Barany' local Fascist Headquarters has gone as well. On 25 July 1943, though, everyone left it well alone. In fact everyone in Littoria left everything well alone, no Fascist symbol was so much as scratched, no portrait of the Duce dislodged from its place of honour – we were the only people in Italy to leave everything where it was, perhaps we felt somehow beholden to the party because of that land – while elsewhere people were already out with their chisels at six in the morning. So no one touched the 'Barany' local headquarters. But after a week or so, seeing that no one was coming to reopen it – but chiefly because a powerful smell of cheese was wafting out from under the metal shutter, a smell which filled the whole square, and people were desperately hungry, hunger ran beside you with a knife and fork in its hand – all the women from the council houses made common cause and broke down the door. And inside it was stuffed with great round cheeses, *provolone* and parmesan. Every room was full of them. The Fascists had stocked up with a vengeance.

My Uncle Adelchi said that it was stockpiled there for imminent distribution. You have to wonder, though. It's anybody's guess.

Anyway, Barany had nothing to do with the cheeses, and even if he couldn't have carried on hoping to have a local Fascist Headquarters named after him, it was quite clear that he had given something to this town, and to his country; his contribution may have been wrong-headed and ill-advised, but when he died in Africa he was at the head of hundreds of Littoria peasant-soldiers like himself. Including my uncles, and goodness knows how many other grandfathers and uncles linked to our family, reclaimers of the Pontine Marshes and founders of Latina-Littoria. *Lares et Penates*.

I'm sorry, what's that you said? That Barany was a Fascist, though?

I know he was. But he's still an ancestor of mine, and that night when he died, my Uncle Adelchi was with him on Amba Aradam. Or rather, not actually right on top of it but on the lower slopes. There were still Ethiopians above him – and all around him – and though my uncle said he had never seen gas being used, he did say that that night on Amba Aradam, while he was hiding in a ravine with his friend Franchini, at one point, when the wind changed, he had noticed a strong smell of garlic and onions which, as you know, is the smell of mustard gas.

It was cold that night on the Amba – even though it was February, which is like our August – and it was only a few hours since Uncle Adelchi and his old friend Franchini had witnessed the death of Barany, their commanding officer. They too had taken part in hand to hand fighting, and every so often my Uncle Adelchi had shouted: 'You rotten load of wogs,' in that piercing shriek of his, though there was more terror in his voice than rage. They'd dodged thrusts from swords and lances. They'd fired shots and dug their bayonets deep into the belly of the enemy, then trampled him so as to be able to move forward and get on to the next man. They'd seen their comrades falling at their sides, men with whom they'd just shared a mess-tin and a glass of grappa. And now, in that ravine – during a lull in the fighting, with that smell of onion and gunpowder, and the sound of cannon echoing around them and hand grenades exploding on other ridges and ravines; dry-mouthed, their hands still sticky with other people's blood – my uncle and Franchini suddenly felt cold.

Up to this point – while they were fighting, foaming at the mouth and blessed with the strength of ten – they hadn't felt a thing. 'It's either you or me, one of us has got to go.' But now – there in the cold – my uncle and Franchini suddenly started to shiver uncontrollably. 'We'd better try to get some rest,' my Uncle Adelchi said, 'or we'll never get home in one piece.'

So they huddled together at the bottom of the ravine, undid their puttees, took off their boots – something they hadn't done for three whole days – huddled up even closer, both shivering – and comforted each other in the only way they could. Then they felt better. The shivering stopped; backs up against the rocky ridge, loaded rifles within arms' reach, they managed a little sleep.

They were awoken some hours later – at the first light of dawn, still with the sound of cannon-fire and bombs echoing beyond the ravine – by the faint snapping of a twig, and the sight of a black face staring at them in surprise from between the branches of a bush, some three or four metres off. Without even stopping to ask him, or themselves, whether he was one of ours or not – because there were plenty of them on our side, too, around those parts: Askaris and Eritreans and Libyans and even Ethiopians, from some rebellious tribe which had been bribed to join up with us – they simply removed that face from the face of the earth. 'To hell with you,' my Uncle Adelchi said. 'Next time I'd be more careful, if I were in your shoes,' added Franchini. Anyway, now they felt as fresh as daisies. Ready for anything. They put their boots back on and off they went, ready to carry on butchering at a rate of knots, even Christians, if it came to it – because Copts were Christians, of a sort – in order not to be butchered in their turn. What else could they do? *À la guerre comme à la guerre.* If you don't want to fight, you'd best stay home.

I don't see anything to laugh about, though. What did you say? Were my uncle and Franchini lovers?

What put that idea into your mind? Not that it's anything to be ashamed of, God help us, I'm no bigot and these days anything goes. I don't know about Franchini, but my uncle was certainly not a homosexual, are you joking? They were just good friends, and they called each other 'godfather', because they'd promised to act as godfather to each other's children when they came home and took a wife, after the war. They'd been soldiers together – been comrades, during the war – and they never mentioned the matter again; they both knew it had happened but they never talked about it, what was there to say? It was love between men in time of war; a way of exorcising death. A magical-religious rite before going into battle. Like Hector and Patroclus in the Trojan war. In my opinion.

Anyway, they took Amba Aradam, the gateway to Abyssinia – *Ianua Aethiopiae* – and now the road to Addis Ababa lay clear. It wasn't exactly the *Autostrada del Sole*, and it took them another two and a half months to travel those five or six hundred kilometres, which they sprayed liberally with arsine and mustard gas, that famous manna from heaven sent to them by the Duce. Then, one May afternoon – after they'd wound their way through an endless wood of splendid eucalyptus trees – my Uncle Adelchi entered Addis Ababa.

That day, back home, all my other uncles and aunts – except for one or two who had to stay behind because, as you well know, cows need to be milked and watered every morning and evening, empire or no empire – had taken the train to Rome, and that evening they were crammed in along with all the others in the square, outside Palazzo Venezia, shouting 'Du-ce, Du-ce,' even before he appeared on the balcony, and when he did, he said: '*Blackshirts, bearers of revolution! Men and women of all Italy! Italians and friends of Italy from beyond the seas: pay heed and listen! Today Marshal Badoglio cabled me as follows: "Today, the fifth of May, at 16 hours, I made a victorious entry into Addis Ababa at the head of my troops." Italy has known many memorable moments during the course of its thirty centuries of history, but never one to equal this. I can now tell the Italian people, and the world at large, that peace has been restored.*'

More shouts of 'Du-ce, Du-ce.' Here, as everywhere else in Italy, the church bells had been ringing and the factory sirens hooting all day, summoning the Italian people to gather around the loudspeakers which had been rigged up in town and village squares. The crowds at a world football championship were nothing in comparison. And four days later we were all back – in even greater numbers, more packed in than ever – and the Duce had said: '*Raise high your banners, your weapons and your hearts, o legionaries, and greet the return of empire to the fateful hills of Rome.*' Yet more shouts of 'Du-ce.' Such things don't happen every day, and all Italian hearts now beat as one: 'Oh, he's a Man all right,' and my Uncle Adelchi too thought that the war was won.

Not a bit of it. The empire was ours, but the others still didn't see it that way and there were pockets of resistance. We'd won over any number of *ras* with our pieces of silver, and the areas they commanded were relatively quiet; but there were also places where our offerings had been refused, and where guerrilla warfare raged. They'd attack any of our units that had been cut off, and if a soldier found himself on his own it was certain curtains, he'd get the works, he'd be blinded and castrated and left to die on the spot, stiff as a board and naked in the sun. Obviously, reprisals were in order, and that's how it went on until we finally left.

My uncle would tell a story about the time they'd been incorporated into a company of *carabinieri* – he couldn't believe it: 'It's not my first time, either,' he'd say to everyone as they walked beside him, though he failed to mention that he'd done a bit of blubbing on the job – and they'd surrounded a village of straw-roofed huts, because there'd been guerrilla action in the region. 'Nobody move! Stay where you are, and don't fire unless I tell you to,' the captain said, after having had them line up in a circle. Then he set fire to the village and ordered them to fire on anything that moved: men, women, children or goats.

Another time – when they'd come upon one of our men who'd been killed on a road somewhere in the middle of the tableland – they went into the nearest village and the section leader – the Apache Sergeant – summoned the village headman and ordered him, in front of all the natives, to hand over the person responsible: 'It's either him or you.'

'I don't know who did it,' the headman said to the Askari who was acting as interpreter.

'All right then,' said our section leader brusquely, and ordered him to come out of the circle of huts – with all the villagers behind him – and go to a great big termites' nest that happened to be nearby. Then he ordered him to dig a hole in it, almost as deep as he was tall, and had him climb into it, with just his head protruding, his whole body smothered in honey. As soon as they scented it, all the termites came crawling out. And ate him alive. And, as they left the village, our men could hear his dying cries. 'But war is war, that's how you treat guerrilla fighters, what else could we do?' said Franchini to us boys whenever he came to call on my Uncle Adelchi, and they'd start reminiscing about the good old days, and laughing heartily. 'How else do you keep an empire going?'

But these reprisals hadn't been carried out just by the soldiers or Blackshirts – I call them Blackshirts, but they'd taken off those shirts the moment they arrived in the port of Massaua, and put on colonial uniforms like the rest of the army, because otherwise they'd have exploded, in that heat – they'd been mainly done by civilians: by the clerks and shopkeepers and truck drivers who'd already poured in from the Fatherland. It was civilians who did most of the work during those three days when we were given a free hand, after the attempt on Graziani's life. They wandered all round Addis Ababa armed with clubs and iron bars and petrol tanks. My uncle saw a truck driver knock down an old black man with a club, and then run him through the head with his bayonet. Another time he met an architect who was there working on the town-plan for the new Addis Ababa, and he complained that he'd thrown so many hand grenades that his arm ached.

Anyway, Graziani had succeeded Badoglio as Viceroy, and he got off lightly – they had to remove 350 little splinters, but they were just skin-deep. But seven people died in the attack,

344

and fifty or so were wounded. It was 19 February 1937 – one year after the conquest of Amba Aradam – and a small group of Abyssinian intellectuals, who had studied in Europe, took advantage of the reception organized to celebrate the birth of a son to Umberto of Savoy, long may he reign. A couple of them scaled a small building, threw down eight Breda bombs and scarpered. Another student was waiting for them at the bottom with a car.

Our reprisals weren't long in coming. Three days of pain for Addis Ababa. Not a black to be seen, as I've already said. And goodness knows how many dead. Some people say six thousand, others thirty thousand. Anyway, after a few weeks the Intelligence Service told Graziani that the Abyssinian clergy were behind the plot – 'It was the Coptic priests, they organized the whole thing' – and that very day the two assailants were going to be taken to Debra Libanos, the main Abyssinian Coptic shrine, a sort of Lourdes, or a Saint Peter's if you like, where thousands of faithful would flood in each day from all over Ethiopia. From there they'd go on to join other groups of partisans, and then take refuge over the border in Sudan. And then the order came: 'Reprisal time!'

Three months had passed since the attack, and my Uncle Adelchi and his old friend Franchini were living a quiet life in quarters. Then suddenly, one day in May, they were loaded on to lorries, and by that same evening – together with their fellow soldiers – they had surrounded Debra Libanos, which consisted of two large brick churches and some thousand straw-roofed huts where the priests lived. Over the days that followed they rounded up any number of priests, bishops, abbots, deacons, seminarians, theology students, altar boys, monks, nuns and the odd pilgrim, and transported some of them to the banks of a nearby canyon – on the plain of Laga

Wolde – at the bottom of which there was a river, almost dry at that time of year. They lined them up on the overhanging rock and mowed down the lot of them with machineguns. Then they went round delivering the *coup de grace* – one shove, and down they hurtled into the void. It was 21 May 1937, and by four in the morning – three o'clock our time – it was all over. My uncle was in a platoon of guards which was reinforcing the machinegunners, and he had orders to fire on anyone who might try and escape.

'But these are priests, Adelchi,' Franchini said, now on the verge of tears.

'Priests they may be, but they're heretic priests! Didn't you hear what the chaplain said? Just pipe down and get on with the shooting, Franchin, before you get shot yourself.'

Five days later, we took the rest – the ones who'd been left behind under armed guard at Debra Libanos – to Engacha, near Debra Berhan, where two great trenches had already been dug out with excavators. We lined them up in front of them – almost all of them were deacons, young boys, young seminarians – and they too got the machinegun treatment.

'But they're priests, they're altar boys,' Franchini beseeched again, but very quietly now, still on the verge of tears.

'Just pipe down, damn you!' my uncle swore back at him.

Had they done a thing like that to us Catholics, we'd still be on our knees in prayer in St. Peter's Square. We'd have made saints of every man-jack of them, and I wouldn't want to disillusion you, but there really isn't much difference between hauling democracy around on the barrel of a gun, and doing the same with empire. But the Duce said we were doing it for their good: 'We brought them civilization.'

But – as you know – that empire didn't provide us with

one single kilo of iron or coal, or any kind of raw material, let alone oil. There was oil galore in Libya, but we never managed to find it. That only happened later. And we found almost as much land for emigrants as we found iron and coal, that is, none. There was very little fertile land, mostly it was a stony wilderness. Believe you me: next time the imperial eagle starts flittering around all over our fateful hills with all that *Imperium* clutched in its talons, I suggest we call in the pest control.

Meanwhile, in the Pontine Marshes – on holding 517, on the Left-Hand Parallel which runs along the Mussolini Canal – on 21 May 1937, at around two, two-thirty, my grandmother was alone in the house, in the kitchen, spinning wool near the window – everyone else was out working in the fields. The cat and dog were playing in their basket at her feet; in our household cats and dogs always played and slept together, always got on; unlike their owners.

At a certain point – the clock was ticking away quietly on the wall – she nodded off, and the wool fell from her fingers. In their basket, the cat and dog were napping too. Then she fell into a deeper sleep, and suddenly a black cloak appeared to her in a dream, covering her entirely, like a layer of asphalt, and she found she couldn't breathe. She tried to cry out, and waved her hands about, trying to make a draught, but still she couldn't breathe, and her throat was burning. She thought that she was dying and she knew, even as she was dreaming, that it was a dream, and she tried to wake herself up, but she just couldn't, that black cloak had her ever more firmly in its grip: 'Holy Mary, Mother of God, I'm dying!' she thought, and commended her soul to God, still in the dream.

Suddenly Armida – Uncle Pericles' wife – came rushing into the kitchen, shrieking: 'What's going on?'

So my grandmother woke up – or rather, finally managed to

wake herself up, to struggle free of that black cloak – and then the dog and the cat woke up too, and shot off like lightning. Outside there was the sound of thousands of bees, whirring and swirling. Armida had been working in the beet-field, and she'd thrown down her hoe to follow them – 'Now where's she off to, always after those dratted bees?' her sisters-in-law had grumbled – and run into the house.

'A black cloak, I was dreaming about a black cloak, I thought that I was dying,' panted my grandmother, and turned round to look behind her at the clock to see what time it was. It was almost three, and my Uncle Adelchi – out there in East Africa, on the edge of that canyon at Laga Wolde – had just fired his last shot in the direction of those priests and altar boys who had been making their doomed efforts at escape.

Five days later she had the same dream again. It was early morning – she was half-awake – and this time she was seriously alarmed: 'Twice in five days? Something must have happened. Oh God, Adelchi, Adelchin!' She had herself driven by cart to the local town to light a candle in the church, and after a few days a letter arrived saying that he was all right, that his period of active duty was almost at an end and that he'd be home within a month at most. 'The Lord be praised,' she said.

But I wouldn't want you to think that it was some sort of permanent open season with us and the priests, and that every time a member of the Peruzzi family ran into one, he'd take a potshot at him. It wasn't like that at all. It was sheer bad luck. We, like everyone else, are straws in the wind of fate. We go where that wind blows us. And once we're where it's blown us – every time – we do what it's blown us there to do. We had no bone to pick with priests. Quite the reverse.

As soon as we got here – the very first Sunday – my grandmother had herself driven by cart into the local town, so she could go to mass. And the next Sunday, and the next. My grandfather would drop her off outside the church and go off to the wine-shop. Then when he saw her coming in his direction he'd say to his friends: 'Wait for me, I'll be right back.' And he'd drive her home and go back and join them, and so it went on for several weeks. 'I wonder what's got into her,' he thought.

Up in the north, she did feel the urge to attend mass from time to time. She'd give something to the priest, and also to the friars when they went from door to door, but she'd rarely go to mass except at Easter and Christmas. Once we were down here, though, she got a bee in her bonnet about going every Sunday, regular as the pendulum clock that hung on our wall. 'It won't last,' my grandfather would say.

Anyway, to cut a long story short, one Sunday morning, when they had all just arrived outside the church, and my grandfather was shouting 'whoa' at the donkey, and waiting a bit impatiently for her to hurry up and get out so that he could carry on to the wine-shop – where his friends were waiting for him, glasses at the ready and cards shuffled, prior to a game of *briscola* – she said to him: 'Wait a minute! You're coming too.'

'What?' he yelped.

'You're coming too!'

'Have you taken leave of your senses? Giddy up,' he shouted to the donkey.

On the journey back he looked daggers at her, and when we were back home – whenever he hove into sight – she shrieked at him like a madwoman all week long.

'What's got into ma?' everyone asked.

'How should I know?' he snapped.

When the next Sunday came, though, she got up at dawn

and started shrieking, so loudly the whole holding could hear her: 'Wake up! Everyone out of bed! It's Sunday! Off to mass, the lot of you!'

'To mass?' someone said. 'But I went at Christmas,' objected someone else. But she was adamant. She dragged them all out of bed and got them all washed, shaved and into their Sunday best, that is, into clean clothes, and with shoes on their feet. Even Uncle Pericles was resigned: 'So it's off to mass we go then,' and he and Uncle Iseo laughed about it together. Armida on the other hand was cock-a-hoop, not about going to mass as such, but about going into town with all the children and husbands decently turned out. So at a certain point even my grandfather smelt a rat and asked nervously: 'Me too?'

'Yes, you too,' my grandmother shrieked back. 'We're making a fresh start in a new place. From now onwards the Peruzzi family always goes to mass on Sundays.'

'The Peruzzi family? It's me who's the Peruzzi around here. Since when were you a Peruzzi? I'm not going anywhere,' and he stayed at home. 'I'll keep an eye on the place,' he added at the last minute, as though to leave open the possibility of a last minute reconciliation.

'Who are you keeping an eye out for?' she asked him, already seated in the cart. 'What are you afraid of, that the people from Sezze might come round and pinch the lot?'

But he stayed put. 'Monti and Tognetti...' he muttered to himself. Then, after a bit, he thought: 'What's stopping me from going to the wine-shop? The people from Sezze, my eye.' And he went straight into the stable, harnessed the only remaining donkey and set off.

But when he got there, and found the place empty, that really brought him up short: 'Where are they all?' he asked the landlord nervously.

'At mass. They've all gone to mass.'

'Bugger that,' said my grandfather, and the following Sunday he found himself going too. He didn't want to be the last of the Mohicans.

He and his friends sat in the back of the church on the men's side – to the left as you went in, whereas the women sat on the right; small children of either sex sat with their mothers and then, after they'd been confirmed, boys joined the men-folk on the left, but in the front, whereas the older men sat at the back – and as soon as the priest had come in and said a couple of prayers, they crossed themselves, genuflected, after a fashion, and rushed off to the wine-shop. They'd put in an appearance. They'd checked in.

Once, though – on the way home – my grandmother said to him mildly: 'I turned round to look for you in church, and you didn't seem to be there.'

'Well, you didn't look properly. There were a lot of people, someone must have been blocking your view.'

'Oh yes?' she retorted: 'So tell me what the priest said in the sermon, after the gospel?'

'That you're one crafty bitch!' he shouted, and the next Sunday he had to sit it out. But he soon learned from his mistake, and he and his friends started leaving early again, even before the priest had finished saying '*Introibo ad altare Dei*,' but when the mass was over – as soon as the first little boy walked past the wine-shop – everyone would ask him: 'What did the priest have to say?'

And the boy would tell them, more or less.

'Well done,' and they'd be in the clear.

From then onwards, though, there was no turning back: everyone in my family was now an ardent Catholic. But so was everybody else. Even the people from Friuli and around Ferrara. Not just those from the Veneto, who'd always been a bit priest-ridden even when we'd been up north. Now everyone was at it, even people who – like us – had never had much of a taste for holy water in the past. But now it started to go down even better than wine, and once you start going to church you get a taste for it, and now we started praying round the clock, even at home, on weekdays. The moment we got up, and before we went to bed at night – my grandmother would wallop us if we didn't – and before every meal. Nor was there any dispensation for my grandfather: 'But what about Monti and Tognetti?' he tried saying to her once.

'May they rest in peace, and not before time, and you can go to hell and them along with you,' and that shut him up – 'Wily old cow,' was all he'd say, but quietly, and only to himself – and woe betide you if a swearword passed your lips when you were in the house. The place was more like a nunnery rather than a farmhouse.

I'm sorry, what's that you said? That in your view this sudden conversion had something to do with the priest from Comacchio?

No, I don't think so. That had happened nine years earlier. If it was just a question of somehow atoning for that, my grandmother had had plenty of time while we were still up north, there was no point in waiting till we'd got down here. And anyway, it was us who'd killed him, not the whole neighbourhood. Who'd they all killed, to suddenly be converted and pray like monks throughout the whole of the Pontine Marshes? You should have been here in the month of May, with every family saying the rosary together – well, even now all you need to do is take a stroll down the roads in front of the holdings of a May evening, and see all the little chapels

352

and statues of Our Lady we've put up at every crossroads. And every family has got a relative who's a priest. It must have been something else – my grandmother was no fool; I think it was more about creating a sense of community.

You see, right from the start we'd pulled together with our neighbours, sharing our tasks, our tools, even our livestock. There'd been an immediate sense of total solidarity, of camaraderie – we were an activist community, as they say nowadays – ever since we'd been on that exodus together. We were the Pilgrim Fathers. Tasks like harvesting, weeding, picking cotton and pulling up sugar beets were things we'd always done together, first on one holding and then on another, just like they do nowadays with grapes and kiwi fruit. All those rows of people singing in the heat, shaded by their broad-brimmed straw hats, bent low over the ground, chatting away as they pulled up the sugar beet – they were a sight to see.

One custom we'd brought with us from the Veneto was that of the so-called *filo* – of meeting up in the evening, after supper, now on one holding and now on another, to tell each other stories and fairy-tales and suchlike, by candlelight, or the light of an oil lamp. In winter we'd go into the cowsheds, together with the animals, because it was warmer there. People would bring along their chairs, or stools, they didn't want to spend the evening standing up. Every so often a cow would lift her tail and we'd all back off in a hurry, to avoid being pissed on. And we'd all burst out laughing. In summer we'd gather on the road, and sit on the parapets on the bridges. And this tradition of the so-called *filo* – going to each other's holdings to have a chat, which originally came from the Veneto, as I've said – soon caught on with other communities as well, those from Emilia or Friuli who hadn't known about such things when they were still up north. Another custom which soon spread was that of having dances on the threshing-floor, but that came from round Ferrara; the people from the Veneto were rather prim and proper, but once they got down here they too became keen dancers, just as the people from Ferrara were always up for a *filo*. Sometimes some local villager would join the dance, and that always spelled trouble.

Anyway, we were a tight-knit group who'd been transplanted from home straight into the heart of the 'land of the wogs' – as my Aunt Bissola used to say – 'and we were about as welcome as a hole in the head.' That didn't mean that somehow or other – with a bit of give and take – we hadn't learned how to rub along together. My Uncle Adelchi for example – as I've already told you – was on close terms with a man from Cisterna. But such good friendships were unusual; almost from the start there were mixed marriages – always an early sign of integration between groups with different cultural backgrounds – but they always smacked slightly of 'imperialism'.

At first these mixed marriages were always, as it were, one way affairs, with a man from the Veneto marrying a woman from the Lepini Mountains and taking her off with him to live on a holding down in the plain. There she would have to forget her own dialect and start speaking that of her new family, as happened with my Aunt Nazzarena, who was from Cori, a village in the hills between Norma and Roccamassima.

They were even more dirt poor than we were, and when we started planting corn down on the plain, the women from the hills would come down to glean, and this Nazzarena was one of them. She was a good-looking girl. My grandmother was courteous by nature, and she wasn't at all standoffish, so when this Nazzarena showed up every now and again – coming and going up and down from the hills – my grandmother would give her the odd day's work. It was she who brought us those first olives, the ones my grandmother threw away. But the one who couldn't take his eyes off her was my Uncle Adrasto, one of the younger ones, who must have been about sixteen or seventeen when we harvested our first corn, in 1933. She herself must have been fourteen or fifteen, and she spoke this strange dialect, but she was good-looking, and my Uncle Adrasto began to go up and down the hills after her – on his bicycle – a couple of times a week. He'd always set off at a great pace, but by the time he got to Doganella, where the road began to run uphill, he'd start swearing like a trooper. When he got near the top – the village was divided into two parts and, as luck would have it, she didn't live in the lower part of Cori, but in the upper part – he'd be pedalling fit to burst, but at a certain point he'd always have to get off and push the bike by hand, and then he'd always say: 'Enough's enough, I'm never coming up here again. I'll get myself another woman from somewhere lower down.' But the moment he caught sight of her, he immediately knew that he'd be going back up again. And after a few more comings and goings he married her and brought her down here, to the holding on the plain: 'That's enough mountaineering for the moment.'

At first she liked being down there, because she loved Adrasto, but after a while – she was only sixteen or seventeen, after all, and there were so many people all over the place, in every room, as well as in the cowshed, in the courtyard and on the threshing-floor, all issuing orders in their own strange dialect – quite understandably, she began to feel rather at a loss.

After a while they actually stopped talking to her, they talked among themselves as though she wasn't there, or else they tried to teach her things by way of gestures – she was a foreigner in a strange land – and when they all went into the cowshed of an evening to carry on with their *filos*, she'd sit outside on the drinking trough and start to cry. What else could she do? But then she learned our dialect – and forgot her own – and nowadays she speaks it better than you or me. Despite all this, she still remained a 'wog'. There was nothing to be done about it, it was just ingrained in her, a bit like original sin.

In patriarchal sharecroppers' families – this may give you an idea of what she was up against – the latest daughter-in-law to join the clan was never called by her first name – Giulia or Francesca or whatever – not even by her husband. She was just known as 'wife', or else 'the wife', and if someone went into town for some reason or other – to the blacksmith or the dispensary, or to the ironmongers or the wine-shop – it was perfectly good manners to ask him simply: 'How's the wife?' She wouldn't get her real name back until someone else in the family married, and a new daughter-in-law entered the fold. And if nobody did, that was how she was referred to for the rest of her life. If they'd had a chance, they'd have put the word 'wife' on her very tombstone. Sometimes the people in the local town would ask after my Aunt Nazzarena, or other local women like herself who'd learned the northern dialects, by saying: 'How's the wog?' and this would set her off into floods of tears, she was so touchy. Anyway, it was always the man from the north who married the wog woman. Never the other way around.

I'm sorry, what's that you said? What about Aunt Bissola and Lanzidei?

What sort of talk is that? I'm sorry, Aunt Bissola was quality goods, as they say, a choice item, a prime cut. Damaged goods are a different matter. Damaged good are hard to get rid of, even at rock bottom prices. It was never quite clear how Aunt

356

Santapace got hitched up with Uncle Benassi, though. My uncles tended to be unforthcoming on the subject, indeed they would give conflicting versions of the story. I don't know for sure, but I think there must have been a touch of the wrong side of the blanket there, otherwise why would my uncles have meekly handed over an eighteen-year-old Peruzzi heifer like Santapace to a thirty-two year-old half-wog like Benassi? Yet in fact my Uncle Pericles regarded him very highly; it was 'Benassi this' and 'Benassi that' from dawn to dusk. He paid no heed to him when he sold the tractor, but nonetheless he admired him greatly. It was mutual. Uncle Iseo admired him too, and so did Uncle Themistocles. I don't know what was behind it all.

It was only after the Second World War – in the Fifties and Sixties – that things started going the other way, with northern women marrying wogs from the Lepini Mountains. But even then, the new family would always settle on the plain. There isn't a single woman from the Veneto up on the Lepini Mountains, apart from the mother of someone called Lidano Sensucci, the editor of *Resistenza Lepina*, who wrote the famous couplet '*The man from Sezze's greatest hope is to find that Latina's been wiped off the map.*' But here too research has shown that it was the father who had had to go down into the plains – to Santa Fecitola – and he, Lidano Sensucci, that is, only spoke the Sezze dialect because every so often his grandfather would come and drag him up to Sezze and have him stay there for a while. Kidnap him, really. Just like in a Western. Wasp against Apache. It would have taken John Wayne to set Sensucci free. These are the sort of marital ties which have always been typical of what you might call 'imperialist' situations. When a territory is conquered, that's how marriages work, and in Eritrea and Abyssinia we had all the black women we wanted – as wives, lovers or concubines – but you can imagine the uproar that would have ensued if an Abyssinian man had taken it into his head to lay hands on an Italian woman.

Regrettably enough, all that we took from our local wogs from the Lepini Mountains was their land and their women. For everything else we were, as it were, at their mercy. We'd come down here without any elite or ruling class. We were the waifs, the landless, the have-nots, and down here it was the others who were the ruling class. The school-teachers, the doctors, the lawyers and the politicians were all wogs from the Lepini Mountains, who'd gone straight down to Littoria to take command. So every time we needed something, or rather someone – a doctor or a lawyer, say – we had no option but to turn to them, bearing gifts of eggs and chickens. But then, as soon as we were off the premises, we'd say to each other: 'How d'you expect him to understand? He's a wog.'

Anyway, nowadays when people talk about the share-croppers in the Pontine Marshes they just refer to them as 'the people from the Veneto'. A lot did come from the Veneto, it's true, but they also came from other places. Of the original three thousand families brought south by the Servicemen's Association, only a third were from the Veneto; the other two thirds came from Friuli and around Ferrara. On the other side of the Appian Way, the private holdings, and those belonging to the Caetani family, were given to people from Umbria and the Marches – like my Uncle Benassi, who was from Umbria – while those belonging to the agricultural cooperatives were settled with people from Bassiano, Cisterna, Sermoneta and Sezze. At a later stage – at Aprilia and Pomezia – the association also gave holdings to families of sharecroppers who had previously emigrated to France, Romania and

358

Bosnia-Herzegovina. In Pomezia there were also families of sharecroppers from the Province of Forli, in Romagna, where Mussolini came from.

Among ourselves, we too refer to each other as being 'from the Veneto', or 'from Friuli', or 'from around Ferrara', depending on our district of origin. But for everyone else we're just 'from the Veneto', as though we'd become a new and separate ethnic group, the 'Veneto-Pontines'. And do you know why? Because all the differences that did indeed exist between us sharecroppers, when we were in the north, were as nought in comparison to the absolute difference between us and the local people of the Lepini Mountains. For us they were all wogs, as indeed were the people from Umbria and the Marches, who were wogs from the north, as you might say.

But – as you know – the devil often makes pots but he never makes lids, he doesn't go in for long-term thinking, and this forging of a collective identity, this creation of a people called the 'Veneto-Pontines', marking out people who weren't originally from the Pontine Marshes, wasn't the only distinction at work around those parts: there was a further distinction, between town and country. Because in Littoria the first inhabitants were middle-class white-collar families who'd been recruited in Rome, and we who lived in the country were all seen by them as 'people from the Veneto'. When we went into town, they'd call us all 'those sharecroppers'. For the town-dwellers in the Pontine Marshes, 'sharecropper' is worse than 'nigger'; according to them, it suggests someone who's ignorant and boorish, like *cafone* in Naples or *burino* in Rome; a lout, an oaf. And if for us the people from the Lepini Mountains were the Apaches, and the people from Umbria and the Marches were the Sioux, for the people of Latina we were and still are wasps, but country wasps. We were Missouri, they

359

were New York. The people from Sezze were the people from Sezze, and that said it all.

So we were just a rural enclave caught between two fronts: surrounded by a great sea of wogs from the countryside, and threatened by an arrogant group of city-dwelling Romans from the towns. What could we do? It was pull together or sink. And so we pulled together. Of course, the Servicemen's Association and the Fascist Party worked towards this same end, encouraging all the country-dwellers to make common cause, to form the critical mass which would ensure the survival of Fascism over time. And then there were the seaside holiday camps for children, the drill you did at the *Balilla*, the *Dux* Camps, the various paramilitary organizations, and cinemas in every village, showing *Luce Films*, and Thespis' carts bringing the theatre into the village square, and travelling libraries, the Fascist version of epiphany, friendly societies, local Fascist activities and Workingmen's Clubs.

Very soon, though, after we'd made our first contacts in the street, and in the neighbourhood – in fact, these usually had their origins in the exodus itself – we also built up contacts in the town: at the post office, in the dispensary, at the blacksmith's and above all at the wine-shop. Some American historians are now saying that there weren't any bars or wine-shops in the villages in the Pontine Marshes until they came along: 'They were forbidden by the party, so that the sharecroppers couldn't socialize or build up any community spirit, and the authorities could keep a firmer grip on them.' But that's complete nonsense. I don't deny for a moment that the Americans brought us freedom and democracy – for goodness sake, as you know, I'm very grateful to them – but to say that they brought us bars and wine-shops is just absurd. They could have had their fill of bars, had they so wanted, and the Pontine Marshes were awash with wine-shops, and you could play bowls outside each one of them – on every street, at every corner – and our old men were always drunk. Old Pellicelli, for example, couldn't get on his bicycle after he'd had a few. The others in the wine-shop knew this, and when it was closing time, or he'd had enough wine and *briscola*, he'd say to them: 'Time to go home,' and a couple of them would put him on his bicycle – one holding the bike, the other holding Pellicelli – and they'd give him a shove and he'd start pedalling for home. Once he got there – on the bridge outside his house – he'd fall off, and his family would come out and pick him up. But if for some reason or other he had to stop en route, he couldn't get on again, and he'd spend hours going from one side of the bike to the other but he couldn't get on to that saddle no matter what he did, at least not until he'd sobered up again. This went on for years without mishap, until finally one night on the Appian Way his luck ran out, and a car ran into him head on.

Anyway, sometimes it seemed to me that in 1928 every one of the twenty-five thousand out-of-work barkeepers in Italy had moved to the Pontine Marshes. There were three bars in Borgo Carso alone – all with bowls pitches in front of them – and any number of crossings on the roads running past the holdings still bear the name 'the Little Stall', in memory of the first ramshackle wooden stalls which sold wine by the glass, put there by various enterprising would-be landlords. The landlords arrived here in the Pontine Marshes even before the drainage people and the sharecroppers.

People also say that Mussolini wasn't a drinker, and that's rubbish too, Nowadays it's said that all he drank was water, plus litres and litres of milk. He may not have drunk in his own home, I can't argue with that, but in the Peruzzi household he drank, and how. And not only in the Peruzzi household either, but on other holdings too, because, as you may know, after he'd refused to attend the opening of Littoria he developed quite a taste for the place and was always hanging around there. Not just on official visits, with his car and escort, but above all on his own, roaring about on his motorbike, a Guzzi 500 Falcone Sport, incognito, to sniff around the place. And when he got back to Rome there'd always be trouble. According to Rossoni, he'd fire off volleys of adverse comments in all directions: '*There's grass growing all along such and such a canal, have it cut immediately. There's a hole in such and such a road, have it repaired. Who was the dolt who pruned the eucalyptus trees in Littoria like that? Have him sent into internal exile.*'

So, he was always hanging about around these parts – he seems to have had a permanent mistress in Littoria, whom he'd set up with a garage and a petrol pump which is a gem of Fascist architecture – and almost every holding has a photograph of the present owner's grandfather or grandmother sitting next to Mussolini, who's drinking a glass of the red wine we used to call *clinton*. Nowadays this type of wine is banned throughout the EU because of the prussic acid it contains, and its high concentration of methanol, which damage the optic nerve and the brain cells respectively. In short, it's more or less a weapon of mass destruction: either you die, or you go blind and mad. But it was good, and I could still lay my hand on a bottle or two for you, if you were interested; there are still a few vineyards producing it in the Veneto, in Friuli and, of course, in the Pontine Marshes; they're kept well out of sight, like illegal immigrants, but they're as pampered as any footballer. Just don't tip the EU the wink.

The Duce called round at our place shortly after the official opening of Littoria. He was going along the Left-Hand Parallel, with a motorcade, together with Cencelli, who was showing him all he'd been doing. As they were going by, he caught sight of my grandmother on the bridge outside the holding: 'But I know her,' he said to Cencelli. Then: 'Stop,' he shouted to the driver, 'go back.'

The driver put the car into reverse – almost crashing into the Servicemen's Association car which was just behind – and back they went to the bridge, and he jumped out: 'Peruzzi! Got any harrows that need sorting out?'

You should have seen my grandmother. She was scared witless – he was the Duce now, not just the callow youth who'd once called by – and so were my uncles, and even my grandfather. But my grandmother managed to keep her feelings to herself; she thrust out her chest and threw back her shoulders and answered him: 'Forget the harrows, there are other things that need sorting out round here.'

According to my Aunt Bissola, Cencelli made a face as though he'd been asked to eat a turd. The Duce, on the other hand, began to laugh, and said to my grandfather: 'The years go by, but she never changes, eh?'

'Tell me about it, Duce.'

Then he laughed some more, and took a walk round her, to see what changes there'd been around those parts – especially around the back. Not many, it would seem. Because he laughed again, and said: 'I'll be back. Right now I've got to be off with these fine fellows, but I'll be back. So have those harrows ready.' And off he went.

So then my grandfather started calling her a 'dirty bitch' again all afternoon, and she started to blush: 'So what's all this, Peruzzi?'

'Dirty bitch,' he'd say, more loudly.

'What's up with those two?' the rest of the family started

363

to ask.

'The Duce had it off with her, when we were still up north,' one of my young cousins must have said.

This earned him a hearty clip around the ears. 'That's quite enough of that.'

But my grandfather had heard what the child had said: 'Wait till I get my hands on him! I'll show him what's what!' he bellowed.

Meanwhile, the child's mother had taken him into her arms: 'But he's only little, he doesn't know what he's saying.'

'I'll show him who's who around these parts!' my grandfather went on bellowing.

'Hush now, Peruzzi,' said my grandmother, 'or they'll take the holding away from us and send us into internal exile.'

In short, this ding-dong carried on until nightfall, until they were curled up in bed, because these things always end up the same way, and she carried on trying to reassure him: 'But are you mad, Peruzzi? When would I have done it? We were never alone together, not even for a moment, you were always there too. And I don't even like the Man,' but on he went at her, hammer and tongs.

'But he was looking at your behind.'

'What behind,' she shouted back. 'I'm an old woman now.' And the next day they were like two turtledoves.

From that day onwards, though, as soon as any child was old enough to understand what was going on around him and could string two words together, all the older cousins and brothers and sisters would gather in the barn and say to him: 'Look, the Duce had it off with our grandmother but you mustn't say so, or grandfather will go off his head. Got it?'

'Yes. The Duce had it off with my grandmother,' and they almost always kept their word. Only once or twice did one of

364

my little cousins go to my grandmother and ask her: 'Grandma, is it true that you had it off with the Duce?'

Then there'd be clips round the ear like you'd never believe. And when he came back all the others would say to him: 'What did we tell you?' and then they'd start laying into him as well.

Anyway, that time, he – the Man – didn't show up again for another month or so. The one who showed up was Rossoni, but Rossoni was another matter for my grandfather, he was almost one of us, a sort of substitute son or younger brother.

But when July came, and it was threshing-time, and someone in high places came up with the idea of having the Duce do his bit too, well, then he said: 'Excellent! A fine idea! We'll do the threshing with the Peruzzi family,' and they all came round to our place with cine-cameras from the *Istituto Luce News Service*. And if you look at the films and photos of the time which are in all the history books, you'll see that the woman wearing a big straw hat and a flowered dress, and passing the sheaves of corn to the Duce, is my grandmother. And the girl holding the plates who is just behind him in another photo, pouring him some of that *clinton* wine, which he is swigging down despite everything the Americans say – except for Mia Fuller, who knows better – is my Aunt Bissola; and the man driving the tractor, who Mussolini turns to and says: 'Come on, driver! Rev her up,' meaning 'Start up the threshing-machine,' is my Uncle Benassi.

But there's also something else to be said about that particular threshing-time. The corn that was being threshed wasn't all our own. Celebrations were in order, because this was the first corn to be harvested in the Pontine Marshes. No arguing about that. After thousands and thousands of years of death and desolation – with swamps, ravines, forests, wild boar,

365

poisonous snakes, tarantulas, anopheles mosquitoes, malaria and anything else nasty that you care to name – suddenly corn now came on the scene, and surely that was something to be celebrated, something worthy of a film, however small, to be shown throughout Italy and indeed the world. It was the first harvest from this virgin land, but you need at least two or three years before you can hope for a good one. The earth needs to be 'christened'; having been purely mineral, it must become organic humus. That takes time. Rome wasn't built in a day, either, and as you know, at that time – our time, that is, not the Roman times – the average yield for corn was between 1800 and 3000 kilos per hectare, 1800 on the least productive land and 3000 on the most fertile. Over the following years we Peruzzi always harvested 3000 and even 4000 kilos per hectare, but in 1933 – at that first harvest – we barely harvested what we had sowed. People were in despair. 'We might as well have stayed up north,' as my grandmother put it.

We didn't realize that it all took time. It was the people from the Servicemen's Association who explained that to us. Then it was explained to us again by someone called Pascale, an agronomist from Naples who was working for a large farm on the other side of the Appian Way which had remained in private hands – it belonged to the family of the Counts of Cerisano-Caratelli – and he would also be called in from time to time by the Board of Agriculture to visit the association's holdings and talk to the sharecroppers. This Pascale was a good man, gentle and nice, he'd explain everything to you in great detail, though he wouldn't leave until he'd got the regulation capon in his hand. Then he'd say: 'No, no, please, I wouldn't dream of it,' and meanwhile he had it firmly in his grip, you couldn't have prised it away from him even if you'd wanted to. Not even with clippers. You'd have had to cut off his hand with an axe. He always went back from his trip around the holdings with his cart brimming with booty.

But there was one thing that he didn't want to hear, and that one thing was often on our lips: 'Ah, the tomatoes you get now are nothing like the ones we used to grow.' That would really drive him mad, and if you harped on a bit – 'Honestly, they're nothing like as tasty' – he'd go all red in the face and start to foam at the mouth and bellow from the seat on his capon-laden cart for hours on end: 'Stuff and nonsense! I won't hear all this rubbish about the good old days! These tomatoes are quite simply better. They're modern, and they're Fascist,' and on and on he'd go, and the only way to shut him up was to give him another capon.

The truth was that he – together with some of his wog agronomist friends – had selected a new type of tomato which they had us plant all over the Pontine Marshes. These tomatoes sprang up like mushrooms, nowhere was safe from them, they were the size of watermelons, and so gleaming and glossy that when the sun was out they positively dazzled you. When it came to their taste, they were juicy all right, that I don't deny, but the skin was so hard it almost broke your teeth, all you could do was spit it out. Indeed, the story goes that during the period of autarky they built factories to extract the cellulose from the skin of these tomatoes, rather than from trees. We sold the patent abroad, too, as we did for Terylene, viscose and moplen.

In our case, though, Pascale had just the one chance to give us the benefit of his opinions about the new tomatoes, because, after that first occasion, as soon as they saw his cart coming along the road all the small boys in the Peruzzi family would stop talking about how the Duce had had it off with their grandmother and would pipe up in unison: 'These tomatoes

367

are quite simply better. They're modern, and they're Fascist.'

'To hell with the lot of you,' he'd say, almost under his breath. But now, I'm told – and this may not be true, you could try looking into it more thoroughly – they use the skins of Pascale's kind of tomatoes to make bullet-proof vests.

Anyway, in 1933 they had to bring in corn from elsewhere for that threshing on our holding, and for the first two or three years it was them, the association, who gave us corn, so much a head per year, and they also paid us so much a day, and allowed us to go and work elsewhere. Or rather, to be more precise, at first they didn't, but my Uncle Pericles persisted with the unions and organized a meeting with all the heads of the various families in the Fascist Headquarters in Littoria, where he said: 'We can't make ends meet like this. Either the association pays us more and allows us to work elsewhere, on the canals and in the vineyards' – because at first we couldn't do that either, we could cultivate only what they'd given us, since the association didn't want to be seen competing with the wine producers in the Castelli Romani, or from Velletri – 'or from tomorrow we sharecroppers will go out on strike.'

As soon as they heard the word 'strike', the people from the association looked as though they'd been struck down by tertian fever. Striking was forbidden by law under Fascism, and Cencelli went wild, he wanted to bring in the cavalry – 'What are you, a pack of Bolsheviks? I'm sending in the Cossacks' – and he immediately asked for a meeting with Rossoni: 'I've got a damned troublemaker on my hands, he's stirring things up with all the other sharecroppers.'

'A troublemaker?' asked Rossoni, who was something of an expert on the subject. 'Tell me who it is, we'll put him straight inside.'

Cencelli flicked through his papers: 'Let's see now... Yes,

here he is: it's Pericles Peruzzi.'

'Pericles Peruzzi? Don't waste my time, Cencelli! Give him everything he's asking for, and fast, and don't let me hear any more such tripe, or you'll be the one who ends up inside. Let's have a little flexibility around these parts, for pity's sake...'

So our request was granted, and that way we managed to get by until the holdings were fully productive. So then, year by year – as the harvests began to give the expected yield, and more – we also began to pay off the sums required to buy our holdings. But we always carried on working as sharecroppers, and we had to do everything they told us. The association was like a military outfit, and you had to hand the harvest over to them – you were completely under their control – and then they'd share out the proceeds. It was quite a performance: at threshing-time the factors and their assistants from the association would note down all the grain that came out of the threshing-machine, sack by sack. Then they'd load it all up on to their carts and lorries, so that it could be added to the stockpile. All they left us was the agreed amount assigned to every family to feed us for the year – so much for each man, a little less for the women, and less still for the children. And it wasn't much, believe you me – a subsistence diet, the barest minimum – and the rest went to the stockpile, because the whole country was on a subsistence diet, and anything left over was used to finance progress, development and the Fascist modernization of the country and the empire. Otherwise, what kind of an *Imperium* would you be looking at? What about all the reclamation work still to be done in Puglia, Campania, Sicily, Calabria?

Still – as I'm sure you'll understand – seeing everything you've worked for during one whole year being carted off before your very eyes is not a pretty sight – sack after sack, all the corn that you've sowed being fed by you into the threshing-machine, sheaf after sheaf, and then picked up by you, sack after sack again, to have them pile it on to their carts and lorries. But off they'd take it, anyway, and all they left you was the barest minimum needed for your survival.

Now and then, though, by means of some ruse or other – a woman offering them a drink, or making eyes at them – the people from the association could be distracted, and the odd sack could be spirited away. The man who'd been holding the sack under the threshing-machine would tie it up and throw it into the wheelbarrow, then his brother would quickly cover it with straw and it would pass from hand to hand until it was safely stowed away in the hayloft, or under the straw-stack that was going up. If they caught you at it, though, that was quite simply that, you'd be out on your ear. No second chances. It was theft. And some people did indeed get caught. Throughout the Pontine Marshes, everyone stole corn at threshing-time. Just ask anyone. It wasn't only the Peruzzi clan. That corn was ours. We were robbing ourselves. And someone – some families – did get caught, and there was nothing to be done, no amount of weeping and wailing would serve any purpose; they would be packed off the very next day, loaded on to trains back to the north: 'Now you can starve away up there.'

But that corn was ours, and until the day she died my Aunt Santapace would tell the story of the year when threshing-time came just a fortnight before her wedding. The priest was free on 17 August, and threshing-time was on the 2 August, and she was so excited to be getting married, but she was also desperately worried because they were as poor as church mice. Then, at a certain point – as she was walking through all that dust, with the tractor roaring and the hammers pounding – she saw my Uncle Pericles tying up a sack of corn and tossing it to my Uncle Iseo, who was standing ten metres ahead of him, and who immediately hid it under a pile of chaff. One hundred kilos, that sack held. Pericles our breastplate. The lion of our people. One hundred kilos of corn tossed ten metres through the air. And as soon as he saw that my Uncle Iseo had caught it – they were both so quick-witted and nimble, Iseo was our family gazelle – and had stowed it safely away in the privy, Uncle Pericles smiled at my Aunt Santapace: 'That's for you, wife.' She was rather taken aback. She hadn't understood at first, it had all happened so fast: they were like two bolts of lightning, those two; Castor and Pollux. 'Did you think I'd forgotten about your wedding?' he said, and smiled at her again.

'Brother,' was all Aunt Santapace said. Then she began to cry. And she cried each time she told the story.

We'd always been a close-knit group, as I've already told you, and that's how we carried on down here. Starting again from scratch in a new land. Work, *filos*, dances, bowls, *briscola*, wine-shop, Fascist activities and religion. But now religion had begun to overshadow Fascist activities. Because of my grandmother. Now it was '*Ora pro nobis*' at every turn. There was no more swearing. Not just in our house, but anywhere. The slate was now wiped completely clean of all painful memories. They all stayed up there, in the north; down here everyone had suddenly mysteriously joined the family of Maria Goretti. Our journey to the south had cleansed us as thoroughly as any pilgrimage to Santiago de Compostela. Benitino Mambrin had taken all our sins upon himself at Ponte Marchi. By now, no one – among the northerners in the Pontine Marshes – had any relative in prison, not even a distant one, nor any illegitimate children within the family: 'These are all

371

virgin cows, as certified by the local vet.'

Anyway, going to Sunday morning mass in town – with the girls all sweet-smelling, and wearing white lace veils, and the women wearing big coloured kerchiefs and black veils – suddenly struck us as the height of enjoyment, you spent the whole week waiting for Sunday. The only trouble was, once you got there, all the sermons were in a language we couldn't understand – all the priests were wogs. All from around these parts. Not a single one of our own. Northern flocks with wog shepherds. When you went to confession they didn't understand a word of what you were saying. At first there wasn't even a full-time priest for every town, they'd come in on Sunday mornings – sent by the local bishops – they'd say that mass of theirs and then go off again. Nice to have met you.

Then finally, in 1933, the big church in Littoria was finished; it was put into the hands of Don Bosco and the Salesians and dedicated to Saint Mark; as patron saint of Venice, he had also been made the protector of the Pontine Marshes, because the sharecroppers came from the Three Venetias. But only until 1950, because after they'd canonised Maria Goretti – she was a local girl who had met her martyr's death at Borgo Montello – they added her as well, and now both of them are patron saints of Latina-Littoria and the Pontine Marshes. Saint Mark and Saint Maria Goretti, a North Italian and a wog, as is our way: a North Italian male and a wog female.

The first parish priest at San Marco was Don Torello – he was from Piedmont – but all his fellow priests, the ones he'd send cycling into the towns, were from Rome, or from around these parts. It's true that now they came into the towns a bit more often, but they always went back to San Marco in the evening. To Littoria. That was their home, and that was where they went back to. For us they were bogus priests, as well as wogs who, like all the others, had difficulty in understanding what we said.

Think of confession, for example. It wasn't just the fact that we had to struggle to make ourselves understood, it was the situation in itself, as my grandmother was now saying daily to Armida: 'How long can we go on like this, telling our business to a wog?'

Then Armida started to pester her husband: 'Your mother wants a priest from round our way.'

'What am I supposed to do about it?'

'You can do something about it all right.'

'Who do you think I am, the Patriarch of Venice? Go to hell, the pair of you.'

But she went on and on – 'Get us a priest, Pericles, one of our own' – until he could take it no longer: 'What am I supposed to do? Me, of all people? Where do you think I can get a priest from – Comacchio, maybe?'

But then the bees got in on the act, buzzing round him all day, with my grandmother and Armida endlessly harping on about 'the priest... the priest', and finally he said: 'The hell with the pair of you,' and went off the Fascist Headquarters in Littoria: 'We want priests from the Veneto.'

'And you come looking for them here, Peruzzi?' they said to him teasingly. 'You of all people, who knows more than anyone about parish priests?'

'You can go to hell with the rest of them,' and off he went to see Don Torello at San Marco. Once again he got the same answer: 'What do you expect me to do about it? Priests have to do what the bishops tell them to, and the bishops are all from round here, and bishops from round here have priests from round here. Priests from up north have bishops from up north. Write to them.'

'Well, thanks for the advice.' And he went back home and started writing letters to all the bishops in the Veneto – 'Send one of your priests to us down here' – and he went round all the holdings and had the heads of the households sign them, and then he sent them off. 'That's enough, though,' he then said to his wife, 'now we're calling it a day.'

One month went by, and then another. No reply. Wife and mother started up again: 'Our priests, their priests...'

'What's wrong with a wog priest, anyway?' he tried saying. But now he too felt a rising sense of fury: what's going on here, I'm writing letters left, right and centre and no one's lifting a finger. The patriarch will be hearing about this. 'Iseo!' he bellowed. 'Aye aye sir,' came the prompt response.

They got into a third-class carriage – they'd still got a bit of money over from the tractor – and went to Venice, where they'd never been in all their lives. I know, they'd lived nearby, but they'd never been there. They might have been all round the world, on active service and so on, but they'd never been to Venice. Come to think of it, that's not really so strange. You've no idea how many of us North Italian-Pontine Marshes dwellers there are, who've been here for seventy years or more, and who wake up each morning to see Cori and Norma and Sermoneta on the hills opposite – when it's a clear day you feel you could almost stretch out your hand and touch them – but who've never been to those places in all their lives. Not to Cori or Norma or Sermoneta; and certainly not to Sezze.

Anyway, my uncles got off at Venice Station wearing their militiamen's uniforms and their Fascist scarves. They took the ferry to Saint Mark's and told the first priest they came upon: 'We want to speak to the Patriarch of Venice.'

'That's out of the question,' the priest told them. 'Do you imagine people can roll up and speak to the patriarch just like that?' It was Palazzo Venezia all over again.

'We'll soon see about that,' said Uncle Pericles. 'So what do you think I came here for, a change of air? Now get a move on and find me that patriarch, otherwise there'll be trouble.' They were in Saint Mark's Basilica, just by the high altar.

'Keep calm, Pericles,' said my Uncle Iseo.

'I'm keeping calm. Unless they really rile me, I'll keep calm.'

Calm or otherwise, the fact remains that the priest said: 'I'll see what I can do.'

He kept them waiting for an hour or two, to see if they'd get bored and go away. But there they sat, as cool as cucumbers, on that same seat where they'd been told to sit. Solid as rock. Still as stone. *Hic manebimus in sempiternum amen.*

'They're here to stay,' the priests must have thought, and after three hours they said: 'All right, then, but just the one of you, not both,' so as not to seem to be completely giving in. Just half.

'Do you want to go?' Uncle Pericles asked Uncle Iseo.

'Are you joking? I always come second, after you.' So it was my Uncle Pericles who went to see the Patriarch of Venice.

They led him up and down various staircases, along countless corridors, then through a series of little dark rooms, each smaller and darker than the last, and finally they opened a door and sent him in alone. It was a large room, with very high windows, and the light pouring in, and you could see the Piazzetta dei Leoni, with Saint Mark's Square in the background. At the end sat the patriarch.

Uncle Pericles walked the length of the room, went up to him and said: 'We want our own priests, people who talk our language.'

'Your wish is my command!' said the patriarch instantly.

375

Then my uncle began to laugh, and so did the patriarch. Then he said to him: 'Come here, my son, and receive my blessing: may the Lord God protect you.'

'I don't think He'll be likely to do that, patriarch,' said my uncle, who had now stopped laughing. 'I've got an awful lot on my conscience.'

'But you've repented?' the holy man asked him gently.

'Yes, I've repented all right. But they're big sins, serious sins...'

'It doesn't matter, *ego te absolvo*, they have been taken from you. Go in peace, my son.'

My uncle retraced his steps, met up with his brother, got back on to the train and came back home again. But the moment they got off the ferry – in the square in front of the new station, which had just been opened, all spanking new Fascist architecture, on the far rim of the lagoon – my Uncle Iseo turned back towards Venice and the Grand Canal, and said to his brother, after a pause: 'Just look at all that water, Pericles! If the Duce gets to hear about it, he'll be round in a flash, reclaiming the lot. I'd like to see the Venetians' faces when they get out of bed one morning and say: "Where's the canal gone? Who's dried up our canal?" '

'To hell with the pair of you, you and your canal,' said Uncle Pericles, his thoughts still with the patriarch.

'Well?' asked my grandmother the minute they got home.

'We'll see,' they said, but before the month was out priests from our parts were flooding in – priests who spoke our language – puffing and panting, streaming into every town in the Pontine Marshes, sent down from every diocese in the Veneto, together with a suitcase and a trunk full of church ornaments and vestments. So now there was a full-time priest in every town, and from the Veneto into the bargain. Someone who understood what you were saying.

'Now I can rest easy,' said my grandmother. 'Now I feel really glad to be down here in these blessed Pontine Marshes. Now I've got everything I could ask for.' He'd have got her teachers and lawyers, too, had she asked him to. But she didn't; all she thought about was the priest. Indeed, until the day she died she always said that she regretted that not even one of the Peruzzi clan had become a priest. 'That way, we'd have broken even,' she'd sometimes add, sadly, but to herself, and my Aunt Santapace, the one who'd married Benassi, even sent her own sons, Accio and Manrico, to a seminary; but they both got themselves expelled, or left of their own accord, I can't remember which. At all events, by now in every town we were one single flock with its own shepherd – the people of God in the Promised Land – and it was as though the whole of the Pontine Marshes were shouting 'Go, Saint Mark's!' when they saw Don Federico cycling off on his way to Borgo Carso and Don Orlando on his way to Borgo Podgora.

In the 1915–18 War Don Federico had been a captain in the artillery; he had a strong, stern voice and his hair was completely white; authoritative and solemn in the pulpit, he was used to holding positions of command – 'He was a captain in the artillery,' we all used to say – but he was also gentle and kindly, at least with us children. Don Orlando too had been in the army, but he was more approachable, more workaday.

Don Bouillon, on the other hand, was the priest in another town that I shan't name. He was known as Don Bouillon because he was extremely gaunt and thin, and when he went from house to house people would ask him to stay to lunch or supper, and he'd always say: 'No, no, I wouldn't dream of it,' just like the agronomist Pascale with the capons. But they'd insist, and at last he would give in: 'All right, all right, I'll

377

stay; but just a little bouillon; I wouldn't want to offend, but anything more just doesn't go down well.' And then the aunt on duty would put on the water, wring a chicken's neck and put it into the pot, and sieve the flour on the table while it was cooking, making a hole in the middle, like a volcano, breaking in five or six eggs and working it into dough. Then she'd roll it out carefully with a rolling pin – 'Just a little bouillon for me, word of honour,' and she'd reassure him: 'Don't worry, this is just for us' – and then, when it was ready, she'd roll it up into a sort of cornet and cut it into rings on the chopping board, lifting them up into the air to disentangle them, and letting them fall back on to the board as *fettuccine*. 'Just a bit of bouillon for me,' he'd keep on saying.

Then, when it was all ready and we were seated round the table, with him at the head – and he'd said grace, standing, head bowed – first he'd drink the bouillon my grandmother had put in front of him, then he'd say: 'Let's try those *tagliatelle*,' and he'd have some more broth with *tagliatelle* in it, then he'd move on to eat all the chicken and the polenta left over from the day before, and half a loaf, with salami or *cotechino* which my grandfather had taken down from the ceiling and sliced up, and then another plate of *tagliatelle*, with the sauce that had been meant for the following day, and then, when there was nothing left at all, he'd have a last glass of that red *clinton* wine with a bit of bread dunked in it.

This Don Bouillon died just after the Second World War, when there wasn't a bridge left standing – they'd all been bombed or blown up from underneath with mines or dynamite, either by the Germans or the Americans – and to get from one side of the Mussolini Canal to the other you had to go down the embankment and walk along until you came to a little dyke on the drainage ditch where there was a makeshift footbridge laid on big stone steps, and make your way across it like a tightrope-walker. Anyway, one winter night at Christmas this Don Bouillon had gone to visit a group of families on the other side of the canal – who'd got together on a holding which was a bit less damaged than the rest – and on his way back, crossing back over to the side where his church and the priest's house were, quite late at night, as he was going across the footbridge he slipped and stumbled and lost his balance. And fell into the Mussolini Canal. The water wasn't very high, and he knew how to swim. But it was night, and winter, and cold. He managed to get out, climbed up the embankment and went home, chilled to the bone.

It can't have taken him more than an hour. But it was late December. He took to his bed, and within a week he was dead of pneumonia. Some people said he'd also had a bit to drink, but that was malicious gossip. What with a few sips of bouillon here and a few glasses of red wine there, to wash them down, it's possible he couldn't see all that well by the time he reached the footbridge. But I think that's just malicious gossip.

The odd thing is, though, that after his death there was always a Don Bouillon to be found in some town or other in the Pontine Marshes. And some of my relatives who stayed up in the north say that there too – in Northern Italy – every so often you'll hear of a priest called Don Bouillon. I wonder why.

Anyway, when my Uncle Adelchi came back from Africa with a chest full of medals – in East Africa everyone got a medal, the new Italy was in need of heroes, just over six thousand men had died, but almost seven thousand medals for valour were awarded, so there were more medals than fallen – when my Uncle Adelchi came back from Africa, Uncle Pericles and

379

Uncle Iseo had already left the holding.

Obviously, they'd discussed the matter before Uncle Adelchi went off with Barany and the Littoria Company. In the Peruzzi family you don't just wake up one morning and say: 'I'm off.' People mull things over, they think about them carefully and then come to a decision. For quite some time – almost from the moment he'd arrived, the first time someone had said to him: 'Do this and don't do that' – my Uncle Pericles had had enough of being bossed around by the factors from the Servicemen's Association: 'One of these days I'll do something I wish I hadn't.' And anyway there were so many of us, too many for that holding. It's true that it was slightly bigger than the others, because there were so many of us they'd given us one measuring fifteen hectares, rather than ten, and it was all very fertile land. But there were still too many of us and above all – thought my Uncle Pericles – as the little ones grew up, let alone their children, where would we all put ourselves? 'What'll we eat?' he'd say to my Uncle Iseo. 'The canal embankment?'

Of the brothers, Uncle Pericles and Uncle Iseo already had wives and children, Uncle Adelchi was still unmarried, Uncle Turati had a wife and a couple of kids too, Uncle Adrasto was about to marry – Aunt Nazzarena, the wog from Cori – and then there was Uncle Treves, and Uncle Cesio who was still quite young and studying to be a surveyor at Littoria; and there were all the girls still to be married off, or with illegitimate children. As you can see, there wasn't much room to spread ourselves, and Uncle Adelchi would always say: 'You're right, there are too many of us,' whenever the subject came up.

'Yes, you're absolutely right,' Uncle Adrasto would instantly agree, because he and Uncle Adelchi were like Uncle Pericles and Uncle Iseo, one fair and the other dark but always of one mind. They understood each other instantly, they were like engines of war which functioned seamlessly – a pair of oxen wearing a single yoke – they thought and acted as one, solid as rock. So Uncle Pericles and Uncle Iseo formed one couple, and Uncle Adelchi and Uncle Adrasto another, even if they were a little less well balanced, because Uncle Adelchi never did much work on the land, he always left that to Uncle Adrasto. His contribution was to give advice. Anyway: 'You're absolutely right,' they'd say to each other. And then they'd fall silent, and wait.

'No, no, let's all stay here together,' said Uncles Treves and Uncle Turati. 'If anything, it's us who should leave,' but you could tell that they were just saying it out of deference to their brother.

'Let's all stay here,' my grandfather would say. 'The holding will be ours in ten years time, and then we'll be able to plant it out with vegetables, and live like kings.'

'No, no,' my grandmother would say, 'they're right, there are too many of us.'

But anyway, after a lot of thought, Uncle Pericles and Uncle Iseo went off on their own. Not to the other side of the world, of course, just three or four kilometres away. Still on the Left-Hand Parallel by the Mussolini Canal, but on the other side of the Appian Way, on holdings not belonging to the Servicemen's Association, but which had remained in private hands. My uncles – still with the help of the local Fascist Headquarters, and Rossoni, and above all the agronomist Pascale – had managed to get a long lease on two holdings of twenty hectares each, with the possibility of eventually buying them, on a farm belonging to the Counts Cerisano-Caratelli, where Pascale was the manager. 'Why do we always have to have dealings with counts?' Iseo had wondered plaintively.

But anyway, off they'd gone. And those Counts Cerisano-Caratelli were decent people, easy to get on with, not like the Zorzi Vilas, may they rot in hell. Once, when my Aunt Ondina had jumped over the ditch between one of our fields and the garden of their villa, to pick a flower, all hell broke loose. My Aunt Ondina was quite small – she must have been about six or seven – and she was minding the cows as they grazed in that field, and on the other side of the ditch she could see flowers and ornamental plants, and shrubs, and little avenues with gravel, and she liked minding the cows in that field, because she could see that garden, and to her it looked like a garden from a fairy story. So once she jumped over the ditch and picked a flower. And that bitch of a countess was standing at the window and she said nothing, just summoned the factor and told him to get my grandfather: 'With the girl, I want the girl here too.' And when my aunt and my grandfather went to the house – my grandfather was even holding her by the hand, she was that small – that woman had the nerve to come out with: 'Is that any way to bring up children? She's nothing better than a common thief! She steals flowers from my garden, just like you steal from us at harvest-time.'

'Forgive her, my lady,' said my grandfather. 'Promise you'll never do it again,' he said to my Aunt Ondina, who was sobbing fit to burst. And she'd still be crying seventy years later, when she told the story: 'I wasn't crying for myself, but for my father, who was a good man, who wouldn't hurt a fly, seeing him put to shame like that over a flower, one single flower, to hell with every Zorzi Vila on this earth.'

The Cerisano-Caratelli were a different kettle of fish, you could talk to them, they were decent people, and every time Uncle Pericles asked them: 'Would you like us to do this, or that?' they'd say: 'Do whatever you think best, Pericles, it's fine by us.' They made all kinds of investments. It was during that time that the local Fascist Headquarters gave them the tractor, and my Uncle Pericles sold it off again – Uncle Benassi is moaning about it to this day – and bought new milch-cows.

The land was good – better than ours, because it had already been worked – and the holdings stood on high ground, so that they were never flooded, even before the reclamation work, and there were vines and fruit trees. My uncles worked from morning till night, but they had a sense of satisfaction – some of the sugar beets they pulled up were as big as your arm – and they were all as happy as sandboys, let alone their wives. The only wives on those holdings were Armida and Uncle Iseo's wife, my Aunt Zelinda, and the farmhouses were quite near one another, so each wife could rock the other wife's child's cradle or deliver a hearty slap, as the occasion demanded. They got on fine, more like sisters than sisters-in-law, the bees made a honey so sweet your mouth would water, there were no more association factors, and when the Cerisano-Caratelli or Pascale came to call they never had any complaints to make, but simply nodded in approval, and even knocked before coming in. It was best not to say anything against Pascale's tomatoes, though.

The only problem was that we were among heathens, *in terra infedelium*, completely surrounded by sharecroppers from Sermoneta who'd shout out: 'Here come the Vikings!' every time they saw us go by with our carts and our beasts of burden.

'Bunch of wogs!' we'd shout back. And every time Armida set up a stall at the fair at Monticchio, selling her honey, a group of local women would gather round – wog women from Sezze or Sermoneta who were selling olives and artichokes in oil, and figs – and start pushing and shoving at her stall:

383

'What's this Viking doing here?' they'd say to each other. 'First she steals our land, then she muscles in on our fairs!'

Armida gave as good as she got. Even if she was in a minority, she answered back, she didn't just take it lying down. But one insult led to another, and at last one of them said to her, to make it clear that it wasn't the honey that was the real *casus belli*, but her dazzling beauty: 'Look at this Viking hussy strutting her stuff.' And indeed the dress she was wearing was just a little shorter than their own, mid-calf, let's say.

Armida didn't have a chance to answer back, because at that moment my other aunts happened to pass by – the Peruzzi women, a whole bunch of them – with the twins, Modigliana and Bissolata, in the lead. And my Aunt Bissola leapt on that local woman like a hyena. 'Who are you calling a hussy, my sister-in-law?' she shrieked, grabbing her by the hair and knocking her to the ground.

Then all the others joined in the fray: 'My sister-in-law?' – to the point that Armida must have wondered to herself: 'Who'd have thought they were so fond of me?' – until the men arrived and sorted things out among themselves. Then afterwards – when they were going home – they all hugged her and made a fuss of her, saying: 'My sister-in-law this, and my sister-in-law that.' The only people who were allowed to insult her were her own sisters-in-law.

Anyway, as soon as he got back from Africa, the first thing Uncle Adelchi did – even before going home to hug his mother – was rush to the town hall with all those medals on his chest and put his request to the *podestà*. Then off he rushed to the new holdings belonging to the Cerisano-Caratelli to see how his brothers had organized themselves. He looked around the house, took a stroll through the fields, checked the cowshed, let out an 'Ooh' when he saw the Friesians and then said: 'It's wonderful! You're well set up... Pericles, I've just been to the town hall with a request to become a municipal policeman. Put in a good word for me.'

'So that's why you called round, you son of a bitch,' said my Uncle Pericles, and started laughing. But he did put in a good word for him. After all, he'd won a lot of medals, he'd got his school-leaving certificate, he'd won the right to wear the 'Fascist scarf', he'd been on the march on Rome and he looked like a god in uniform. 'Who do you want for your policeman...' my Uncle Pericles said to the people at the town hall, 'the Prince of Piedmont?' So Uncle Adelchi became a policeman; one of the first in Littoria. There were five or six of them, always sporting their pistols and holster-belts, and pith helmets and spotless white uniforms in summer, and black ones in winter. He was an authority figure, a sheriff. At first he went around on a bicycle, but later they gave him a motorbike – the first police motorbike in Latina-Littoria, a Gilera 125 – because he'd also learned to ride a motorbike in Africa, and he'd been discharged with the rank of sergeant or section leader, I can't now remember which. Anyway, he rode all around town and he was an authority figure because – in those days – a municipal policeman in Littoria could command respect.

In the evening – after he'd gone off duty – he'd come back to holding 517 on his own bike, and go back on it to Littoria in the morning. There he'd pick up a municipal bike, or motorbike, but only for use when he was on duty, because my Uncle Adelchi was a stickler for doing things by the book, and he'd never have bent the rules to his own advantage.

At home, on the holding, he was now the oldest male, but it was clear that never again would we be seeing him wielding a pitchfork in the cowshed, or out in the fields. I can remember seeing him out in the fields only once – when I was a little boy – and we were pulling up the sugar beets. It was in the early Fifties, and we were all out there in a row in the field. He and his colleague passed by on the road. It was the early Fifties, as I've said, and Latina had become something of a serious town, it didn't have just four or five policemen but a whole motorized patrol of them, and they always went round in twos, like *carabinieri* or traffic policemen.

Anyway, they were going along the Parallel, and at a certain point they stopped. They left their motorbikes on the road and came to say hallo to us. 'Remember when even you used to pull up sugar beets, Delchi?' my Uncle Iseo said to him teasingly. Then – to show his friend what he was made of – my Uncle Adelchi took off first his pistol and holster-belt, then his jacket and shirt and then, when he had stripped down to his singlet, but still wearing his uniform breeches and motorcyclist's boots, he grabbed a hook and said: 'I'll show you!' and started pulling up a couple of sugar beet. And that's the only time I ever saw him do such a thing. But only one or two, because, as he put it: 'Unfortunately now I've got to go back on duty' – amidst much laughter – 'otherwise I'd show you how it's done.'

And, of course, he was still the first to wake up – by now he had a right to a small room of his own – and wash and shave, meticulously, and apply his brilliantine, and put on the spotless white shirt and uniform my grandmother always had ready ironed for him, and then, his glossy quiff sticking out from under his peaked cap, he'd start to throw open the doors and bellow into the rooms, particularly those of his sisters and nieces, married and unmarried alike: 'Wake up girls, the sun's well up, it's time to go and get out into those fields.'

'Go to hell, Adelchi,' my uncles would say to him each

morning.

Anyway, it was 1937, my Uncle Adelchi had come back from East Africa but – as you know – by now the Spanish Civil War had well and truly broken out. That was a war to the death. On the one side the reds, supported by thousands of volunteers from all over the world, and backed by weaponry from the Soviet Union. On the other – apart from the putschist generals themselves – Italy and Nazi Germany.

'Aren't we fighting in enough places already, without having to go to Spain as well?' my grandmother would ask.

'Don't start worrying your pretty head about politics, ma,' my uncles would say, laughing. 'If you don't get them, sooner or later they'll get you. It's called supremacy.' According to my uncles, the Duce wasn't stupid: was he going to allow the Bolsheviks to dig in right there on the other side of the Mediterranean, the *Mare Nostrum*? You're mad, the Duce said, and sent our troops in straight away. Now as long as Uncle Adelchi had been in Africa, we could say to the Fascist Headquarters: 'Well, we've got Adelchi in Africa.' But the moment he was back, we too had to send someone – a volunteer – to Spain: 'Who's going this time?' And this time it was Uncle Treves, because he hadn't yet got married. Uncle Turati wanted to go with him – to keep him company – even though he had a wife and two young children: 'The pay's good,' he would assure his wife, 'and we're so strong, there's no possible danger. And we could put some money aside.'

'Yes, but I'd be here on my own,' she said, sobbing.

'You're staying right here,' said my grandmother, and Uncle Turati stayed. At home.

Uncle Treves, on the other hand, went off to fight in Spain, and we carried on the war to reclaim our holding, and the Pontine Marshes, which by now, were almost totally reclaimed.

387

Meanwhile, on 19 December 1934 – having declared Sabaudia open for business that same April – the Duce and Cencelli had gone on to found Pontinia, and we put in an appearance there too. Actually, Cencelli almost didn't make it. A few days earlier, he'd been involved in a car accident. I don't know exactly where he was, somewhere on a road between the holdings, when a Maremma cow suddenly appeared from nowhere, and he hit it head on. So there was one dead cow, and him and his car, which had run headlong into a parapet on a bridge and knocked it into the canal, and he'd ended up in the ditch. Some peasants pulled him out, swearing like a trooper: 'Gently does it, damn you; gently, I said, or I'll have you sent back to the Veneto.' He'd fractured his chin, and cracked a pair of ribs. But he wasn't going to miss that opening: 'What, you think they can found Pontinia without me?' he started shrieking all over the hospital at Velletri, until they found him a stretcher and carried him on it to Pontinia. You can still see photographs of the Duce laying the mortar on the first stone with a trowel, with Cencelli beside him, looking like a mummy, wearing the uniform of the militia and a black shirt, but swathed in yards of bandages, with white gauze draped all around his neck, under his chin, and over half his face and head, under his black fez. He looks like Tutankhamen.

Anyway, it was 19 December 1934, and the place was going to be blessed by the bishop, and the first stone laid, and it was a right shambles, as always – with the whole Peruzzi clan all present and correct, of course – and it was bucketing down in Pontinia as well. But as soon as the Duce arrived, the sun came out. (I can't imagine why you're laughing; if you don't believe me, that's your business, but that's the story as my uncles told it to me. And they were there.)

The person who wasn't there on 18 December of the following year, though – 1935, when they declared Pontinia officially open – was none other than the luckless Cencelli. It had been his idea, he'd been present at the founding, albeit on a stretcher, he'd had all the projects drawn up and had checked the various firms involved, but when the time came to see it all there in bricks and mortar, and have it officially opened, he wasn't there. He'd been struck off the books.

The Duce was like that: one minute you were his blue-eyed boy, the next minute your name was mud. It's true, Cencelli tended to push his luck. He was from Rieti, after all. He would pick quarrels left, right and centre: with the former landowners, the noble families, the contracting companies, the navvies on the canals, the sharecroppers on their holdings, the union members and the saints in Paradise. All in all, he was the most hated man in the Pontine Marshes, more hated than the anopheles mosquito and the people from Sezze.

To be honest, the Duce seemed to have become a little jealous of him. That was how he was, one moment he'd praise you to the skies, and then – the moment your star seemed to be burning a bit too brightly – he'd cast you out again into outer darkness. Look at what he did to Balbo – even when they were old my uncles couldn't understand it, and they were on Rossoni's side, not Balbo's. Balbo had set us up with an air force which was the envy of the world, he'd obliged us with two transatlantic flights, the second one with twenty-five seaplanes flying in close formation, crossing the Atlantic to reach Canada, then the USA. The eyes of the world were on us. No one had ever managed a feat like that before, it took not only great courage but also immense powers of organization and technical skill. We were in the forefront of world aviation, or at least that's what my uncles said. And indeed the Americans gave him a welcome – first in Chicago and then in New York – which in Italy you could only dream of. Even now, if you go to Chicago, there's a great big Balbo Avenue, and they kept the name even after we'd declared war on them. That's quite something.

But the Duce seemed to think nothing of it, there was no pleasing him: 'Just who does Balbo think he is, anyway?' he kept on saying to Rossoni. As you know, there wasn't much chance of Rossoni saying: 'Come off it, Duce.' If anything, he'd have said: 'It's me you're asking? It's you who've always rated him so highly' – and anyway, as soon as he got back from America the Duce sacked him from the government and sent him to Africa to be governor of Libya.

Now I don't know if we had the finest air force in the world in 1933, as my uncles claimed, but seven years later – after we'd entered the Second World War – we certainly had the worst. Everyone else had progressed by leaps and bounds, and we'd stood still. All we'd got was Balbo's biplanes. In just seven years, we were still at the starting post and everyone else was up and away. All because the Duce suffered from fits of jealousy. It was the same story as with Rossoni, all in all.

Now I don't know how things really went with Cencelli. But the fact remains that the Duce knew perfectly well which of them was the true founder of Littoria – even if he'd taken all the credit for it – and which of them had been so set against it. Above all, though, each of them knew that the other knew. Of course, Cencelli didn't say as much to his face; what he did say to him, to his face, was more along the lines of: 'It was all your doing, Duce, all your idea, I didn't lift a finger, I don't remember a thing about it, word of honour, Duce.' Guilt-stricken as the Duce must have been, how could this business not have left a nasty taste in his mouth?

Be that as it may, one fine day the Duce said: 'Enough,' sacked him from the Servicemen's Association and went off to declare Pontinia open with just Rossoni for company; Cencelli was kept well out of the picture, eating his heart out, now, at Magliano Sabina. It was 18 December 1938, as I've said, and you can believe me or not, it's up to you, but there's still an old copy of the Naples *Mattino* lying around somewhere in the holding which will tell you how – after the downpour of the night before, with the sky all dark and threatening – the moment he arrived the sun came out: 'The sky was one mass of cloud, but at that very moment a sudden gust of wind drove the mist towards the snow-covered Lepini Mountains. It even caused a small patch of blue sky to appear, and it was at this patch of blue that Mussolini looked before turning his gaze upon the crowd'.

It was 18 December 1935, as I've said, we were three months into the war with Abyssinia, and thirty days had passed – as we learn from the deathless words of the memorial tablet set into the tower at Pontinia – since the world, that is, the League of Nations, had laid economic siege to us with its sanctions, in universal protest against, and condemnation of, our brutal assault on Abyssinia.

My uncles were incensed: 'Oh yes? You can have all the empires you like, and all I get is sanctions?' Never mind that they lifted those sanctions as early as July 1936 – when the whole thing was a *fait accompli*, as they say, and Ethiopia was ours – and went back to sending us everything we asked for: iron, oil, coal, rubber; all we had to do was pay for it. But that was something my uncles didn't mention, for years our propaganda machine carried on talking about sanctions and economic blockades – everyone had it in for us, they were all at our jugular – and such propaganda was making giant strides.

You couldn't move for cinemas. Now every town would show a film on Sundays – in Littoria they'd show one every day, or rather every evening – and before the film there'd be a documentary by the *Istituto Luce News Service*, showing the Fascist conquests and all the outrages inflicted on us by the rest of the world. The rest of the world didn't want to grant us our God-given right to that famous *Imperium* which – if you recall – we were laying claim to in their own interests, to take them our *pax romana*. But no, they wouldn't hear of it, and all discussion at the Fascist Headquarters – but also in our own home, or at the wine-shop – always ended with talk of sanctions: 'The hell with them and their sanctions.'

'Just what are these *sancheons*, though?' my grandmother once asked.

'It's hard to explain, ma,' said Uncle Adelchi. 'Let's just say that they're worse than that new 90 exchange rate.'

'Holy Mary!' she said.

Anyway, no one ever told us that those sanctions had been lifted as early as July 1936. Or if they did, we didn't understand. And when, in 1954 or 1955 – ten years after the end of the Second World War – my Uncle Iseo went out and bought a new wireless and brought it home saying: 'Wife, I've bought a wireless,' my Aunt Zelinda was pleased as punch and looked it up and down in great delight, as an object, I mean, not just because it emitted sounds and songs. It was only small, a new type – CGE was the make, and it was made out of laminated plastic – more or less the size of a shoe box. Not a wooden cabinet, like in the old days. 'What a lovely wireless,' said Aunt Zelinda. But then, after she'd had her daughter read what was written on the back, she looked thoroughly flustered and ran to ask her husband: 'But where did you buy this thing?'

'From the wireless shop,' said Uncle Iseo. Then, a bit later,

'Why? What's wrong with it?'

'It's foreign!'

'So?'

'What about the *sancheons*? How did you get round the *sancheons*?' And it was 1954 or 1955.

Anyway, sanctions or no sanctions, Fascism was carrying all before it, and on 21 April 1936 the Duce came to the Pontine Marshes – or rather to their northern border, the Roman Plain – to found Aprilia.

All my uncles were there, of course, and they saw the Man in person, getting on to a Fiat tractor – a spanking new orange model with caterpillar wheels – and driving it off, with the plough behind it, to mark out the sacred furrow within which the town would rise.

And this time too – and don't start laughing, otherwise I'm off for good – it had poured with rain all the previous night, and until the Duce arrived the sky was overcast, but the moment he showed up, at nine in the morning, the sun came out again: '*The fields were glinting with puddles, the ground was sodden and raindrops were still dripping from the trees,*' according to the newspapers.

Anyway, he got on that Fiat tractor, pulled on the cord attached to the plough, put the tractor into gear and marked out his sacred furrow, just like in the times of Romulus and Remus. In those days cities were still founded following the Roman custom, you marked out a furrow according to the rites of the ancient Etruscan augurs, and the city would rise within it. Woe betide anyone who went beyond that furrow, and Romulus himself had put everyone on their guard: 'He who goes beyond it meets certain death.' By way of a dare, his brother started hopping to either side of it: 'See, I've gone over it! See, I've gone over it!' What could Romulus do? He slaughtered him. And when he found himself with his brother's innards in his hand, he said: 'Oh Lord, what have I done?' But by then it was too late – 'What's done is done,' there was no turning back – he cleaned his sword of his brother's blood with a tuft of grass, put his brother's body in the ditch, made the sign of the cross or said some other prayers that they had in those days, and started to pile up stones and build up walls. Otherwise, what sort of figure would he have cut in front of his friends? And he created Rome.

So, following in his footsteps, on 25 April 1936 the Duce ploughed the sacred furrow that would run around Aprilia – it was the first time he'd done this business with the furrow, and we were all there, the Peruzzi, the Benassi and the Lanzidei, the lot – then he laid the first stone and went back home to Palazzo Venezia.

Eighteen months went by, and on 29 October 1937 Mussolini came back to Aprilia for the inauguration. It was finished. Every stone in place. And he was well pleased, because he'd got himself a real jewel there. Then – just seven years later – it was bombed into non-existence during the war, and it'll never be the same again, you should have seen it. Four people had been involved in the planning of it – two engineers and two architects, and the two architects were Jewish; ardent Fascists the pair of them, just like poor Barany. At that time, no one had yet started to take any special notice of the Jews, they were just people, Italians and Fascists like all the rest.

The Duce took Rudolf Hess along with him to the inauguration, he was second-in-command in Hitler's mighty Germany. Just one down from Hitler, then, and by now we were good friends. At first, the Duce hadn't reckoned him at all. Rather it was him – Hitler – who wanted to tag along with the Duce, and kept on asking for meetings: 'Duce, you're a star, where you lead I follow, all that I know I've learned from you, I want to be just like you.'

'Give us a break, Adolf, you're always hanging on to my coat tails,' and he fended him off with one arm, because Hitler was always touching him, he stuck like a burr, and the Duce didn't like being touched. Except by women. 'Don't they teach people manners where he comes from?' he asked Rossoni, who was at his side. 'What a buffoon.' Then when Hitler told him he'd got it in for the Jews, the Duce felt that enough was enough: 'He's off his head! What harm did they ever do to us, those poor old Jews?'

But then Hitler really started to make it, and we joined up with each other in Spain – side by side, fighting the Bolshevik reds – and he started coming up with the most terrifying modern weaponry: Dorniers, Messerschmitts, Junkers Stuka Ju-87. It was in Spain that they perfected the techniques later used in the Second World War. It was there that they tried out carpet-bombing, too, at Guernica – on 26 April 1937 – razing it to the ground just when we in the Pontine Marshes were building Aprilia. Well, that's how life goes, first you give someone a wide berth and then you get into bed with them. And we got into bed with Nazi Germany. In October '36 we signed the 'October Protocols' for foreign policy – the Rome-Berlin Axis – and from that moment on it was one long love-in, up to the Pact of Steel: '*Two peoples one faith*,' as it said on the postage stamps.

The fact is, during the war in Abyssinia we'd found ourselves up against France and England, which were putting spanners in the works – they'd already got their empires and we, as I've already said, apparently had to stay out in the cold – and even comrade Roosevelt had started to back off: 'Hey hey, aggression's just not on!' Nazi Germany, on the other hand, was much more helpful: 'Please, help yourselves! You've got right on your side, in spades, from now onwards we're your friends and brothers, go ahead, we'll give you a hand.' And, while we were fighting that war, they were the chief suppliers of arms to the Negus, but let's leave that out of things for the moment. Business is business, as Tony Soprano says. But one thing leads to another, and even if they lifted the sanctions after the war, and everything went back more or less to how it had been before, the more France and England looked askance at us, the more the force of circumstances drove us to into the arms of Germany.

They, meanwhile – the Germans – were going from strength to strength, with both their economy and their military preparations. We couldn't hold a candle to their organizational skills – there's nothing in this world as precise and perfect as German mechanical equipment, that's what my Uncle Benassi used to say, and he should know – and they were like one great machine which just carried on growing, proliferating, multiplying before your very eyes. Geometric progression, it's known as, and the Duce would go to Germany to review the military parades and each time he'd come back more flabbergasted than the last. Now it was he who was hanging on to Hitler's coat tails, and it was 'Hitler this', and 'Hitler that', and it was Hitler who was saying: 'Keep your distance, Duce, stop pawing me.' And he winced and drew back a bit, saying to Goebbels under his breath: 'Some manners they've got, these eyeties!'

Anyway, Rudolf Hess was there with the Duce on 29 October 1937 for the inauguration of Aprilia, and the Duce was all cock-a-hoop because he'd managed to pull off the sun trick yet again – in front of Rudolf Hess, into the bargain: 'Tell that to Adolf. Let him have a go.'

But the oddest thing is that exactly two years later – on 28 October 1939, when Pomezia was declared open for business – at Pomezia too it was pouring with rain, and the sky was like a leaden cloak. The Duce arrived from Rome at midday in an open car, and no sooner had he appeared on the horizon than the sun instantly started peeping out from behind the clouds: 'As the motorcade crossed the bridge and came towards us in the square,' said Lanzidei, who could wax lyrical when he'd had a glass or two, 'all of a sudden the sun appeared in the heavens in all its splendour and set everything aglitter.'

'Everything aglitter my eye,' my Uncle Adelchi would butt in at this point. 'You should have seen the place.'

But that was the last time he pulled off that particular trick. Which was a shame, because by now it was the only one he had left up his sleeve, none of the others had been working for quite some time. But he was still as cocksure as ever: 'Every number I pull out of the hat is a sure-fire winner, Mussolini is always right.' In fact, though, all the numbers left in the hat were duds, he'd run through all the good ones, but he didn't want to admit as much. Indeed, every time he pulled out another dud, he'd say: 'It doesn't matter, the next one will be a winner,' and off he'd go, putting his hand in the hat and pulling out another, even duffer one. There was no way of staying that hand of his – it had become a sort of mania – because, as the ancients say, whom the Gods would destroy they first send mad.

Anyway, he inaugurated Pomezia on 29 October 1939. And that was another gem. It had been designed by those same four friends – two engineers and two architects – who had designed Aprilia.

Oddly enough, it was just when they started work on Pomezia – 22 April 1938 – that the *Manifesto of Racist*

Scientists came out, and a review called *Defence of the Race* started to appear. Then, between September and November, a series of anti-semitic rules and regulations came into force, and by the end of 1938 Jews were virtually outlawed in Italy, they were no longer citizens like everybody else, they couldn't teach or hold any public office, nor – Heaven forfend – be in the army or the Fascist Party, or practise certain trades or professions. Now they couldn't even send their children to school.

To be honest with you, to our family it was like water off a duck's back. So it was to the rest of the Italian people, let's be clear about this. Have you ever heard of anyone in Italy in 1938 or 1939 getting up and saying: 'Hang on a minute, that's no way to treat the Jews.' No one. Not a word. What the Italian people did say was: 'What do I care? I'm not a Jew.' Indeed, thinking back on what priests and the Catholic Church had said and done in Italy over the last five hundred years – it was they who'd invented the ghetto, and the first one was around our parts, in Venice, in the north – you won't be surprised to learn that my family, and the rest of the Italian people with them, quite soon went back to saying: 'Damn all these Jews, they're a positive curse.'

But you'll also recall that two of the four men who'd designed Aprilia and Pomezia were Jews. Ardent Fascists, but Jews. Like Barany, come to that. And then, from one day to the next, you turned on them and stabbed them in the back.

Indeed – years later – every so often my Uncle Adelchi would say: 'Take Barany, for example! If he'd lived another two years, it would have been us who'd have done for him. Just as well he died on Amba Aradam, he got off lightly.' First we'd have driven him out of the Servicemen's Association, then out of the party and then – no two ways about it – we'd have loaded him on to a sealed wagon and sent him to Mauthausen; that's where Petrucci's step-son died – one of the architects of Aprilia and Pomezia. And all because the Man had bound himself head to foot – body and soul – to his new German ally.

'Are you completely mad?' Balbo had shrieked – Italo Balbo, all honour to him, but he'd been a lone voice – together with De Bono at the Grand Council of Fascism: 'What did the Jews ever do to you? In Italy they're more Fascist than we are.'

'You don't understand anything about politics,' the Duce hissed at him. And everyone kept mum, even Rossoni. You could have heard a pin drop in the Council Chamber. '*Mussolini is always right,*' was written on walls all over Italy, and they'd written it so often that they'd started to believe it. Indeed, what's worse is that he believed it himself. The only time he hummed and hawed or shilly-shallied was when he was with his mate Hitler: 'Ever known him to be wrong?' He was jealous of him, but by now there was no turning back: 'Adolf is always right.' By now, he was completely under his thumb.

Anyway, while we were starting to build Pomezia – and cooking up that tasty morsel for the Jews – the war in Spain was drawing to a close, and my grandmother was pleased as punch because Uncle Treves would be coming home.

He wasn't, though. 'Where are you going then?' they asked Uncle Treves. 'There won't be much demobilizing going on round here, not with all this bedlam.' And indeed the Duce's German chum had already annexed Austria, and just thirteen days before the war in Spain came to an end he'd started on another one by marching into Czechoslovakia.

We, in the meantime – so as not to have our noses put out of joint – had gone off to invade Albania, on 17 April 1939, and annexed it to Italy: 'That bit's ours.' There wasn't anything there, but at least now – when our king was being introduced to some bigwig or other – we could say: 'This is His Majesty Victor Emanuel III, Emperor of Ethiopia, and King of Italy and Albania.' That's quite something, surely?

Then, on 1 September 1939 – less than two months before we finished building Pomezia and the Duce came to inaugurate it – Hitler invaded Poland and started the Second World War. The world caught fire again, although, for the moment, we were in the clear. Indeed, Adolf had told the Duce in no uncertain terms: 'You keep out, in terms of trade you're more useful to me out than in. If you were in, you'd only be a nuisance.'

'All right, Dolf, we'll stay out,' he said. But secretly he was worried: 'What kind of a figure am I cutting?' he asked himself. What he wasn't worried about, though, was us, or rather my grandmother, who'd had enough of wars: 'With all the work we've got to do round here?' But we boys were all for it: 'Eight million bayonets! What are we waiting for?' By now we were convinced we were unbeatable.

Anyway, that was the situation when the Duce came to inaugurate Pomezia on 29 October 1939: the world was at war. But what may strike you as strange is that for the Peruzzi clan, that wasn't the worst of it – the war, I mean – but the fact that that day at Pomezia, inaugurating the town, a certain figure was no longer at the Duce's side, namely Edmondo Rossoni. The hour had struck for him. He was out on his ear.

A few days earlier, he'd been summoned: 'Comrade Rossoni, I've decided to accept your resignation from the Ministry of Agriculture.'

'Eh?' Rossoni gulped.

'Sign here and go in peace,' the Duce'd said, thrusting a pen and paper under his nose. 'Tomorrow you'll be replaced by Comrade Tassinari.'

For a year now, Rossoni had been working with this Tassinari – a young Under-Secretary who was still a nobody– on the problem of the Sicilian *latifondi*. Five hundred thousand hectares – half a million – to be divided up into so many holdings and given to the peasants, plus fifty or so towns of various sizes, all to be built from scratch. A gigantic undertaking – ten times the Pontine Marshes – with all the Sicilian barons and landowners to be put on the rack. They were all set to go. In a few days their plan would pass into law, and they'd be able to get started.

And start they did – building towns and holdings at breakneck speed throughout the war years, until 1943; they only stopped with the American landings, at which point Sicilian barons and *mafiosi* alike heaved a sigh of relief – but they started without Rossoni: 'Sign here.'

Now I don't know if he sacked him because he was getting too big for his boots – 'At this rate people will think it's him who's giving the land to the peasants, not me' – or just because that's what he was like, which wasn't very nice. Or perhaps – who knows? – he was still irked by the business of Tresigallo.

As you'll recall, the place where Rossoni had been born was just a hamlet – three houses and a little church – in the Commune of Formignana. Well, after he became a minister, Rossoni had a new town built there too – a town of five thousand souls – and made it a commune in its own right; you should visit it if you're ever around those parts. And Mussolini too – as we all know – had Predappio Nuovo built round the hamlet of Dovia where he'd been born, but it can't hold a candle to Tresigallo, and maybe when he saw it Mussolini felt that he'd been outclassed: 'Son of a bitch!' because it's an architectural gem. People come from all over the world to look at it – for Rossoni, it was to be a sort of anti-Ferrara: 'I'll show him,' he'd said – and he'd been personally responsible for every detail, compulsory purchase, tenders, the lot. A square in the form of a colonnaded hemicycle – 'You ought to go and see it,' he'd say to my grandfather when he came to call – and factories of all kinds on the outskirts, making tractors and threshing-machines and processing agricultural produce: the 'corporative city', he called it. In the middle of the cemetery he'd put up a huge mausoleum with the word '*Rossoni*' on it: 'I'll put you in there too, after you're dead,' he'd say to my grandfather.

'No, that's for you,' my grandfather would say. 'I'll be fine on the Mussolini Canal.'

Anyway, the fact remains that when Mussolini had said: 'Sign here,' Rossoni objected timidly: 'But Benito...'

'Who are you calling Benito? Who do you think you are, one of the family?'

'I'm sorry Duce, but really...'

'Really my eye! Just take a look at this,' and he pulled out a thick wodge of paperwork going back years. 'You made a mint out of Tresigallo, you fleeced your fellow townsmen, and you had your hand in the till in the Pontine Marshes too...'

'What do you mean? That's slander, pure and simple.'

'Slander?' shrieked the Duce, thrusting the paperwork under his nose. 'Take a look here! The union funds! You even stole from the workers.'

'Not that again? But it's not true,' said Rossoni entreatingly.

'And what about your wife? Just take a look at this!'

'My wife?' and now Rossoni went quite pale and dizzy as the Duce pulled out a report from the Servicemen's Association which said that his wife – she was quite a lot younger than he was – had been having it off with one of his cousins.

'One evening while you were in the town hall in Tresigallo, she was in a hotel with your cousin's son.'

'But it's just not true,' wailed Rossoni.

Then the Duce changed tone. He stopped shrieking, pointed to a page from *Defence of the Race*, and asked him gently, purringly, almost affectionately: 'Rossoni, why did you never tell me that your mother was Jewish?'

'Jewish? My mother? What's she got to do with anything?'

'Sign here and be off, and just thank the Lord I'm not having you shot into the bargain,' he said, reverting to his harsher tone.

'Thanks, Duce,' Rossoni said. He signed, and went off home.

'So now I'm Jewish too,' he said to my grandfather, almost weeping with rage.

But now things weren't going too well in the Peruzzi household either, as a matter of fact. Or rather, things were all right on our branch of it, on holding 517 on the Mussolini Canal. As indeed they were in the next one, the one where my Uncle Themistocles lived. And Aunt Bissola and Lanzidei had finally gone to live near Aprilia, taking his father and brothers with them. She'd turned them all into good peasants – and everyone was very pleased, because that way at least they could be sure of their daily bread – and there it was my Aunt Bissola who was in charge, because none of Lanzidei's family had ever seen a farm animal in their lives. He of course was still an anti-Fascist, but now they'd given him a holding, Aprilia was a fine place, the land had been reclaimed, his wife was what she was, and now he too would go to the local Fascist Headquarters for Saturday activities, wearing a black shirt and a militiaman's uniform, his rifle shouldered, ready for drill.

'Comrade Lanzidei!' my uncles would greet him whenever

they met him.

'*A noi!*' he'd answer back, and start to laugh. But one or other of us was always round at their place – some child or other – and they were always round at ours. There was a continual coming and going, on carts or bicycles, and not only did we do each other all kinds of favours, working for each other and generally helping each other out, we also seemed to want to be together, one big family. Aunt Bissola was quite capable of turning up unannounced at our place – with a crowd of children on that bicycle of hers which even her husband wouldn't have ventured out on when he was selling underpants – and start shrieking like a madwoman if someone had so much as moved a mat on a bedside table: 'You can't leave the place for a moment without someone turning it upside down.'

'Haven't you got a home of your own?' my grandmother would say. 'Why don't you just stay there?'

'So, you want to get rid of me?' she'd say. But there she'd always be.

'Why don't you get rid of her once and for all?' all the children would say.

'Quiet, now, she's your aunt.'

No, the people for whom things weren't going all that well by now were my Uncle Pericles and my Uncle Iseo. They were fine as far as their health was concerned, and their wives got along together like sisters. At first it was as though they'd found the land of milk and honey. Their land produced sugar beet as big as your arm, as I've already told you, and thousands of kilos of grain, hay, cotton, maize and whatever else they planted. Then one fine day in late May or early June, in 1939, my grandmother woke up saying: 'I dreamt about a figure all in black.'

'Not again!' they all groaned.

Uncle Treves – the only member of the family who wasn't home at that moment – couldn't be in any danger, because the war in Spain was over and he was doing his army service in a barracks somewhere in Piedmont. 'Never trouble trouble,' my grandfather said to her. 'Say a prayer and pipe down.'

Then there were Armida's bees, which had been taking strange flights since the previous evening. 'Bzz, bzz, we want to move over there,' they told her.

'Where do you want to move to? You just stay put, you dratted creatures!'

But in the early afternoon – just after lunch, when the sun was on our holding – there was nothing to be done, the bees had gone off on their own, and they'd all come to our place, to a hive she'd left on the embankment.

After that there came a hailstorm to end all hailstorms. But only on their side, at Ponte Marchi; on our side, nothing. Hailstones as big as eggs. Like stones. One of the younger ones didn't make it into the barn in time, and was hit on the head by one of these monsters, making a gash that poured with blood. And there were broken tiles and the crash and dazzle of thunder and lightning from all directions, and when the storm died down the sky was so black it seemed like night.

On our side, the sun shone on, but on their side – not more than three or four kilometres the other side of the Appian Way – there was this dense mass of dark cloud as far as the mountains, riven from time to time by lightning flashes spindly as skeletons. 'It's over Pericles' way,' said my grandmother, holding her head in her hands, 'it's the figure in black.'

The whole harvest was ruined. All the corn was flattened, all the maize, and all the fruit on the branches, just ripe for the picking. Now I don't know whether you realize what a ruined harvest means. It means you won't be getting a lira in wages

405

for the whole of the coming year. It means you'll have to look after the family, pay the rent, pay the hire-purchase on the car and your children's school fees, and go to work for nothing – not a lira at the end of the month – for one whole year.

But – unlike the Zorzi Vila – Count Cerisano-Caratelli was a decent man, and he summoned all his sharecroppers and said to them: 'Okay, the harvest is ruined, we've lost the lot. Now let's roll up our sleeves and try to have things back to normal by next year, I'll meet you halfway and suspend all your debts. You'll have to try to keep paying at least the mortgage installments, though, because that's the bank's business, not mine.' And they all muttered agreement, swearing under their breath the while, but shaking each other by the hand: 'Well, you Viking?' 'How about that then, you wog!' before they went their separate ways.

Obviously, my Uncle Pericles and my Uncle Iseo got help from the rest of the Peruzzi clan, not just in terms of physical assistance, but also in the form of grain and flour and even the odd bit of cash, from Uncle Treves in his barracks and from Uncle Adelchi's wages as a policeman. My Uncle Pericles accepted these offerings, but unwillingly, because he was rather touchy by nature – like all the Peruzzi, come to that – and he didn't like the idea that the others might be saying: 'See? Why couldn't you have stayed on our holding in peace and quiet, and then nothing like this would have ever happened!' though it's hard to imagine who would have been fool enough to say such a thing to him. And not just because he was Pericles, but because such things just aren't done, even the Peruzzi know you don't rub salt into other people's wounds.

But Uncle Pericles was no fool either. He knew what they were thinking, and – because he felt responsible for having dragged him away with all his family – he turned to Uncle

Iseo, and said to him, when no one else could hear: 'Iseo...'

'Pericles!' my Uncle Iseo butted in before he could get any further. 'Don't say a word about it. I'm with you to the end. And I don't want to hear another word, damn you,' and they set to work again like Castor and Pollux.

But when November came, just after the inauguration of Pomezia – after that unexpected burst of sunshine – it started to rain again every blessed day. Not in buckets, admittedly, just drizzle, up and down the Pontine Marshes; but the sky was always dark, and from time to time there'd be a heavier shower. On the Alban Hills, on the other hand, it poured. It rained so much from 2–3 November onwards that the *Fosso di Cisterna* and above all the Teppia almost burst their banks.

The bees had been flying around in a state of agitation since the evening before. But everyone – the experts from both the association and the consortium, and Pascale the agronomist – had said there was no danger: 'Don't worry, it can rain as much as it likes at Velletri, but this time we've got our eye on the water level in the Mussolini Canal, it can take all the water God throws at it. You can sleep easy.'

Hearing the way her bees were buzzing, though, Armida wasn't having any of it. She looked at the rising water level in the Mussolini Canal, told Pascale to mind his own business, called her sister-in-law – 'Zelinda!' – and they picked up their hives and children and rushed over to holding 517.

Once they'd got here, though, they felt guilty about having left their husbands: 'A wife should stick by her man.' So they left their children and the bees with my grandmother and retraced their steps. It was pitch-dark by the time they got back home, Pascale had left and their husbands were glad to see them. But ominous gurgling and swooshing sounds were coming from the direction of the canal. 'Nothing to worry about,' my uncles said. 'That's one big canal, it can take anything God throws at it.' In fact, though, on the night of 4–5 November the Mussolini Canal burst its banks a second time – but only on my Uncle Pericles' holding, everywhere else the embankments held firm, just as the experts had promised. Only on his holding. But it was his fault; and also the fault of that Pascale.

After the hailstorm which had ruined the harvest at the beginning of June, my uncles had let Pascale convince them that what was needed was more investment. 'It's like with the lottery,' he said – he was from Naples, after all. 'When your number doesn't come up, what you have to do is double it. Plant peaches.' So they planted a peach orchard. 'Plant my tomatoes in the peach orchard.' So they did, and they borrowed the money for the seedlings from the Cerisano-Caratelli. The peach seedlings – selected by Pascale himself, as they learned afterwards – cost an arm and a leg. What's more – and this is where the trouble starts – since they didn't have enough land for all that planting, my uncles also planted peach trees on the embankment, which wasn't their land. 'No one will notice,' said Pascale. 'Plant away, and you'll be rich.' He also had them uproot the eucalyptus from the strip that served as a windbreak, so they could use that as well: 'What the hell are those eucalyptus doing there? They drink up all the water, and anyway, they're foreign.'

So they ploughed the embankment up and sowed peaches there, and as the Mussolini Canal started filling up, the force and weight of its waters began to press up against the sides. Then, in the places where the earth had been disturbed, the water started to seep in and, as its level rose, so did its weight, and it carried off all the earth, washing away the top of the embankment and opening up a slight gap. Then all the rest of the water seeped in through that gap, gaining in speed and power and carrying off the other, more solid layers – the lower ones – and it was through that gap that the Red Sea burst into my uncles' holding and stayed there for over two weeks before subsiding.

Only their holdings had been flooded, though, together with the two or three further downstream. Their neighbours – the wogs from Sermoneta – offered their help, and their wives brought them food. When they were alone, though, they kept on saying to each other: 'These damned Vikings.' The consortium sued my uncles, and claimed damages. And now everything had been destroyed, lost, once and for all; even the corn which they'd just sowed.

At the beginning of December – once the ground had put on a show of drying out – they tried again, sowing a bit of barley and oats and quick-growing forage crops. But it was late in the year, and the sodden ground was hard to work. There was no point in deluding themselves. There would be a poor harvest this year too.

My uncles didn't know which way to turn. They were up to their necks in debt. They went to Pascale for advice, but they couldn't find him anywhere. He was lying low. He'd flown the coop. 'What shall we do?' my uncles asked.

'Come back to us,' my Uncle Adelchi said immediately, and so did all the other Peruzzi brothers.

'But what about the debts?' said Uncle Pericles and Uncle Iseo. Mainly what they were thinking of was the mortgage payments. One failed harvest, two at a pinch, even the other debts – it wasn't the end of the world; but not to keep up with the mortgage payments, not to become the owners of the land they already considered theirs, that was out of the question. So then they said: 'One ruined harvest doesn't spell disaster,

409

these things happen. But the debts and the installments have to be paid,' and they went off to the militia barracks in Littoria to sign on as volunteers in the first war that might conveniently crop up.

By now there were enough wars to go round, all over the place, and sooner or later we too would enter the Second World War – so everybody said – and it would be child's play, we'd win it on our own, together with that German ally of ours who was a real force of nature, no one could keep up with him. After a fashion – its own rather slipshod fashion – Italy was making preparations. Regiments and divisions were being reinforced, and they were also looking for volunteers, and paying them quite well. So my uncles said: 'Let's volunteer, the pay's quite good, we're bound to win and then we'll pay off the installments and all our debts.'

'Okay!' they said to them at the recruiting office. 'Get enrolling, then. Departure time: end of month. Destination: East Africa.'

'Okay then!' said my uncles. 'If Adelchi got all those medals in Africa, just imagine what we'll come away with!'

Their wives were less keen. Armida wept like a fountain: 'Don't you be going – don't you be going, Pericles.'

'I've never seen you like this, woman! What's got into you?'

'Don't you be going!' she kept on wailing, until finally even her sister-in-law – my Aunt Zelinda – told her to stop being such a silly goose: 'You're behaving like a little girl.'

'I'll give you little girl. I've got my bees, and all day long they're telling me: don't let him go.'

My grandmother wasn't too keen, either: 'I dreamt about a figure all in black again.' But that's life: 'We've got to go,' said my uncles, 'we're going, but we'll win, and we'll be back soon enough. We'll be home within the year.'

Meanwhile, the party – or rather Count Cerisano-Caratelli, who was a bigwig at the local headquarters and who had intervened on my uncles' behalf – had somehow managed to get the consortium to drop its claims for damages; he made out that the embankment had collapsed of its own accord, rather than because of their illegal doings. That didn't solve everything, but it was definitely a step in the right direction, because if they'd also had to pay third party damages, not even star wars would have been enough to save my uncles. They were on their beam ends all right – clean out of gas, as the Americans would say nowadays, but in those days there was no gas, at least not on our holdings – but little by little they'd make it, that was what my uncles thought. 'A Peruzzi never gives up, goddamn those Zorzi Vila.'

The women of course would stay on at the holding, otherwise they'd lose possession of it. They'd have to get by as best they could. In spring they'd plant the sugar beet, sell off such fruit as there was – for the rest, they'd manage with my uncles' soldiers' pay – and tend the cows, although there weren't many left now, what with all that water one Friesian had died of pneumonia or galloping consumption, I no longer remember which. Another one had eaten too much wet grass and her stomach had swollen up so much that she died. So there weren't many cows left, and one of us – from holding 517 – would go over every now and again to lend a hand.

'Don't you be going,' Armida had wailed the whole night long – before they left – scratching my Uncle Pericles viciously on the back. 'Don't you be going.' At Littoria Station, the following morning, guess who was there to see them off? Pascale the agronomist. There'd been no sign of him since that evening of 4 November when he'd gone off with the last capon

411

two hours before the embankment came down. Now there he was at the station, saying: 'Peruzzi, I'm sorry.'

'Get out of here, you!' said Armida, spitting on the ground.

My Uncle Pericles, on the other hand, just took him gently to one side and said to him: 'Pascale, this time we'll let bygones be bygones. Be careful, though, because I've given my family orders to get their guns and shoot you on sight if they see you anywhere around.'

'But Peruzzi...'

'Get out of here, otherwise the shooting will start right now,' and he took his rifle from his shoulder and had already started loading it, while Uncle Iseo started yelling: 'And those modern tomatoes of yours aren't fit for pigs!'

Then – as the train was already about to leave, and the band was playing *Giovinezza* – all the black-shirted soldiers leant out of the window and shouted: 'Yes, we want the old tomatoes back!' because by now he was known the length and breadth of the Pontine Marshes.

It goes without saying, we never clapped eyes on him again. But my Uncle Pericles' orders stayed etched on the minds of generations of Peruzzis, and even now, each time a Peruzzi is old enough to understand what's going on, the first thing he's told isn't that the Duce had it off with my grandmother – we stopped telling them after his death, and then hers – but rather: 'Look, there are just two names that make a Peruzzi reach for his gun: the first is Zorzi Vila and the second is Pascale. The moment you hear them, son, you get your gun and fire, you'll have all your ancestors behind you. Actually, it's the other way around: Pascale first and then the Zorzi Vila.'

Anyway, my uncles left for Africa while Italy was still at peace. She wasn't yet a belligerent. And if on the one hand they hoped that things would stay that way – so that with a

412

couple of years' pay they'd have sorted things out – they also thought that if we did go to war, we'd win it in a trice: 'It can't last long.' And that was the view of the whole Italian people.

They, on the other hand – from the king and the Duce to the last party leader or general, from Ciano, the Duce's son-in-law who was Foreign Minister, to Badoglio and Cavallero – knew how things really stood: 'What's all this about going to war? The army isn't ready.'

'Well, Adolf's ready, and we're right behind him,' said the Duce. 'What else are we to do, sit by and watch?'

'Fine, Duce! The Duce is always right.'

My uncles were sent to Naples, and took ship from there. Then, on 10 June 1940, when the Duce appeared on the balcony at Palazzo Venezia and said: '*The hour of destiny has struck in the skies over our Fatherland: now is the time for irrevocable decisions. Our declaration of war has been handed over to the British and French Ambassadors. We go into the field against the plutocratic and reactionary democracies of the West, who have repeatedly blocked the march of the Italian people and even threatened their very existence,*' everyone in the square applauded fit to burst. And so we went to war.

But my uncles had already been in Abyssinia for some time and in the meanwhile – that is, from January, when they'd left, until June – even if they were unprepared, our General Staff had noted that the Duce meant business and had started calling people up and bolstering the troops. We were waiting for Uncle Treves to come home – he'd come back on leave just once since he'd been back from Spain – but what actually happened was that Uncle Themistocles and his son Paris were called up, too – Paris was the oldest of the Peruzzi cousins, he'd been born in 1918 while his father was away fighting in the First World War. Now both of them – father and son – were

413

off fighting in the Second, not in the same place and the same unit, but thousands of kilometres apart. Then my Uncle Turati went off too – this time his wife's tears were of no avail – and so did Uncle Cesio, the youngest, the one who was studying to be a surveyor. There wasn't a single male Peruzzi left on our holdings except for my grandfather, who was getting on a bit – he must have been nearly seventy by then – the sons of my Uncle Themistocles, who were fifteen and sixteen, and my Uncle Adrasto, who had just married and been allowed to stay at home because they must have thought to themselves that at least one man had to be left on every holding, otherwise what would they all eat? And then of course there was my Uncle Adelchi – because there had to be one or two policemen around Littoria, they'd pared them down to the bone, three had been called up but three had to be kept on – though, as you know, when it came to working the land you couldn't really count on Uncle Adelchi: 'I've got to get to work! Wake up, girls, it's time to go.'

So, knowing that men were rather thin on the ground, my Uncles Percles and Iseo wrote to their wives from Port Said – even before they'd gone through the canal – telling them to lease out all the land, or, better still, to sell up, if they could find a buyer. Then, on 7 June 1940 – three days before He declared war – my Uncle Pericles wrote from Addis Ababa:

Assa Baba 7.6.

very dear family Parents and Armida

we are fine Armida tell me how things are going in connection with our intrests, by receet of the present you should have finished harvesting so I'd like to know how it went and how are the sugar beet the maze the

414

cotton the cows how is the forridge and let me know how our children are what is Adria saying. As far as our intrests go try and do the best you can, always talk everything over with my brothers. and keep everything well weeded. even if you have to spend a bit on getting some extra help. Dear brothers those of you who are still at home, as to my little scheem do what you think is best even if you have to sell everything and take my family to Podegora just do it, but if you can carry on as you are that's fine too talk about it among yourselves, Adrasto if you find yourself in a bit of a muddel about my intrests, go and see Rinaldo he'll advice you your brother Pericles. Dearest Armida do your best to repay them for their help, Adrasto and the others too.

On another sheet, in the same envelope, Iseo wrote:

Addis Ababa 7.6. 1940

Dearest Parents and Family

I hope this finds you as well as it leaves me at present after a long voyidge we arrived in Addis Ababa, the cliptas are just like Adelchi said but we're not staying here, we don't know where we're going but we'll write to you and keep you informed. Zelinda when you receeve the present tell me if your up to date with the payments if you've moan the hay have you started cutting the corn, how is the harvest coming on? Tell me if you've found a hand if you havent try and find one: that way I'll feel better about things too I no you cant manidge it all on your own, speshially the cows they can be dificult, tell me how its going in the feelds not well I don't suppose?

415

*Zelinda keep going itll all be over soon, When you write
let me no everything about our skeem, if you've still
got the two heffers if their too much trubble sell them,
Adrasto keep an eye on my house do your best as far
as the intrests go if your in trubble write to me and tell
me what its about. Ill leave you now greetings to all the
family.*

Peruzzi Iseo.

Three or four more letters arrived, then silence. And we'd only
gone to war on 10 June 1940 because he – the Duce's German
chum – already seemed to have the upper hand. Norway had
been occupied, Belgium, Holland and Luxembourg had been
invaded, he'd given the joint Anglo-French armies a drubbing
and was about to enter Paris. Such English as were left were
huddled on the beaches at Dunkirk, waiting for all kinds of
craft, even little rowing boats, to pick them up and whisk them
home to safety as indeed they did. A total rout. France alone
and on her knees. And it was then that our Duce – the Man –
suddenly started to say: 'What are we waiting for? Let's join
the fray, that way at the price of a couple of thousand dead I'll
be sitting at the table along with the victors.' So we attacked
France, which had already lost her own battle and was on her
knees. Talk about hitting someone when they're down. We
attacked her from below, from the Alps, and my Uncle Treves
was there too and he thought that it would be a pushover, just
as the Duce did. We'd be pouring in. But it didn't turn out that
way at all, and it was them who gave us a thrashing. When
we came to sit at that famous table it was only because the
Germans had done for the French completely in the meantime.
'What are you doing here?' Adolf must have felt like saying to

the Duce. 'Have you no sense of shame?'

Anyway, we'd beaten France, we'd joined the winners and now it was just a matter of beating England and then we could all go home. Now – as you know – the first years of the war didn't go badly for us, all in all. We had a powerful ally in the Germans – Germany was a terrifying engine of war, churning out cannon, planes and tanks like our fields churned out sugar beet – even if we did our very best to make them lose. When we invaded Greece – he'd already said to us: 'Give the Balkans a wide berth, don't start opening up a new front there, concentrate on North Africa and we'll get Suez and Egypt' – Adolf almost went into a swoon: 'But why the hell have you gone into Greece without letting me know? You might at least have warned me.'

'Well, did you tell us when you went off to invade Poland and Czechoslovakia and then Romania?'

Indeed, on 12 October – going down through Hungary – the Germans had also sent a 'military mission' to Bucharest, to prevent the oil from Ploesti falling into the hands of the Russians, who weren't yet our enemies, though Hitler knew that they soon would be. 'Could I have left that oil in their hands?' he asked the Duce in an attempt to excuse himself for not having alerted him. Italy had read about it in the papers. The Duce had been really riled: 'Oh yes? Well, now I'll show you.' Much of the blame, though, lay with his son-in-law, Galeazzo Ciano, who'd said to him: 'Greece? We'll have it for lunch.' And we invaded it – if you could put it like that– just to show him we could. Who did he think he was: the only person who could do invasions? 'Two can play at that game.' And he – Hitler – flew into a towering rage: 'You pack of boobies, there's no oil there. In Greece, there's nothing. They're even poorer than you lot, you just went there to spite my face, goddamn you.'

But there was nothing to be done. By now we'd gone and invaded Greece, and my Uncle Themistocles was there as well – there's always a Peruzzi on every front – but the Greeks gave us such a thrashing, and we left so many dead there on those hills, that they drove us back immediately and went on to invade Albania, which was where we'd moved in from in the first place. They drove us into the sea – or almost – and they were already nearly at the gates of Tirana, only a hundred or so kilometres away. Then we had to go asking the Germans for help – 'Sorry, Dolf, give us a hand' – because if they didn't come along with their tanks and open up this other new front, then pretty soon it would have been us surrendering to the Greeks. Do you remember that song, that lament, really, that used to be sung by the Julia – the Alpine Division – about the war in Greece? It was on the bridge at Perati that the Julia met with disaster, and the flower of Italian youth was cut down in its prime.

And do you know where Perati is? It's not in Greece, as you might think – after all, it was us who were doing the attacking, and the Duce had gone out on to the balcony at Palazzo Venezia and said that we were going to give Greece a proper thrashing. In fact, though, Perati is in the heart of Albania. As for the thrashing, it was them who clobbered us, and if the Germans hadn't showed up on the scene it would have been them, the Greeks, who'd have landed in Italy, and that might have been no bad thing, at least the whole business would all have been over and done with. But no, the Germans turned up on the scene and it was the Greeks who surrendered. And we occupied Greece, down to the last hamlet and island. We didn't pull our punches, either. We were merciless. Forget the idea of Italians as a happy-go-lucky people, and films like

Mediterranean.

Anyway, the last letter from East Africa was dated 27 September 1940. After that, nothing. At that point – as I've already said – it still seemed that we were bound to come out on top, everywhere, and at first it looked that way in East Africa as well. We immediately went on the offensive, and at the beginning of July we went into Sudan and also into part of Kenya. The English retreated without a shot being fired. At the beginning of August we went into Somaliland – British Somalia, up in the Horn of Africa – and there too the English cleared off, they did us a fair bit of damage but then they cleared off, taking ship from Berbera. In Italy, the propaganda-mongers and the *Luce Film Service* had a field day. 'We've as good as won already,' everyone was saying in the Pontine Marshes.

Meanwhile the offensive in North Africa was also getting under way – in Libya, where Uncle Cesio was, the youngest brother, the one who was studying to be a surveyor – and we'd also invaded part of Egypt. All we had to do was to get to Alexandria – 'Easy as pie,' we thought – seize the Suez Canal, drive the English out of the Mediterranean and bingo, we'd have made it.

But we never reached Alexandria. First they drove us out of Cyrenaica. Then we went on the attack again, but now too we had to call in the Germans – Rommel and his *Afrika Korps* – and by May at last we'd got to El Alamein, just sixty kilometres from Alexandria: 'That's it, we've as good as taken it.' In fact, that was as far as we went. We fought bravely – not just at El Alamein, but also at Tobruk, at Bir el Gobi and everywhere else – and, as it rightly says on the memorial tablet to the parachute regiment at El Alamein: 'It was good fortune, not valour, that was in short supply.' Actually, what was really in short supply was cannon, planes, petrol and tanks. Or, to put it another way, what was in short supply was common sense, because – as my grandmother always said – it's madness to go to war, but it's even greater madness if you haven't got weaponry and munitions to equal those of your enemy. 'If that's the case, you stay at home!' my grandfather would say. 'Where's the sense in wandering all over the place if you're not up to it? If that's the case, you stay at home, damn you and the Zorzi Vila.'

'But look, I thought Adolf would take care of everything, and that all we had to do was follow him,' was what the Duce said. Or at least what Rossoni said he said. Franchini, on the other hand – who came from Cisterna, and who'd gone out to conquer an empire with my Uncle Adelchi as a young man, and who went on to make a hobby of studying the Second World War – always said that it wasn't true that we were so defective in terms of armaments and equipment: 'It was us who made the first prototype for a jet plane, and we were also experimenting with an aircraft carrier; the latest models of our fighters were superior to theirs, as were our bombers. Our latest cannon, and our tanks and radar and submarines and pocket submarines were every bit as good as theirs. We had a pool of designers and technicians that they could only dream of, we were quite simply first-rate...'

Now – as we know – when a man from Cisterna starts to talk big, and spins out of control, the only way you can stop him is to shoot him, and my Uncle Adelchi was quick to cut him down to size: 'Get off with you, you goon! While you were building one piffling submarine, the Americans were churning out a hundred thousand. What counts in war is numbers. If we lost, there must have been a reason, and it wasn't bad luck or betrayal, Franchin, it was a total lack of common sense.'

But my Uncle Adelchi said all this later – many years later, in fact. While it was all going on – there on the spot – he too believed that we'd have an easy win: 'It'll be a walkover! Our faith is stronger than iron and gold.'

In North Africa – in Libya – we Peruzzi were represented by my Uncle Cesio, as I've said, and he ended up as a prisoner in India. He was wounded at Tobruk, then taken prisoner and sent on to India by ship. We saw him again in 1946. He'd gone off as a boy of eighteen, but the English had roughed him up so much while he was in prison in India that when he came back, he looked like an old man. A terrifying sight. The one who didn't come back, on the other hand, was my Uncle Pericles. The sword of the Peruzzi. The lion of our people.

In East Africa things hadn't gone any better than in the north. Indeed, straight after our offensive, the English had troop reinforcements sent in from India and South Africa. All fresh as daisies, and well-equipped. We had three hundred thousand men out there. They had sixty thousand. That was some mismatch. Our air force was inferior not just in terms of speed and manoeuvrability and weaponry but also, more crucially, in terms of numbers, because many of Balbo's old planes – which by now were so decrepit as to be virtually useless – had never been replaced. It was the same with the ground troops. We'd been the first to fight a mechanized war in Africa, using lorries and tanks; but they too were the same out-dated models. We didn't even have spare tyres or inner tubes. Our pieces of ordnance were mostly antiquated and our munitions dated back to 1918. Once they'd been fired, a lot of grenades failed to explode. You'd throw them and they'd make a puffing sound and that was that.

The English, on the other hand, came in armed to the teeth, and all their weaponry and equipment was absolutely up-to-the-minute. All that was missing was Ray-Bans. There we were on foot with our carbines, and there they were, covered from the skies by a sea of planes, with tanks and armoured cars and all-terrain vehicles – forerunners of the Land Rover – and more light guns and machineguns than you could shake a stick at. The 'Gazelle Force' they were known as. In January 1941 they launched a simultaneous attack from north and south. And there were sixty thousand of them, as I've said. There were three hundred thousand of us. Three hundred thousand jokers.

We couldn't call in the Germans to help us in East Africa. They couldn't get there. Suez was as closed to them as it was to everyone else. Otherwise we'd have prolonged the agony there too. No help arrived, not even reinforcements from the Fatherland. We held out for as long as we could and fought, bravely at times. The Duke of Aosta got dug in on Amba Alagi and held out until 17 May 1941. When we surrendered, the English granted us the honours of war.

'We'll be back!' the Duce said. 'The empire's out there, it's ours and no one's going to touch it. Soon we'll have won the war in Europe, we'll break their backs once and for all and then we'll be off again and take back that empire.'

What can I say? At that point, we still believed him. Of course we weren't all that happy about things, and above all we were terribly worried about our people who were out there and who we hadn't heard from. There was no internet – no satellite phones – and letters sent by air mail hadn't a hope of getting through, not with the English in complete control. At one point wireless communications for the troops themselves broke down. Months went by without any news at all. Just war bulletins and the Duce bawling: 'We'll be back!' Where my uncles were, God alone knew, as my grandmother would say.

Then, early on the morning of Christmas Eve, 1941 – she'd got up to make the *cappelletti* for the next day – just after she'd killed the chickens for the broth and the filling, just after she'd wrung their necks but just before she'd started plucking them, she said to my grandfather as he came downstairs: 'Last night I dreamt about a figure cloaked in black.'

'To hell with you and your figures cloaked in black, doom-merchant that you are,' he said to her, but gently, not sharply, and he took her by the shoulders and made as if to kiss her, his eyes already full of tears, because he too had a lump in his throat, for all those sons scattered throughout the world, but above all for those two in Africa, Pericles and Iseo.

She fended him off, using one of the chickens: 'I'm busy,' and she carried on with what she was doing. She put wood on the fire, tested the heat of the water in the pot with her finger, prepared the barley and boiled the milk for everybody's breakfast, and then plucked the two birds.

Once that was done, she took the pot off the stove for a moment, stirred up the fire and held each chicken over it – to singe what remained of the feathers – and then started to clean them, cutting into their necks, opening them up and taking out their innards. She cut each into two big chunks and put them on to boil. Then she busied herself with other matters, and by ten o'clock – when the broth was almost ready – she kneaded the flour with the eggs she'd broken into it. She rolled out the pasta dough with a rolling pin and hung it up to dry. Once the chickens were cooked she took them out of the pot and stripped the flesh from their bones, then chopped it up finely on the chopping board. She also chopped up a *cotechino* and a salame. She mixed them all together – with a bit of parsley and nutmeg and herbs – added another couple of eggs, and the filling was ready. All the children were standing around,

423

waiting.

She took a strip of pasta dough from the top of the bread chest – where she'd put it to dry – and rolled it out again on the table. Then she poured on another sprinkling of flour and cut it all into little squares with the tip of her knife, drawing big vertical lines from top to bottom, then horizontal ones from side to side. Like a chessboard. She placed a dollop of filling on each square, and then said: 'Go!' Then all the children rushed forward to top the squares with other squares, over the filling, until the table was covered with little hats, with the filling rising in the middle, and broad brims round it. You always had *cappelletti* at Easter and Christmas – otherwise it wasn't Christmas, or Easter – and this was specially exciting for us children because it was the done thing to put a button into one of them, into the filling. Then the next day – on Christmas Day – you'd wait and see who found it and said: 'Ouch!' amidst much laughter. That was how my grandfather lost his last upper tooth. He spat it out, together with the pasta square, and stared at it blankly as it lay in his hand. Once – but it must have been after the war, I was quite small – we put in a whole lot of buttons: 'That'll be a laugh!' – but in fact the laugh was on us, because she walloped us good and proper: 'You only put in one!'

'Why only one?' we wailed.

'Because that's how it's done,' followed by more thumping. Just one. One's a laugh, any more and you'll get a pasting, because just that one reminds everyone that today is Christmas and you're eating fit to burst, but watch it, bad luck is always just around the corner, nothing in this world is for free and in any case tomorrow it won't be Christmas any more and real life will be back waiting for you, everyday life, pain and sacrifice and not much wine. That's what that button's telling you. Just that one, though. Not one more. Too many buttons can ruin even Christmas.

It must have been about eleven o'clock – on that occasion – when we heard someone saying: 'May I come in?'

It was Don Orlando, the priest from Borgo Podgora, who came from the Veneto, and my grandmother said: 'Please, do come in, will you have lunch with us, Reverend Father?'

'No, I've just come to bring you a letter.'

In fact it was a postcard, with 'P.O.' written on it in big letters – post office, that meant – and 'P.O.W.' prisoner of war. It had been sent on to him by the Vatican, or the papal welfare body which had links with the International Red Cross. It had been posted in Kenya, though goodness knows what highways and byways it had gone through before reaching us.

It was from Uncle Iseo, who said that he had been wounded but was all right now, and that he was in a prison camp run by the English. He asked after us all, and after all his brothers who were in the war: Themistocles, Treves, Turati and his nephew Paris. At the end, though – after he'd wished us well – he also asked for news of Pericles: 'Lost contact with Brother Pericles, what news.'

'He's asking us?' my Uncle Adelchi started shrieking when he got back from work. 'He's out there with him, and he asks us for news?'

'Now you're blaming my Iseo,' wailed Zelinda – his wife – clutching her children to her skirts. Armida – Uncle Pericles' wife, and they'd both been back with the rest of the Peruzzi clan for quite some time by now – Armida hugged her and said: 'Nonsense, we're not blaming you, we're just thanking God that your man is safe, at least.'

'So's yours!' shouted my grandmother, but she looked grim, and not at all convinced.

Indeed, by now everyone was on tenterhooks, because so many of us had fathers and husbands and sons wandering around the globe and something might happen to any one of them at any moment, because war is war – as we all know – and in war it may happen from time to time that somebody actually gets killed (even if we Italians hadn't got this into our heads all that well, and every time we sent people wandering around all over the place, in the Congo or Iraq or on the moon, and someone got killed, we'd immediately say: 'Blimey, why did those cowardly murderers have us in their sights, all we're doing is bringing peace! Let's go home!') But as long as nothing happened to our fathers and husbands and sons, we didn't worry all that much – 'At least he's alive, and anyway God will provide' – and now that Uncle Iseo had been taken prisoner, a great weight was lifted from our minds: 'He's been taken prisoner but he's alive; things may not be easy but sooner or later he'll be back, and then he won't have to do any more fighting.' Now we knew where he was; but God alone knew what had happened to Pericles.

Now the Peruzzi clan were on the road to Calvary. Backwards and forwards, asking people things: to the recruiting office in Littoria, the Fascist Headquarters, the militia, the Red Cross; to Don Orlando in Podgora, to Don Federico in Borgo Carso and then, with them, to the bishop in Velletri. And backwards and forwards to see Rossoni in Rome – though he didn't count for anything any more, and they'd kept him sweet by letting him carry on being the boss of the Farmworkers' Union and a member of the Grand Council, even though it was an age since the Duce had convened a meeting: 'I'll do it all myself, where's the need for the Grand Council?' – and Rossoni too was going backwards and forwards, to see the odd friend he still had at the Ministry of War. No dice. Uncle Iseo appeared on the lists

426

of prisoners – because every so often there were exchanges of prisoners, even between enemy armies, organized by the Vatican or the Red Cross – but Uncle Pericles didn't show up anywhere, neither among the prisoners nor among the dead and wounded. Nowhere. Missing.

'But what does missing mean?' my grandmother asked my Uncle Adelchi.

'Missing means missing. They don't know what's happened to him. He might be dead or he might be alive.'

'But... more dead or more alive?'

'It depends! They don't know. They might learn something at some point.'

'Does that happen?'

'Sometimes, ma,' but he knew quite well that it almost always doesn't. Or very rarely. Very rarely indeed. Mostly, in war the missing are just dead men without names, people you haven't managed to put a name to – people who've lost their identification tag – or who have been mangled beyond all recognition. Every now and again, though, as we know, someone turns up, comes back; but that's a miracle, a real one-off.

The Peruzzi clan, though, clung to that one-in-a-million hope, starting with my grandmother and Armida, who, when no one else would listen, would ask her bees: 'So, is he alive or is he dead?'

They just carried on buzzing and pretended not to hear.

Then she'd become impatient: 'I said, is he alive or is he dead?'

More buzzing. 'He's neither alive nor dead,' they said. 'He's missing!' and off they flew, but in a strange way.

'To hell with the lot of you!' and, as you know, there's nothing worse than uncertainty, because what crushes people is not bad news as such, but doubt, and above all the waiting to hear the worst. You can face up to bad news, and when you've heard it, one way or another you'll pick yourself up and carry on. But if it doesn't come – and you're left in a state of doubt – how can you pick yourself up? It's like when someone dies at sea, and can never be given burial because he's never found, and his relatives don't know where they stand. If the drowned man's body never turns up, you'll never see him – his corpse – and you'll never be able to dress him in his funeral clothes, slip a coin into his pocket, lower him into his grave and place a stone upon him. He's neither alive nor dead, he's homeless, he's neither in this world nor that – he hasn't crossed the River Acheron – and he's still shouting to Charon: 'Carry me over, take me to the other side.' And that's a grief you'll have for ever, every day of your life until you yourself leave this world, and find your dear one among the wailing souls of the unburied, where you can say to him at last: 'Look, here I am! Give me your hand and we'll cross together, I've got obols for the two of us to give to Charon.'

I don't know whether Uncle Iseo ever received the letter in which we explained that we didn't know where Pericles was either; if he didn't know, as my Uncle Adelchi said, there wasn't much chance that we would. Anyway, he didn't say anything more about it in those few messages – all postcards with 'P.O.W. – P.O.' stamped on them – which we received between then and 1945. He asked after all of us, but he stopped asking about Uncle Pericles. He never mentioned him again, for good or ill. He did mention Armida, though. He never failed to ask after her and her children, and always with the utmost affection. But not a word about Uncle Pericles, and every time a letter or postcard arrived from Kenya and someone started to read it aloud, when they got to the point where Uncle Iseo talked about her and her children – but not a word about her husband – Armida would begin to cry. And of course the more time went by, the less hope there could be, even if she and my grandmother never gave up hoping. They prayed, and she carried on asking her bees: 'So, is he alive or dead?'

'Zzz... Zzz. He's neither alive nor dead, end of message.'

Uncle Iseo came back from the prison camp in late autumn 1945. My Uncle Themistocles and Adrasto had sowed the corn in several fields which had just been cleared of mines, and they were going over the ground with an ox-drawn harrow to make sure the seeds were properly covered. He arrived from the Mussolini Canal. The bridge was no longer there – they'd blown it up, I can't remember whether it was the Germans or the Americans, immediately after the Anzio landings – so he used the footbridge. He was walking along the top of the embankment, and when he saw them – they hadn't noticed him – he shouted out: 'Hey there, you lot!... hey, Peruzzi boys!'

My uncles froze on the spot at the very sound of his voice – they let go of the harrow, turned around and ran towards him. He too was running, stumbling, rolling down the embankment, picking himself up again and running. 'Brother!' they shouted at him as they rushed towards him, flinging their arms around him.

And while Uncle Adrasto was turning round and streaking off in the direction of home: 'It's Iseo, Iseo's back!' he was shouting – Uncle Iseo himself, shaking off the embraces of a tearful Uncle Themistocles, didn't immediately rush off in the direction of his mother and wife and children, but went into the fields, and then into the cowshed, to see his oxen and his harrow and to weep, his arm around their necks and his head between theirs. He drew them to him, one to each side of him, and stroked them; then, still with his knapsack on his back, he took the handle of the harrow in both hands and: 'Ah!' he

429

said, and the oxen started off and he with the harrow behind them. But after a few steps, 'Hey!' he said, and took his hands off the handle, the oxen stopped in their tracks and he fell to the ground and, crouching on his knees with his face in the churned up earth, mixed up with a few grains of wheat – the seed – he cried and cried, and my Uncle Themistocles, who was crying too, tried to pull him up, to clean his face, and said to him: 'Don't take on so, Iseo, please don't take on so.'

Meanwhile, there was shouting all along the road. From all the holdings: 'He's back. Iseo's back!' – even though they all had worries of their own, on every holding, what with the dead, the wounded, the missing, and family wandering all over the globe – and when he and Uncle Themistocles arrived at holding 517 the whole Parallel was there on the threshing-floor, to put their arms around him and to weep with him.

The only one who wasn't weeping was my grandmother, who was in the kitchen, and as soon as she heard my Uncle Adrasto shouting 'Iseo!', out there in the fields, she'd suddenly felt faint – 'Oh my God, I'm dying!' - and she'd sat down on a chair to stop herself from keeling over. Then she'd got up, called out: 'Peruzzi!' sternly to my sobbing grandfather – 'Go to hell,' was what he'd said, though he quickly dried his eyes with his big handkerchief – and then she'd gone out too.

As she appeared, everyone stood aside – to form a corridor down to the bridge on to the holding, and it was there that my Uncle Iseo was still standing, together with his wife Zelinda and their children – and everyone fell silent.

My uncle dried his eyes. He straightened up, ran his hands through his hair and went towards her. She took a couple of steps in his direction. He bent down to take her in his arms: 'Ma.'

'Son!' she said. And then the shouting and weeping started up again – 'Iseo! Iseo!' – and every family from along the road was there, the Toson, the Zago, the Mambrin, the Pellicelli, the lot, and people carried on arriving and then Uncle Themistocles said to him: 'Tell us about it.'

They wanted to go inside, but people said: 'No, tell us about it out here, then we can all listen.' Then chairs were passed out through the windows and everyone formed a circle, and people who didn't have anything to sit on stayed standing, or sat on the drinking trough or the well, or crouched on the ground, even if the grass and ground were wet because it was November, as I've said. Then my Uncle Themistocles said again: 'Tell us about it.'

'Where's Armida?' asked Iseo, because she didn't seem to be anywhere around.

'Never mind Armida, tell us about it!' said Uncle Adrasto, and Uncle Iseo knew what they wanted to hear, but he began by telling them about his time in the prison camp, and it seemed as though he'd never come to the point. He was fine – he said – and they could all see that for themselves. He wasn't fat, it's true, but he was sunburned and muscular. The English hadn't treated him badly in Kenya. No rough stuff. At any point. Indeed, they'd even tended to his wounds. In India it had been another story – as we learned the following year from Uncle Cesio when he too managed to make his way home, and he looked a fright, just like a scarecrow, all skin and bone and old before his time, more dead than alive – in India the English had doled out thrashings and beatings from morning until night.

Now I can't swear to you that this is God's truth. But it's what my Uncle Cesio said and – for my part – all I can tell you is that my Uncle Cesio, the youngest of my uncles, the one who was studying to be a surveyor, was not the sort to tell tall stories; if he said they'd beaten him up, you can be certain

431

that they had. But then if you were to point out that my Uncle Cesio was younger than Uncle Iseo, so he was even more hot-headed, and reckless, like all the Peruzzi clan, and he didn't like kowtowing to anyone, and maybe even in prison he wouldn't take orders and might have answered back or been impertinent to the English – and earned himself a thrashing – well, there I really wouldn't know how to answer you. 'Everyone has their reasons,' was what my Uncle Adelchi used to say, but Uncle Cesio's camp in India was certainly what was known as a Fascist Criminal Camp, just as my Uncle Iseo's was in Kenya. These are the facts, and I'm telling them as such.

The main thing about that camp in Kenya, though – according to Uncle Cesio – was that you went hungry. More hungry than you or I could ever imagine. All there was to eat was extremely watery soup and soft white bread, and very little of that, either. They were well-treated, as I've said, there were no beatings, but practically nothing to eat. 'We haven't got much ourselves,' was what the English told them.

'How come you look so well, then?' asked Uncle Themistocles.

'Rats. I've eaten so many rats that I'm not sure I could manage any chicken.' Even if, later that same evening, he ate a whole one all by himself: 'My goodness, it certainly beats rats.' (Sorry, what did you say? What do rats taste of? A mixture of rabbit, pork and partridge. With an added touch of rabbit and partridge.)

He and his friends had made little traps and nooses out of string. They spent hours lying in wait for their victims – they were prisoners, after all, they hadn't got a lot to do – and as soon as a rat appeared they'd pull on the string, cut off its head with a knife they'd made by filing down the handle of a spoon, take out its innards, thread it on to a stick, hold it over the fire and there was your Sunday roast. That was how my Uncle Iseo came back hale and hearty after four years' imprisonment in Kenya. Then he asked again where Armida was.

'Never mind Armida,' said Uncle Adrasto. 'More to the point, where's Pericles?' said Uncle Themistocles, uttering the dreaded name at last, and silence fell all over holding 517 and over the whole of the Left-Hand Parallel. Beyond the embankment, the canal too fell silent.

Then my Uncle Iseo made a despairing gesture, and only after what seemed like an eternity did he say: 'About Pericles, God rest his soul' – and as soon as she heard that 'God rest his soul,' my grandmother turned pale again and seemed about to faint – 'about poor Pericles I know nothing... I never saw him again. Vanished... Missing,' while my grandmother, seated upon her chair, almost relieved, regained her self-control.

Meanwhile Uncle Adelchi had also arrived, on that black Gilera Motorbike which went with the job. After spreading from holding to holding – 'The Peruzzi have got their Iseo back' – the news had finally reached Littoria. He'd darted off like a madman, skirting round the wartime potholes as speedily and deftly as Giacomo Agostini. He too was crying. 'My Iseo,' he kept repeating, holding him close.

Uncle Iseo carried on with his story, but he remembered almost nothing about the battle. All he remembered was that at one point, while he was going on the attack amidst the usual explosions, and smoke – my Uncles Pericles and Iseo would move forward by fits and starts, and every so often they would be almost crouching, one beside the other, among their fellow soldiers as they fell and shouted, while the lieutenant carried on shrieking: 'Go on, advance!' – at one point he'd found himself on his knees, and then on the ground, but without knowing why, and almost completely breathless. And then he put a hand to his side, and didn't seem able to find it. So he brought his hand up to his face and looked at it. It was red. He put it down to his side again, but all he felt was pain. Then he shrieked: 'Pericles, Pericles, Periclin!' like he'd done when they were children and he had need of his older brother.

Uncle Pericles saw him and heard him immediately, and immediately lay down beside him. 'Keep calm,' he said to him.

'They've got me good and proper,' Uncle Iseo was saying in the meantime, and then: 'It's no good, I'm dying, it's you who'll have to take care of my children, to hell with the Zorzi Vila,' and Uncle Pericles dragged him out of harm's way, behind an upturned lorry, and plugged his wound, while the others kept on coming and going and everything was just a nightmare world of explosions and flames and smoke and shouts. Uncle Iseo was afraid, he suddenly felt very cold and it was then that he started saying: 'Don't leave me alone, Pericles, don't leave me, stay here with me.'

But all the others carried on coming and going and shooting, and Uncle Pericles couldn't stay, he had to leave him where he was, out of harm's way, relatively speaking. 'Keep calm, Iseo, it's nothing; you stay here, I'm going on the attack and I'll be back for you soon. Wait for me, brother, I won't be long, and to hell with the Zorzi Vila.'

And Uncle Iseo said: 'I'll wait.' And that was the last thing he remembered.

He woke up – he didn't know how many days later – in hospital. Here too his memories were confused. At first he thought it was an Italian hospital, a field hospital, with Italian doctors. But then later on in his memories the doctors changed and became English, and the hospital changed too – it became a proper one, made of bricks and mortar – but he couldn't say how or when these changes occurred. Then gradually he got better, and they took him to a prison camp. But even when he was in the hospital – when he'd started to be able to move a bit, and speak and understand – he immediately began asking everyone he knew whether by any chance they'd seen his brother Pericles Peruzzi; and he asked even more people when he arrived in the prison camp, because there were a lot of men from his own unit there.

Some people said they'd seen him before the attack but not after. Someone said he'd seen him while it was going on, but with all his clothing torn off, and smeared all black with oil. This someone wasn't even a hundred percent sure that it was him, but he thought so. There'd been an explosion – he said – but oddly enough Pericles was still on his feet, although he'd lost all his clothing, apart from his boots and his helmet. And it certainly looked like him. He took a few stumbling steps, all smeared with oil as he was, and his face all black, but his white eyes were rolling and he was smiling a crooked smile, and after a bit he started to go slowly but firmly about his business there in the midst of all that chaos, as though he were taking a stroll through the streets of Littoria, and every so often he'd stop and gesture towards the soldiers he met on his way – whether Italian or English – as though to say: 'Have you got a cigarette, by any chance?' But not even this man knew what had become of him; in fact, he was the only one to give this version of events, and he wasn't even completely sure that it was Pericles – 'It looked like him' – while most of the others remembered him in battle, fighting, and nothing more.

Two men had seen him jump on to an English tank, lift up the trapdoor, throw in a grenade, close the trapdoor and jump down again. And while it was exploding inside the tank, and stopping it in its tracks, he'd immediately climbed on to the tank behind. And so on. Hand grenades against tanks. My

435

uncles were in the *Arditi*, the assault troops. But no one saw him after the battle. No one at all.

Or rather, someone from Borgo Montenero who was a good friend of theirs – they'd taken ship from Italy together, from Littoria in fact, but he'd died in the prison camp in Kenya – had asked Pericles to stick with him, and they'd shared hand grenades and munitions to the last, or perhaps it was him who'd given Pericles some hand grenades because he'd gone through his own, and this man from Borgo Montenero had seen him, clear as day, on top of a little mound – some thirty metres away, near a lone acacia tree, with two spreading branches and no leaves, so that they looked like outstretched arms – being struck full on by a howitzer. A 152/13 – according to the man from Borgo Montenero – a Howitz-Echaurren. And when he'd heard it whizzing through the air he'd thrown himself flat on his face. Then after the explosion – when he'd looked up again, and the smoke had gradually cleared and was rising up into the sky, all mixed with dust – there was no longer anyone there on top of that little mound, only a hole, but absolutely no sign either of my Uncle Pericles or of the acacia tree with the outstretched arms. They'd vanished, together, into the smoke which had enveloped them like a great black cloak, and which was now clearing as it rose towards the sky.

What is there to say? Nothing, except that my grandmother – and Armida too, for that matter – continued praying for Pericles' return until the day they died.

'Missing,' was how the authorities put it. That was what was written in the regimental roll and in his pension book.

'Where's Armida?' my Uncle Iseo asked again at this point, because her children were right there in front of him, but there was no sign of her.

'Later,' said my Uncle Adelchi, looking grim, as though to

say: 'This is not a matter to be aired in public.'

'Poor Pericles,' was what Iseo said.

They'd already given Armida her marching orders. They'd taken her children from her – at least the older ones – and they were still here, on the Peruzzi holding. She on the other hand was staying in a little house at Doganella. In exile. Quite a way away. They'd allowed her to keep her two youngest children. Or rather, they'd wanted to leave her just the one. They'd wanted to take Menego from her too. To keep him on the holding. It was my Aunt Santapace – the one who'd married Benassi – who managed to see to it that she was allowed to keep him, beseeching her mother – my grandmother – saying: 'But ma, you can't take such a little child away from its mother, show a bit of mercy, ma, for heaven's sake.'

But my Aunt Bissola was baying like a hyena: 'Take him away from her!'

One or two years later, though – when they were all a bit older, and above all when things had started to sort themselves out, and everyone who was ever going to come back had come back, and the post-war era had really got under way – all her children were taken from her. One here, another there, but all under the watchful eye of the Peruzzi clan: Adria with my Uncle Adelchi, who had rented a house in town – 'Right from the start, the moment I saw Littoria, even when it was still being built, I said: this is the place for me!' – and who was now married; Onesto with my Uncle Delfin at Borgo Hermada, where he worked as a farm-hand; Florinda and Pisana first at boarding school, then on the Peruzzi family holding; Tarcisio, too, went first to boarding school, but he kept on running away and my Uncle Adelchi would go and pick him up from his mother at Doganella and take him back to school, or bring him

437

back to us here on the holding. Once he took him to stay with Aunt Bissola, but she refused to have him, because when she beat him he answered back by kicking her on the shins: 'I want my mother! Take me back to my mother, you ugly sow.'

All her children were taken from her. And she was exiled to Doganella, and told she couldn't leave the house. She couldn't visit them. Except Adria, once a week, in Littoria, because there my Uncle Adelchi could keep an eye on things.

But all this happened in 1945 – November 1945, when Uncle Iseo finally got back from Kenya – and in the years that followed. And we – if I'm not mistaken – hadn't got further than Christmas Eve of 1941, and the first postcard from my Uncle Iseo when he was a prisoner in Kenya, asking for news of Uncle Pericles, and all East Africa and the empire had gone to blazes, and Aunt Zelinda and Armida had left those damned holdings near Ponte Marchi and come to live with the Peruzzi.

They'd managed to sell the holdings on to someone who'd been found by Pascale, as it happened. To pay their debts, though, they'd had to sell all they'd got, even the heifers and such other livestock as still remained to them, not that there was much. They came back to the Peruzzi empty-handed. Except for the bees. And it had been my Uncle Adrasto and my Uncle Themistocles' sons who'd had to go and pick them up with their carts and donkeys, because they hadn't got a cart and donkey of their own – all they had in the world was a few bedsprings and mattresses, a couple of chairs, a bit of linen and a wheelbarrow. And even so they hadn't managed to pay off their debts entirely. Anyway, back they came, and on holding 517, too – back on Peruzzi territory, which was where they'd started off from – they wanted to be together, since they were more like sisters than sisters-in-law, just as they had been on the holdings at Ponte Marchi.

But, when they arrived – even before they'd started unloading the carts – someone piped up: 'Perhaps it would be better if one stayed here and the other went to Themistocles' place, that way there'd be more room for all of us.'

They gave us a doubtful look, they wanted to be together: 'To tell the truth, we'd thought...' ventured Aunt Zelinda, Uncle Iseo's wife.

'No, no, this way we'll all have more room, it'll be better for you, we're only saying it for your own good,' put in Uncle Adelchi hastily.

'Oh yes, we're only thinking of you,' added Uncle Adrasto, quick as a flash, 'it'll be better for you that way.'

'Oh, yes, much better: one of you here and one of you there,' chimed in the Peruzzi sisters-in-law – with Aunt Bissola, who happened to be there at the time, leading the chorus, followed closely by Aunt Nazzarena, the wog from Cori, Uncle Adrasto's wife – as they began to unload Aunt Zelinda's linen and other possessions.

'No, that's not right,' my grandfather was saying to his wife: 'They shouldn't be separated, tell them they can both stay.'

'But that way it's better for them,' said my grandmother. 'One here, one there.'

I can't even begin to describe Armida's response. Aunt Zelinda just began to weep. That holding was theirs. Or rather, truth to tell it belonged to Pericles, because he and Themistocles had been the only ones to have fought in the 1915–18 War and, as veterans, it had been they who had caused the Servicemen's Association to assign those holdings to them, and hence to the whole family, in the first place; furthermore, it had been them – and surely this was no minor matter – who had cycled to Rome to see Rossoni. But you know how these things go: if you've gone off and then come back with your tail between your legs, you can't expect any prodigal son treatment and killing of fatted calves. That only happens in the Bible. In the real world they're more likely to start stoning you, at best. And if they don't start stoning you but come to pick you up in their donkey carts, you just say yes – yes thank you, in fact – to everything they come up with, and sit down meekly in whatever corner they choose to put you in. You grin and bear it, as they say. You certainly don't start putting up objections and taking matters into your own hands.

But then there was Clelia – my Uncle Themistocles' wife, who'd been our maid-of-all-work up in the north of Italy and who my grandmother couldn't stand – who was all too keen for Armida to go and live with her: 'Come to my place,' she'd said, because she had only boys and just one little girl. 'Come to my place, you can give me a hand and we can sort it out between us,' because Armida got on like a dream with her too.

Sorry, what did you say? I told you earlier that Armida also got on like a dream with my grandmother, so why didn't she keep her on there with her, as my grandfather had wanted?

I don't know what to say. My grandmother did indeed get on like a dream with Armida – she loved and made a great fuss of her, and thought she could set her own daughters a good example – but she got on even more of a dream with my Uncle Adelchi.

So that was how things were, and that was how they stayed: Aunt Zelinda and my Uncle Iseo's family in holding 517, and Armida and Uncle Pericles' family in holding 516, also on the Mussolini Canal. 'When Pericles comes back, he can sort it out with his brothers,' was what Armida thought. She took her possessions, her hives, her bees and her children and went to live with Uncle Themistocles and Clelia.

440

But all this had happened several months, almost a year, before that Christmas 1941 when we'd already lost a chunk of East Africa and received Uncle Iseo's postcard telling us that he'd been taken prisoner, and was alive and well, but that he had no news of Pericles.

But even earlier – during the course of that same year, 1941 – the international scenario had become yet more complicated. Meanwhile the United States – which had been neutral – had started saying that they weren't equally neutral towards everybody. No, they weren't coming into the war now nor did they want to do so in the future, but, 'when it comes to comrades' – Roosevelt now thought – 'I feel more comradely towards the English, seeing that my *Mayflower* left from Southampton.' Not from Copparo or Ferrara. It was all about blood ties. And they started supplying them with all the reinforcements they asked for.

Then the Germans also invaded the Soviet Union. We were now in 22 June 1941, and the Russians – call it enlightened self-interest, if you like – had allied themselves with Great Britain, with whom they'd previously not got on at all. What else could they do?

'See if I care,' Hitler had said to the Duce. 'Anyway, I'll be gobbling up the both of them!'

'Fine, Adolf, whatever you say. Can I come along as well?'

'Of course!' and we sent an Italian expeditionary force to Russia too. As I think I've already told you – though maybe not – if that imperial eagle ever, ever starts flittering over our history-laden hills again, we ought to intercept it right away, bring it straight down with our crack Italian fighter planes. If you're a featherweight – I don't know how much you know about boxing – you don't suddenly take it into your head to go and compete in the world heavyweight championship. Or

441

if you do, you're nothing but a featherbrain. And that was how featherbrained our fateful eagle had become.

But anyway, by October we were just outside Moscow. A *blitzkrieg*, that's what it had been. 'See? What did I tell you?' said that braggart Fuhrer.

'Blooming heck Adolf, you're always right and no mistake.'

But at the beginning of December our offensive, and that of our German ally, was halted, bogged down by Soviet resistance and above all by General Winter – as they call him – by the cold and the snow and the ice, and the temperature, forty degrees below. 'Holy smoke,' my grandfather said when he heard the news bulletin in the wine-shop. 'At this rate we'll be ending up like Napoleon.'

'And how did he end up?' his friends asked him.

'The same way as a goose.'

Then his friends all lowered their heads and put their fingers to their lips and shushed him: 'Hush, Peruzzi, if they hear us they'll do us for defeatism.'

But one or two days later – on 7 December 1941 – our imperial eagle must have started flittering in the skies all over Tokyo, as well. Our other new ally –the Nips – now decided to play a truly fateful card, one that would carry all before it. At seven forty-eight in the morning, without any warning, the first wave of Japanese Air-Sea Forces attacked Pearl Harbour, in Hawaii. The second wave came at eight fifty. Much of the American fleet was sunk, or at least put out of action.

'So what do you think of our Nip ally?' the *Führer* apparently said to the Duce. 'They won't get back on their feet again after that thrashing.'

'Son of a bitch,' the Duce said back. And he immediately declared war on America as well. 'We've as good as won already. What sort of a fool d'you take me for? A stay-at-home?'

442

But when they went to Senator Agnelli – the man from Fiat – to tell him that the Duce had just declared war on the USA, all he said was: 'For heaven's sake, has no one shown that blustering big-head a New York telephone directory?' He knew – from personal experience – that in the time it took us to build one new plane, over there in America they would have churned out a hundred thousand. They won the war not so much with armies, but with factories. The Duce on the other hand thought we were back in the times of *The Grapes of Wrath,* when they were still dying of hunger and as backward as when comrade Roosevelt was sending the New Deal experts to the Pontine Marshes to see how things were done. He hadn't wanted to believe Balbo, that time when he'd come back from his transatlantic flight and told him: 'Duce, they're light years ahead.'

'You can go to hell,' he'd said, and sent him off to Libya.

Anyway, that was how things stood on Christmas Eve, when the Peruzzi household learned that there was no news of Pericles of any kind, alive or dead. The Axis troops were on the attack on every front – except in East Africa, of course, East Africa was a lost cause by now – their advance seemed unstoppable and victory was within our grasp. 'Who can stop us now?' my Uncle Adelchi would say when he heard the news bulletin on the wireless. '*Victory! Victory! Victory! We'll be victorious on earth and sky and sea,*' was what everyone was singing, and meanwhile life went on as it always had done in the Pontine Marshes. Work, work and more work. Even more work than before, of course, and round the clock, all done by old men and women and children, because there was hardly an able-bodied man anywhere to be found.

The Peruzzi were scattered all over the globe. Uncle Cesio was in Libya; Uncle Treves had gone from France to Russia with my Uncle Turati – despite all his wife's weeping, he too was now at war, together with his brother; Uncle Themistocles had left Greece and gone to Yugoslavia; my Cousin Paris was going from Dalmatia to Albania and back again with the harbour militia; Lanzidei's brothers were all fighting on some front or other; and the oldest of the Dolfin brothers, my Cousin Ampelio, was in the navy in China, no less, on a battle-cruiser in Manchuria. There was nowhere in the world where you wouldn't come upon some member of the Peruzzi clan risking life and limb for his country.

Those members of the Peruzzi family who'd stayed behind in the Pontine Marshes – boys and girls – spent their days pushing and pulling carts and trying not to think of those who were overseas, but thinking of them all the time anyway, and praying to God to keep them safe and sound, and above all praying for Pericles. 'Oh Lord, let him come home safe and sound,' was what my grandmother and Armida were thinking the whole time.

We had our noses to the grindstone. Now it was my grandfather who was the first to get up in the morning and go into the cowshed – at his age – and take the hay to the animals, and milk them and clean the place out. The women would be in the cowshed too, and sometimes they'd also do the ploughing, and you should have seen the strength of them – sometimes two at a time, with their stomachs right up against the ploughshare, holding the plough so that it bit deep into the ground, and they were knocked this way and that as the oxen pulled and tugged. There wasn't much to eat, because by now everything was rationed. Now corn wasn't stockpiled just by us in the Servicemen's Association, it was hoarded by everyone all over the country. One of the last and most important things that Rossoni did before the Duce sacked him was in this connection. Now, he decreed, anyone producing corn – from the smallest peasant to the biggest landowner – could no longer sell it on the open market to anyone he pleased. He had to hand the lot over to the state, and fast, at a set price – the same for everyone – and now he couldn't keep a stash for himself, hidden in his barns while the price was low, waiting until there wasn't much around and then bringing it out only when prices went sky-high, which was tantamount to speculating on poor people's hunger. Now, when you'd done the threshing, you had to hand the lot over to the state, and the state would handle it for you: the same price for everyone, all the year round. The farmers were shrieking like stuck pigs: 'But this is Communism! Where are we all of a sudden, in the Soviet Union?' It was because of all this – because of the stockpiling, and what Rossoni had done about it – that Ezra Pound too became a Fascio-Communist. Whereupon the Duce sacked him in 1939; Rossoni, obviously, not Ezra Pound.

Anyway, our life was all work and no play, and not much eating either; praying for the safe return of those who were overseas, bringing up the children, going to mass in town on Sundays, and sometimes also to the cinema, then getting back to work again, and praying: 'Please God, let them all come back safe and sound. Specially Pericles.'

But the more time went by, the fainter these hopes became. 'What shall I do without my man?' was what Armida kept saying to herself. And she kept asking the same question of her bees. They pretended not to hear, and just buzzed about, now this way, now that. From time to time, though, one would say to her, in as many words: 'Armida! If one drone dies, there's always another.'

'Be quiet, damn you!' and she'd crush it between her fingers. Stone-dead. The bees learned their lesson.

445

But, as I'm sure you'll understand, despite her great grief for her beloved man – the father of her children, the rock on which she lived and moved and had her being – the flesh is weak, and Armida, as I think you'll have realized by now, was not the sort of person who could put certain matters out of her mind entirely. She didn't want to think about them, but she did. How other women managed I don't know, and nor did she, but every so often she would think: 'What shall I do without my man?' And in bed in the evening – particularly when she could hear the queen bee's love-song wafting up from the hives below the canal embankment, when she was starting to get her drones' blood up so that they would go after her the next day, foaming at the mouth and champing at the bit – Armida would toss and turn there in her bed: 'Dirty little whores that you are,' clutching her children to her, having brought them with her into that big bed so as not to think about such matters. In desperation, she'd put a cushion between her legs. Well, why don't you try not thinking about such matters?

We were now into June 1942. Rommel had dug in at El-Alamein, just sixty kilometres from Alexandria. We were winning. In Italy, the daily bread ration was down to 150 grams a day. In Russia the Axis was making good progress towards Stalingrad and the oil wells in the Caucasus. The Italian troops were already scenting victory – we had a cousin in the cavalry there, from the Dolfin side of the family, and my Uncles Treves and Turati were in the Blackshirts. On 24 August a certain cousin of mine, Argesilao Piva from Borgo Montenero – he was a cousin because he'd married the Dolfin's oldest daughter – took part in the last cavalry charge in the whole history of the Royal Italian Army against regular troops, in the steppe near Isbushensky, at a bend in the Don. The force in question was the Savoy Cavalry, and on more than one occasion – at a gallop, sabres drawn – they charged against the mortars and cannon and machineguns of the Siberian 812th Infantry Regiment, positioned in their trenches among fields of sunflowers. In history books, it's known as the Charge of Isbushensky, and my Cousin Argesilao Piva came back alive to tell the tale. Now there's no need for me to tell you that the Russians were on their own home ground and that it was us who'd gone out there to seek them out – you've heard that often enough already: 'Everyone has their reasons,' as my Uncle Adelchi used to say. The Duce sent us to Russia, and to Russia we went.

The one who didn't come back from Russia, though, was my Uncle Turati. He too fell beside his brother – 'They've got me, good and proper' – and his brother, my Uncle Treves, lay down beside him and said: 'Keep calm, just keep calm.'

'What d'you mean, keep calm, I've had it, goddam the Zorzi Vila,' and his whole face suddenly went all white as the blood poured out of him.

'Don't die on me, Dirty Dog Turati!' and my Uncle Treves was already in tears.

'I'm counting on you to take care of my children... and my wife!'

'What sort of talk is that? Of course I will, you dog.'

'Swear on it...' and those were the last words he ever spoke.

'I swear on it,' said Uncle Treves, but Dirty Dog Turati, the hero of the Peruzzi clan – its rescue plane – was already out of earshot.

Then my Uncle Treves dried his eyes, closed those of his brother and went off on the attack again. And, throughout the retreat from Russia, three hundred and fifty kilometres of forced marches in the middle of all that snow and ice, Napoleon had had it easy in comparison – General Winter,

447

at it again, the temperature between thirty-five and forty-two below, and they were underdressed, boots made of cardboard and puttees made from rags, and people who'd nearly reached their breaking point saying: 'I've just got to sit down for a moment,' and who froze to death the moment they did so – my Uncle Treves always managed to keep going, to hang on to the bitter end and get home safely if only because of that one thought lodged in his mind: 'I've got to get home in order to take care of that wife and those children of that poor brother of mine.' And the first thing he did when he got to Shebekino – safely behind the German lines – was to write home: 'Tell the sister-in-law that from now on she can count on me to take care of her and those dear children of hers for ever and a day.'

'What's he mean, he'll take care of them? What about us lot?' said my Uncle Adelchi, while all the women were screeching and my grandmother was pulling out her black mourning clothes. And she wore those mourning clothes for the rest of her life, indeed, as she was putting them on, she thought: 'These will do for Pericles as well,' even as she tried to suppress the thought, and replaced it with: 'Lord, at least let him make it home safe and sound.'

My Uncle Treves – after a series of trials and tribulations the length and breadth of Europe – finally managed to make it home towards the end of 1945, and the first thing he did, even before he'd greeted her properly, was to marry his sister-in-law, the wife of his brother Turati, in church, with all her children and relations gathered round. Only in church though, not in the town hall. Don Orlando married them in secret, both dressed in mourning – except for a little white veil on the bride's head – in the small church in Borgo Podgora, and it was only afterwards that they greeted each other properly, now let's see what stuff you're made of and if we'll get along together. There was no room for wondering. They had to get on – but above all they wanted to – and indeed they did, adding children of their own to those she'd had with my Uncle Turati. He didn't marry her just because he'd sworn he would, he married her because it's a commandment, it's right there in the Bible. But my uncle married his sister-in-law only before God and the Peruzzi clan. Not before the state. Were we going to hand back her widow's pension? If his widow remarried, it would be pension, bye-bye. So blow you, state, if you're such a churl.

Meanwhile, though, in June 1942, we were still winning on every front – almost – except in East Africa, needless to say. We were virtually starving, we were desperately overworked, the only thing we weren't short of was worries – about those who were away fighting – but then Themistocles came home, and we couldn't believe our luck. Not just his wife Clelia – and before she locked herself into the bedroom that night with her husband she was smiling a little smile that made even Armida laugh, but then when she heard the sounds that came out of that bedroom, or thought she heard them, she had to take all her children back into her bed and put that cushion back between her legs – but all of them were pleased as punch, because now there was one more man, and what a man. The Servicemen's Association had managed to get him discharged: 'Someone's got to be in the fields for the sowing and the harvest, otherwise the soldiers can win the war as much as they like but there'll be no one to have won it for, they'll all have died of hunger.' So they'd sent him home, and we could breathe more freely for a bit.

But now it was June 1942 – halfway through the year – and even if at that point we were winning, there are always twelve months in a year; after spring comes summer, and summer, as you know, is usually followed by autumn and by winter. Those who don't wrap up well in advance will feel the cold.

In America, the factories had started working at breakneck speed. They'd clap their hands, and cannon would pop out. They'd utter the word 'Tank' and out would come droves of tanks, whole divisions of the things. They could have sunk us with telephone directories alone, had they felt so inclined. And then they set to supplying their allies all over the world, from the Atlantic to the Pacific, from the South Pole to the North, and apart from armaments they threw in the flower of their youth, because they too had such a thing – we weren't the only ones – and you could be sure they wouldn't just stick bayonets in their hands, and leave it at that; there might have been eight million of us, but all we had was bayonets. In less than a year – put on their mettle – they whipped up the most powerful army ever seen on the face of the earth. They were pilgrims like us – Pilgrim Fathers, who'd set off from Southampton on the *Mayflower* – and you'd be well advised to give them a wide berth. By this juncture, the Lord of Sabaoth – the Lord of Hosts – was undoubtedly on their side. The fortunes of war had gone topsy-turvy.

By mid-November 1942 the English had already dashed all hope of victory in Africa. Then, in February 1943, Stalingrad had fallen, so there too it was goodbye Dolly Gray. The first survivors started coming back to Italy. People saw them and talked to them, and rumours began to circulate. There'd already been a few air-raids in 1941–42, but now our cities began to be subjected to massive bombardment, particularly the ports and the industrial cities in the north. It was the RAF's 'autumn air offensive'. And when people receive news from the front just by letter or wireless bulletin, however bad it is, that's one thing, but when whole tons of bombs start raining down right on their heads, that's quite another matter. That's when people start getting hot under the collar.

So, by March 1943, people throughout Italy were beginning to express more than a few doubts about how things were going, and at Fiat Mirafiori in Turin the workers went on strike – for the first time in twenty years – asking for more pay but, more importantly, for peace. The strike spread to Milan and the other northern industrial centres, but now you could no longer send in the Fascist Action Squads to shut them up. Of course they didn't say as much on the wireless, but what with those returnees all over the place, the wounded, soldiers who'd been recalled or relocated, the rumour began to spread: 'There's been a strike at Fiat.' And at the time, no two ways about it, the very word 'strike' was taboo.

Then in May they also drove us out of North Africa – so long to Tripoli, fair land of love – and promptly started making preparations to come up through Italy. On the wireless, the powers-that-be kept saying: '*We'll be back! We've got strongholds in Pantelleria and Lampedusa which will stop their armies in their tracks,*' particularly Pantelleria, which was some stronghold, equipped to put up limitless resistance to any and every attempt at a landing. Well, after a few days of aerial bombardment, Pantelleria surrendered without a fight, without even waiting for so much as a single dinghy to attempt a landing. When they arrived, they found underground hangars stuffed to bursting with planes in perfect readiness for action. 'Blow me down!' was what the English said.

'Never mind,' was what the Duce said. 'We'll stop them on the beaches. Out there in the waves. They'll perish to a man.'

But in fact, on 10 July 1943, they strolled into Sicily as cool as cucumbers – or almost – under the command of General

Eisenhower. What the Italian people must have thought, I leave to your imagination: 'Hang on, weren't we supposed to be the top dogs who were to extend their *Imperium* over all the peoples of the world? So how come it's them who've walked straight in through our front door, without us lifting a finger to defend ourselves?' It was true, the Italian troops didn't put up much resistance. Within ten days the allies had occupied two-thirds of the island. By 22 July they were in Palermo and people everywhere, all over Italy – including the party bigwigs, the ministers, the king himself and all his generals – started to say: 'Come off it, Duce, the game's up. Let's call a halt right now, before it's too late. Just press for peace.'

And on 19 July he – the Duce – went off to Feltre, mid-way between Rome and Berlin, to meet the *Führer* and say to him outright: 'Awfully sorry, Adolf, but we want to press for peace.' That, after all, was why he'd set up the meeting. And all his generals and subordinates were waiting with their hearts in their mouths: 'Let's hope for the best.'

But when he got back Ambrosio, the chief of staff, asked him how things had gone: 'Well, Duce, how did it go? What did he say?'

'I couldn't get a word in edgeways. It was him who did all the talking, shrieking like a madman,' and he, the Duce, hadn't said a word, he hadn't had the nerve. Paltry, that's what he'd been made to feel. 'But he did tell me that they've got a whole load of new secret weapons, of unimaginable power, capable of altering the outcome of the war from one moment to the next.'

'And what do you think, Duce?'

'Blowed if I know,' was all he said.

Meanwhile, though, that same 19 July when he'd been in Feltre, they bombed Rome for the first time ever. Four thousand bombs. We'd heard the planes going over the Pontine Marshes, and we Peruzzis had asked one another nervously: 'Where do you think they're going?' Then after a bit there was a terrific booming sound coming from Rome, like that of a distant storm. The whole district of San Lorenzo was razed to the ground, as were those of Tiburtino, Prenestino, Casilino, Labicano, Tuscolano and Nomentano. Three thousand dead and eleven thousand wounded. Could things really go on like this?

Then, in the early morning of 25 July 1943 – when my grandfather had just got up to go into the cowshed – as he opened the door of the anti-mosquito passage, he saw a car parked on the bridge. And seated on the parapet was Rossoni. Wearing civilian clothes. In a blue suit. Smoking. And as soon as he saw my grandfather put his nose out of doors he threw the cigarette into the ditch, leapt to his feet, rushed up to the gate and called to him beseechingly: 'Save me, Peruzzi, save me!'

'Holy smoke, Rossoni!' said my grandfather. 'Not still that business at Copparo?'

'I'll give you Copparo, damn your eyes,' Rossoni said to him. 'Just let me in, will you? If he gets his hands on me, I'm done for.'

He'd been out there since four – even earlier, possibly, half past three – waiting out on the bridge for any sign of life. He didn't want to sound his horn or make any other kind of noise. Indeed, he was worried that the sound of the engine – out there alone in the night, on the dirt roads of the Pontine Marshes – might already have aroused suspicion. And it was true that he had indeed been heard by my Cousin Paris and by Armida, she with the smallest child in her arms and he holding the trawl-net, while they'd been coming home through the fields from

453

the embankment of the Mussolini Canal, where they'd been fishing, below the little waterfall. 'Who on earth can that be?' they'd asked each other, but it didn't occur to them to go and see, they were more concerned with getting back into bed, fast, before it started to get light.

Rossoni's wife – the evening before – hadn't wanted him to go to the meeting of the Grand Council: 'Don't be going.'

'But how can I not? What shall I say?'

'Just don't be going, he's a swine.'

'But that's just why I have to go.'

'All right then, but watch it.'

'You watch it, more like, and don't wait up for me. If things take a nasty turn, it's each man for himself and God help us all.'

'Edmondo...'

'Darling...' and he gave her one last kiss. 'Keep out of trouble for my sake.' He'd put a change of clothes in the car – that civilian suit – because you can say what you like about Rossoni, but you can't say he wasn't practical, and ready for every eventuality, particularly if there was a possibility that he might be going to have dealings with guards and policemen – and at five in the afternoon, on 24 July 1943, he'd gone to the meeting of the Grand Council in Palazzo Venezia wearing his black bush jacket.

That lousy Grand Council hadn't assembled since 7 December 1939, and even now it was only being convened because things had reached such a disastrous pitch. The situation was catastrophic and all the bigwigs were desperate to find a way out that would save their bacon: the Duce had more or less bowed out, so it was them who talked to the king, and discussed surrender, and peace, and then everything was back to how it had always been, with them at the helm. 'He's in agreement,' they told Rossoni, 'and so's the king, and that way we've got everything sorted out.'

'Seems odd to me,' Rossoni thought to himself, 'so I'm bringing along my blue suit, just to be on the safe side.'

And indeed, deep down, the Duce now didn't seem to be as much in agreement as all that, even if nowadays all the historians say that he was, and that's what Rossoni also told my grandfather – that, deep inside himself, at least at first, he really was, in agreement, that is. Then he must have had second thoughts. 'I know him,' Rossoni said, 'he'll never give up an inch of power, not even if the whole world is falling around his ears.'

Anyway, when he arrived, just before five o'clock, the Duce greeted him with a booming 'Edmondo!' as though they were bosom chums. 'How goes it, my dear Edmondo?'

'Well, Duce, let's see now... So so, I suppose,' but deep down he was thinking: 'Just go to hell, why don't you. So I'm your dear Edmondo all of a sudden?' And when the time came to vote on the motion of the day – which was to restore military command to the king – he voted for it, together with Grandi and Ciano and all the rest.

The meeting broke up between two-thirty and two-forty on the morning of 25 July. At least some of the so-called 'plotters' seemed calm and satisfied when at last they left the chamber: 'Tomorrow the king will sort it all out, and we'll all be back in the saddle again.' Others – such as Ciano – were worried: 'He'll have us all arrested.' And indeed there were no fewer than four divisions of the militia out and about in Rome. As it turned out, though, they all went quietly home, as though they'd been at a poker game in the local bar: 'See you tomorrow, then.'

Rossoni on the other hand had got into his car: 'You, my friends, are living in a dream world. Watch your backs,' and from Piazza Venezia he'd gone straight to San Giovanni – he lived right on the other side of town – and then he'd taken the Appia to Albano, then on to Ariccia, Genzano, Velletri, Cisterna di Littoria, the Mussolini Canal and, finally, the Peruzzi holding 517 on the Left-Hand Parallel.

My grandfather opened the gate and rushed off to open up the barn behind the house and then pushed the car – so Rossoni wouldn't have to turn on the engine and wake up the whole neighbourhood – shifted a big load of hay, had Rossoni drive the car under it, covered the whole thing up, got the ladder down from the wall, told him to climb up it into the hayloft and locked him firmly in.

Nobody was to know a thing about it – not even his own family – because in such cases word gets about, and fast. Except my grandmother, who made his meals, and would take them to him when no one was around, creeping warily up the stairs with a covered plate, knocking on the trapdoor with a broom handle, waiting for him to open it and take the plate and close it up again. He'd come out every now and again at dead of night to stretch his legs, and my grandfather would lean the ladder for him up against the outside of the house. No one was to know anything about it. The only ones who saw him going up and down from the roof were Paris and Armida – when they came back from the embankment, one carrying the trawl-net and the other the smallest child, as always, before it started getting light: 'There he goes.'

But whenever some child or other from the other holdings came to play in the courtyard, all the children in the Peruzzi household would whisper in unison, but so you quietly that you could hardly hear: 'Rossoni's staying in the loft, only you mustn't say so or grandfather will get furious, because when we were up in the north of Italy he had it off with our grandmother.' And then one of the littlest ones went and said to my grandmother: 'Grandmother, is it true that you had it off with Rossoni too?'

She felt like throttling him, believe you me – whichever child it was, not Rossoni, obviously – and she stuck his head into a drawer in the sideboard, and left him hanging there, flapping his arms the way the chickens for the *cappelletti* flapped their wings. The others rescued him at the last minute, and my grandfather said in amazement: 'Holy Virgin, woman, he's only a little mite.'

'Little mite?' she shrieked. 'Did you hear what he said to me?'

'And what did he say to you, damn it all?'

'He asked me whether I'd had it off with Rossoni, too.'

'Get him over here,' and now my grandfather was shrieking too, 'and I'll give him what for.'

Anyway, the fact remains that Rossoni stayed in hiding in our loft for three or four days without anyone knowing – apart from the whole of the Left-Hand Parallel from Borgo Carso to Borgo Podgora, that is – until he and my grandfather were quite sure that he'd fallen, the Duce that is, and wasn't likely to be getting up again. Only then did Rossoni come down from the loft.

My grandfather had been backwards and forwards to the wine-shop every day, to listen to the news bulletins on the wireless. When he came home he was almost always half-cut. 'You and your wireless,' my grandmother would say.

'He drinks to down his sorrows,' was how my little cousins put it.

The king had the Duce arrested, and not long afterwards it was the turn of the bigwig plotters. Now they were sent packing too. Fascism had fallen and that was that. End of story. All

Italy went berserk. Until the previous year everyone had been going: 'Du-ce, Du-ce, victory will be ours.' Now no one had ever been able to stand the Man. Just like with the Socialists in 1919–21. And with the Communists and Christian Democrats around 1994. Now Craxi was rubbish, and soon – you'll see – it'll be the same with Berlusconi, and in a hundred years it'll be the same with whoever's in power then: 'What, me? D'you think I'd ever have voted for a nincompoop like that?'

And so, on 26 July 1943 – when the wireless just couldn't stop telling us that '*His Majesty the King and Emperor has accepted the resignation of His Excellency Benito Mussolini from his post as Head of Government, Prime Minister and Secretary of State, and has appointed His Excellency and Marshal of Italy, Pietro Badoglio, to replace him in those functions*' – everyone rushed down into the streets to celebrate. Real mass demonstrations – 'oceanic' was the word used for them at the time – the length and breadth of Italy. Everyone dashing up ladders, hammer and chisel in hand, and prising the Fascist Party symbols off the walls. You couldn't move for busts of Mussolini flying out of windows into the street, and people spitting on them, and passing soldiers even took potshots at them. Now there wasn't a single Fascist to be found, for love or money. Not a uniform in sight. They'd all vamoosed. Except in the Pontine Marshes.

In the Pontine Marshes all we said was: 'Big deal! Let's wait and see how things turn out,' and it was business as usual. Certainly no one started dislodging things from walls. That was well beyond the call of duty. Indeed, in the Pontine Marshes we even wondered: 'How will we manage without him – without a Man like that?'

'There's always the king.'

'Er, yes, I suppose so...'

In the hill villages, though, there were wild celebrations, for days on end; once again, as you'll understand, they had their reasons and we had ours.

Around our way, in Littoria, a small group of recruits and shirkers from the 82nd Infantry tried to gather in front of the town hall, intending to hack off the Fascist emblems from the façade of the tower. But when they went up to the main door they were met by my Uncle Adelchi, who was on guard there – all rigged out in his white summer uniform and sun helmet – who said to them: 'What's all this about? Off with the lot of you!'

'Fascism's fallen,' said the boys from the 82nd, while a small crowd of local people murmured their disapproval. 'Fascism's fallen!'

'See if I care!' said my Uncle Adelchi. 'Fascism or no Fascism, this is Littoria Town Hall, and anyone who lays a finger on it had better watch out,' and he pulled out his pistol and released the shot into the barrel.

They turned tail, and shouted 'Fascist,' at my uncle before beating a retreat.

'And proud of it!' he retorted, while the crowd of locals cheered him on – particularly the women, who were out doing their shopping, and he was as handsome as the young Sylvester Stallone, as I've already told you: 'Well done, Adelchi, that's the spirit.' Then he got quite worked up because he'd done his duty – or at least what he thought was his duty – but, truth to tell, inside himself he was also worried, since he'd been confronted by at least a dozen soldiers, some of them armed. And then – all worked up as he was – he saw that one of the soldiers was a member of the Ciammaruconi family, who were from Sermoneta and lived on a holding on the other side of the railway, and he shouted to him: 'Just you watch out,

459

Samarucon, I saw you and I've got my eye on you, you dirty wog.'

'That's the spirit,' shouted the women.

Anyway, the Duce was done for – under arrest – and no one knew where he was being held. Not a bleat from the militia, of course, with all their Blackshirt armies and divisions, they'd simply transferred their loyalties to the royal army, cool and orderly as you please, they'd removed their Fascist insignia and the badges on their hats and replaced them with the five-pointed star, end of story. And then my grandfather came back from town one morning and said to Rossoni: 'Everything's quiet out there. If you want to stay, stay by all means, but you don't need to stay up on the roof.'

'I'm not convinced, Peruzzi. Bring me the parish priest.'

'The parish priest?' said my grandfather. 'What are you planning on, dropping down dead right here and now?'

'Cut it out, Peruzzi. Just bring me some damned priest and a spare cassock, so when the time comes to make a run for it I've got my cover.'

Then my grandfather went off and came back with Don Orlando and a spare cassock. Rossoni put it on – 'He became a priest to atone for that business with our grandmother,' was what my cousins would say quietly to each other – and they all three got into the cart and my grandfather drove them to the station at Cisterna, with Don Orlando on one side and Rossoni on the other, also dressed as a priest.

'What about the car?' asked my grandfather as the train was pulling out.

'Do what you like with it,' and, acting the part, he made a great big sign of the cross, a blessing, out of the train window.

When they got to Rome he didn't even call in at his house. He went straight to the Vatican. There he was told: 'You're in

460

no danger, Marshal Badoglio is someone you can trust.'

'No danger? That's what you say! I'm not budging from here,' and they had to take him in.

Less than two months had gone by, and – the moment the Italian Social Republic was declared – even the people in the Vatican were obliged to start saying: 'You have to hand it to him, Rossoni's always right.' Together with the other treacherous plotters of 25 July – even if the first plotter seems to have been none other than the Duce himself because, as I've told you, initially he seems to have gone along with the new plans – Rossoni had become public enemy number one. The first thing the Salò Republicans had done when the Germans put them back in the saddle was to go and track down these traitors, one by one, to put them on trial at Verona. But they didn't get them all, only a handful: Galeazzo Ciano, De Bono, Marinelli, Pareschi and Gottardi. They were all sentenced to death on the evening of 10 January 1944, and the sentence was carried out the following morning. The others – the ones who had got away – were sentenced to death for treason *in absentia*. They shot them as they got their hands on them. 'Now do your damnedest to get Rossoni,' the Duce had said to Pavolini. 'Be careful, though, he's slippery as an eel. That's one rogue's death I want to witness with my own eyes.'

'It's as good as done, Duce,' Pavolini had said. He was the secretary of the Republican Fascist Party, the founder and leader of the Black Brigades. At first he'd been a close friend of Ciano's, and indeed when he'd been in prison in Verona – Ciano, that is – awaiting trial, he'd kept on saying: 'You'll see, any moment now Pavolini will be on the job, he'll sort things out.'

Ciano had no idea of what he'd done, of what a hornet's nest he'd just stirred up. He'd breezed on to a German plane

461

– just after the Germans had freed the Duce at the Gran Sasso and taken him to Germany – and had himself taken there too, with his whole family: 'Now I'll have a word with the father-in-law and we'll get everything sorted out. It was all a joke.' But when he got there – apart from all the Germans and Republican Fascists who were baying for his blood like so many maddened hyenas – he discovered that the most maddened hyena of all was none other than his mother-in-law, Rachele, who immediately said to her husband, the Duce: 'We'll have to have him shot, right now, otherwise I'm really going on the warpath.' Her daughter started weeping: 'But he's the father of my children.' 'You should have thought of that earlier.'

He, on the other hand – Ciano, that is – really still thought that the Duce was playing games. He couldn't imagine that Pavolini – 'Everyone's got their reasons' – was deadly serious. But Alessandro Pavolini was staking his all on his next move – his desperate, carefully calculated last move – and he knew just what he was doing: 'I don't care what it costs me.' He was a good writer and a good father, but by now his blood was up and he felt pity for no one, himself included. Of all the bigwigs, he was the only one to put up any resistance, to try to fight back and to flee, weapon in hand, when the partisans took them captive in July 1945, on the road which runs around the upper branch of Lake Como from Menaggio to Dongo; that's where they shot them early the next morning, 28 April 1945. It was he who led the file when they were taken to their place of execution, and he was also the only one who'd been wounded the previous day, the only one who'd tried to resist. All the others, including the Duce, had simply given themselves up. Indeed, he – the Man – had himself captured in a German lorry, hidden under an overcoat belonging to an ordinary German soldier. His famous refrain – 'If I advance, you follow, if I retreat, kill me' – seemed to have gone by the board. Then, as you know, on the morning of 28 April the bodies of the Duce and his party bigwigs, all of whom had given themselves up without fighting back – together with that of Pavolini, who had – were taken by lorry to Milan. Together with that of Clara Petacci. And then hung up by the feet – so everyone could get a good view – from the cantilevered roof of a petrol station in Piazzale Loreto, where less than a year before they themselves had done just the same thing, killing fifteen anti-Fascist partisans and exposing their bodies to ridicule. 'Everyone has their reasons,' as my Uncle Adelchi used to say. 'In this world, as you give, so shall you receive.'

Anyway, there was going to be trouble if Pavolini got his hands on Rossoni. But he never did. Not even cannon-fire would dislodge Rossoni from the Vatican as long as there were Salò Republicans and Germans on the loose in Rome, and he had a death sentence hanging over his head. But when they went off and the Americans arrived, his wife came running to Saint Peter's Square to wait for him: 'Edmondo my darling, it's over at last!'

'Over? Are you mad?' and he rushed home to pack his bags and then dashed down to Naples to queue up for the first ship bound for the distant Americas.

'But what danger can there be in Italy, now that we're free?'

'Shut up, you simpleton, I'm the expert around here when it comes to making a getaway,' and off they went to Canada. Just as he'd done twenty years before.

Well, you won't believe me, but the ship wasn't even out of territorial waters when our courts in that new free Italy slapped a life sentence on him as a Fascist criminal, responsible along with all the others for all the misdeeds of those fateful twenty years. In the meantime, he'd got to Canada – 'Catch me if you can' – and didn't come back until 1948, when everything came to an end with a general amnesty. He retired from public life and no one ever heard any more about him. He didn't go back to Tresigallo, either. He never set foot in the place again, because it seemed that there was still someone there – someone who'd suffered from his compulsory purchase orders – who had it in for him: 'Best keep out from under his feet.' But he ended up there anyway after his death – in 1965 – in that mausoleum that I told you about. As long as he lived, no one ever saw him again in public, anywhere. He lived alone in his house in Rome, or sometimes with us in the Pontine Marshes, for as long as my grandfather was alive. He'd turn up in his car, sound his horn on the bridge, get out of his 1100, lean up against the door and start to yell: 'Save me, Peruzzi, save me!'

'You again, damn you,' my grandfather would say, and go up and throw his arms around him.

Sometimes he'd stay for days on end. Not up in the roof, but in the little room that was to have been a bathroom. They'd chat for hours, he and my grandfather – 'Do you remember that time we did such and such?' – and if there was work to be done he'd come out too, to cut the hay, or dig up the sugar beet, with his straw hat on his head, and go and drink out of the ladle in the kitchen. He was here when my grandfather was taken ill, and he stayed on till the end: 'Only if I'm not in the way.'

'Don't be silly, Rosson,' my grandmother would say. 'We're glad to have you, you've always been like a younger brother to my man.'

'And him to me. An older brother,' Rossoni would say, and during those three weeks when my grandfather was laid up in bed and my grandmother was caring for him, backwards and forwards, night and day, as though he were a child, he'd always be sitting there beside her, helping her to turn him over, wash him and turn him over again, while every so often my grandfather would say: 'Monti and Tognetti.'

'Monti and Tognetti,' Rossoni would say back. And when he wanted to stretch his legs, he'd come out with us boys into the fields. Amongst ourselves, we'd say: 'They're brothers! Grandfather's father had it off with Rossoni's ma.' And he was also there that evening – seated on the other side of her – when my grandmother sat down for a moment to this side of him, and my grandfather looked at her and said: 'If I felt better tomorrow and went out and bought myself another horse, girl, what would you say?'

'A horse? Buy yourself as many as you like, boy, that's what I'd say.'

He smiled, and after a bit he said to her – weakly, it's true – 'You're such a beauty.'

Quick as a flash, she answered back: 'No, love, it's you who's the beauty,' and then he died.

Rossoni stayed on until the funeral – he was always at her side, and she never shed a tear, she was distraught but she never wept – he ate with us in the evening after they'd buried him and then he went back to his house in Rome.

He came back three weeks later for my grandmother's funeral, because that same evening, after they'd buried him, she too had gone to bed and stayed there. So back he came, and this time too – it was to be his last visit – he stayed to supper, telling new generations of Peruzzi children the whole story of the cart and the beatings and the horse, that time at Copparo, and how he'd shouted: 'Save me, Peruzzi,' and about the time Uncle Pericles and Uncle Themistocles had cycled down to see him in Palazzo Venezia. Then he went off, never to return. And every December, just before Christmas, one or other of us would go to Rome – particularly Uncle Adelchi, if he needed some advice – to take him a couple of chops, some pork fat and a *cotechino*, all from the pig that had just been killed. Adelchi's wife was at his funeral in Rome, in 1965, and so were at least two members of every branch of the Peruzzi clan. He may have been a Fascist but he was our brother, a builder of cities and reclaimer of the Pontine Marshes. And it was he who had brought us here, Edmondo Rossoni from the nowhere hamlet of Tresigallo, on the road that runs from Codigoro to Copparo in the Province of Ferrara.

Sorry, what's that you said? You want to know if it's true about my grandfather's father and Rossoni's mother?

What do I know? Why don't you go and ask the Duce?

Anyway, to go back to the morning of 25 July 1943 when, after some twenty years of dictatorship, the Fascist Regime had fallen, thanks to Rossoni and Ciano and their friends – not to mention the king – and now everyone in Italy was expecting peace to follow. But on the radio, the following day, probably to avoid arousing German suspicions, the new head of the government – Marshal Badoglio – had said: '*We shall fight on at the side of our German ally. Ever mindful of her age-old traditions, Italy keeps faith with her given word.*' What traditions he was talking of, I can't imagine. Those of every ignoble bully who's ever walked the earth, perhaps. But we still believed him – he had the king behind him – and above all he was still Marshal of Italy, Pietro Badoglio, who'd entered Addis Ababa at the head of his victorious troops, together with my Uncle Adelchi and his good friend Franchini. How could you doubt his word? So we would fight on too, alongside our

466

German ally.

And so it was that when his leave was over, my Cousin Paris – good little soldier that he was, like all the Peruzzis, come to that – put on his uniform again, took up his kitbag and, one morning in mid-August 1943, some three weeks after that 25 July, kissed everyone goodbye and rejoined his unit. Nobody paid any attention to Armida, who was crying; they were all crying, why should anyone have any thought for Armida? 'Don't be going, son,' was what his mother said to him through her tears.

'Ma, that would make me a deserter,' he told her gently.

'But can't you see what a mess it all is?' his mother said, obviously meaning both the end of Fascism – 'Yes, what a mess!' chimed in Armida – but also the course of the war itself, now almost lost. 'Anything might happen.'

'You women! Come what may, no one has ever heard of a Peruzzi being a deserter. Give me a kiss and pray for me.'

He came back in mid-June, on so-called summer leave – his first leave in three years of war – because such leave was sometimes granted to peasant soldiers who would be needed at home to help with the harvest and first ploughing. Requests for such leave would be put forward by their families through the Servicemen's Association and the Board of Agriculture, and everybody made them. Every so often leave would be granted, and since he'd been with the harbour militia for over three years in Albania, he struck it lucky and came back in mid-June, handsome as only someone called Paris can be in this fine world of ours.

Our Paris was very tall, broad shouldered and narrow-waisted. Rippling with muscles. Dark as dark could be – as I've told you, the Peruzzis alternated between fair and dark: Pericles was fair, Uncle Adelchi was dark – so, dark as dark,

467

but with blue eyes and glossy hair like my Uncle Pericles, but his face and all his features, and his hard body and above all his character, were those of my Uncle Pericles. Paris was the flower of the Peruzzi clan, the first of the new generation, the pride of all the bunch, the most adored by all the cousins. You should have seen him walking through the fields, stripped to the waist, with a whole crowd of little boys tagging behind him, all the cousins – 'Paris! Paris!' – one on his shoulders and another in his arms, one hanging on to his breeches and another running in front of him and then turning round to shout: 'Paris, listen to me!' And he'd listen to everyone, he'd tell them stories, give them cuffs round the head and kicks up the backside – and they'd all laugh – but he was also quick to comfort them, if they fell down and hurt themselves, or if their mothers or indeed my grandmother had given them a thrashing: 'Come here, I'll tell you a story.'

Strong as an ox, once, for a bet with his brothers, and I remember this because I was there too, I was quite small at the time, he put himself between the shafts instead of the oxen and started to pull the plough, and his brothers pressed down on the ploughshare to make it harder for him, but he managed to move forward anyway, by fits and starts, with his brothers behind him, jumping this way and that, and he made it to the end of the field and took me into his arms and threw me up into the air. He knew any amount of stories, any number of jokes, and he was the life and soul of the party at any gathering in town or at the Workingmen's Club. But he too was a true Peruzzi – not just a buffoon – and he was single-minded and determined and knew how to fight his corner. I don't know whether I've ever told you about that night in the wine-shop at Casal delle Palme when my Uncles Pericles and Themistocles had words with the Di Patroclo brothers, wogs

468

from Sermoneta who lived on the other side of the Appian Way. It was something to do with a card game – politics didn't come into it, I promise you – even if after the war they started saying that it had been to do with politics, that the Peruzzi had had a go at them because they were anti-Fascists, and indeed one of them was awarded a pension because he was a victim of persecution during the Fascist Era. But in fact it was just about a card game, and perhaps they'd had too much to drink, and they were trading insults between 'wogs' and 'Vikings' while they were playing, and then they came to blows. My Uncle Cesio was there too – the one who was studying to be a surveyor – and so was my Cousin Paris, though they were both younger than the others. So, four members of the Peruzzi clan, two adults and two youngsters. But there were six or seven of the other bunch, and when the landlord said: 'Cut that out, and kindly leave the premises,' it was Paris who was the first to start pulling up the fence posts – or perhaps the little supports holding up the young pine trees they'd just planted along the Appian Way, I can't remember which, anyway posts of some kind or other – and the others followed suit, and they gave those wogs such a going-over with those posts that they remember it to this day. One of them still draws a pension because he was a victim of persecution – by the Peruzzi. 'Go and play cards with someone else,' my uncle would say to him each time they met. And you almost felt he was still looking round him for another post.

But with us Paris was as kind and gentle as a prince in a fairy-tale – you'll have to take my word for it – he was good and sensitive and he'd listen patiently to whatever twaddle you cared to tell him. But he was also biddable – if you knew how to handle him – and helpful. My grandmother only had to say his name, and he'd come running and whatever it was would be done in a trice: 'Pleased, grandma?'

'Very pleased,' she'd say.

The first to catch sight of him as he arrived on the bridge that day on leave – they were in the hives under it – were the bees, and they all flew towards him, buzzing happily. But when they got near him, they instantly buzzed off again.

'What's up with them?' he wondered, and went straight off to holding 517, where he was promptly greeted by my grandmother and all the rest, and then to his own home on holding 516, where he was met by his father Themistocles, his mother Clelia, his sister and her children – her own husband was away at the war – a sister of his mother's with a whole crowd of children of her own, and lastly by Armida – Pericles' wife – with hers. Hugs and kisses all round: 'Paris, Paris.' It was only when it came to Armida's turn to kiss him – and you should bear in mind that Paris was almost like a son to her, because when Armida first arrived in the Peruzzi household at Codigoro she was about seventeen or eighteen and he was five, and goodness knows how often she'd bathed him in the tub, perhaps along with her own children, and cuddled and comforted him, and spanked him and looked after him when he was ill – well, when her turn came, she drew back in disgust: 'You've got lice, to hell with you and the Zorzi Vila.' Lice.

'Lice! Paris has got lice,' shrieked all the children, laughing.

The tub was brought out on to the threshing-floor. Hot water by the bucketful. Another potful on another fire near the stove, to boil his clothes. His head was given a thorough going over with paraffin, his clothes were whisked away and there he stood in his underpants, then got into the tub: 'Give yourself a thorough soaping!' – with all us children clustered round, and Armida and his mother, both of them laughing. The children were shrieking: 'Tell us, tell us about the motorboat you had in the war, what sort of noise does it make? Does it go *vroom vroom*?' all climbing on to the tub and splashing the water.

He laughed. He looked around and laughed. Then he caught Armida's eye: using the voice he'd used as a little boy, he said to her: 'Aunt Armida! Will you wash my back...'

Then Armida started to soap his back, and she was laughing too. But as she washed him, running her hand over his neck and back and sides, feeling his muscles, the dip between each rib and the strong upright column of his backbone, Armida felt she was about to faint, and then she felt some damp between her legs. So she pressed them together, and leaned up against the tub for a moment. Meanwhile, her hand had stopped moving. She started soaping him again, taking his back in a grip that was almost vice-like. Then suddenly she drew back, and now she wasn't laughing any more. She threw the soap into the tub and stepped back a pace.

'What's going on here, Aunt Armida?' Paris asked. 'Come on then, wash my back...'

'Get your ma to wash it,' and off she went.

'Now what have I done?' Paris asked everyone, in vain. But things went on like that for several days, because the more he played with her children – 'Yes yes, some time, one of these evenings, I'll take you fishing with me' – and the more he tried to get close to her, the more sulky she became, fending him off with a sour look: 'Keep your distance, you!'

'Whatever have I done?'

'Just keep your distance, I said.' It was the same when they were out in the fields, he'd be working in the same row as all the others, and she'd be on her own, trying to keep her eyes on the ground, trying to keep them well away from him, but every so often, inevitably, she'd look up and see his shoulders – those shoulders – and feel that same pang between her legs.

Now the bees had to keep their distance too – 'Just go to hell, the lot of you!' – and on those occasions when she could no longer avoid going to the hives, to collect the honey or scrape out the wax, she would do so in some haste, without wasting any time to stop and chat with them. She even thought of putting on her hat with its protective veil, and that wasn't something she often thought of doing.

'Goodness she's rude,' they'd say. 'No manners at all.' Later, though – at dusk, when he was washing himself in a tub near the watering-trough, stripped to the waist, splashing the water up into his armpits or soaping his neck, and she would be coming back from feeding the hens and would cast him a sideways glance – she couldn't help herself, she'd feel that same sensation between her legs, coming back as sure as a bad penny, and then one of the bees would swoop down on her from above and buzz into her ear: 'You dirty little bitch...' and she'd have to dodge sideways and backwards, ducking and weaving in her efforts to avoid it.

'Go to hell the lot of you,' she'd say, trying in vain to snatch at them in mid-flight.

'Dirty bitch,' her bees would buzz gleefully; though sometimes one of them would come back and say to her, more gently: 'Watch out, Armida, take care.'

She did watch out – she avoided him as best she could. He kept on trying to remonstrate with her: 'But what is it I've done?' and all she ever said by way of reply was: 'Just keep your distance!' But there he was. He couldn't simply vanish into thin air. And he would talk and laugh, joke with the neighbours when they called by, and with his cousins and his brothers. Then, in the evening after supper and the *filo* on the bridge, when most of the family had gone to bed, he'd take his fishing net and acetylene lamp and go off to fish in the

Mussolini Canal.

You could catch all kind of fish there, in those days. The water was clear and clean, you could even drink it, and the Mussolini Canal was full of fish. As many eels as you could eat, and big ones at that. But there were also roach, chub, tench, carp, crayfish and whitebait. You know, those little fish, less than a finger long – with a silver streak on their sides – which you eat by the spoonful, fried. Well, all you needed to do was to lower your net on to the surface of the water and in they'd jump of their own accord, just for the joy of it; if you wanted them out, you'd have to tell them so. And the carp would never weigh less than ten or fifteen kilos; on occasions we would catch one weighing twenty.

Later – in 1960, when prosperity arrived, and factories too, at least in Cisterna – there wasn't a fish to be had in the whole canal, and at the dyke, where there was that little waterfall, there was a mountain of foam which ran right down to the bridge on Via della Sorgente. The fish have been back in the canal for some years now – ever since they installed purifiers at Cisterna – and even yesterday I saw that those big white herons were back too, lying in wait for fish on the steps of the dyke, on the big basin. I don't know if there are any salmon nowadays. The carp and chub are here again, but my Cousin Paris said that once there were also salmon, which swam up the Mussolini Canal from the sea, taking the dykes in great leaps and bounds – a metre high, clearing the steps and the waterfalls – and going to lay their eggs at the foot of the Lepini Mountains. I saw them myself once, and when I'd tell this story at my boarding school everyone would laugh and tease me, because on Children's TV – which the priests would let us watch once a week – there was a programme called *Along the St. Lawrence River*, which had just informed us that all the

473

salmon in the world, whichever sea they might be in, when the moment came to mate, would go up the Saint Lawrence River in Canada and lay their eggs there. That documentary must have been wrong because my Cousin Paris said that in those days they also came to the Mussolini Canal. To the Saint Lawrence River and the Mussolini Canal. What's so odd about that?

Sorry, what's that you said? That salmon likes cold water and an arctic climate?

So, what kind of climate does the mammoth like, a warm one? And how come there are mammoths beneath the Mussolini Canal? Or at least their bones, like the ones Carlo Alberto Blanc found at the dyke at Plick plock? And if there are mammoths beneath the Mussolini Canal, could you explain to me why there shouldn't be salmon in it? Please, if you carry on like this I'll plonk some polar bears down on those steps – instead of the heron – to eat up those dratted salmon.

Sorry, what did you say? That those mammoth remains would have dated from the ice age?

That's right. But if it was the ice age, then there would have been salmon too, wouldn't there? And these salmon would be the sons of sons of their sons. Didn't they also tell us in *Along the Saint Lawrence River* that the salmon goes to mate, to build its nest, to lay its eggs and all the rest of it, only and always in the place where it's been born? From there – the moment it's been born – it sets off throughout all of the world's seas, but as soon as it feels a strange pang between its legs, it lowers its fins against its back and starts peddling homewards, to its place of birth: 'I've got to mate.' And that's the only place where it can do it, that's all there is to say. For centuries and centuries – for millennia – they've clearly carried on coming to these parts, even though the water's heated up and turned the place into a marsh; and now that what they find at Foceverde is no longer the *Fosso Moscarello*, but the Mussolini Canal, they swim up that instead. That's all there is to say. My Cousin Paris sometimes caught salmon weighing a hundred and fifty kilos on our dykes in the Mussolini Canal; the size of the pigs in our pigsty, they were. Flying pigs, in fact.

Anyway, when Paris got back from some fishing-party with one or other of his brothers – he was the most badly bitten, he'd caught the passion from my Uncle Pericles as a child, and Pericles himself had caught it up in Codigoro – it would be pitch-dark. They'd light the acetylene lamp in the entrance and then come up the stairs. Everyone would be asleep. All the doors and windows would be open. Only the mosquito nets would be closed. Beds all over the place. He slept on his own – he was the oldest – in the little room which was to have been a bathroom. She – and her children – slept in the big room opposite, on a big bed pushed up against the wall. Paris' sister, Themistocles' oldest daughter, slept by the window with her own young children. As soon as she heard them coming back, Armida would immediately be thoroughly awake. Not that she'd ever really been asleep, not with that fire she'd got raging in her belly. That churning frenzy. Watching the reflections of the lamplight ahead of them as it crept up along the walls and the ceiling of the stairs, she felt her stomach gradually knotting up.

Now they themselves were coming up the stairs. She'd turn over in her bed. She'd hear the other brother – the younger one – groping his way towards his bed in the darkness in the big room, feeling for his own bed between those of his brothers. Paris on the other hand would undress in the lamplight, in his little room – between the foot of the bed and the door – and she couldn't help but look at him, each time, from beneath her cushion, while he was in his underpants. With his broad shoulders – which somehow seemed even bigger in the lamplight – he looked like a giant. Armida grabbed hold of the cushion and put it back between her legs, weeping soundlessly: 'Where can he be? Is he alive or is he dead? He's dead, I know it...'

Then one day – perhaps a week after Paris had come home on leave – while they were out in the fields, a plane crash-landed. It was a fighter, and it was going back with the others to the airport, which – as you know – was some four kilometres away from our holdings. It was flying low, there was clearly something wrong, it was rising and falling and giving out smoke, but above all the engine was losing revs, and a friend of the pilot's was circling around slowly above it. It didn't make it. Sinking gradually, it aligned itself with the embankment and tried to land in the wide bed of the canal, but by now the engine was hardly running. There was a dull thud as it hit the ground, then an explosion and the first crackle of flame. We all rushed up. Paris said: 'Get back, all of you!' and he and Uncle Themistocles went to pull the pilot out and drag him on to the embankment, while the petrol tanks exploded and the plane went up in flames. His friend circled above him one last time, then, flying extremely low, went off to land at the airport. Just four kilometres away, as I've already said.

An ambulance and a lorry arrived on the scene almost immediately. But there was nothing to be done. The pilot – a fair-haired young man – was dead. Kneeling down beside him, Armida was cradling his head in her lap. All he said to her was: 'Ivana...?'

'Yes, it's me.' Armida had said, and had given him a kiss. Then he had died, and she had stayed there holding him.

His friends doused what remained of the fire, and carried him away: 'We'll be back for the plane in a couple of days.' As soon as they'd gone, we trudged wearily back into the fields. Only Armida stayed on for a bit, down there on the grass where she had held him in her arms and kissed him as he died. He was young, fair-haired. 'Ivana,' he had said. How she would weep for him. Then she would cease her weeping, and start to laugh again. Ivana is young. She'll fall in love again. 'Be careful, Armida,' said the bees as they buzzed around her. 'Careful, Armida!'

'Go away. To hell with the lot of you.'

That evening no one would go fishing with Paris: 'I don't feel like it,' 'Neither do I.' Armida's children asked if they could go: 'Take us then, Paris, take us along.'

'No, you're going to bed,' was what Armida said.

Even Paris didn't really feel like going. But then he thought: 'When my leave's over I'll have to go off and fight again, and I might even die. So I'm going fishing!' and he picked up his net and the lamp he used to dazzle the fish and set off on his own for the dyke further up the canal.

When he returned, they were all fast asleep, as usual. Doors and windows open. Only the mosquito nets were closed, and only Armida was tossing and turning in her bed, unable to get to sleep, thinking about her husband – my Uncle Pericles – who might be dead, and about that other boy, the fair-haired young man whose head had rested in her lap that morning, and who was definitely dead, though his Ivana didn't know it yet, and now perhaps she too was in bed thinking about him, smiling, dreaming of their next meeting.

Then Armida thought back to that other time – at Codigoro, all those years ago – when the neighbour she'd just seen at lunchtime had shouted '*Briscola*,' in the wine-shop and then collapsed on to the table; and she had cleaned his nails and laid him out on the bed, and that same evening that madman Pericles had suddenly turned up, and at first she hadn't wanted anything to do with him. And while she was tossing and turning – and the children lying beside her started tossing and turning too, and fretting and fuming, because she was so restless and kept on waking them – she heard him coming up from downstairs, the fizz of the match as he lit it and the first lamplight creeping upwards over the walls and the ceiling above the stairs. Now suddenly completely motionless, there in her bed, Armida held her breath.

He started coming up the stairs. He was whistling *Lili Marlene.*

From underneath her cushion, she watched him undress, stand there in his underpants – stripped to the waist – lift up the sheet, slide under it and blow out the lamp. Now it was dark. Except for the moonlight coming through the windows, disturbing Armida's unlikely dreams and falling upon every wall of my Uncle Themistocles Peruzzi's holding 516.

Armida heard Paris turn over once or twice, as you do when you've just lain down and are trying to get to sleep.

Now, like everyone else on the holding, Paris was asleep. Moonlight on the walls. An owl hooting from the branch of a eucalyptus tree. The chirring of a cricket on the roof of the cowshed. A faint mooing from the cows. A mumbled 'Ma...' from a sleeping child. Uncle Themistocles' intermittent snoring. Only Armida lay awake, and in despair.

She got up.

She tiptoed into the little room. She closed the door behind her. She pulled her nightdress over her head. She let it fall to the floor. She lifted up the sheet and slipped, naked, into the bed. She stopped his mouth with one hand, and drew the sheet over herself with the other.

Paris opened his eyes.

Then she removed her hand. He put his hands on the small of her back. She pressed her heavy breasts against his mouth: 'Have a nibble,' she said. And he did.

When it was over, he said to her: 'Thank you, Aunt Armida. I've dreamt of this moment ever since I was a child.'

'You pig!' she said.

'You sow,' was what her bees had been saying to her all day long, though. And they'd all laughed, and so had she. 'Life's meant for living,' was what the queen bee said.

'Careful, though, Armida, careful now!' was what the eucalyptus tree out there was saying.

'Be careful now,' one worker bee joined in.

That evening, Armida's children were finally allowed to go fishing. All of them. In the afternoon, he'd rigged up a hut just below the dyke, up against the embankment, with eucalyptus branches and leaves by way of a roof. He'd laid a blanket on the ground – against the damp – and after a couple of hours, when the novelty had worn off, one by one they'd all curled up on it and gone to sleep. The two of them – once they'd checked that all of the children really were asleep – had gone off to bathe naked in the waterfall, and they'd made love time and again, with the fishes darting all around them, laughing, and saying to her: 'You filthy sow!'

'Just keep your distance, you!' she'd said, laughing and laughing, stretched out with her shoulders on the stone at the top of the drainage ditch and the rest of her body in the flowing water, while Paris made love to her.

'None of that scratching, now,' he said.

'You're the image of your uncle,' she'd say to him afterwards – almost every time – as she gently stroked his face.

479

'My poor uncle,' he'd say, sadly.

And so it went on; but after a couple of evenings the children started to tire of it: 'I've had enough of fishing, I'm going to bed,' and one after another they trooped off – boys and girls both – and by the end there were just the two of them and the youngest boy, Menego, who'd been born just two months after my Uncle Pericles had gone off to the war. He must have been about three and a half. She always took him with her – Paris didn't feel he could object – and they set out for the Mussolini Canal every evening with her carrying the child and Paris carrying the net.

'How come it's been going so badly lately?' his mother and brothers would ask Paris. 'You've never caught so little.'

'Well, fishing's a matter of luck,' he'd say. 'It's probably the moon...' But anyway, moon or no moon, he had to bring something home to show for his efforts – just an eel, a couple of carp, three chub and a few kilos of whitebait, to show willing, you understand, but even so they couldn't get through it all at Uncle Themistocles' place. So most of it was shunted on to holding 517, where it was divided up and sent on to every branch of the Peruzzi clan throughout the Pontine Marshes. With all the hunger that there was around, we were the only ones to have a surfeit of protein. There wasn't one Peruzzi child – in all the families in the Pontine Marshes – who didn't come in to lunch or supper saying: 'What, fish again? I'm sick of eating fish.'

Luckily for them, when mid-August came – 'Say what you like, there's never been a deserter in the Peruzzi clan' – Paris had to pick up his kitbag and go back to Dalmatia: 'Give me a kiss and say a prayer for me.' It was 16 August 1943 – a Monday – and the date remained for ever fixed in the Peruzzi family memory because the next day, the 17th, was the anniversary

480

of my Uncle Benassi's marriage to Aunt Santapace, and she'd been looking forward to having him there for lunch at their place. But he'd had to leave the day before.

The last night on the canal – stretched out on the stone paving of the drainage ditch, after having scratched his back until it almost bled, and bitten his neck and shoulders in every manner she could dream up – Armida had said to him, gently but very firmly: 'Paris, swear to me that you'll never mention any of this to anyone.' That same afternoon, in fact, several worker bees had started to buzz around her: 'Buzz buzz, Armida! Where's it all this going to end?'

She didn't need the bees to make her wonder about that. She herself knew what trouble she'd be in if rumours started to circulate. But coming from a bee's mouth, if you can put it like that, the warning took on another hue entirely. So, there on the canal, before they said goodbye, she made him swear an oath: 'Come what may, you'll never tell anyone on God's earth that you have been with me. Swear it on my head, on that of your Uncle Pericles, on that of poor Dirty Dog Turati and on those of all our relatives, living or dead. Promise me, Paris!'

'I promise.'

'Whatever anyone says, always deny it!'

'I'll deny it, Armida.'

'Don't forget, you've sworn on oath!'

'I won't forget,' and the next day off he went.

But – as I've said – it was 16 August 1943. With trains and ferries disrupted by the war, it took him two or three days to get to the other side of the Adriatic – to Dalmatia, which is now Montenegro. Anyway, after he'd calmed down a bit, he put on his harbour militiaman's uniform and resigned himself to spending all day glued to his Colt 6,5 Machinegun in his little reconnaissance motorboat – a 14-metre Svan, like those used by the Mas – patrolling the Dalmatian coast from Ragusa to Cattaro: 'Who knows when I'll next see my Armida?'

In fact, though, just three weeks went by, taking us up to 8 September – 'The death of the Fatherland,' as they call it nowadays. After signing the armistice with the Anglo-Americans – without a word to anyone – the king and Badoglio were finally gracious enough to impart this information to the Italian people, the royal army, the various institutions and the state machinery at large, to every subject and subordinate, of high or low degree and, after all, why not, while they were about it, to their old German ally, by leaving a record running on the wireless; then they hot-footed it out of Rome, each man for himself and God for us all. 'When it came to the midnight flit,' my grandfather would say, 'they could leave Rossoni standing.' Unlike him, they gave the priest's cassock a miss, and while the record was playing endlessly on the wireless: '...*all acts of hostility by the Italian forces against the Anglo-Americans must now cease on all fronts. The Italian forces will however continue to fight back against any forthcoming attack, from whatever quarter*' – they were already on board the *Cruiser Baionetta* on their way from Pescara to Brindisi – 'Kick him where it hurts' – into the arms of their new Anglo-American ally. Never did a ship bear a more fateful name: it was a Bayonet that would forever skewer the heart of what we'd once called the Fatherland. Patch that up if you can, because if Italy is now riddled with *mafia and camorra*, if the politicians steal everything that's not nailed down, if people double-park and no one pays their taxes, it's 8 September that's to blame – the death of the state: 'Each man for himself and God for us all.' If you're an artful dodger, don't expect me to toe the line.

Left to their own devices, without any hint of a plan, or

orders, or directives, six hundred thousand Italian soldiers on the loose were disarmed by the Germans, loaded on to trains and taken to Germany, to concentration camps. The ones who escaped this fate couldn't wait to dump their uniforms and go underground before the Germans could get their hands on them as well.

On the Left-Hand Parallel there were small scattered groups of airmen who were trying to make it from the airport to the station at Cisterna, and then on to who knows where. They too were dumping their air-force jackets and badges and asking the sharecroppers for civilian clothing. They asked us, too. 'What's all this then, Caporetto?' my Uncle Themistocles would say to them in disgust, and he'd give them short shrift – 'Off with the lot of you!'– rifle in hand, mounting guard in front of the windbreak that ran along the edge of our holding: 'Keep off my cliptas, you layabout deserter.' At Caporetto – I don't know if you remember – his job had been to shoot them.

My Cousin Paris, on the other hand – that same 8 September – had come back into harbour at Ragusa while we were still at war, or at least so he and his friends thought. So they filled up with fuel and got everything ready for the next day's patrol around the Straits of Cattaro as though nothing had happened, and then, all of a sudden – at 19.42 – they heard that record on the wireless , and they all threw their berets in the air, shouting: 'The war's over,' fit to burst.

But scarcely an hour had gone by – it was dark by then – than two lorries full of Germans armed to the teeth rolled into port. They jumped out and set up two MG Machineguns on the quay, together with a self-propelled cannon. Our commander didn't know what to do. He made enquiries here and there, but no one knew any more than he did. The Germans, meanwhile, fired a couple of shots into the air and then started ordering the Italians to line up. My Cousin Paris and his friends looked at each other and then rushed off into their motorboat, which was moored nearby. Before putting on his 6,5 though, he'd had the bright idea of throwing a bicycle into the boat – it belonged to the harbour office, and it just happened to be lying around: 'That's mine,' he said. They started up the engine and off they went. The Germans shouted '*Alt! Alt,*' from the shore, and then started firing. Paris fired off a couple of rounds, but then the Colt jammed. The Germans started up with their MGs, one great stuttering roar. But by now it was pitch-dark, and they were already well clear of the coast: 'Catch me if you can.'

'Where are we going?' asked the helmsman once they were out of the harbour.

'Home!' they yelled in unison.

Off they went hell for leather down the Adriatic, like illegal immigrants. By three in the morning they were off Molise, between Termoli and the Lake of Lesina. They threw the breechblock into the water, put all their weapons out of commission, together with the engine, took an axe to the keel, said a last goodbye to the Svan, walked up to the nearest houses, asked which roads were relatively safe and then they too started up: 'Each man for himself... and good luck to us all.'

At this point though I have to be absolutely honest with you, there's no way I could do otherwise. You see, my Cousin Paris – pedalling along towards the Apennines on the bicycle from the harbour office in Ragusa in the darkness, or rather in the first light of dawn – my Cousin Paris couldn't have cared less about the death of the Fatherland. I'm sorry, but that's the fact of the matter. All he was thinking about was his legs, and Armida's tits. He was in seventh heaven. That 8 September, he was the happiest man alive: 'To hell with it, I'm going back to her!'

My Uncle Themistocles had his first glimpse of him three or four days later – it was early morning, and he was out on the bridge near the road, putting out the milk churn to be picked up by the dairyman when he came by with his lorry – and he glimpsed him in the distance, at the point where the Parallel crosses the Via della Sorgente. By now that bicycle was a tangle of filthy, clanking, stinking metal, and he himself wasn't much better – he was wearing civilian clothes given to him by some shepherds from the Abruzzi.

My uncle suddenly felt faint. He leant against a eucalyptus for a moment, then said to him: 'What on earth... I never expected any son of mine to be a deserter...'

'Me, a deserter? I leave that to the king! Should I have let myself be taken prisoner by the new enemy?'

'No, son, not that, no!' and my Uncle Themistocles put his arms round him.

The ones who didn't put their arms around him, though – indeed they seemed even more taken aback than my Uncle Themistocles, and for longer – were my young Peruzzi cousins. The moment they saw him, they all went quite white: 'Oh no, not more fish?'

'Couldn't you find a way of catching sausages?' was my grandfather's suggestion.

So off they went again each night to the embankment. 'My God!' Paris said to himself: 'This is just paradise.' It lasted a day or two.

Then, on 16 September – shortly after nine in the evening – when Paris and Armida had just reached the Mussolini Canal and exchanged their first kiss, all hell broke loose from the

485

direction of the airport. It went on until midnight.

Eighty-five Wellington Bombers flew over in successive waves – RAF planes, one coming and one going, in rotation – dropping ton after ton of bombs on our airport in Littoria. It went on for three hours. There's no way I could describe that night to you. From the Peruzzi holding it was bright as day, and from the first-floor windows you could see the bell tower at Podgora as clear and sharp as on a sunny morning. The flares lit up the mountains behind Littoria as though it were midday.

We could see great flashes and huge leaping flames coming from the airport itself, darting right up into the sky – it wasn't just the bombs but above all the fuel reservoirs and tankers, which were exploding and catching fire. Now we knew what the flames of hell looked like. And endless rumbling and crashing, so that you thought the house was about to fall down at any moment. With all the windows wide open, and the panes jingling and then sometimes shattering. Beams, walls and floors juddering. They came back later to bomb other places in the Pontine Marshes, indeed they'd been here on previous occasions, but there was never anything quite like that night at the airport. Very few civilians were killed – it was a surgical strike, as they say nowadays – and not a single bomb fell on the nearby holdings; they all fell on the airport, on the runway and the hangars and the airport buildings and the canteen, leaving one huge crater and nearby wreckage that had been the planes.

But of course we didn't know that it was a surgical strike – here everything was exploding all over the place – so everyone was rushing out of their houses, and all along the Left-Hand Parallel people were running with children in their arms, saying to one another: 'Everyone to Ponte della Madonnina,' which was just beyond holding 517, a bridge under the Parallel some

486

ten metres long, and not more than two metres wide, but set deep into the embankment, with very strong parapets of living rock. A burrow. But those twenty or so square metres of burrow under the roadway – our very own air-raid shelter – now found themselves occupied by the entire population of the Left-Hand Parallel, jammed up against one another cheek by jowl. On top of each other, in fact. A hundred or so people crammed into twenty square metres, and old Ma Toson weeping to herself: 'Take me back to Zero Branco.'

My Aunt Santapace and Benassi, on the other hand, were on the far side of the airport, midway between Littoria Scalo and Tor Tre Ponti. In front of their house there was a transmission station – or a beacon transmitter, I'm not sure – which was used by the airport and a German anti-aircraft artillery battalion. The Italian airmen had gone off on 8 September, but the Germans had stayed on and were continuing to do their own work and that of the Italians as well. There were probably some five or six of them, I don't know how many exactly. But for my own family they were still the German ally, boys just like us, some in fact rather more civilized and educated than our own. There was one – his name was Hans – who was studying fine art in his own country, he was an artist, and the Peruzzi houses are still full of his pencil portraits and drawings. Sometimes they'd come and ask my aunt to heat up the food in their mess-tins, and they were always extremely respectful and polite, and in the evening they'd sit down and chat and take my cousins on their knee, and whenever they got a parcel from home, they'd immediately call on my Aunt Santapace and give her a bit of chocolate or real coffee, and she'd jump for joy because there was no real coffee to be had for love or money, only the stuff made from barley or chicory.

Well, just imagine what it must have been like at their

place, that night of 16 September 1943 when they bombed the airport. They were right in the bombers' line of fire, on the route that the Wellingtons took as they flew in from the sea. They'd change course and lose height – lining up to take aim at the landing strip – as though they too were about to land. But then they'd drop their bombs and pull up, circle around and come back again, until they'd got nothing left to throw at us. Imagine what it must have been like, with all those planes roaring around above our heads, bombs raining down on the airport less than two kilometres away, the flashes and the flames, the fire from the light cannon and machineguns of our own German battery and their bombers dive-bombing, hoiking and turning, seeking us out in the trail of our own tracer bullets and letting fly the odd bomb intended just for us.

As luck would have it, none of them hit home. 'This is the day of reckoning,' said Benassi, and all he was thinking of was his children. Not that there was much that could be done. If you left the house – in his opinion – you'd only be worse off, because you were more exposed to the machinegun fire and flying splinters. The best thing to do was to stay indoors – they lived in a pretty little house belonging to the agricultural cooperative; it had just one floor, and a timber roof, and in the afternoon you could see fine dust in the air, caught in the sunlight filtering through the gaps between the tiles – and if you didn't want the roof to come crashing down on your head the best thing was to take refuge under the kitchen table. So that's what he did, and he took the extra precaution of piling the mattresses on top of it. Then he put himself under it, with his two older children, Norma and Tosca, beneath him. 'I want to be the first to die, goddam it.'

But there was no way that she – my Aunt Santapace, that is – could be persuaded to join them. She helped him put things in place and pile on the mattresses, but that was as far as she would go; she stayed well away, or rather kept on going in and out of the house with the youngest in her arms – my Cousin Othello – who can't have been more than about one and a half, and who was still being breastfed. In and out she'd go, with the anti-aircraft battery just nearby, shrieking: 'Give it to them! Come on, you can do it!' at the German who was firing at the enemy planes. 'Look out, here comes another one! Come on, Hans, go for him!'

My Uncle Benassi would shriek back at her from under the table: 'Come on back in, goddam you.'

'I'm just coming,' she'd say as she carried on with her comings and goings.

'Just come in here right now!'

'I'm coming.'

'At least give me my son, goddam you and the day I met you. Give me my son!'

And finally she did, and he stowed Othello away with the other two, with him on top: 'I want to be the first to die... But if the Americans don't do for you, Santapace' – because he was convinced that it was the Americans, though in fact it was the English – 'when all this bedlam is over, when I get out of here, I'll do the job myself.' So out she went again, and this time she didn't come back. Now she wasn't just screeching: 'Give it to them,' she'd actually joined the gun crew, now she was at the head of the line of German soldiers as they passed ammunition to each other under the turret. She'd show up in the doorway every now and again – throughout that three-hour-long bombardment – just in order to reassure the children: 'How's it going, then?'

'Get off with you,' my Uncle Benassi would say to her from under the table, and she would laugh. Then she'd start screeching: 'Give it to them,' again, and go back to the action.

Sorry, what's that you said?

Yes, this time it's you who's right, I must admit: all those Peruzzis were a bit touched (although, believe you me, they weren't the only ones. There's a psychologist in Latina who's come up with a theory about the 'pioneer syndrome': if you start acting the pioneer, reclaiming the marshes, subverting the forces of the cosmos, of the gods, of nature, you're bound to have a screw loose; you're bound to be a bit unhinged. Here we're all a bit that way. Including that psychologist, I shouldn't wonder). In defence of my Aunt Santapace, though, you have to understand that just a few days ago they'd been our German ally. Do you remember that song they used to sing at the time – about that new bosom pal of yours, Richard, he was called, and he was just your age, and you knew in what street he lived in Berlin, and he'd met your first child, and goodness how glad your ma would be if she knew what a fine new chum you'd got; you were twin souls, men of two nations sharing their last crust of bread, together to the last, united in adversity.

Now surely there comes a point when you might rightly say: 'Look here, it's not my fault if the Duce and Adolf have gone soft in the head. And if you lot have made me believe a whole load of codswallop. It's time for a bit of fighting back, and you'll be getting it where it hurts,' as Lanzidei and Benassi would put it in their rough-and-ready way. Well, forget that swearing of endless oaths and talk of deathless camaraderie and the like: what that new bosom pal of ours, Richard, now found himself risking his life defending was the land and the holdings which the Duce had given us, and which we had reclaimed. Now I'm not going to say anything about dictatorship or the race laws or the harm they did to the country, and all the utter tragedy that followed. I'm just saying

490

that you have to try and put yourself in our shoes. Every one's got their reasons. So, according to you, who was the enemy, from our point of view: the people who were defending our reclaimed holdings, or the people who were bombing us? You see what I mean?

Anyway, that evening the day of reckoning was approaching for Paris and Armida, as well as for my Uncle Benassi. Her bees had been flying around her ever since she'd gone to see to them in the afternoon, and they'd kept on saying: 'Don't go to the canal today, Armida... zzz... just don't go.'

'D'you think I don't know what's good for me?' she answered them back with a laugh. 'I'm going come what may, you nasty jealous insects.'

But when that bedlam broke out at around nine in the evening – and she'd just lit the acetylene lamp and put her youngest, Menego, into the hut, and Paris had lowered his net into the water – she suddenly remembered: 'My bees told me not to come!'

The child had fallen asleep in her arms on the way there, and when she'd laid him down and covered him up, he'd stretched and smiled and turned over on his side and gone back to sleep. She'd looked at him, and she'd smiled back. Then she'd set off to go down to the waterfall to start smiling at Paris too. But before she'd got there, Menego had burst out crying and she'd instantly turned tail and started running back to the hut. But just at that same moment – or rather, one split second after Menego's first cry – it was suddenly as light as day, and the reflections of the flares were chasing each other like lightning flashes along the surface of the Mussolini Canal, which itself now looked like one long endless lightning flash, streaking from our dyke on the drainage ditch down as far as the bridge on Via della Sorgente and beyond. Then came the stuttering sound of explosions from the airport, and flashes and leaping flames from the other side of the embankment.

'My children!' shrieked Armida like a Fury, and she snatched up Menego and started running along the embankment and then on through the fields, losing her clogs as she did so and carrying on barefoot: 'My children, my children – you told me so, you bees.' And Paris went running after her. All the way home.

The other children were already on the threshing-floor. Clad in a white nightdress, Adria, the oldest – she must have been eleven or twelve – had gathered her wailing brothers and sisters around her. 'Here I am!' gasped Armida, clutching them to her.

Paris – behind her – stood stock-still, and the threshing-floor was awash with relatives rushing hither and thither amidst the flashing and roaring of the planes flying over our heads and gaining height prior to coming back again, and everyone was yelling: 'Everyone to the bridge,' that little bridge which served as an air-raid shelter for the whole of the Left-Hand Parallel.

Now my Aunt Clelia and Uncle Themistocles – him in the long drawers he wore to bed in summer and winter alike – suddenly froze as well. Two pillars of salt they were, there on the threshing-floor. They stared at them – Aunt Clelia at Armida and Uncle Themistocles at his son – and it was as though they could see guilt written in huge letters all over their faces. Like a knife-wound to the heart. Until that moment no one had noticed anything. Not even the brothers. Now they were looking things straight in the eye.

Meeting his father's gaze, Paris looked away. Not so Armida. She carried on looking straight at my Aunt Clelia, and then she turned to look straight at Uncle Themistocles as well – her father-in-law, my Uncle Pericles' older brother. And her look meant that she took all blame upon herself, and that she was asking desperately for forgiveness.

'Everyone to the bridge!' said my Uncle Themistocles, and not another word was spoken.

'So that's what my bees wanted to tell me,' thought Armida. Then everyone ran off to the bridge, and in every stable along the Left-Hand Parallel the animals were howling, the hens were squawking and the dogs were baying like wolves, running off in desperation to take refuge under the bridges outside the holdings just like their masters.

Once her children were safely under the bridge, Armida ran out again – 'Stay here, you,' said Aunt Clelia, 'you just stay here!' 'No, I've got to go' – in search of her bees, who were buzzing madly around in their hives: 'I'm here, bees,' she said, 'calm down, I'm here.' Paris was desperate to go after her – to keep her safe in all that merry hell – but he could feel the eyes of the whole Parallel upon him, all crammed together in that burrow with the sole purpose of judging him, or so he felt, whereas in fact even his own father had stopped looking at him, so little did he want to think about the matter. His mother, on the other hand – after a particularly loud rumble from the airport, promptly followed by a screaming from under the bridge – even put out a tentative hand to reassure him. And he drew all Armida's children to him, and tried to tell them stories and make them laugh.

She came back again all out of breath, but with a hive in either hand, and started to push her way in under the bridge along with the rest of them. One of the sisters-in-law – not Clelia but one of the Peruzzi women from holding 517, the sister of her poor husband Pericles – said to her: 'You keep your distance, you and your bees!'

'Keep off, you!'

Even during the days that followed, my Uncle Themistocles and his wife never said a word about what had happened, either to her or to their son. They talked about everything else as though things were perfectly normal, but they never said a word about what they'd just discovered, not even when they were alone. Never. Totally locked in their own silence. Each man for himself. And everyone tried to protect them and cover for them, so that no one – not even the brothers – could suspect that anything was amiss.

Naturally enough, they – Paris and Armida – made no mention of it either. Indeed, Paris seemed positively to be avoiding his parents, he jumped to it when he was asked to do something but he avoided meeting their gaze, he'd immediately lower his eyes. Armida on the other hand looked at them long and hard, continuing to ask for mercy and forgiveness. When they were alone, though: 'What will become of us?' Paris would ask her.

'Nothing. Nothing will happen. You'll get married and have a family of your own, love.'

'No I won't! I'm going to tell everyone.'

'No. If you love me, you won't say anything to anyone, you swore as much on your poor uncle's head.' And then, at the end of October, or rather the beginning of November, when they'd already started sowing and she noticed that her stomach was getting bigger – she was already in her fifth month – one day at last she came upon her parents-in-law, Uncle Themistocles and his wife, alone in the little room where the seeds were kept, selecting which ones to sow. She went in and shut the door behind her. They looked up at her – they were sitting down on some sacks – and she said: 'Perhaps it would be better if you sent him away... Paris, that is.'

They rose to their feet – Aunt Clelia sighing, as if in relief – and they said: 'Yes, Armida, you're right... Thanks.'

'And never tell anyone that it was him. No one. Ever.'

'Never, Armida, never!'

'Swear that you won't. On oath. On Pericles!' and Armida was crying.

'We swear. Thanks, Armida, thanks again,' and the next day my Uncle Themistocles went off to Littoria to the new Republican Fascist Headquarters, which – as you know – was the first one to be set up anywhere in Italy.

Soon after 8 September – when the king and Badoglio had said: 'Down tools! Armistice! We're scarpering,' and put that record on the wireless and scarpered as fast as their legs would carry them – the Germans, reasonably enough in their view, had gone off to free Mussolini who'd been held prisoner by Badoglio on the Gran Sasso; they'd taken him off to Germany where Pavolini was waiting for him, along with the more disgruntled of the party bigwigs, and had him set up a new party and a new government. On 16 September an announcement had gone out from Radio Munich informing whoever cared to listen of the birth of a new republic in the Italian territory still controlled by the Germans – the RSI, the Italian Social Republic – and telling them that war was now resuming, alongside the German ally. So now we had two governments: one in the south – that of the king – allied to and under the command of the Anglo-Americans – and one in the north, under the command of the Germans.

But people all over Italy were not convinced – 'That's just an announcer, that's not the Duce's voice. Badoglio must have done for him long ago' – and even the most ardent Fascists were somewhat sceptical. It wasn't until two days later – 18

495

September 1943, at five in the afternoon – that the Duce spoke to the nation on Radio Munich with his own voice: '*Blackshirts! Men and women of Italy! At last, after long silence, I am speaking to you once again, and I have no doubt that you will recognize my voice: it is the voice which rallied you in times of trouble, which rejoiced with you in times of triumph...*' and from that moment onwards, as you know, we all set off again, lickety-split, on the last leg of that fatal journey.

That was on 18 September, as I've said, but two days earlier – that is, on the sixteenth, the day they bombed the airport – bypassing the pettifogging need to hear the Duce's own voice and putting their trust in that of the announcer, the party faithful in Littoria had already set up the new Republican Fascist Headquarters. The Peruzzi, you won't be surprised to learn, had promptly re-enrolled in the militia, even if at first there wasn't much to be getting on with, and all they had to do was lend a hand clearing up the wreckage in the airport, filling in the holes and tidying up the landing strip. But there'd been a lot of disagreement – within the RSI Government itself – about the role of the new militia and the Republican Armed Forces.

Graziani, the minister of defence, wanted there to be conscription. You had to enlist – the Graziani Proclamation, it was called – and failing to do so was tantamont to deserting. His fellow ministers, particularly Renato Ricci, had ideas of their own: 'Grazia, let's have just volunteers; let's let all the others be, they've been through hell and back and they're already dragging their feet. Do you want them back in the army if they don't want to be there? Let's just have the ones who want to join.' No dice: 'They've got to enlist,' said Graziani. So people ran off into the mountains, because they were well and truly fed up with the Fascist Party and with a war which was as good as lost: 'That's enough of that,' was what people were saying. If at that point he'd left them in peace and carried on with what he wanted, but just with volunteers, that might have been the end of it. But oh dear no, he sent his soldiers up into the mountains after them and lined them up against the wall to be shot as deserters, if they didn't come straight down again and carry on fighting along with him and the Germans. 'Enough's enough,' they said, and then they too started shooting – resisting – and that's how the civil war began. But – as you know – if you start shooting at me, and I shoot back, the whole thing tends to turn nasty, what with your German friends joining in the fray and burning villages which have given me shelter. And the ensuing vendettas can go on for ever. That's civil war for you: family pitted against family, and all because of the Graziani Proclamation. What on earth got into you – after everything you'd put me through already – to force me to enlist against my will, and dig me out and have me shot up there in the mountains?

Anyway, that morning in early November 1943, after talking matters over with Armida, my Uncle Themistocles went to the Fascist Headquarters in Littoria and said to the first man he came across: 'Have my son sent overseas.'

'Bravo, Peruzzi,' they said. 'That's the spirit. I wish there were more where you Peruzzis came from.'

He got back on his bicycle and went back home.

His wife was on the threshing-floor – just near the drinking trough – making some mash for the pig. She took one look at him and said: 'He's in the cowshed.'

His son was in the cowshed, hosing down a cow. He stopped as soon as he saw him, recognized the form he had in his hand by its colour and asked: 'When am I leaving?'

'Tomorrow.'

Then Paris went up to his father and took the form from him, to see his destination. Then – for the first time for over a month and a half – he raised his eyes and looked his father in the eye. 'Pa...' was all he said.

'Son,' said Themstocles back to him, and held him in his arms. And that was it – that was all they said to one another – and Paris went to have a wash and get his things together, and then he went to holding 517 to say goodbye to his grandmother, his grandfather and all the rest of the family: 'I've been called up again.'

'Watch out for yourself, son,' was what my grandmother said.

'At least we won't be eating any more fish,' was what my cousins said.

'Couldn't you learn to catch sausages?' was what my grandfather said, again, holding out his hand.

'No no, grandfather, don't be giving me money.'

'Take it, son – you're barely out of short trousers.'

Meanwhile, on Uncle Themistocles' holding, 516, his mother and Armida were darning his woollen socks and under-shirts; using the big fire-tongs, they took embers from the fire, put them into the iron and ironed his jacket, his shirt and his handkerchiefs. There were no paper ones in those days. 'Give me that handkerchief, my love' – sang my aunts – 'for I'm off to the fountain, washing.'

That same night, after a bit of *filo* with all his friends and his Peruzzi relatives, who'd come over from holding 517 to say goodbye to Paris, who was leaving – when everyone was at last starting to say their goodbyes – my Aunt Clelia picked up Menego and said to Armida: 'Go out for a bit, you two, I'll put this lot to bed,' and Paris and Armida went back to the Mussolini Canal, this time without either a lamp or a net.

It was cold by now, it was November. They were wearing coats. They were walking down the middle of our country road – on the grass, where it was less muddy, clear of the ruts made by the wheels of passing carts. There was no sign of the paved drainage ditch, its bed was now completely filled by the first flood waters, which rushed along, streaked by moonlight. The sound of the waterfall too was now just a distant murmur. They were sitting on a stone at the top of the embankment, under a eucalyptus tree. Further downstream, the hut had been carried away by a particularly powerful rush of flood water. All that was left of it were a few branches from what had been the roof, which had got caught up on the bank, and even they were already all twisted and bent crooked by the current. 'What will become of us,' said Paris, 'will we get bent all crooked, like those branches?'

'We'll do what those branches have done, my love, we'll go with the current.'

'And what about my son?' he asked her, laying his hand on her stomach.

'He's not your son, Paris, he's Pericles' son.'

'Don't talk nonsense, Armida! Are you trying to take him away from me as well?'

'But it's true. It's you I love now, but Pericles is the father of all my children, because he made me pregnant with them all on that first occasion, just as my bees do.'

'Don't talk nonsense, Armida, you're only making a fool of yourself.'

'It's you who's making a fool of yourself. This child is Pericles' son.'

'That child is mine, Armida, and everyone is going to know it.'

'You're not to tell anyone, ever, Paris, and least of all that

499

child. Ever. You swore to me that you wouldn't. Anyway, you've got your own life to lead.'

Now Paris was crying hard. 'Armida! Armida!' he gasped between his sobs, as they lay together one last time.

She was scratching his back beneath his undershirt.

'From tomorrow onwards, and for the rest of your life,' she said to him just before they went back into the house, 'you must go back to calling me "Aunt Armida".'

He left early the next morning, before dawn. He said goodbye to his brothers when they were still in bed. 'Come home on the winning side,' one of them said to him. 'Come back in one piece, more to the point,' said another. Then he went to kiss Armida's children, one by one, and they immediately stirred in their sleep. Adria woke up: 'Bye, Paris, give me another kiss.' Othello woke up too, but he was still half-asleep: 'Is it time to go fishing?'

Downstairs – in the kitchen – were his parents, and Armida. All three stood there looking at him in silence – he was now seated at the table, eating polenta and drinking coffee, made with barley, though, not the real thing. Then he kissed his father and mother, and Armida went out with him on to the bridge. They exchanged one final kiss. 'Thank you, Aunt Armida,' he said to her.

'Thank you, my beloved, and God bless you, and thank you for everything, for always... and may God bless whatever pain may come from my wrongdoing, and to hell with the Zorzi Vila and all their kind.'

Paris left from Littoria some time between the end of October and the beginning of November 1943, together with six or seven hundred others, who had volunteered for service at the Piave Barracks in Orvieto. You can still see the building,

500

above the *Autostrada del Sole* – as you come down from Florence – perched on its rock, to the left of the town, on the other side from the cathedral, with its big long windows, topped by great red arches. Graziani didn't need to come to the Pontine Marshes to winkle us out, we enlisted en masse of our own accord. Indeed, he would have had to shoot us to stop us enlisting (and I sometimes think that if the men who went up into the mountains had been given land and holdings, as we had, perhaps they'd never have joined the resistance at all, perhaps they'd have re-enlisted and laid their lives on the line again as we did; it all depends on how you treat people: 'Everyone has their reasons') and there were even mere boys of fourteen or fifteen, who changed the date on their birth certificates with ink eradicator to get themselves taken on; and then their mothers would go off after them and bring them home again, cuffing them around the ears along the way; but some managed to run away again and went off to fight, sometimes as far away as the north, like Luciano Bonanni from the council houses, and he never made it back, and his mother weeps for him to this day.

At the Piave Barracks, Paris and the others did a brief period of training and then they were incorporated into units in the militia, which was now known as the Republican National Guard. And back they went to fight, whether against our old enemy, the Anglo-Americans – who were now the new ally of the Italian government in the south – or against those Italians who, because they had gone up into the mountains, now came to be seen as traitors. So, back they went to fight, and a lot of them never made it back. 'For the honour of Italy,' was how they put it.

And Paris went back to fight with them. First in an M Battalion – the 'IX September' – on the Anzio-Nettuno front, as luck would have it, when the Anglo-Americans landed.

But we'd already been evacuated, and we saw him only once, when he visited us when he was on leave, and we were in the mountains above Cori, where some relatives of my Aunt Nazzarena – my Uncle Adrasto's wog wife – had set us up in a sort of cave with a wooden canopy in front of it, normally used by the local shepherds. And that's where we stayed – scattered over the mountainside with lots of other sharecroppers, evacuees like ourselves – waiting for the war to end. He came to visit us there after the child had already been born. He had trouble finding us, because the village was empty – the people from Cori had also been evacuated, and were now living in the mountains – and he kept asking for the Peruzzis as he made his way up through the hills, but no one knew who he meant or where we were. Until finally someone said: 'Oh, you mean the Vikings with the bees. You turn left, then right, then carry on up,' and at last he found us.

He didn't give Armida much of a welcome, he greeted her coldly – 'Hello, Aunt Armida' – as the others expected him to, and they too seemed to avoid her like the plague. And – as he thought they would expect – he also seemed surprised by the presence of this baby: 'And where's he blown in from?' Now I can't tell you whether the others had really fallen for it, or whether they were just putting on a show, but that's how the story was told to me and that's how I'm telling it to you.

So all that he and Armida could exchange was looks. He saved his hugs and kisses for his mother, grandmother and his other aunts. And for the child, of course, which the others seemed to avoid as much as they did his mother, poor little thing. They say he held that baby in his arms for the whole of the two hours that he was there, and every so often he would throw him into the air and catch him: 'My little cousin,' he'd say. Then: 'What's he called, Paris?'

'No, Pericles.'

So, 'Little Pericles,' he said to him: 'My little Pericles!' and he threw him up into the air again, and then put his grey beret with the red M for the M Battalion on the baby's head – the little thing practically drowned in it. The baby laughed – Aunt Bissola had a face like thunder – and he threw him into the air again: 'Little Pericles.'

There in front of everyone, Armida – his aunt – had to steel herself to say: 'Paris! You're making him bring up his milk!'

Aunt Bissola put on her best false smile: 'Paris has always loved babies.'

Then there were more hugs and kisses, and off he went – and all Armida got was a brief glance: 'Bye, Aunt Armida' – and from the front at Nettuno they sent him up into Northern Italy, to the Apennines, to hunt down partisans, the ones who'd gone up into the hills to get away from Graziani. As I said, it was civil war. And off they went, up hill and down dale, along the coast and over the plain in search of these partisans. Up in Northern Italy, Paris had met up with another of our cousins of his own age, one of the Peruzzis who'd stayed up there – our relatives on my grandfather's brother's side who'd lived with us both in Codigoro and when we were with those damned Zorzi Vila, but who were still Socialists, they hadn't become Fascists as we had, nor had they come down to the Pontine Marshes, they'd stayed up north – and this cousin was a partisan. A Communist. And you know how it ended up between him and Paris amidst all that bloodbath and murder up there in the north, and even if you don't know, whether Paris ever made it safely back home – and yes, he did come back; even if he was never the same again – I'll tell you about it at a later date, there's no time now. We're dealing with another story, and we've got to see it through to the end. I'll tell you the other stories – if God gives me the time and the good health – at another *filo*.

The real drama, though, was when they learned from my grandmother that this baby was on the way. That was catastrophe. Greek tragedy.

The Christmas novena had just begun. The previous evening we'd all been to church in town. The Anglo-Americans were now just below Cassino, up against the Germans' Gustav Line. The first attack was imminent, and you could already hear the crump of distant shelling. Armida was now into her seventh month, and air-raids on the Pontine Marshes were becoming increasingly frequent. People were saying that the land war had already begun in the Province of Littoria – at Formia, Gaeta and Minturno – and bombing was now our daily bread. Indeed, it was more daily than our bread, because now you couldn't get flour even on the black market. We weren't leading a life of luxury, but we still had a bit of this and that, and that day at the start of the novena we on my grandfather's holding 517 were slaughtering a pig.

We'd killed it. We'd drawn off the blood and collected it in basins for the blood-pudding. Poured boiling water over its body to soften the bristles and then pulled them out. Hoisted it up with the block and tackle. Cut it in two and cleaned it up. Cleaned all the guts with boiling water. Hoisted it up again and stripped the flesh off it. Sliced up a few chops. Salted the sausage-meat. Rolled up the belly pork. Minced all the meat and put it into different piles: the leaner meat for salami and the rest for *cotechino*. We'd boiled and stripped the head and minced the meat and cartilage for pressing. All we had to do now was stuff the meat into the casing. My grandfather's family and Uncle Themistocles' family were both there, and the night before – as my grandmother told us while they were dealing with the pig – the night before my grandmother had again had that dream about the figure cloaked in black. The only people who weren't there were my Aunt Clelia and Armida, and in fact she hadn't been there for some time. 'How come you never come to see me nowadays?' my grandmother would ask her from the cart, whenever she passed her going into town.

'I've got so much to do,' Armida would say, 'but I'll be over soon,' and would smile at her from the courtyard. But she kept her distance.

'Well, I'll be waiting for you,' my grandmother would say, but as soon as they set off again her daughters would mutter: 'Tell her to keep out from under our feet, more like.' All of them, with the possible exception of Aunt Santapace, Benassi's wife.

'Don't talk like that!' my grandmother would say to them reprovingly. 'She's a good girl. I wish you were more like her.'

'What?!' they'd all say, and it would be cuffs all round.

Anyway, on holding 517 – that day when they'd been dealing with the pig – there wasn't enough string to tie up the salami, and while a pair of German or Republican planes were flying over our heads on their way back to the airport, limping and hawking, my Uncle Themistocles said that there was plenty of string on holding 516: 'Go and get it, someone, Clelia and Armida know where it is.'

It was one of my girl cousins who went, I can't remember which. She must have been about ten. And when she came back, all laden with rolls of string, she also said: 'I think Aunt Armida must be pregnant, she could hardly move and she was holding her back, I think it'll be a big one.' An x-ray couldn't have made things clearer.

Forget the war. Things were far worse on the domestic front.

The sound of the bombing from around Cassino was even louder now, and nearer, too, coming from around Anzio and Terracina but also from Velletri, some American plane was dropping sweeties from the skies there too. But it was nothing in comparison with what was happening at holding 517.

My Uncle Adelchi was smashing all the chairs on to the kitchen floor – 'Now we'll have to buy new ones,' my grandfather said quietly, to no one in particular – and banging his head against the wall, and crying. 'The shame of it,' he shrieked as he banged his head against the wall, 'The shame,' and he was weeping like a baby.

'Who was it? Who did it?' yelled everyone around him – particularly the womenfolk – but not with a question mark, as though they wanted to know who it was, but with an exclamation mark, as though they wanted to know how whoever it was had dared, the scoundrel.

My grandmother told someone to go and get her. It was Aunt Santapace who went, and she was crying too: 'Now what have you gone and done, Armida...'

'May God forgive me,' was all she said. And out she came: 'Whatever will be, will be.'

Meanwhile – on holding 516 – my Uncle Themistocles and his children were now at it hammer and tongs: 'What about you lot? How could you not have noticed anything?'

'I don't know anything about it.' 'Me neither.'

'What do you mean, you don't know anything about it?' shrieked Uncle Adelchi at his older brother. 'You should have kept an eye on her! You were the keeper of the Peruzzi family honour, we put her in your care.'

'In my care? Why didn't you keep her over there with you,

where she belonged? Why did you send her off and dump her on me?'

'What's that to do with anything?' my Uncle Adelchi was shrieking, like one possessed. My Uncle Adrasto and his wife Nazzarena immediately joined in: 'Yes, what's that to do with anything? It was she who wanted to go, we kept telling her to stay here, isn't that so, Zelinda?' and they all turned to look at Zelinda, my Uncle Iseo's wife.

'I don't know anything about it,' said Aunt Zelinda. She was a good friend of Armida's, almost a sister to her, but she was a guest in their house, on sufferance, as you might say.

And Uncle Themistocles, whose blood was up by now – though he was still cold and calm and self-controlled – said to my Uncle Adelchi: 'You're a crafty one, Adelchi, but watch your step, I'm not so stupid either.'

'What d'you mean, crafty?' said my Uncle Adrasto. 'He's only telling the truth.'

'Keep quiet, you!' Uncle Themistocles said to him threateningly, all red in the face.

Meanwhile Armida had arrived, with Aunt Santapace on one side of her, still crying, and Aunt Clelia on the other; she was on the warpath now, with the air of someone who's going to fight to the death to defend the honour of her son and her son's son: 'Fire away, Peruzzi, I'm ready.'

'You whore!' my aunts began to shriek, especially Bissola. 'You filthy sow.'

Meanwhile the bees were starting to fly off towards their hives. 'Time for bed,' they buzzed.

My grandmother now had Armida by the arm, and she started to shake her violently. In the meantime my Aunt Zelinda had gathered together her own children and those of Armida and was hustling them out after the bees, towards the canal, but Adria and Onesto, the two oldest, refused to budge and started wailing: 'Ma, ma,' but Aunt Zelinda shoved them out anyway: 'You come along with me!' Then my grandmother let go of her and slapped her hard around the face, and Armida didn't move an inch, and my grandmother said: 'Who was it, you filthy whore?'

Not a word.

'Who was it?'

Silence.

'Who was it?'

'No one.'

'What d'you mean, no one?' said all the brothers and sisters-in-law in unison. 'It must have been one of Themistocles' sons, come on, own up!' chimed in Aunt Bissola and Uncle Adelchi, speaking as one.

'You leave my sons out of this!' thundered Uncle Themistocles, picking up one of the knives they'd just used on the pig. 'It's me you're dealing with! Tell them, Armida, tell them it was me!' 'Yes, it was him, it was him!' piped up his wife, my Aunt Clelia, quick as a flash. 'Armida, tell them it was him,' but all she would do was shake her head – 'It was me, and there's an end to it,' said Uncle Themistocles, looking daggers, knife in hand, 'you leave my sons out of this or there'll be a massacre,' and he now had his knife trained on Uncle Adelchi's stomach, and his blood was up.

'No, it wasn't any of your sons,' Uncle Adelchi agreed. Then he turned again to Armida: 'So, who was it then?'

'Pericles. He's Pericles' son.'

'You leave my brother out of this, you whore!' screeched Aunt Bissola. 'What did he do, come to you in a dream and make you pregnant?'

'And how many times has that happened to you, I'd like

508

to know?'

'What are you talking about? There's no comparing you to me and my brother. You don't even know how to read or write, but I, my dear, am a Peruzzi!' and now Aunt Bissola lurched towards her and tried to join in the slapping, screeching: 'You whore, you filthy sow,' at the top of her voice as she did so.

'You keep your hands off me!' shouted Armida, but now she too was picking up one of those murderous knives from the table – 'Never start an argument when there are knives on the table,' said my grandfather, who was standing beside her – 'say anything you like, but use words, not hands,' and now he was looking straight at my grandmother, 'or I'll be doing a bit of massacring myself.'

My grandmother made a gesture, and everyone instantly fell silent. Then she said to her, quietly: 'Just tell us whose child he is.'

'It was me, it was me, he's my child,' repeated Uncle Themistocles.

'Be quiet!' ordered my grandmother. 'Who's child is he?'

Then Armida seemed to pause for thought, and finally, in a voice that was at once resigned and firm, she said: 'He's Pericles' child, may the saints be my witness...'

'Be quiet, and don't blaspheme,' and my grandmother crossed herself. 'Leave my son and the saints out of this...'

'We made him,' continued Armida in that same tone of voice, 'we made him the way bees do, at the same time as all his brothers and sisters, that night he did for the priest at Comacchio,' and believe me, she was absolutely serious. 'May the saints be my witness,' she repeated.

'You're mad,' said my grandmother, crossing herself again. 'Mad and bad! From now on, I advise you too to start praying that Pericles really is dead, and that he won't be ever coming home... Because if he does...' And from that night on my grandmother – who, until the previous evening, at the novena in town, had always prayed: 'Lord, bring my Pericles safe home' – from that night on, until she died, she prayed: 'Lord, don't send him safe home, not ever, give him peace where he is.'

But the die was cast. It was exile for her. My grandmother immediately sent for Uncle Themistocles' cart to collect their possessions, Armida's and those of her children. She was going to stay here, under her eagle eye, on holding 517. 'She might have thought about that earlier,' Aunt Clelia and Aunt Zelinda said to one another. 'We all know about the horse and the stable door.' 'We're Christian folk, so you can stay here till you've given birth, but after that you're off! You and your bastard both. Out of our sight once and for all,' said my grandmother.

Armida stayed where she was, and didn't say a word.

'The other children will be staying on here' – Armida turned pale – 'Those children belong with the Peruzzi family,' and that was what they did, take them all from her. The only one they left her was Menego – the littlest – but only because Santapace intervened, beseeching her: 'You can't take the little one away from her, ma. Leave her the little one.' But they took all the others away and shared them out among each branch of the Peruzzi family.

Sorry, what's that you said? They couldn't do that?

Of course they couldn't, not legally – even I know that. But she'd have needed a lawyer. And in this world – not to mention in Italy! – there are a lot of things that you can't do legally, but you still do them, if you have half a chance.

All Armida needed now was a scarlet letter on her forehead. She couldn't go into town. She couldn't go to mass on Sundays, not even at Christmas. If someone called round, she had to be shut away. Kept out of sight. And if anyone did meet her by chance – particularly the womenfolk – they'd immediately look away and call her 'whore'. If anyone in town happened to ask: 'Has that cow given birth?' it never even entered our Peruzzi heads that they meant Venezia, the black and white cow who was expecting a calf, we immediately thought that they meant Armida. A sense of shame weighed down on all of us: 'That filthy sow.' Only my grandfather, when he came upon her alone in the house, would address her with affection. Just him and Santapace.

She – Armida – would walk through the fields alone with her swollen belly in front of her and the bees behind her. Now they were starting to keep her children from her, not letting them go out with her. 'But what have you done, ma, what have you done?' Adria would ask her, clinging to her tearfully. 'Forgive me, love,' was all Armida said. One day when Aunt Santapace was looking out of a first-floor window and saw her down on the threshing-floor, in front of the well, which happened to be uncovered, she said to her mother, my grandmother, who was in the room with her: 'Ma! She wouldn't, would she?' 'If only!' said my grandmother. 'Her and her bastard both!' And then she prayed: 'Lord, don't let my son come back, or there's no knowing what might happen.'

What did happen, though, on 22 January 1944, was that the Anglo-American forces landed at Anzio. Now I'm not saying anything against them – far from it – they had good reasons of their own for doing so, it had been us who'd gone and made nuisances of ourselves around their parts, and if everything was going up in smoke the fault was ours alone; ours, and that of our German-Nip allies. But they hadn't landed at Anzio to give us the time of day, they'd landed there to break our bones. Break them good and proper. That's a historical fact. There's no denying it.

The first great battle of Montecassino had begun on 12 January. It raged for one whole month, but it was stalemate. All the allies could do was wait there, below the abbey, until 19 May 1944. It took four months of fighting – with thirty-two thousand allied dead on their side, and eleven thousand Germans – before they could move on from Cassino.

Cassino was the stronghold on the Gustav Line, the line of defence which ran from the Tyrrhenian Sea, from the mouth of the Garigliano, to the Sangro on the Adriatic, cutting Italy in two. On one side was the Kingdom of the South – with the so-called legitimate government headed by the king – in an Italy now conquered by our new allies and former enemies, the Anglo-Americans, who were desperately trying to advance and conquer the whole country. On the other side were the Germans – and the so-called puppet government of the RSI, the Fascist Republic in the north – who were trying desperately to resist them.

Now if you look at a map of Italy, you'll see that this Gustav Line ran through nothing but mountains. Imagine it with bunkers and fortifications. The only point where the Anglo-American armies and armoured vehicles could get through was the valley below Cassino, along which the high-speed train and the *Autostrada del Sole* now run. But this valley was overlooked by Montecassino, the hill on which the abbey stands. It was impassable. As you were moving forward, the Germans were right smack bang in front of you, they could practically throw stones at you – 'strategic advantage', it's known as – and indeed it took four months and forty-three thousand dead before they pulled it off.

But it wasn't as if they – the Anglo-Americans – didn't have a back-up plan. 'I know, let's make a landing on the Pontine Plain,' they said, 'between Mount Circeo and Terracina, push on with tanks through the Pontine Marshes to Cori-Giulianello, then swing eastwards at Valmontone and take the Germans from the rear.' The only trouble was, Admiral Canaris' secret services had got wind of their plan – even if in the circumstances you didn't need assistance from an admiral, you or I could have got there just by looking at a map – and so the Germans called in the experts from our Servicemen's Association and the consortium which had done the reclamation: 'Comrades, this calls for a bit of flooding in the Pontine Marshes.'

'*Jawohl,*' we said, what else was there to say? As every schoolboy knows – and it's not just in von Clausewitz, you'll find it much earlier, in Livy– the advancing enemy must find nothing ahead of him but scorched earth, you mustn't leave him anything that might be of any use to him, you even have to kill and bury your cattle if you can't take them with you, you mustn't leave them there for him to get his hands on. Some historians have been shocked that the fields should have been flooded. Well? We couldn't just let them breeze in without our lifting a finger, could we now?

We went out and deactivated all the pumping equipment. It's not true that it was the Germans who sabotaged it or blew it up with TNT. That's all rubbish. The Germans didn't touch a thing, not so much as a door or a vine. It was us – our technicians – who deactivated the pumping equipment and took away the parts. We re-flooded our fields – we turned them back into marshes – to stop the enemy landing and getting through. That was our doing.

On the Lepini Mountains, though, as you know, our wogs

513

did put up resistance to the Germans, and not just passive resistance either. Princess Caetani in the meantime – the days of serving coffee to the sharecroppers were over – was dispensing hospitality to the agents of the Oss; from up there in her castle on the hills near Sermoneta they could observe the movements on the plain and transmit the map references to the enemy bombers. But there were also acts of sabotage and armed conflict. On our side of the hills alone there were two small partisan groups active at Sezze and Sermoneta, the Zaccheo Group and the Fiacci Group, and they were engaged not just in sabotage but also in armed conflict, and people were killed and wounded. It wasn't much, there weren't any great battles or deployments; but our wogs in the Lepini Mountains did resist the Germans, and that's a fact. We, on the other hand – us northern sharecroppers from the Pontine Marshes – resisted the English and the Americans. 'Everyone has their reasons.' That's all there is to it.

At all events, now the allies couldn't land in the north and take Cassino from the rear – they'd have been caught in the crossfire. Or at least that's what the Germans thought: 'Tanks can't cross lakes and marshes, and they wouldn't be as stupid as to land at Anzio and then have all that way to go to Cassino. So, no landings then,' was what the Germans thought. 'Let's concentrate on Cassino.'

But – as I've told you – Cassino was a tough nut to crack, and when the first battle began on 12 January 1944 the Anglo-Americans too started saying to each other: 'Damn the Zorzi Vila, this isn't looking good.' Then Churchill said: 'I tell you what. It may seem a long way away, but I'm going to land at Anzio anyway, so at least I'll be putting a cat among those Germans' pigeons and a spanner in their supply lines, and they'll have to leave Cassino undefended, while my cat will

514

make for Valmontone on the one hand, which is to their rear, and head for Rome via Aprilia-Campoleone on the other, and that way it'll bye-bye to the Gustav Line. I can't wait to see my cat among those German pigeons,' and Winston Churchill rubbed his hands in glee.

So – what with one lot saying 'There won't be any landings,' and the other lot saying 'I'm going to land at Anzio anyway,' – when 22 January came and the allies landed at Anzio there wasn't a soul waiting for them, there were hardly any German troops or tanks in the whole region. There were just two battalions of veterans from the Gustav Line in the whole of the Pontine Marshes, and they were stationed on various holdings along the coastal strip, on leave. On a winter break. But only something over a thousand men, at most.

But there were fifty thousand Anglo-Americans, and five thousand armoured vehicles. And thirty-two kilometres of ships – three hundred and seventy-four of them, strung out along the coast between Astura and Tor San Lorenzo, spewing out soldier upon soldier at a rate of knots, and tanks and cannonades. There was a sea of them there on that beach, all jammed up together, and every one of them – starting with the American general who was in command of Operation Shingle, as the landing was known – was wondering: 'Now what?'

He – Major General John P. Lucas – had been through the mill in Sicily, as well as in Salerno and on the Garigliano. He'd seen his men mowed down in rows under a barrage of German fire: 'I wonder how many it'll be this time. God knows what we'll have to go through this time round.' It would never have entered his head that there'd be no one there to welcome them. 'What's this monkey business then? Where are they all lurking? It's Germans we're dealing with here, they're craftier than foxes, and they play a dirty game.' So they proceeded cautiously. On all fours, feeling their way with their hands. But all they heard was the odd desultory shot: 'See? What did I tell you? They were waiting for us.' So they brought on the artillery and let fly – stock-still where they were – in the hope that the Germans would go away and let them pass. But no. After their artillery had ceased firing, there was another solitary gunshot from the other side. So they said, again: 'What did I tell you? We're in trouble.' And they set their artillery blasting once again, stock-still where they were, strung out along the beach.

On our side – as I've already said – there were just a thousand soldiers. And the sharecroppers from the Pontine Marshes.

The first Anglo-American vehicles had landed on the night of 21–22 January, at Riviera Zanardelli, between Anzio and Nettuno. Then – gradually, over the first twenty-four hours – more than thirty-five thousand men followed, all along the coast from Tor San Lorenzo to Torre Astura, and that was the first wave. For at least thirty hours, if not more – until the German divisions which had been driven out of Cassino and the rest of Italy started arriving on the scene – they were the only armed men in the Pontine Marshes. The world was their oyster, at that juncture. Poor old General Lucas must have eaten his heart out for the rest of his days.

According to one story – though some historians say it's not a story, but the truth – as soon as it landed, one English light lorry took the coast road to Nettuno. Not a living soul to be seen anywhere along the route. 'What shall we do?' asked the man who was driving. 'Let's go on a bit further,' said the others. They were only young men, as you know, and before landing they'd been liberally plied with whisky and cognac and benzedrine, as happens in every army in the world. So on they went. They drove on as far as Aprilia and there wasn't a *Kraut* to be seen for love or money. They went on to Campoleone. Same thing there. On they went to Ciampino and Quarto Miglio and finally to Rome, without encountering so much as a hint of a German. They themselves couldn't believe it, and it was only when they got to Piazza San Giovanni, right by the arches of the Aurelian Walls, that they went into reverse and back to Anzio. 'Phew, not a soul to be seen.'

Now I don't know whether anyone believed them or not. Or whether they believed them but sent someone else to have another look, and perhaps that someone else had a different tale to tell. Certain it is that those few thousand Germans who were taking their winter break – the 71st Battalion and the scouts from the 29th Panzer Division on leave from Cassino – immediately got down to business. They started rushing all around the place with three or four self-propelling light cannon, and every so often they'd stop and fire. But they never seemed to be aiming at anything in particular. They'd stop and fire off a few rounds at random, then get back into their lorry and go off again; carry on for another two kilometres and start firing again – aimlessly, all around – then off they'd go yet again, to convince the unseen enemy that the place was crawling with cannon. And they succeeded.

But it must also be admitted that what they were saying in the RSI newspapers wasn't true. It was just propaganda. If you take a look at the cover of the *Domenica del Corriere* of 13 February 1944 – we've got one lying around somewhere on holding 517 – you can read as follows: '*In the Pontine Marshes, alongside German soldiers, groups of country dwellers from Romagna, armed with rifles and shotguns, are defending the land which they themselves have reclaimed; holed up in their farmhouses, they are opening fire on Anglo-American reconnaissance patrols,*' and there's a drawing of our holdings, and of those sharecroppers who were supposed to be doing the shooting. Well, that's complete nonsense. It's propaganda. They said that they were from Romagna because that's where the Duce came from. But in fact – together with the Germans – the people who were doing the shooting were us, the Peruzzi, and all the other sharecroppers in the Pontine Marshes, from the Veneto and Friuli and around Ferrara, not just the ones from Romagna. The Veneto-Pontine Vikings. Who else?

When the Anglo-American ships' cannon had started to spew out fire and flames at two in the morning, all of us in the Pontine Marshes had woken up immediately, and seeing and hearing that the fire was coming from the sea, we didn't need a rocket scientist to tell us that someone was landing. My Uncle Adelchi woke up suddenly in the house he'd rented from the Social Security people in Littoria. He went to the window and said: 'Holy smoke'. Then he put on his uniform and his holster-belt – he was still serving as a policeman – and went off to the police headquarters, in the town hall. There he met up with his colleagues, and they were promptly sent off all over Littoria to check on the shelters, and to try and get frightened people to calm down, and he and a mate got on their Gileras, drove past the militia barracks to pick up the odd rifle and set off towards the towns and along the coast to see what was happening. Then they began to drive up and down on their motorbikes, together with the Germans with their light guns. At dawn – around five-thirty or six – they were somewhere near Borgo Piave, and they saw an American jeep coming towards them very slowly in the distance, surrounded by a patrol of infantrymen.

They threw their motorbikes to the ground and started shooting. The others threw themselves down, too, and followed suit. My uncle started to shriek: 'Manzon! Manzon! Manzon!'

'What's up, Adelchi?' someone shouted from inside the Manzon holding. They'd recognized his voice.

'Come out and get shooting, you son of a bitch, or they'll take your holding too.' Then – 'Sweet Jesus, the holding!' and the Manzon family came out as well, to be followed by the Rivoletto family from the holding opposite, and then several others. Some armed with carbines they'd got from the militia, others with shotguns they'd hidden in the loft – because after 8 September the Germans had banned civilians from bearing arms – a group of sharecroppers now took up positions against the Americans on either side of what is now the E42 Pontina. Hearing a hail of bullets, the German scouts with the light guns also turned back, even if they didn't make it before the jeep had done an about-turn and rushed back towards the canal: 'Resistance! We're encountering resistance!' they must have said into their radios.

The same sort of thing was happening on the other side as well – towards Aprilia-Pomezia – because almost at the same time on the morning of 22 two or three English light lorries appeared just outside the holding belonging to my Aunt Bissola and Lanzidei. The road – the present-day E42 Pontina, which was under construction at the time, all there was of it was the macadam – runs just below it, slightly sunken. On either side of the road – above it, on the two hillocks between which it runs – are my Uncle Lanzidei's holding and that of his neighbours opposite, who are from Romagna and are called Maltoni, like the Duce's mother, indeed they claimed they were related. 'Well, we're related to Rossoni,' my Aunt Bissola would snap back, not to be outdone. Anyway, they were on one side and we were on the other when these two or three light lorries appeared at the end of the road and the firing started. Us from above and the English from below. They were caught broadside on. One lorry skidded off the road and landed in the ditch, blocking the others' way, so out they all got. 'You keep clear of my land, don't you touch my holding!' shrieked my Aunt Bissola, firing from where she lay, stretched out on the ground in the lee of a drainage ditch.

'Let me have a go, ma, I'm a better shot,' the oldest of her sons begged her.

'You just pipe down, or you'll be next in the firing line!' she said. 'Keep quiet and pass the ammunition, damn you.' My Uncle Lanzidei and his father – old Lanzidei from Nettuno, an anti-Fascist who now had a holding of his own, if you don't mind – were wearing helmets dating back to the 1915–18 War. We Peruzzi and our neighbours from Romagna were at it like you've never seen, not even in a Western. We had the strategic advantage. After a quarter of an hour or so they put up a white flag, loaded up their wounded – 'Keep shooting!' my aunt was shrieking, but my Uncle Lanzidei told her to lay off, 'or it's me who'll be shooting you' – turned their lorries around and hared off back to Anzio to report: 'You can't get through that way.'

That was how the first twenty-four hours went after the Anzio landings. Then the next day our German ally arrived in full force – together with a few units from the RSI – and the professionals took over. And that was as far as our resistance went – we fired off a few rounds and made a great deal of noise, and that was it – and we weren't the only sharecroppers to put up resistance. But what with the cannon fire and a few bursts from the machineguns – fired off every now and again at random by those thousand Germans here on their winter break – for over thirty hours, until the real army arrived, that is, we managed to convince the enemy that they had quite some army to contend with. They were so scared, our every bang sounded like ten. And when at last they realized that what they were up against was just a thousand Germans and us sharecroppers – against thirty-five thousand of them – it was too late, the Axis forces were all in place. Their offensive was halted, the bridgehead was surrounded, they found themselves penned into an area between the front on the Mussolini Canal to the south, and *Fosso Moletta* to the north, down to its mouth at Tor San Lorenzo. They were penned in there for four months – over fifty thousand of them, stuck there in the mud – whereas during those first thirty hours, if they'd felt like it, they could have breezed all the way up to Rome and Cassino. Churchill had to go before the House of Commons and make an awkward confession: 'At least we've got their forces away from Cassino. I thought we'd set the cat among the pigeons at Anzio, but, I admit, there we still are, like a beached whale.' Stopped in their tracks by a thousand Germans and the share-croppers from the Pontine Marshes.

What's that you said? That none of this is in the history books? That historians mention only the Germans, not the sharecroppers from the Pontine Marshes?

Yes, I'm quite aware of that, but what can I say? It's not my fault if the historians have based themselves solely on the military archives; where, unsurprisingly, our names do not appear. As you'll agree, it's more dramatic – and less embarrassing – to refer to 'brutally determined Germans' than to 'a handful of scruffy sharecroppers'. And anyway, excuse me, but do you really think that on the night of 22 January 1944 – and also in the hours that followed, given the state of panic they must have been in – they'd have taken down the details of everyone who happened to fire a shot at them? 'It's the Germans!' they'd say, and then turn tail. What can I do about it, if in fact we too were there among those Germans?

Do I have to deny it, just to keep you sweet? Make of it what you will. But you'll find it in the *Domenica del Corriere* and – if I may say so – it's engraved in the memory of the Peruzzi clan, and in those of other sharecroppers from the Veneto. I heard about it from my uncles. But, believe you me, they only whispered it under their breath, because after the war – when at last they liberated us, and we saw that the devil wasn't as black as he'd been painted, because not only did they not take away our holdings, but they even helped us with supplies and DDT – it suddenly didn't seem such a good thing to go round harping on about the part we'd played. Then we joined in the chorus: 'The Germans did it all.'

Once, during one of the first meetings held in Aprilia to celebrate the Resistance – when democracy was back after the liberation, and my Uncle Lanzidei had rejoined the Socialist Party, together with my Uncle Dolfin – at a certain point my Aunt Bissola stood up and said: 'We were in the Resistance too, you know.' My Uncle Lanzidei immediately took her by the arm and tried to make her sit down again: 'Hush now! That's enough.' But she shook him off and repeated, even more loudly: 'Tell them! Tell them that we were in the Resistance too.' Then, addressing the whole assembled company: 'My man here,' and she pointed a finger at him, as he cowered and wished the ground would swallow him up – 'my husband here, he shot a lot of those Americans'; who of course were English, just to make matters worse.

'Well, comrade,' said the speaker, who'd come down from Rome, 'that's not the Resistance we're here to celebrate today. We're here to celebrate the Resistance against Nazi-Fascism.'

'Don't talk such piffle,' said my aunt. 'An educated man like you, coming out with that tripe, I'm surprised at you. We fired on them – Germans, Americans, what's the difference?

It's Resistance, whichever way you look at it!' she carried on, while my Uncle Lanzidei dragged her away, making signs to his friends and comrades with his fist closed and his thumb in the air, raising it up and down in front of his mouth – though without her seeing him – as if to say: 'She's had a jar or two.'

As I've said, these are the facts – that's what I've been told, and that's what I'm telling you. You can believe me or not, it's up to you, that's what my Aunt Bissola and my Uncle Adelchi would say.

On 7 February, though – in 1944 – the Germans had us evacuated. The allies had appeared on the canal on the morning of the landings, 22 January. At Borgo Podgora, an American fighter plane had just machinegunned the local bus, on its way from Cisterna to Littoria – people had set off to go to work as though it was just another day – when other, bigger planes started arriving, and a cloud of parachutes was floating down on to the Mussolini Canal, just beyond the last curve of the Left-Hand Parallel – the American 504th Parachute Regiment. They landed on both sides of the canal, in the little grove of eucalyptus trees at the end of the Mambrin's holding. Together with the Germans who were now pouring in from the nearby town, the Mambrin and their neighbours started shooting at the first parachutists who were emerging from the trees. They did an about turn and took up positions in the bed of the canal – beyond the embankment – and by the time my grandfather and Uncle Themistocles and all the rest of the Parallel arrived on the scene with their shotguns, it was all over. But, as you know, the Americans were there for four whole months: on the other side of our embankment – in and beyond the Mussolini Canal – stuck in the pocket of their bridgehead.

They stayed there until 23 May, after Cassino, when the

allies – the Anglo-Americans, that is – launched an offensive here as well, and after they'd smashed through all our defences, they liberated Pontinia, Littoria and Cisterna on 25 May. Then they were all over the place. After joining up with the forces from Cassino, they went on to liberate Aprilia and Velletri, and on 4 June they entered Rome '*at the head of their victorious troops*'. It was 1944, as I've said, and it was the Mussolini Canal that had served as the front line – trench warfare for four months – with the Americans on the far side of the canal, and the Germans and RSI Italians on our side. Imagine the blood that must have flowed down that canal; washed down through the drainage ditches, over the dykes, around the embankments. Imagine the patrols skirmishing in the nearby fields. Thirty thousand dead altogether, on the Nettuno-Anzio front. Young men just out of their teens, who'd come from all corners of the earth to die round our canal. Their mothers are weeping for them to this day.

But – as I've said – on 7 February the Germans had us evacuated. We couldn't stay put. By now the line of defence was firmly established, the enemy bridgehead blocked on the canal. The German and RSI Units – well dug in this side of it – took turns in the line of fire. They'd come and shoot and kill and be killed and then they'd be relieved, albeit briefly.

Our holding was now more or less a thing of the past. Stove in from every side. The roof had no tiles on it. The doors and windows had been torn out. We spelled trouble, both for ourselves and them. So they sent us away. My grandfather didn't want to go. He stuck to his guns. He wanted to stay right there. They said to him: 'No, *danke kamerad*, thanks pal, now it's us who's doing the fighting,' because, down to the very last day – to make himself seem useful – he'd hung on there with them, behind the privy, carbine in hand. Indeed, at one point they'd even given him a sub-machinegun – 'How does this damn contraption work then?' he'd asked, turning it over in his hands – and then he said to them: 'What's all this talk of fighting, *kamerad?* This is my land, this is my holding, this is where I stay.'

'*Raus, raus!* You evacuate,' they said to him, rather less politely by now, when they saw that politeness wasn't going to get them anywhere. We took a cart and our last remaining donkey – most of our livestock had been got through, mainly by the Germans – and we set off by night, towards Cori, and the mountains: 'My relatives will give you a hand,' my Aunt Nazzarena had said.

We spread white sheets over the top of the cart, and painted them with a red cross, so people would know we were civilians. But, as I said, we also took the precaution of leaving by night – by now we were on our guard. Two days earlier the Mambrin had been fired on from the canal by the Americans while they'd been moving out, despite the fact that they too had everything covered in white sheets. No one trusted anyone by now: an ox-cart had set off from our side – along the Parallel – all draped in a fine white sheet with a red cross on it, as though transporting the wounded behind the lines. But suddenly the wind got up, the sheet probably hadn't been properly secured and it blew off, to reveal a piece of ordnance which the Germans were trying to move elsewhere. The Americans had started firing, and from that moment on – sheets or no sheets – they fired at everything that moved. The Mambrin included.

So we Peruzzis left by night, taking the Parellel in the direction of the Appian Way. At one point, though, the German police wouldn't let us through: '*Nein, nein.*' So off we went through the fields towards the canal. We'd almost reached the Appian Way when our hunting dog, Gina – the black and white bitch that had belonged to my Uncle Pericles, God rest his soul, who was walking some thirty metres ahead of us, wagging her tail – was suddenly blown up. She'd stepped on a mine. We were in a minefield. Everybody froze: 'Now what do we do?'

My grandfather was in favour of to waiting until daylight: 'Then we'll be able to see better.'

'Yes, and so will the Americans,' put in my grandmother, adding 'Goddam the Zorzi Vila,' for good measure. And so – by the grace of God – we managed to make it safely through that minefield and across the Appian Way, and on to Doganella and then to Cori, where my Aunt Nazzarena's relatives organized a place for us to stay up in the mountains, above the village, on the slopes of Mount Lupone, among the holm oaks. In a kind of cave, as I've told you, with a wooden hut in front of it, where shepherds would shelter with their flocks. We stayed there for four months, together with a lot of other share-croppers on those same mountains. It was a life of poverty all right – we lived mainly on berries, on roots, and even on the charity of the wogs. Without their help, we wouldn't have survived. They would turn up and call out: 'Hey, Vikings!' and bring us some small offering.

Meanwhile, in our cave, the baby had been born – as I've already told you – and my grandmother didn't send Armida packing straight away: 'We're Christians, like I said, and you and your bastard can stay here until the war is over and we go down home again. Then you'll have to get out from under our feet for good and all.'

'Thanks, ma.'

'And give over calling me ma!'

'All right, if that's what you want.'

As time went by, though – and every minute of our waking

hours, even in the bitter cold of February and March, was spent wandering the woods and mountains in search of something to eat, mushrooms, herbs, nettles, wild endive – simply by virtue of proximity, like it or not, my grandmother grew used to that bastard baby. When she thought of Armida, my grandmother's only comment would be: 'That cow!' but this baby – you'll have to take my word for it – never cried except when he was hungry. Never. All he did was gurgle and laugh and smile at whoever picked him up, and more especially at the bees, which were always buzzing around him and trying to make him smile and telling him stories and crawling over his hands and face. In the end my grandmother started smiling back. She became fond of him.

Later, though – on 19 May – we had to leave Cori in a hurry, because a rumour was spreading throughout the region that the real wogs, the ones from Morocco and Algeria, were going round raping people. They'd come to these parts in the wake of the French troops, first to risk their own lives at Montecassino and then to threaten those of our own poor wogs – particularly the women – from the Liri Valley and the mountains that ring the Pontine Marshes. They'd raped two thousand women aged between eight and eighty-five, the French themselves confirmed as much – though rumour had the figure as sixty thousand – and eight hundred men, including a priest, and killed eight hundred more because they'd tried to protect their women or refused to stand by and watch. 'Just like we did in Africa,' said my Uncle Adelchi later on. 'What you give, you get.' So we too left Cori in a hurry – 'If we've got to die, let's die in our own home' – because rumour had it that the real wogs were moving over the mountains in our direction. So off we rushed – 'The sooner we get home the better' – along the mountain-tops towards Norma and our own Pontine Marshes, where the Germans were doing battle with the Americans.

We reached the crag where the village now known as Norma stands – the ruins of the Roman town of Norba, that is – on the night of 23–24 May, still with our cart and that donkey which my poor grandfather had fought for tooth and nail throughout those four months of our evacuation. He scarcely slept at night, for fear that my grandmother or someone else might slaughter it. We were all hungry. 'Let's eat the donkey,' my grandmother would say.

'You must be mad! Eat me, if you like, but not the donkey.'

We stayed up there – hidden in the caves and the remains of the old temples – for the whole night of the 24 May and the one that followed, with the sound of fighting rising from the plain below: bursts of machinegun fire, the sound of cannon, tanks and hand grenades.

On the morning of 25 May 1944 – 'Let's go home,' my grandmother kept saying, 'before the wogs arrive,' and this time she meant the real wogs, the ones from Morocco, not 'our' wogs, who had taken the bread from their own mouths to feed us – well, on the morning of the 25 May we climbed to the top of that crag, on to the walls of Roman Norba, and beneath us we could see the whole of the plain of our Pontine Marshes. With Littoria and the sea in the background, and the chain of lakes of Sabaudia and Fogliano, with Monte Circeo to the left, twelve thousand hectares of flooded fields turned into marshland once again by the Germans between Pontinia and Terracina, and then the plain, with smoke and fires and the sound of gunfire here and there, but, right ahead of us, the tiny bell tower of Borgo Podgora still standing there defiantly and, beside it, towards Cisterna, the sharp, clean-cut furrow of our own Mussolini Canal, its silver ribbon of water sparkling in the sunlight. It was a sight to lift the heart.

'Let's go home,' my grandmother had said, and off we set down the ridge.

There was still the 'Barbarigo' to contend with, the Barbarigo Battalion of the X Mas, the last to leave the Pontine Marshes, with its sailors – all of them mere boys, some local, all volunteers – gradually falling back along the slope, from foot to ridge, dodging from one olive tree to the next, from prickly pear to protruding rock, and then turning round to fire at the American infantry, who were advancing in a similarly cautious fashion; they were the last rearguard covering the retreat of the German divisions towards Rome. On the other side, too, as you know – to the north of the Pontine Marshes, beyond Aprilia and Pomezia – it was the parachutists of the Nembo and the Folgore who made up the rearguard engaging in the *last defence of Rome*. In the valleys and upland plains of Castel di Decima they attacked the advancing tanks with hand grenades – like my uncles in Africa – opening the trapdoors and hurling them inside. Sometimes they succeeded; more often, though, they didn't; and their mothers, too, weep for them to this day. Then the tanks would roll forwards and there was nothing to be done.

So, down we came from Norma, and at a certain point – pausing for a moment on a slight rise, waiting for the Americans, and our sailors from the Barbarigo, who were a few hundred metres below us, to stop firing at one another and move off in the direction of Cisterna so that we could get past – my grandmother turned towards the baby, who was in his mother's arms, babbling away and playing with the bees. 'I've been thinking,' she said to Armida. 'When he's a bit older, he'll be staying with us too. Not you, though. It's over with you and the Peruzzis.'

Armida froze: 'So, these snakes want to take him from me

529

as well?' But at the same time she also felt happy for her child, who was being welcomed back into the fold.

'Ma,' she said – calling her 'ma' for the last time, while my grandmother turned grimly round to hear her out – 'Ma, I was in the wrong and I'll pay for it as long as I live, but I swear to you, he's Pericles' son, you must believe me, we made him like the bees do, together with all the others, at Codigoro!'

'You're mad! I'll believe that the day donkeys fly,' and at that very moment a stray bullet – I don't know whether it was the Barbarigo or the Americans – struck my grandfather's donkey right on the head and it keeled over on to the ground. And while my grandfather was kneeling down to put his arms around it and trying vainly to coax it back to life – 'My donkey, they've got my donkey' – our donkey's soul was flying up to heaven.

But we all got down that mountain safe and sound, the Lord be thanked, together with our carts, and bags of linen on our shoulders and children in our arms, and so did all the other sharecroppers who'd spent those months as evacuees on the Lepini Mountains, where they had met with kindness. Our second exodus. And now once more we were Pilgrim Fathers on the plain, this time with the blessing of our wogs: 'Good on you, Vikings.'

By now the Germans had left Cisterna. The Barbarigo had joined up with them and left as well. For better or worse, it was over. We had been liberated. And, as I've said, we fought against it to the bitter end. But now it had happened. 'Long live our liberators!' and they also brought us all sorts of good things to eat, kinds of food we hadn't seen since goodness knows when.

My Aunt Santapace, who was now staying with Benassi in my Uncle Adelchi's house in Littoria – and who, two days earlier, as soon as we'd learned that the Germans had left Terracina and that the enemy was also hotfooting it up from the south, had already started to shriek 'Oh my god, what will all those blacks do to us women?' and had sharpened all her knives to kill her daughters and then herself, so as to be ready before those blacks arrived – when she'd looked out of the window and seen a lorry full of Englishmen unloading sacks of flour as white as the driven snow, and everyone rushing up to lay their hands on it and the flour swirling all over the place and everyone laughing and shrieking for pure joy, Englishmen included – well, then Aunt Santapace had gone along to join them with her daughters, and started shrieking together with the rest: 'Long live the Americans,' even if they were English. 'Long live the Americans, and to hell with the Zorzi Vila!'

So home we all went – wandering here and there together with the other sharecroppers through fields edged with barbed wire and helpful notices put up by the last Germans or Salò Republicans: '*Achtung minen*,' 'Minefield' – to our Peruzzi holding 517 on the Mussolini Canal. All that was left of it was the main walls. The roof of the holding had collapsed, as had that of the cowshed. Indeed, you could say that the whole of the reclaimed Pontine Marshes had collapsed. Aprilia had been razed to the ground down to the last stone – built just seven years earlier, an architectural jewel, as I've told you, designed by Jewish architects whose sons died in Mauthausen – and so had almost all the holdings in the Pontine Marshes. The fields were flooded. Nearly all of the coast was mined. The pools along the coastal strip were marshland all over again. The anopheles mosquitoes, maddened by all those years of abstinence they'd been put through – during those ten years since the first reclaiming – were now at it like mad in all those

531

new swamps, and malaria set in even worse than before, and people died like flies. It was the Americans who saved us, using those same planes with which they'd bombed us to spray the whole of the Pontine Marshes with DDT. DDT is manna from heaven, take it from me: blessed be its inventor, and to hell with the Greens and the Zorzi Vila. And they brought us penicillin too, let's not forget. Of course they brought us freedom and democracy as well, I'm not complaining. We're grateful to them for that too, but – truth to tell – we Peruzzis hadn't seen much freedom and democracy even before Fascism, indeed it was with Fascism that we came in for a bit of attention for the first time in our lives. Anyway, thanks, Americans, for that freedom and democracy. But thank you most of all – if it's all the same to you – for prosperity. That was truly something we'd never seen before. All that we'd seen till then was hunger.

But we returned to utter ruin. Our fields untilled, and pitted with bomb craters. Dead bodies still lying around. Canals and drainage ditches filled with earth. Roads impassable. The Mussolini Canal itself beggared description: all the stones on the dykes and central low-water section all over the place; the banks torn up or mined; the whole bed filled with earth, so that the fields would be flooded at the first drop of rain. Cisterna too was razed to the ground, as was most of Littoria, the blocks of flats had been gutted and the tower of the 'M' Building had vanished into thin air. Everything had to be rebuilt from scratch. The whole of the Pontine Marshes had to be reclaimed from scratch. Clearly, all the coins thrown into the foundations by the humblest workman or carpenter, or indeed by Cencelli, Rossoni or the Duce himself, had not sufficed. They had been of no avail in the face of such an *adynaton*. What was needed was blood. The blood of all those who had come first from the Veneto, Emilia and Friuli, and then from the whole of the rest of the world – from India, New Zealand, the USA, England, France, Morocco and Algeria, as well as from our own local mountains, to die in and around the Mussolini Canal – and who now had to roll up their sleeves and start again from scratch, redigging the canal, drying out swamps and marshes for a second time, rebuilding Littoria and all the others towns and holdings, making new roads and cowsheds, the lot, but this time in peace and freedom, for ever, it's to be hoped. That's how our Pontine Marshes started off on their second life, that's how they truly became the Garden of Eden, the Promised Land, our own Veneto-Pontine Nation.

Sorry, what's that you said?

Where do I fit into all this?

Well, you remember I told you that we'd been evacuated, on the night of 7 February 1944, when the Germans sent us off from the Peruzzi holding 517 with our cart and a white sheet? You do? And do you also remember that at a certain point I told you that we found ourselves in a minefield, and my Uncle Pericles' black-and-white hunting dog, Gina, got blown up by an anti-personnel mine?

Anyway, we were standing stock-still in that minefield, and you know how it goes the world over in such cases, when a family or a group, a clan, a tribe like our own suddenly finds itself in a minefield unable to move either backwards or sideways, but can only cross themselves and go ahead, cost what it may – only go straight ahead.

In such cases it's the old who have to go ahead first, first the old people and then – as they get blown up but, in so doing, show the way to the others – the men, and then the women who are still of child-bearing age, and then the children. That's how it's done, because here what's at stake is the survival of the group, or of the species. First the old, and then all the rest.

So, when the dog Gina got blown up, and my grandmother said: 'Now what do we do?' my grandfather had said: 'Let's wait till it gets light,' because that way, he thought, we might actually be able to make out the odd mine, and take steps to avoid it, and generally be able to see better. But when she said: 'Yes, but so will the Americans,' my grandfather resigned himself: 'Given the circumstances, what's one day more or less?' and he lit his cigar, inhaled deeply and went ahead.

My grandmother put out an arm and blocked his way, holding it taut and firm across his chest.

He tried to shake it off so that he could go forward on what he felt – on what he knew – to be his way.

She wouldn't budge. And when he and all the others started pulling faces as though to say: 'What's got into you?' my grandmother simply said: 'No, not you!'

'Who, then?' the others thought to themselves, but no one said a word. Everyone stood stock-still, frozen with panic, wondering whose turn it really was.

My grandmother didn't budge. She just stood there without saying a word.

And then the penny dropped.

It was the work of a moment.

Armida handed little Menego over to Aunt Santapace who was already weeping, holding out her arms to take him to her. 'Be brave, Armida,' whispered a eucalyptus tree on the drainage ditch at the field's edge. And Armida went up to the cart – which was last in the line with the donkey, behind us all – and took a hive, and said to her bees: 'Let's go,' and walked forwards through that whole Peruzzi clan which stood aside to let her pass. 'Come on, bees,' and off she went across the mines.

The bees went buzzing around her over the damp earth, sniffing things out as they did so, trying to shift the clods of earth with their feelers and stings, and buzzing loudly whenever they came upon anything odd. Then Armida would stop and take the path they seemed to be suggesting. Meanwhile – dipping into a sack of flour which she held perched high on her swollen stomach, and which my grandmother had given her, without a word, before she set off among the mines – she left a trail of flour, to tell those who were following some thirty metres behind her which path to take. 'Can't she get a move on?' said one of my aunts.

Armida was sweating. The bees were buzzing, zigzagging as they went. At a certain point, she and the bees found themselves beneath that eucalyptus tree by the drainage ditch. To the east, from behind the chain of the Lepini Mountains, towards Sezze, the first glimmer of dawn was coming up. Armida felt a sharp pain in her stomach and her waters broke. She felt them warm on her wet legs as the bees flew buzzing round her.

Then Armida crouched down near the eucalyptus tree – 'Take your time, Armida, easy does it' – and I was born. Together with the whole placenta. And that's how I came to be born in a minefield. The bees immediately settled on me – that's what my mother would tell me – while she tried to get her strength back, leaning against the tree. She used her teeth to bite off the umbilical cord.

I gave one little gasp as I lay there on the ground, just enough to draw my first breath, but I didn't cry. I was covered by a black cloak – that's what my mother would tell me – or rather a black-and-yellow cloak, formed by all the bees as they crawled over me, cleaning up the placenta.

'Now what's she up to?' asked my aunts impatiently, as

my mother scooped me up into her arms, all newly clean, and laughing, with the bees buzzing around me. And that's how I came to be born. In a minefield. And, just like Scarlett O'Hara, my mother got to her feet and said: 'Thank you, bees. Tomorrow is another day,' and walked off with me in her arms and her bees behind her, leading the Peruzzi clan to safety.

Sorry, what's that you said? According to you, it's my Cousin Paris who is my father?

You're mad. In that case, you haven't understood a thing. As my mother always said, I am the son of Pericles, and they conceived me together with all my brothers and sisters – as our bees do, as your god Krishna did with Satyabhama – on the night my father killed the poor priest from Comacchio, God rest his soul.

That's the end of the *filo*. Signed, Don Pericles Peruzzi, parish priest in the Pontine Marshes.

To be continued in our next... God willing. Amen.